THE SPANISH REVENGE

ALLAN TOPOL

This is a work of fiction. Names, characters, places, and incidents are the product of the author's imagination or are used fictitiously. Any resemblance to actual events, locales, or persons, living or dead, is coincidental.

Vantage Point Books and the Vantage Point Books colophon are registered trademarks of Vantage Press, Inc.
FIRST EDITION: September 2012

Published by Vantage Point Books
Vantage Press, Inc.
419 Park Avenue South
New York, NY 10016
www.vantagepointbooks.com

Manufactured in the United States of America
ISBN: 978-1-936467-56-3

Library of Congress Cataloging-in-Publication data are on file.

9 8 7 6 5 4 3 2 1

Cover design by Victor Mingovits

THE SPANISH REVENGE

ALSO BY ALLAN TOPOL

FICTION

The Fourth of July War

A Woman of Valor

Spy Dance

Dark Ambition

Conspiracy

Enemy of My Enemy

The China Gambit

NON-FICTION

Superfund Law and Procedure (co-author)

For Barbara, with appreciation
to my partner in this literary venture.

"All the same, confrontations between the Eastern forces of Islam and the Western forces of Christianity have never completely abated."

—FROM *MYSTERIES OF THE MIDDLE AGES* BY TOMAS CAHILL, P. 179, 2006

"This multicultural approach, saying that we simply live side by side and live happily with each other has failed. Utterly failed."

—GERMAN CHANCELLOR ANGELA MERKEL, OCTOBER 18, 2010.

PROLOGUE

MARCH, AVILA, SPAIN

At five minutes to midnight the heater in the battered gray Renault van died. Omar, in the front passenger seat, was astounded that the vehicle had made it all the way from Clichy-sous-Bois, the suburb of Paris.

They were parked outside the gate of the Franciscan Monastery. Thirty minutes ago, the last light had gone out.

"Cut off the engine," Omar said to Habib, seated behind the wheel, puffing on a foul-smelling Turkish cigarette. "Time to move."

Omar got out of the van, stretched his legs, and checked the pockets of his black leather jacket. Gun and map Musa provided in one pocket; knife and flashlight in the other. He grabbed the two shovels from the back and tossed one to Habib.

The air was cold for this time of year. The moon full in a cloudless sky. The light would make their job easier, but increase the risk of someone spotting them. It could only be one of the monks. The monastery was surrounded by woods.

With Habib at his side, Omar walked swiftly along the dirt road toward the monastery entrance. The black wrought-iron gate was padlocked. He reached for his gun, then reconsidered. The monks inside the building might hear the noise. He pointed to the six-foot stone wall. Habib nodded.

Omar easily scaled it, then moved away while Habib tossed over the shovels, following behind. No need to consult Musa's map. He had committed it to memory. That bastard Tomas de Torquemada's grave should be fifty meters away at the end of the road leading from the entrance gate. He walked swiftly along a narrow path bisecting ancient weather-beaten stones.

Approaching the spot, he recognized from pictures the large stone cross.

"We dig here?" Habib asked.

"One thing first."

Omar unzipped his pants, pulled out his prick and peed on the cross. "For all those Muslims you killed cruelly and without mercy," he said softly.

Then he grabbed a shovel.

Fortunately, it had rained yesterday, and the ground was soft. Still it was tough work. On one side, they created an incline to get out. Once they were down three feet, Omar's face and shirt were soaked with perspiration. Drops ran down his cheeks and into his eyes.

He drew strength from the importance of his mission. The cause he and Musa had labored so hard for over many months was now at a critical point. With the parchment, their success would be assured. Europe and the world would be irretrievably transformed.

"The dead man's spirits are talking to me." Habib was trembling. "Telling me it's wrong to disturb a grave."

Omar pulled out his Glock and aimed it at Habib. "You fool. No Christian spirits are talking to you. You dig or this will be your grave too."

Reluctantly, Habib resumed.

Forty minutes later, Omar's shovel struck a metal box about a meter from the coffin, as Musa had said. He could barely contain his excitement.

The parchment will be in the box.

Suddenly, he heard the rustling of leaves. Footsteps near the building. Now getting closer. It might be an animal. Or ...

"Stay in the hole and keep quiet," he whispered to Habib. Then he climbed out and slipped behind the cross. A black-clad monk was approaching, lit torch in hand, making a beeline for the open hole. He shined his light down and looked into the hole. As he did, Omar, shovel in hand, circled behind him. He watched the monk calling to Habib, who was cowering in a corner of the hole, "Who are you?" Omar raised the shovel and swung it like a baseball bat, with all his might, striking the monk on the side of the head. He crumpled to the ground away from the hole, blood pouring down the side of his face. "Help me," he mumbled. "Help me." Omar ignored his pleas, lifted his shovel, and smashed the metal against his face. The monk stopped moving.

Omar stepped over the body and climbed back into the hole. He had to work fast, or others might come looking for the dead monk. He dug around the box, being careful not to damage the old metal. When he got closer, he handed his shovel to Habib. With his fingers, he clawed furiously, grabbing the soil, pushing it aside until he freed the box.

Cradling it in his arms, he climbed out and placed it carefully on the ground. The box was sealed shut. Using his knife, he pried the top open. Habib was leaning over Omar. He felt Habib's hot garlic breath on the back of his neck.

He pulled the top off, then grabbed his flashlight and shined it inside. For an instant the light blinded him, the reflection from jewels and gold coins. He reached in and moved the contents around, searching desperately for the parchment. He came up empty.

"No," he wailed. "No!"

I have to get the parchment. I can't face Musa without it.

Musa didn't tolerate failure. He won't understand. There must be another way.

Eyes bulging, Habib was staring at the gold and jewels. "Let's take what's here and leave. Nobody will ever know."

"We can't do that, you imbecile. If we're caught by the police with that stuff, we'll be tortured. You'll lead them to Musa, and all will be lost."

"Then let's just go."

"No. Somebody inside must know where the parchment is. Musa said there are five monks altogether."

Omar looked at the stone building. Dark inside. He raced toward the nearest door. Habib was right behind him. The door was ajar. He opened it carefully and shined his light inside. The room was deserted, its stone walls muting the reflection. They must all be asleep. He spotted a bell and rang it.

Minutes later, four monks stumbled out of the wing on the right, in night clothes. Omar held up his gun and herded them toward four wooden chairs in the reception area. One was praying. "Shut up and listen." Omar called out.

"No comprendo," one monk said in Spanish.

"Any of you speak French?" Omar asked.

A tall, thin, gray-haired monk said, "I do."

"Good. I'll talk to you. A parchment was buried in a box next to Tomas de Torquemada's coffin. We dug up the box, but the parchment isn't there. I want to know where it is."

The tall, thin man was flabbergasted. "You disturbed his grave?"

"Someone already had. The parchment was gone. I want to know where it is?"

"I have no idea."

"Then ask your colleagues in Spanish. One of them must know."

The tall, thin monk said something to the others. All shook their heads in denial.

Omar didn't believe them. He was becoming angry. "This monastery has been here since before his death in 1498. At some point one of your monks must have taken it and hidden it. This must be a secret passed down here through the ages."

"How can you be sure it was buried with him?"

Omar raised the Glock and aimed it at one of the other monks. He fired at his head, blasting it apart. Two others wailed.

"Don't you challenge me," Omar said. "Tell me where it is."

"You can kill us all," the tall, thin monk said, "but you won't get the information."

"Because you don't know—or because you won't tell me?"

"That's your riddle to solve," he replied in a taunting voice.

Omar used his knife to gouge out the eyes of one of the other monks. Despite the man's screams, nobody said a word.

Omar killed that one and the other, leaving only the tall, thin monk. "I'll make you suffer more than you can imagine," Omar said.

"I am a man of God. I have no fear of mere mortals."

Omar knew it was hopeless. He shot and killed the man. Then he and Habib searched the building. Even the basement, beneath a concealed trap door. No sign of the parchment.

To extend the time before they were discovered and pursuit began, Omar decided to move the dead bodies down the stairs. "While I do that," he told Habib, "Rebury the box. Toss the other dead monk in the hole and start to refill it. I'll be out in a couple of minutes to help you."

He searched one more time, then dragged the bodies across the floor, flung them down the wooden stairs, and closed the trap door.

After leaving the building, he crossed the grassy swale back to the graveyard. He couldn't believe his eyes. Habib was stuffing gold and jewels into his pockets. Omar stood behind a tree and watched. Once his pockets were full, Habib ran toward the wall. As he began scaling it, Omar raised his gun and fired, dropping Habib with a single shot. Enraged, Omar raced over and pumped three more bullets into Habib's dead body. Then he removed Habib's ID, dragged him back to the hole, and kicked him in.

For the next two hours, he worked until he was so exhausted he could barely lift his arms. But it was all done. Habib, the monk, and the metal box all buried.

Walking back to the car, he had an overwhelming sense of gloom. With the parchment, they could change the map of Europe—even the world alignment between Muslims and Christians. But he had failed. They would have to find another way to get the parchment.

PART ONE

OCTOBER,
SIX MONTHS EARLIER

1

PARIS

When Craig Page agreed to become Director of the new European Counterterrorism Agency a year and a half ago, he persuaded the EU to put the agency's headquarters in Paris. That choice was fortunate right now, he decided, as he waited for Jacques Dumas, the head of the French Intelligence Service to arrive at his office.

Craig got up from his desk and walked over to the double-glass wall with a view of the concrete courtyard, fifteen floors below. The building was part of the complex of modern commercial office buildings known as La Defense, at the end of the Avenue de la Grande Armée, shooting out like a spoke from the Arc de Triomphe. In the dim late afternoon light, he spotted heavyset Jacques, mid forties, with a shaved head, walking fast, almost racing from his limo toward the building. And indeed he should be. Craig had told him on the phone, "We have an urgent situation involving the American President."

This won't be easy, Craig realized. Jacques, reluctant to cede any authority, had been opposed to the creation of a European counter-terrorism agency. And the idea of an American as director had made him nearly apoplectic with rage.

Immediately after Craig's appointment, he had arranged a dinner with Jacques, just the two of them at L'Ami Louis, to break down Jacques opposition. At the beginning of the meal, Jacques told Craig he appreciated that Craig's twenty years as a CIA field agent, fighting terrorists in the Middle East, dwarfed his own experience. He understood that Craig's bitterness toward his scheming CIA masters and the American bureaucracy led him to resign from the CIA and open a private consulting firm in Italy, where he had roots. Despite all that, Jacques bluntly declared, "We don't need a pan-European agency, and if our brilliant leaders insist on it, then the director's job should have gone to one of us, not some American."

But they kept talking, eating, and drinking in the noisy bistro, with gargantuan portions of outstanding food and rude waiters. By the second bottle of Bourgogne Rouge, and midway through their thick steaks, as they traded war stories, Craig believed he had Jacque's grudging respect. One professional for another. That was as much as he hoped for.

Now Jacques pushed passed Craig's secretary and barreled into the office. "What's the great crisis?"

"I've learned from an informant that an Iranian group is planning to assassinate President Dalton when his motorcade goes from the American embassy to the Elysee Palace for dinner with the French President. I told Agent Bardolino, my liaison, who's traveling with Dalton, and asked him to brief the American President, to find out whether Dalton wants to change his plans for this evening."

"What'd he say?"

"The answer was a resounding 'No.' In Dalton's words, 'that's why we pay you guys. To keep me safe.'"

"Nice."

"Yeah."

"Who's the informant?"

"His name's Hakim. An Iranian. A holdover from my CIA days."

"I don't know him."

"He's proven extremely reliable in the past."

Still feeling prickly, despite their peace dinner and moderate cooperation ever since, Jacques said, "And I'm supposed to take your word in blind faith?"

"We're on the same team. Aren't we?"

"Humph," the Frenchman snarled. "Everybody in Europe hates your President Dalton."

Craig didn't argue. Six months ago, when President Brewster died of a sudden heart attack and his Vice President, Owen Dalton, succeeded him, Craig had been appalled at his neo isolationist statements. Dalton's much-heralded trip to Paris was to advise the French President that the old Atlantic alliance was over.

"He's not my President."

"Well, you are an American."

"I haven't lived there for years. C'mon, Jacques. We have to act on what Hakim told me."

Jacques waited a long minute before responding. "Let's assume Hakim is right. What do you want me to do?"

Craig was ready for the question. His title sounded impressive, but, in a typical EU compromise, he had no troops of his own. He was dependent for fire power on the country in which a terrorist attack would occurr.

"We have an hour until the motorcade leaves the American embassy. I want you to station sharpshooters on the roofs of the buildings lining the route, set up video cameras to monitor the entire area, and send the feed into my IT center."

The Frenchmen linked his fingers together, closed his eyes, and scrunched up his large, round face. "You're asking quite a bit, based on one informant. If nothing happens, I'll look like an idiot."

"You can put the blame on me. But if you thwart an attack, you'll be a hero."

"I just don't know."

Craig thought it wise to remain silent. He had made his case. Finally, Jacques whipped out his cell phone. "OK. I'll do it."

Forty-five minutes later, Craig and Jacques were in the IT center of Craig's counter-terrorism agency. Eight thirty-inch screens lined one wall. A dozen computer geeks, whom Craig recruited from across the EU, manned workstations in cubicles. When they weren't responding to a crisis, they were analyzing and digesting information forwarded from intelligence agents around the world.

Hans from Amsterdam was monitoring the video feed. "All the cameras are in place," he said. Craig's eyes ran from one screen to another, seeing French army sharpshooters on the roofs lining the fashionable Rue Saint-Honoré—home to some of the most expensive boutiques in the world.

Craig checked his watch. Then called Bardolino. "What's your status?"

"We're moving in ten minutes. You ready for us?"

"Good to go. We have the whole route covered. If the troops see a sniper, they have orders to shoot to kill."

Craig had divided the route into eight segments, each with a separate camera and screen. Now he studied the screens one by one. Nothing out of the ordinary. Tourists, shoppers, business people walking along the sidewalk. The flow of traffic looked normal.

What if Hakim's wrong?

Craig realized he'd look like a fool, creating so much disruption and cost for nothing. And Jacques would make sure information of Craig's failure was widely known throughout the EU.

On the first screen, Craig watched President Dalton leave the American Embassy and walk toward the black Cadillac limousine. Supposedly bullet proof. That was a joke, with powerful new weapons like grenade launchers.

"Close up," Craig said to the technician working the screen. That made Dalton big as life. Thin lips and a wart on his right cheek. Christ, doesn't that guy ever smile?

Craig watched Dalton climb into the car. It began moving slowly out of the driveway from the American Embassy compound.

Jacques was standing next to Craig, intently studying the screens.

Craig was moving his eyes from one screen to the next, looking for any tiny movement. Not a thing.

On the fifth screen, the Presidential motorcade turned on to the Rue Saint-Honoré. That began the area of greatest risk. If I were positioning a sniper, Craig thought, I'd put him in the window of one of the buildings lining the street. Craig didn't see anything in a window or on screens five through eight. He looked at the street. Traffic had been halted on the cross streets. The motorcade had the Rue Saint-Honoré to itself. Pedestrians stopped walking, waiting for the motorcade to pass, hoping to catch a glimpse of the American President. Craig studied the pedestrians. Their faces. What they were holding.

A man, Middle Eastern-looking, an Iranian or Arab, in a suit and tie, was standing alone, a cell phone on his hand. "Close up on the guy with the cell phone," Craig cried out. The man was looking at the approaching motorcade at a distance of fifty yards. His eyes moved from the motorcade to an old, battered motorcycle parked on his side of the street, about twenty yards away. Seated on the motorcycle was a man in a brown leather jacket, collar raised in the back. Face barely visible behind the guard of a heavy helmet. The Middle Eastern man raised his hand almost imperceptibly at the motorcycle rider, who climbed off and walked away.

Craig said to Jacques, "Have your men follow the guy in the brown leather jacket and motorcycle helmet."

"Will do."

"Don't arrest him. See where he leads us."

Hooked to the back of the motorcycle, Craig saw a large Hermès box with its distinctive orange color. Messengers delivered those on motorcycles all the time, but not on motorcycles this battered. And a real messenger wouldn't walk away from his package with several thousand dollars of merchandise.

Craig looked back at the man with the cell phone. Now fingering it nervously. Starting to raise it. The motorcade was only twenty yards from the motorcycle with the Hermes box.

"What do you think?" Craig asked Jacques anxiously.

"Your call."

Craig picked up his cell phone and called Bardolino. "Halt the motorcade right now. Hold it in place."

He turned to Jacques. "Tell your nearest man to order the guy with the cell phone to drop it on the ground. If he refuses, shoot to kill."

"Are you certain?"

Of course I'm not certain.

"Yes."

Craig watched a French soldier in a helmet and bulky body armor approach the man. He raised his gun and shouted in French to the Middle Eastern man. "Drop the cell phone now and put up your hands."

The man looked mystified.

What if he doesn't understand French?

The man lifted the cell phone and began punching in numbers. The soldier cut loose with a barrage that blasted into the man's chest. The cell phone fell to the ground. His body next to it. His whole body gave a sudden jolt. Then he was motionless.

Gun in hand, the soldier rushed over and checked the man. "Dead," he said and began searching for ID.

Craig turned to Jacques. "Get the bomb squad to examine the Hermes box."

Bardolino was on Craig's cell. "What the hell's going on?"

"I'm worried about a bomb further down the road. Turn the motorcade around, go back to the embassy compound, and hold until I give you an all clear. Also tell Dalton he doesn't have a choice. This isn't his country."

"Roger that."

Watching the screen, Craig held his breath while the bomb squad opened the Hermes box. What if a dress was inside and nothing else?

They worked slowly with meticulous care to avoid setting off the bomb—if there was one. Craig felt moisture forming under his arms.

After several minutes, they lifted off the orange top. The video camera peered inside. Craig saw a metal object. Unquestionably a bomb. Using precision tools, they disassembled the bomb. Jacques's cell phone rang. "Yes," Craig heard him say. "Yes."

Jacques turned to Craig. "A powerful bomb laced with nails and broken glass."

"What'd they find on the dead man?" Craig asked.

A few seconds later, Jacques had the answer. "No ID on his body. Fingerprints removed."

Craig watched them load the pieces of the bomb into a van and drive away.

He called Bardolino: "The bomb's disabled. The terrorist's dead. You're clear to go."

Then Craig and Jacques turned back to the video screens to follow the motorcade's progress.

Once they passed through the gates into the Elysee Palace, Jacques was on the phone. "What happened with the guy in the brown leather jacket?" Craig heard him say.

Jacques put it on speaker.

"He walked two blocks then got into a car. He's alone and driving. We're following in an unmarked car. You want us to stop him?"

Jacques looked at Craig. "Negative. We're hoping he'll lead us to the planners of the attack."

"Got it. We'll keep you posted."

Fifteen minutes later, they received an update. "Suspect is on the A-1. proceeding north. Very fast. We have a chopper in the air. I'll give you real-time feed."

Craig watched the suspect cut in and out of lanes, driving recklessly. He had to know he was being followed, particularly with the chopper overhead. The pursing car kept pace.

The suspect was in the center of three lanes. They were approaching an exit. Suddenly, without a signal, he cut to the right trying for the exit ramp. At a hundred and forty kilometers an hour, he missed it and smashed into a concrete retaining wall. His car exploded in flames. Craig knew they wouldn't find any hints of his identity by the time they pulled his charred body from the wreckage.

"What now," Jacques asked.

"While Dalton and your President are feasting in the Elysee Palace, I'll have a secretary order take-out for us. At the end of the evening, we'll watch Dalton's motorcade go back to the American Embassy."

"You think they'll make another try?"

"Hakim didn't say that," Craig shrugged. "But who knows, after they struck out?"

They were finished eating ham and cheese stuffed into baguettes, washed down with Perrier, when Craig's cell phone rang. Caller ID flashed: "Elizabeth Crowder." He moved into an adjacent empty office.

"I just got off the plane at JFK and saw the news on TV about the attack on President Dalton's life. I assume you were the one who thwarted it."

"Working with Jacques and the French military."

"Was that skinhead actually helpful?"

He smiled. "You have a great way of expressing yourself."

"Come on. I don't like him because he's done everything to sabotage you."

"I'm prepared to cut him some slack. Lately, he and I are doing better."

"So what happened?"

He responded in a low voice, "I got a tip from an informant that an Iranian group planned to assassinate Dalton on his way to the Elysee Palace. We killed the assassin before he could activate the bomb."

"Well done. Do I get the details, so I can write it up for tomorrow's International Herald?"

"It's still a work in progress. We have to get Dalton home and tucked into bed safely after dinner. Besides, you have something else to worry about in New York."

"For sure. I'm having dinner with Harold this evening. We have a meeting at Wellington Books, tomorrow morning at eleven. With Virginia Tolbert, the Publisher."

"That's a good sign."

"I hope so. I'd like to lock this up tomorrow and get back to Paris."

"If you have to stay longer, don't worry."

"Are you kidding? Once word gets out about your newest success, French women will be fighting with each other to get my place in your bed."

He laughed. "Hey, that sounds like fun."

"Yeah, well. It better not happen."

"You're safe. Nobody like you. Break a leg tomorrow."

"Thanks. I really want this."

Craig put down the phone. Before returning to Jacques, he closed his eyes and thought how ironic that Elizabeth had come into his life at his moment of greatest pain and loneliness, a year and a half ago. He had never fully accepted his wife, Caroline's, death, twelve years earlier. Then he received that call in Milan, where he had been living and working after ending his CIA career because of Director Kirby's jealousy and resentment.

He hated even thinking about the call. A bolt from the blue telling him that Francesca, his only child, his only family, had been killed driving in Calgary, Canada on a snowy night on the way to the airport. The result of a hit and run with a large truck, according to the police. He knew she was on the verge of uncovering a big story as a reporter with the *New York Tribune*. He was convinced her death was a homicide.

When he met Elizabeth, Francesca's editor, after the funeral, they decided to join forces to discover what happened.

They not only succeeded, but, as he spent time with feisty Elizabeth in Washington, Tehran, and Beijing, he rediscovered feelings he thought had died with Caroline.

When Craig returned to Europe to assume the position of Director of the EU Counterterrorism Agency, eighteen months ago, it seemed natural for Elizabeth to relocate to Paris and to take a job as a foreign reporter with the *International Herald*. They rented an apartment on the top floor of a building on Montmarte, with a fantastic view of the city.

He wasn't sure where they were going next. They hadn't ever spoken about marriage or children. She was thirty-seven. He was eleven years older.

They were a couple of expat Americans loving Paris and enjoying each other, while fully committed to important jobs.

He noticed Jacques standing in the doorway. "Recess is over. They're finishing up dinner. Dalton's getting ready to leave."

Craig and Jacques were back in front of the video screens, watching carefully as the motorcade pulled out of the Elysee Palace and headed toward the American Embassy. This time the ride was uneventful. Craig breathed a huge sigh of relief when President

Dalton's car entered the embassy compound. Mission accomplished. Thank God they're safe.

"Great irony here," Jacques said. "The American President who hates Europe owes his life to a French bomb squad."

Craig raised his hand and Jacques clasped it. The show of camaraderie pleased Craig. "Life would be wonderful without the politicians," Craig said.

"So what's our next act?"

Craig shrugged. "You can be sure some whacko or self righteous ideologue somewhere is hatching a plot."

NEW YORK

Walking along Park Avenue and hustling to keep pace with Harold Gorman's long strides, Elizabeth felt nervous, yet confident. Nervous because this was her first book deal negotiation and Harold was asking for more than she ever imagined. Confident because Harold had been an agent for forty years and knew every nuance of the business.

At sixty five, he still had a thick head of wavy black hair sprinkled with gray, spilling over the collar of his weather-beaten, tan raincoat. He had once played basketball at Cornell and maintained the athlete's shape. Last evening at dinner at Jean Georges, he'd given her the detailed background on whom they were meeting with at Wellington Books. Virginia, in Harold's words, "Is very smart, but tough, no nonsense, strictly bottom line, so cold blooded she'd freeze the mercury in a thermometer. Now Ned, your editor, if we cut a deal, is just the opposite. A big teddy bear. Warm, friendly, wouldn't kill a fly if it settled on his arm."

Harold also told her, "When he's in a meeting with Virginia, Ned rarely opens his mouth. But he happens to be one of the best editors in the business."

A secretary led them into the publisher's glass-walled corner office, looking down Park with a view of Grand Central. Virginia, wearing a dark gray suit, had her dark brown hair tied up and wound tight in the back. She was smiling warmly as she shook Elizabeth's hand. "Don't be deceived by that," Harold had warned her.

Ned, standing across the room, did remind Elizabeth of a teddy bear. Mid forties, curly brown hair, five six, protruding stomach.

They settled in to a living area in one corner, pot of coffee with china cups on a marbled top table. Virginia clutching their book proposal was in a straight-back chair. Ned was on her left, Harold and Elizabeth on a sofa facing Virginia.

Ned pointed to the coffee. When Elizabeth nodded, he poured a cup.

"I read the proposal," Virginia said. No pleasantries. Right to the point.

The word, "And?" almost popped out of Elizabeth's mouth, but Harold had said it was better for him to take the lead. "I'll tell you when to talk." So she kept still. Harold was waiting for Virginia to continue.

"I like the concept. Europe does face a serious problem from its growing Muslim population. I even like your title, *Heads in the Sand—Europe Ignores the Islamic Threat.* But an advance of eight hundred thousand dollars in this market is ridiculous."

"We're offering world rights," Harold said calmly. "Not just US"

Virginia waved around the proposal. "I can read."

"It's the hottest topic in the world. Muslims versus Christians."

"That doesn't mean it'll sell books."

"Thilo Sarrazin's book claiming that the Muslims are bringing about Germany's downfall sold over a million copies in the first month, in Germany alone."

"He was a celebrity in Germany."

"He was a banker for God's sakes. Bankers aren't celebrities. Elizabeth was a widely read and respected foreign affairs writer for many years with the *New York Tribune.* For the last year and a half with the *International Herald.* She won a Pulitzer for her coverage of the war in Iraq as an embedded journalist with our troops. I'm sure your sales projections back me up."

Virginia was looking at Elizabeth. "Why'd you leave New York for Paris?"

"I was ready for a change and I'm in a relationship with someone there."

"I know all about Craig Page. And I have powerful friends in Washington. People who were close to President Brewster. I've heard what you and Craig did to stop General Zhou in China. All very hush-hush. Why don't you do a book about that?"

Elizabeth smiled. "I don't know what you're talking about."

Virginia laughed. "I can give you a hundred thousand for *Heads in the Sand.*"

Elizabeth's chin dropped.

Harold fired back. "That's insulting."

He stood up. Elizabeth guessed she should do the same.

"OK, we're out of here. It's been swell." He sounded angry.

As they started toward the door, Virginia said, "Tell you what, Harold, to go above two I need Board approval. Let's break for lunch. Come back at three. I'll make some calls. See what I can do."

Elizabeth exhaled with relief. Harold took her to lunch at the Four Seasons restaurant. His usual poolside table. "I refuse to eat in the Grill Room, with all those publishing power players. It's enough I see them the rest of the day."

When the waiter came over, Harold told her, "Have a drink. It'll relax you." Though she almost never drank at lunch, she ordered a cosmo.

"What do you think?" she asked.

"We'll end up around six hundred K. That gives her something to save face."

"Are you serious?"

"I never joke about something like this. You'll notice she didn't argue when I said her marketing projections support my position. Your topic, Muslims versus Christians, is so timely. They know they can sell books. The large advance will make sure they do."

She ordered a lobster salad, but her stomach was churning. She moved it around with her fork. As she sipped the drink, Harold asked, "What was this China business with you and Craig and General Zhou, Virginia was talking about?"

Elizabeth put down the glass. "I promised President Brewster I would never divulge it."

"Brewster's dead."

"I know. But …"

"OK. Is that how you met Craig?"

"Yeah. His daughter Francesca was working for me as a reporter at the *New York Tribune*. She was killed in Calgary. Craig was formerly with the CIA. He and I hooked up trying to get to the bottom of Francesca's death."

When they returned to Virginia's office, the publisher was smiling. "Good news. I have approval to give Elizabeth four hundred thousand."

Elizabeth wanted to scream, "Take it," but Harold was shaking his head. She thought about asking Harold for a recess to discuss Virginia's offer.

Before she had a chance, Virginia said, "Dammit, Harold. You're being unreasonable."

"I don't think so. This is the hottest subject in the world. My client is a Pulitzer Prize-winning author. You're getting world wide rights."

Virginia's face hardened. Oh, oh, oh, Elizabeth thought.

"Tell you what, Harold. I'll split the difference between your eight and my four. That's my best and final. Take it or leave it."

He looked at Elizabeth.

"Yes," she said.

Virginia was smiling again. "Good. We have a deal at six. Thirty days for a detailed outline. Twelve months for a complete draft."

On the way out, Elizabeth chatted with Ned and told him he could expect the detailed outline in three weeks.

Out on Park Avenue, she threw her arms around Harold. "Thank you so much. You're the world's best agent." She was on the verge of crying with joy.

A black Lincoln Town Car pulled up at the curb. "He'll take you to JFK," Harold said. "You can get the next plane back to Paris."

"Thanks. I have a stop to make first."

"He's yours. Wherever you want to go."

She gave the driver an address on the North Shore of Long Island. Then she took out her cell phone and called Craig. "I'm coming back on the ten thirty this evening. For dinner tomorrow, book the best restaurant in Paris. I'm buying, and we're celebrating."

"Fabulous." He sounded elated. "How much did you get?"

"I'll tell you at dinner. Make it a surprise."

"I love surprises like that. I'm so happy for you."

The car exited the LIE and wound its way north, until it reached a middle class neighborhood of modest red brick two-story houses with small, but tidy, front lawns. Her parents had moved out here from Brooklyn six years ago, because her dad, then sixty-three, had recently retired from the New York Police Force and wanted to be close to the water to use his boat. Her mother died a year after the move.

Two blocks from the Sound, the car slowed down.

"That's the one," Elizabeth said pointing. An American flag hung from the roof.

Before Elizabeth was out of the car, the front door of the house opened. Her dad limped down the stairs, the result of a bullet he took in the leg in on a drug bust a year before retirement, after he had been promoted to Senior Detective. A large smile lit up his craggy face. She met him half way up the stairs and hugged him.

"What a nice surprise, you calling, Elizabeth."

He always insisted on using her full name. "I didn't give my daughter a beautiful name so I could call her Liz, as if she were some reptile."

She followed him into the living room. "What can I get you to drink?"

"How about if I join you for a Jack Daniels and soda? I have reason to celebrate."

While he fixed the drinks, she looked around the room. Nothing had changed since the day her parents moved from Brooklyn. Above the fireplace was a photograph of the mayor presenting the Distinguished Service Award to her father, Brian Crowder. She was twelve at the time. Her brothers, fourteen, sixteen, eighteen and twenty, were all in the picture, along with her mother.

On an end table was a picture of Elizabeth in her high school baseball uniform on the mound, pitching to a boy at the plate. Beside it, one of her dad in a Marine uniform when he returned from Vietnam. Then a picture of the whole family at her Harvard graduation.

He returned with the drinks. "Let me guess," he said. "You and Craig are getting married."

"Not that. I just made a deal to write a book for a huge sum of money."

He raised his eyebrows. "A hundred thousand?"

"Six hundred."

His face lit up with pride. "Alright! Good for you. I'll drink to that."

He raised his glass, pointed it at her and sipped. "What's your subject?"

"The problem Europe is having with Muslims."

"Why Europe? We're having problems here, too."

"Maybe I'll do that next."

He put a steak on the grill in the back. While they ate and sipped beer, he gave her a report on her brothers, all of whom were policemen, also her nieces and nephews.

"I like that Craig," her dad said. "He appreciate you?"

"Yeah."

"Then you should marry him."

"We're not quite there yet, Dad."

"But you're thirty-seven, Elizabeth. Don't let that biological clock stop ticking."

She loved her father for always saying what he was thinking.

"I don't mean to be nosey. I'd just like to see a little Elizabeth running around."

"Craig and I will come for Christmas."

"That's great. We're having it at Tommy's. They'll all love to see you. You like living over there in France?"

"Mostly. Some of the time I miss the United States."

She offered to help him clean up. "Where are you going now?" he asked.

"I'm on a ten thirty from JFK back to Paris."

"Then you better get going."

"I have time. How are you doing financially, Dad?"

"Clear sailing. Another forty thou on the mortgage. That's all the debt I have. Not many people can say that these days."

She took a deep breath and swallowed hard. Ready to skate on thin ice. She had to be careful. She was worried her father might get angry, but she had to try.

"As soon as I get my first installment on the book deal, Dad, I'm sending you a check for your seventieth birthday. Enough to pay off the mortgage."

"Oh no you're not."

"Please Dad. I want to very much. I can afford it. I've never forgotten how you sacrificed to help get me through Harvard."

"You had a scholarship."

"But that only covered part of it. You know that."

He shook his head. "You're something, Elizabeth. God bless you."

He stood up and hugged her. She glanced at her watch. "I guess I should be going."

At the door, he put an arm around her. "Listen, honey, be careful. Lots of them are good. But some of them are dangerous people. Those Muslims. And they hate us."

3

ATLAS MOUNTAINS, MOROCCO

Musa was sitting behind the desk in the one-floor, thick-walled brownstone building he had constructed to be his headquarters. His eyes were glued to the large-screen television on a table across the room. Mesmerized, he watched as CNN replayed over and over analyses of yesterday's assassination attempt on President Dalton and how Craig Page thwarted it.

The CNN announcer was droning on. "Craig Page has enjoyed his greatest victory. There was some dissent when an American was picked for the position of director of the newly established EU Counterterrorism Agency. With yesterday evening's action, those dissenters have been silenced."

Musa assumed that the media only knew about half of what had happened. Even then, Craig had done an incredible job, Musa had to admit. Though he had nothing to do with the Dalton attempt, Musa realized Craig would be Musa's primary adversary for the Spanish Revenge.

Once he came to that conclusion last evening, Musa had used the internet to develop an extensive bio on Craig. From his birth in Monessen Pennsylvania to his chemical engineering degree at Carnegie Mellon, two years in the oil business in Houston, followed by twenty years with the CIA, running some of its most successful actions, rising to become head of Middle Eastern Operations. And finally a sudden and unexplained dismissal from the agency a year and a half ago.

Though Craig was experienced and good, Musa was confident that Craig would never stop Musa's Spanish Revenge. "Craig Page, you're about to suffer your most serious defeat," Musa said aloud.

Musa's operation had been carefully and precisely planned. Nothing could go wrong. Still, with Craig likely to be involved, Musa wanted one final check.

He picked up the phone on the battered wooden desk next to the Beretta and summoned Omar.

His deputy appeared a minute later. "Yes, Ahmed."

"I told you not to call me that. There is no more Ahmed. Only Musa Ben Abdil."

"I'm sorry. Old habits die hard, my friend."

"I can understand that." It was an old habit. He and Omar had grown up together as close boyhood friends in adjacent buildings in Chichy-sous Bois, a suburban slum outside of Paris, populated by Muslims whose families, like their parents, came from Algeria and Morocco.

"I want to go over the details one more time," Musa said. "Before they leave tomorrow. Bring Kemal, Ibrahami, and Yasir over here."

"Right away."

Waiting for them to arrive, Musa, stroking his neatly trimmed beard, paced on the terracotta floor stained by the blood of a traitor whom he shot last week, going over the operation in his mind. He had brilliantly conceived it. Now the implementation had to be flawless.

The three of them entered behind Omar. Kemal, who had grown up with Musa and Omar, a lifelong friend, though not as close as Omar, now looked hesitant and fearful. Not Ibrahami and Yasir. The Somali and the Algerian, both of whom Musa met in Clichy during the '05 riots, stood tall, looking eager. Ready for what lay ahead in the next two days.

Nobody sat. They all stood around Musa's desk.

"Yasir," Musa said. "In the morning, you'll fly to Paris. Stay with friends in Clichy whom you can trust and don't tell them why you're there. Then Friday morning, from eight a.m. on, you'll be in the area of Paris near the pont de l'Alma. Walk around. Stop in brasseries until I call. You have the number of CNN?"

"Committed to memory," Yasir said.

Musa reached into his desk drawer, pulled out a micro CD player and handed it to Yasir. "All you have to do is hold it up to the phone and press the play button."

"I understand."

Musa turned to Kemal and Ibrahami. "Tomorrow morning, the two of you will fly to Madrid. You'll pick up the bomb and remote from the locker in the train station. Tomorrow evening at eight, deliver the note to the Spanish Defense Ministry. Then drive to Seville. I want you both in place early Friday morning when the Spanish school vacation begins. Then …"

Kemal interrupted. "Is it wise to provide advance notice of the attack? Won't that increase the chances of our being stopped?"

Musa couldn't believe Kemal was questioning him on an operational matter. The success of an organization like the Spanish Revenge depended on tight discipline and the chain of command.

"I shouldn't have to explain it," Musa said slowly, as if he were speaking to a child. "Giving advance notice shows our strength to the world. We're telling the Spanish government that they can't stop us even if they know what we've planned. We'll gain greater respect. And will be able to raise funds more easily for future operations."

Kemal persisted, "But …"

Musa cut him off. "I said we're doing it that way. Now let's look at the map of Southern Spain. You can take it with you, but I want to focus on the spot for the attack. I selected it myself after visiting the area."

The five of them moved up close to Musa's desk, their eyes on the map. Musa pointed to a red "X" along train tracks running from Madrid to Seville. "This is it."

He glanced at Ibrahami, who was nodding. Kemal had his lips pursed together. Mouth drawn tight.

"I expect you to escape," Musa continued. "But remember, under any circumstances you can't let them take you prisoner. Craig Page is likely to be involved. He'll interrogate you. Force you to divulge the location of our base and who else is involved. All will be lost."

Musa delivered his warning in a stern voice.

"If necessary, I'm prepared to die for the cause," Ibrahami said.

"And you, Kemal?" Musa asked.

"Why do you need two of us to do the job?"

"We've been over that. One to set and detonate the bomb. The other to drive the get-away vehicle."

"Ibrahami could easily do it all himself."

Musa felt a surge of resentment against Kemal, the coward. Afraid and unwilling to die for the objective of the Spanish Revenge. Though Musa kept his anger in check, he realized he couldn't risk sending someone like that on an important mission.

Musa looked at Ibrahami. "Could you do it all?"

"Absolutely."

"Then that's what we'll do."

He reached into his pocket, took out a key and handed it to Ibrahami. "It has the number of the locker in the train station. Close to where tickets are sold."

As the meeting broke up, Musa asked Omar to remain behind. When they were alone, Musa said, "Watch Kemal. I don't trust him."

Omar nodded and left. Alone, Musa paced again. He was worried that he had made a mistake letting Kemal live. Perhaps he was being too lenient because of their history.

Once there were three boys in Clichy: Ahmed, Omar, and Kemal. Only twenty five years ago. It seems like eons.

That was the only world Ahmed had ever known until Madam Cohen, his math teacher, discovered when he was twelve that he had a remarkable gift for mathematics. Despite his father's opposition, Madam Cohen arranged a scholarship for Ahmed to attend an elite private school in Paris. Riding a train home in the evening meant enduring the taunts and fists of neighborhood boys. Omar and Kemal were his only friends. Each night he went home bloodied and bruised. Life was unbearable until a vicious sixteen-year-old bully came after with him with a baseball bat and the cry, "I'll murder you, traitor." In the twilight, Ahmed knew he meant it.

A circle of neighborhood kids rapidly formed around the two of them. Ahmed realized only one would walk away alive. In front of the circle, he heard Omar shout: "Kill him, Ahmed."

The bully was bigger and stronger, but Ahmed was faster. Each time the bully swung, Ahmed ducked. He reached to the ground, grabbed a handful of pebbles and tossed them into the boy's eyes. His adversary blinded, Ahmed grabbed the bat. Savagely, he smashed it against he bully's ribs knocking him to the ground. Then he pounded away at the bully's skull, again and again, unleashing the frustration of long weeks of misery, until the bully stopped moving. Horrified, other boys pulled Ahmed away, still holding the baseball bat.

They left the bully's dead body on the ground. An hour later, the police came and made only a perfunctory investigation. A code of silence of the neighborhood held. No one told the police what happened. From that day on, Ahmed carried the baseball bat with him to and from the train to school. No one ever bothered him again.

Thinking about the private school, he immediately saw Nicole, so young, so beautiful, the blonde hair cascading alongside her strikingly beautiful white face. Between classes and the study, they slipped into the woods near the school and kissed. His first love. His only love. The gold cross around her neck. She was afraid to tell her parents about him.

When he graduated from private school, Madam Cohen, who had followed his progress, arranged a scholarship to Columbia University. He traveled around the United States. Saw how Americans hated him and all Muslims because of 9/11. Their bigotry and hatred made him glad it happened.

But not everyone despised him. In New York, those knee-jerk liberals saw him as the dark-skinned Muslim poster child from the Paris slums. They pretended to love him. It made them feel better.

He abandoned engineering for world history and slept with the lightest and blondest women. He dabbled for a while with pro-Palestinians helping to organize a protest against the Israeli foreign minister, but he quickly realized he had no interest in their cause. His people didn't care squat about Jerusalem or the West Bank. They were the despised Arabs and Berbers from North Africa living in poverty and subjugated by the Christians who had stolen their land five hundred years ago.

After receiving a degree in history, cum laude, he returned to Paris, moved back to Clichy, and organized youth programs. Money was no problem. He raised over a million euros from French liberals who supported him to salve their conscience.

The best was Nicole. She had waited for him. With a degree in psychology from the University of Paris, she worked with him. They moved in together, still concealing their relationship from her parents. Socially prominent Parisians. They would never understand.

He was so happy. Then it all came crashing down in the riots in the Paris suburbs of October 2005.

The police were brutal. Blood flowed on the streets. The blood of his people. And Nicole marched next to him. Always close by, until that thug of a red-faced policeman fired tear gas right at him, then pulled Nicole away, the only white girl in the crowd.

Eyes burning, restrained by two cops, Musa watched helplessly as the red-faced monster smashed his truncheon against her blonde head over and over, smiling sadistically the whole time.

Musa arrived at the hospital after the ambulance. "She's in a coma," the doctor said. "The result of a brain hemorrhage." He sat next to her bed, willing her to regain consciousness. Then her parents came. "Get your ugly black face out of here," her father screamed. "You destroyed our daughter."

For the next week, he remained downstairs in the hospital, out of their sight, seeking reports from the nurses about Nicole while watching on television the police brutality aimed at defenseless Muslim youth.

A week later, a nurse told him: "Nicole died." He cried for an hour. Not being a believer, he couldn't seek solace in prayer. Action was his only response to what had happened: Nicole's death, the riots. It was his destiny, he decided, to begin his own movement, demanding justice and equality for Muslims in Europe. Seeking revenge for Nicole. Violence was the only way to obtain it.

PARIS

Craig rushed through the briefing he and Jacques gave to Pierre Morreau, the Defense Minister, about the attempted assassination of Dalton. He didn't want to be late for his eight thirty dinner with Elizabeth.

His car was waiting in front of the Ministry. When Craig took one look at the Boulevard St. Germain, which resembled a parking lot, he said to his driver, "I'm taking the Metro. Please meet me in front of the Bristol Hotel in a couple of hours."

As the crowded train rumbled along, Craig, standing and clutching a pole, thought about Elizabeth. He was thrilled for her. She had sounded so excited when she called early in the afternoon to say she had arrived. Happily, the Bristol had had a cancellation.

The train stopped. He exited the Metro station at Avenue Franklin Roosevelt. Walking swiftly in the chilly autumn air, he covered the four blocks to the Hotel Bristol, only a hundred yards from the spot on which the Iranian with the cell phone had intended to activate the bomb in the Hermes box.

A hotel doorman nodded to Craig and turned the revolving door, catapulting Craig from the busy Rue Saint Honore to the quite elegance of Paris's most luxurious hotel. Craig glanced at the clock above the concierge's desk. Eight thirty-five. He cut across the marble-floored lobby to the circular, richly wood-paneled dining room—the height of opulence and sophistication. The incredible food and meticulous attention to detail made it Craig's favorite restaurant in Paris.

The maître d' greeted Craig and said, "Madame is already here."

Craig spotted Elizabeth across the room, seated at a round table adjacent to the side wall. A glass of champagne in front of her, she seemed preoccupied, deep in thought, looking radiant, her honey brown hair pulled back, the magenta suit snug enough to reveal her good figure.

"Mind if I join you?" he said.

She snapped back to reality. He kissed her on the lips, then sat down.

The tuxedo-clad sommelier wheeled over a cart with half a dozen bottles of champagne on ice. "I'll have what she's drinking."

When Craig had a glass, he raised it, "Congratulations. Now tell me about the book deal."

"I will in a minute. First, I want to know what happened with Dalton. Did they try again?"

He shook his head. "Nothing else. As I just told Pierre Moreau, it's over."

"Do you know who was responsible?"

"I understand why you're such a good reporter."

"I take that as a compliment."

"According to my source, the Iranian government. If they try again, it won't be on my turf. Since Dalton hates Europe, I doubt if he'll be back."

"Did Dalton thank you for saving his life?"

"Yeah, right." Smiling, he pulled the cell phone from his pocket. "Maybe I missed the call when I was in the Metro." He glanced at it. "Nope. No call."

"Dalton's a jerk."

"So you and Jacques are in agreement about something."

A waiter came over with menus. They ordered. He selected an '05 Chambolle Musigny from Dujac.

"Okay," he said. "I won't wait a second longer. What's the deal?"

"Harold got Virginia to agree to an advance of six hundred K." She was flushed with excitement.

"Yes!" he cried out. Too loud for the dignified dining room. People stared at them. He didn't care. He ignored them. She had put a lot of work into the book proposal.

"That is fabulous," he said.

"So I'm buying dinner this evening."

"You won't get an argument from me. What's your deadline?"

"You always ask the practical questions."

The wine arrived. He tasted it. Perfect for their seared fois gras with caramelized apples, which came right behind. They paused to eat.

"This is spectacular," she said. "I'm glad you picked this place."

While he sipped wine, she said, "They want a detailed outline in thirty days. A draft in twelve months."

"Can you do that while working at the paper?"

"I talked to Rob, who's now running the foreign news department. He said they'll lighten my reporting load. Even give me a little time off to do research and write, if I need it."

"Very generous."

"He said he's not being altruistic. They want me to have the expertise. The topic will become even more important over time."

"I agree. Rob's being smart."

"If it's okay with you, I'd like to turn the study in the apartment into my writing center."

"Sure. Whatever works. I'll do anything to help."

They were midway through the fois gras when Craig felt the cell phone vibrating in his pocket. Sometimes, he hated that phone. As he yanked it out of his pocket, she said, "Dalton, calling to thank you."

"I doubt it." He checked caller ID. General Jose Alvarez, the Spanish Defense Minister.

"Sorry," he said to Elizabeth. "I have to take this. I'll keep it short."

"Don't worry. I understand. If you take too long, I'll drink all the wine."

"Hold on a minute," he said to Alvarez. Then with the phone plastered to his ear, he headed out of the dining room and into a quiet corner of the lobby.

"We have a situation," Alvarez said. "And Prime Minister Zahara insisted that I call you."

Alvarez sounded hostile. Craig got the drift. Regardless of the threat to Spain, Alvarez would never have called for Craig's help. But Prime Minster Zahara was a different matter. On the two occasions they had met, Craig and Zahara hit it off.

"Tell me about it," Craig said.

"About two hours ago, a messenger dropped off a typed note at the Defense Ministry, warning that one of the trains from Madrid will be bombed tomorrow morning. The note was signed 'Musa Ben Abdil.' We haven't been able to locate the messenger. I think it's a prank and nothing will happen, but Zahara doesn't want to take a chance. He wants your ideas of how we should deal with this situation."

Craig hated cutting short his dinner, but Zahara wanted his involvement. "Send a plane to Paris for me. I'll drop everything and come to Madrid."

"I don't think that's necessary," Alvarez said. "It's late. We'll hook you in by phone as needed. I'll tell Zahara you're busy in Paris."

I'm sure you will.

"Listen Jose, Madrid is an hour away. This sounds like a major terrorist attack. If Prime Minster Zahara wants my involvement, it will be more effective in person."

"But ..."

"You know I'm right."

A deep sigh. "I guess so. I'll send the Prime minister's plane to Orly. Be there in an hour."

Craig checked his watch. He had twenty minutes before leaving. Time to explain to Elizabeth. First, he had one more call to make. To Giuseppe, his deputy in Rome. After describing the Madrid situation, he told Giuseppe, "Use one of the Italian government planes to fly to Madrid. I'll meet you there."

Back at the table, Craig whispered to Elizabeth what he had heard from Alvarez. At the mention of Musa Ben Abdil, she gave a start. "The man was an historical figure," she said.

"I've never heard of him."

"Let me give you the background. The short version ... from the tenth through the fifteenth century, Muslims ruled Southern Spain and much of the Iberian peninsula. During this period, science, arts, and learning prospered. Generally, a spirit of religious tolerance prevailed with Muslims, Christians and Jews living in harmony, then internal dissention in the Islamic leadership and disputes among Arabs and Berbers weakened the governing structure. At the same time, Christian armies were moving south from France and conquering Northern Spain."

Elizabeth paused to take a breath. "In the Fifteenth Century, Queen Isabella and King Ferdinand solidified their rule over Christian Spain and formed a close alliance with Pope Innocent VIII. Armed with the Pope's blessing, they vowed to drive Islam out of Spain. Muslims would have a choice: Expulsion, conversion, or death.

"Methodically, Isabella and Ferdinand moved their army south, conquering the countryside town by town. In 1491, much of the remaining Muslim population was gathered in the Alhambra, their magnificent palace of Islam near Granada. The Muslim leadership wanted to surrender, but one famous general, Musa Ben Abdil, argued for fighting to the death, despite the odds. When he was overruled by the leadership, Musa refused to accept their decision.

"He grabbed his sword and mounted his horse. Accompanied by only a few supporters, he stormed out of the Alhambra. He fought valiantly, killing as many Christians as he could, until they finally killed him."

"How do you know all this stuff?"

"I majored in medieval history at Harvard ... Remember?"

"Oh yeah. So you're telling me that the terrorist who sent this note has a keen knowledge of Spanish medieval history."

She was on the edge of her chair. She liked to play baseball. Right now she reminded him of a batter getting ready to hit the ball out of the park.

"More than that," she said. "You're not dealing with an ordinary terrorist. You're facing an Islamic fanatic who's declaring war on Christians in Spain."

"And if that's the case, whoever we're dealing with won't limit himself to a single train bombing."

"Correct."

"Can you fly with me to Madrid this evening? Your knowledge of Spanish medieval history will be valuable."

"Sure. All I was doing was having a celebration at the best restaurant in Paris. Maybe they'll pack the rest of our meal to go."

5

MADRID

Craig wasn't surprised that the two a.m. meeting took place in the ornate residence of Prime Minister Zahara or that the Prime Minster was not only attending, but was seated at the head of the polished wooden table in the library. From their prior meetings, Craig concluded that the handsome sixty-year-old politician with coal black hair, slicked down and parted in the center, was very much of a hands-on leader, and the stakes were now high.

For the Spanish government, the Prime Minster was joined by General Alvarez and Carlos Sanchez, Alvarez's Deputy Defense Minister, whom Craig knew from his resume to be forty-two, but who had a young man's face, making him look like twenty-five.

When Craig, Elizabeth, and Giuseppe entered the room, Alvarez and Carlos were seated at one side of the table. Two walls with floor to ceiling shelves were filled with books, so neatly arranged that Craig doubted anyone ever took one off its shelf.

Craig made the introductions. "Giuseppe Maltoni, the Assistant Director of the EU Counterterrorism Agency based in Rome, and Elizabeth Crowder, a personal friend who has expertise which I believe will be valuable."

Alvarez was twirling his mustache and glaring at Craig. "You omitted to say that Elizabeth is a reporter with the *International Herald*. We're having a confidential meeting on a critical issue. Not a press conference." He was raising his voice. "It's outrageous of you to bring her."

Craig refused to let Alvarez intimidate him. "As I said, she's a personal friend." Craig was speaking calmly. "She has something to contribute and her confidentiality is assured."

Now Alvarez turned to the Prime Minster. "We can't let her stay."

Zahara looked at Elizabeth. "I know who you are. I read your articles and usually like them."

"Usually," she said.

"I didn't appreciate the one a month ago about the weakness of some of our banks."

"Actually, I thought I was being kind."

"Perhaps. Back to this. I understand Jose Alvarez's concern. On the other hand, Craig says you have something to contribute. Will you promise not to report anything about this situation unless I give you approval?"

"Absolutely."

"That's good enough for me."

Alvarez was fuming. "This entire meeting is ridiculous. All for a prank. The note was prepared by some kids or a nut. I can't tell you how many threats I get every day that turn out to be nothing."

"I don't think so," Craig said with confidence. "Not this time."

"Why?" the Prime Minster asked.

"The name typed at the bottom of the note was Musa Ben Abdil."

Craig's words were met with blank stares by the three Spaniards.

"Tell them who Musa Bin Abdil was," Craig said to Elizabeth.

Everyone was looking at her.

"In 1491, when the Muslims were surrounded in the Alhambra, the Islamic leadership wanted to surrender to Queen Isabella and King Ferdinand. Musa Ben Abdil, a famous Muslim general, insisted on fighting the Christians to the bitter end. On horseback, he stormed out of the Alhambra with his sword and killed as many Christians as he could, until they killed him."

"That doesn't prove a thing," Alvarez said. "The prankster could have read a history book and picked up the name."

Craig turned to Zahara, "My gut tells me we're dealing with a viable threat made by an Islamic fanatic intent on declaring war on Christians in Spain."

"That's ridiculous," Alvarez said.

"And this train bombing may be only his opening salvo. He has to be stopped early."

Alvarez scoffed. "We're dealing with kids playing a game."

With his eyes, Alvarez was shooting poison darts at Carlos.

"How do you propose to stop this bombing?" Zahara asked Craig.

"That won't be easy. A huge number of trains leave Madrid every morning."

As if on cue, Carlos reached into his briefcase and pulled out a stack of papers. "The train schedule for tomorrow," he said, and slid it across the table to Craig. "The beginning of a school holiday."

Glancing at the schedule, Craig confirmed his instinct. Scores of trains were scheduled to leave Madrid tomorrow morning, heading in every direction. Craig was impressed with Carlos, who was conscientious and organized. What a contrast to his boss, that bag of hot wind.

"How do you propose to stop this terrorist who calls himself Musa?" the Prime Minister asked Craig.

"Thwart the train bombing and capture one of the perpetrators, who can lead us back to Musa."

"That won't be easy," the Prime Minster said pointing to the schedule Carlos handed Craig.

Craig was ready with the plan he had developed with Elizabeth's input on the plane ride from Paris. "Soldiers with bomb detectors will check each train in the Madrid station before we let passengers board. Other army units around the country will examine train tracks leading from Madrid. Finally, high tech body and baggage scanners will check passengers before they board."

Alvarez groaned. "You know how long that will take? None of our morning trains will leave before noon."

"Perhaps, but I don't think Prime Minster Zahara wants a disaster."

The Prime Minster nodded.

"Nor does he want the political fallout from chasing pranksters," Alvarez shot back.

Zahara was rubbing his hand over his chin, looking at Craig "You're the expert. If you're telling me I would be foolish to brush off this threat, then I have to follow your advice. Is that what *you* are telling me?"

Craig gulped hard. "Yes, Mr. Prime Minster."

"That's good enough for me."

"We'll have a public relations nightmare," Alvarez said. "We'll never be able to conceal the reasons for the extra security from the people. Rumors will fly."

"I don't want to conceal it," Craig said. "Quite the contrary. I think we should inform Madrid radio and televisions stations that a threat has been made to blow up a morning train and the government is trying to stop it. Let people planning to travel decide whether or not to chance a train."

"That's ridiculous," Alvarez said.

"Having Prime Minster Zahara conceal the information would be a lot worse."

"Agreed," the Prime minister said with a ring of finality. "Carlos, you prepare a statement for Craig's review. I want you, Carlos, to be a spokesman with the Spanish media."

Craig glanced across the table. Carlos looked pleased, but a little embarrassed. Alvarez was scowling, twirling his mustache, definitely not having a good night.

"One other thing," Craig said. "Elizabeth, can you still get a short piece in the *International Herald's* morning edition?"

She glanced at her watch. "If I call in the next fifteen minutes. But regardless, it'll be on our website."

"I'd like you to publish the note from the man calling himself Musa Ben Abdil. Also, include your name and contact information at the bottom. Would you be willing to do that?"

"Sure, if it would help," she said without hesitation.

"What do you hope to accomplish?" the Prime Minster asked.

"An alternative route to Musa. We'll try to trace any call she gets. Route it into the Defense Department's IT Center. Also, pick up the originator of an e-mail message. These people may want to make a statement. We'll hang Elizabeth out there as the bait."

"I thought he was your friend," Zahara said to Elizabeth.

She smiled. "I thought so, too."

If Elizabeth were reluctant to do it, Craig knew she would have said so. Nothing shy about her. And she was never intimidated by him.

She took the laptop from her bag and drafted the article.

Craig said to Carlos, "I'll work with your IT people to set up the logistics to trace calls and incoming messages."

"Meantime, I'll assemble a military liaison for you," Alvarez said, now wanting to be part of the team. "For the security checks."

"I'll be available to help at any point," the Prime Minister said. "Nobody sleeps tonight. We have to stop that bomb."

ATLAS MOUNTAINS, MOROCCO

With the sun rising in the eastern sky Friday morning, Musa sat down at the desk. He removed the Glock pistol from the holster strapped to his waist and placed it at his right hand. Then he booted up his computer. He was eager to get online. Why the hell did it take so long?

He had learned years ago that the Western media could be effectively manipulated to support any cause. Reporters—print and television—were like pigs at a trough in a constant feeding frenzy. Their sustenance was the stories or, even easier, the handouts anyone cared to give them to fill hours of airtime or the pages that separated advertisements.

He had carefully thought through his media plan for the Spanish train bombing. Now he had to see if he was receiving the attention he craved.

He stroked his neatly trimmed beard, waiting for that damn

computer. Let's go. At last he was online. He began with the *Madrid Times*. On the front page he saw a short item entitled "Possible Train Bombing."

It's more than possible, you fools, he thought. Then he read on: "An unidentified terrorist has threatened to bomb a train leaving Madrid this morning. Authorities have increased security at the station and on trains. Speculation has centered on Basque separatists groups."

That was all. The whole article. He re-read it and bristled. Why didn't they publish his note? Why didn't they include the name Musa Ben Abdil? And he wasn't a terrorist. He had a cause. He was seeking justice for Muslims in Europe. He despised being called a terrorist.

He went to another Madrid daily. Exactly the same article. Verbatim. And ditto for a third.

The Spanish government was managing the news. Issuing their own story and requiring all the papers to publish it. Conspiring to deprive him of the attention he deserved for this daring attack. Well, they'll suffer in a few short hours.

There was another possibility. He went online with the *International Herald*. There, under Elizabeth Crowder's byline was an article entitled: "Spanish Train Bombing Threatened." He continued reading: "Spanish Authorities received a note this evening stating: 'One of your trains leaving Madrid tomorrow morning will be bombed.' It was signed by Musa Ben Abdil."

Now Musa was pleased. His name was in print. And Elizabeth Crowder had written the article. Musa knew from the internet, purveyor of intimate details of peoples' lives, the greatest privacy invader in the history of the world, that Elizabeth was Craig Page's lover. Her byline confirmed that Craig was involved. Not merely that fool Alvarez. They were taking him seriously.

His eyes dropped down to the bottom of the article. Elizabeth provided her contact information.

That made him smile. They were inviting him to call her and take credit for the bombing, so Craig could use his high-tech tracing equipment to locate Musa. Did Craig really think Musa was such a fool?

No, he had his own plan for media manipulation to take credit for the bombing. Yasir was in Paris, ready to move as soon as Musa called him. He had the tape. By this time tomorrow, everyone in the world would know who Musa Ben Abdil was. Who the Spanish Revenge was. Their objective. And Craig Page, the great counterterrorism expert, would be tearing his hair out.

He heard a knock on the door and looked up. "Yes?"

"It's Omar."

"Come in."

"We have a problem," Omar said.

"What happened?"

"You asked me to watch Kemal."

"What's that sniveling coward doing now?"

"Planning to quit and leave the base. He's in the barracks packing."

"When we came here, I told him quitting was not an option."

"I reminded him of that, but he says he doesn't care. He told me that this morning he called his sister, Lila, in Marseilles on his cell phone. He wouldn't tell me what he said to her."

Furious, Musa shot to his feet. "I gave an order. No cell phones. Unless used properly, they'll permit our enemies to locate us. Bring Kemal over here. I'll talk to him myself."

Musa's tone was hard, and cold as ice. He watched Omar cringe, then look at the ground as he marched out. He knew Omar wouldn't dare defy him and help Kemal escape. Omar had always feared him. Done what Musa told him.

Ten minutes later, Omar returned with Kemal, who looked belligerent and defiant.

"I hear you're leaving," Musa said.

"Yeah. That's right. We're heading for a disaster, because you insisted on giving the Spanish advance notice of the train bombing."

"I've explained to you a couple of times why I'm doing that. It shows our strength to the world. We'll gain respect. It'll help us raise funds for further operations."

"That's nonsense. It was a mistake. They're on alert. They'll arrest Ibrahami. He'll tell them all about us. When the bombs start falling here, I don't want to be looking up into the sky, then running for cover."

"Don't worry. You won't be."

"What do you mean?" Kemal said, anxiety in his voice.

Musa picked up the gun on his desk and walked toward Kemal.

Retreating, cowering, Kemal said, "If you feel that strongly, I won't leave."

"What did you tell Lila on the phone this morning?"

"I didn't talk to her."

"Don't lie to me."

Kemal glanced at Omar. "Bastard," he hissed.

Musa felt betrayed. "I told you no cell phone calls."

Kemal pulled the phone from his pocket and held it out.

Musa ignored it. "What did you tell Lila?"

"Nothing."

Musa grabbed the gun by the barrel and savagely smashed the handle against the side of Kemal's face. Blood poured from his nose and mouth. He dropped to his knees, the cell phone falling from his hand.

"What did you tell her?"

"I asked if she heard about a Spanish train bombing today. She said it was on the news."

"Did you tell her where you were?"

"No. Not a word. As Allah is my judge."

Musa didn't know whether Kemal was telling the truth. But he was convinced he'd never find out. He was also convinced that Kemal was now a huge liability, with the potential to destroy everything Musa had worked so hard to establish. He raised the gun and pointed it at Kemal.

"Please, Ahmed. We grew up together. The three of us. We've been friends since we were five years old. We ..."

Musa pulled the trigger and fired a single shot to Kemal's heart. As he collapsed, Kemal's arms were flailing on the ground, his movements spasmatic. And then, in death, he was still.

"Get his body out of here," Musa said to Omar. "He disgusts me. And clean up the blood from my floor."

Watching Omar take away the body, Musa thought how completely he had severed his ties to the past. He refused to be distracted. Now was not the time for sentimentality.

Once Omar cleaned the floor, Musa returned to his desk and thought again about the logistics for this morning's train bombing. Everything was in place. Ibrahami knew what he had to do. And he couldn't be taken alive. With Craig Page now involved, Ibrahami would never be able to hold out if captured. He'd disclose Musa and the location of their base. Operation Spanish Revenge would be wrecked before it ever swung into high gear. But he was confident that wouldn't happen. Ibrahami wasn't Kemal. Craig Page would be helpless to stop the bomb. It would kill scores of people.

Musa Ben Abdil and the Spanish Revenge would be known around the world. And this is only the beginning of our struggle for justice and equality.

7

MADRID

At ten minutes to ten in the morning, the central railroad station in Madrid was a beehive of activity. Craig was standing in the stationmaster's cluttered and overheated office, with a view of the waiting area and tracks below. Notwithstanding disclosure of the threat, and extensive delays, only about twenty percent of the passengers canceled their trips. But so far, not a single train had left the station.

Looking down, Craig saw thousands of people milling around, including lots of children, because of the school holiday, jamming the cafés, where supplies were exhausted. Fighting for sitting space, smoking cigarettes, and cursing the delay. Frayed nerves led to pushing and shoving. Patrols of armed soldiers kept order. One helluva mess.

Despite all of that, Craig was pleased with the progress that had been made. By seven, the first morning trains had all been carefully searched. No bombs were found. Passengers and luggage were then passed through metal detectors. It was a long and arduous process, supervised by Spanish troops. Meantime, under Giuseppe's direction, soldiers were checking train tracks leading out of Madrid. So far nothing. Craig's hope had been to get trains rolling by ten. That looked doable.

He called Alvarez on his cell to get approval.

"You didn't find a thing. Did you?" the Defense Minister said gleefully.

"Not yet."

"So this whole effort which you instigated, organized, and directed has been a massive waste of resources and a huge burden for thousands of people. All in response to a prank."

Craig got a sick feeling in the pit of his stomach. Alvarez might be right.

"I did what I thought was reasonable to save lives."

"I hope you'll at least go on television and let the people know you were responsible."

Craig felt anger welling up inside. "I'm sure you'll let them know. But don't start gloating over this publicly yet. It's far from over."

"You're a stubborn prick. Aren't you?"

"I've been called worse. Now can the trains start rolling?"

"As far as I'm concerned, they could have all left on time this morning. But the Prime Minister wants the final approval. I'll call him and get right back to you."

A minute later, the approval came.

Craig gave the order to the stationmaster. The first trains left the station. Everything seemed normal.

The next part of Craig's plan called for him and Giuseppe to be in military helicopters, following train tracks and looking for suspicious activity.

Craig decided initially that they should focus on high-visibility vacation destinations with many passengers. He told Giuseppe to fly over tracks leading to San Sebastian while he took the route to Barcelona.

Julio, an air force pilot, was already in his Apache on the roof of the train station parking garage. Craig climbed in and buckled his seatbelt. They circled northeast of Madrid for an hour, up to Barcelona and back. Craig didn't see a thing.

He called Giuseppe, "I'm coming up empty," his deputy said.

Craig wondered if Musa had decided to call off the bombing once he learned of the government's preparations.

No, he decided. Fanatics like Musa think they're invincible.

Then it hit Craig. He was missing what should have been obvious. He tried to put himself into Musa's mind, based on what Elizabeth had said, Musa was an Islamist focused on the fifteenth century, who wanted to make a statement. Where would he make it? In the South of Spain. Of course! Where the bitter final battle between Islamic and Christian forces had occurred. That meant Musa would hit a train en route to Andulusia. He told Giuseppe to head toward Granada. "And I'll cover the tracks from Madrid to Seville."

Craig consulted his blackberry, which had the schedules of all the trains that left Madrid and their destinations. Train 123 pulled out at ten o'clock, heading to Cordoba. There it would turn west to Seville.

"Let's find train 123," he said to Julio. "It should be about fifty kilometers north of Cordoba now. We'll follow it for a while."

A few minutes later, they picked up the fast-moving train. It was barreling through fertile agricultural land devoted to crops and vineyards. Most had been harvested. The sun was shining brightly. No sign of trouble on the tracks. Craig told Julio to fly to Cordoba, then turn around and fly above the track toward train 123. As they got closer, Craig saw a number of tractors and other farm vehicles. Farmers were loading hay and digging trenches. One farmer took off his hat and waved to Craig. Suddenly, something caught his eye. A dark-skinned young man was standing next to a pickup truck holding an object in his hand and looking at the tracks in a northerly direction from which train 123 was coming.

Craig grabbed the binoculars from the seat and held them tight against his face. The man didn't look like the farmers.

Craig shifted his gaze to the track. Holy shit! He saw a flat metallic object in the center of the tracks. Had to be a bomb. And the man standing next to the tracks must be planning to detonate it when the train passes over it in about two minutes. Craig had to get that train to stop before it reached the bomb.

No time to work through military channels. Fortunately, he had asked for cell phone numbers for all the engineers this morning listed by train number. He pulled up train 123 on his Blackberry and dialed.

One minute to go.

Frantically, he yanked out his cell phone and called the engineer. "Stop your train now." He shouted.

"I can't hear you. The connection's bad."

"Stop your train. I said." Craig was screaming. "Right now."

"Who is this?"

Thirty seconds, please God.

"Craig Page with the Spanish military. Just do it."

"I can't hear you."

Oh Christ, no!

He was too late.

In horror, Craig watched the train race over the metal object. Then heard a deafening blast ripping the train apart. It came to a sudden stop. Fragments of metal, people, and luggage flew through the air. Flames shot up. He called his Defense contact in Seville and told him what happened. "Get emergency medical people here immediately. I'm going after the bomber."

Craig now had one objective: To capture the man who detonated the bomb. He was climbing into a pickup truck.

Craig pointed him out to Julio.

"I could hit the truck with rockets," Julio said.

"No. No. I have to take him alive."

The bomber was Craig's only way of getting back to the man who called himself Musa Ben Abdil.

The pickup truck was driving fast over a dirt road that cut between vineyards, kicking up a cloud of dust in its wake. They were close enough that Craig saw the driver leaning out of the cab raising his eyes toward the chopper.

When they were was overhead, Craig pulled out a microphone and shouted. "Stop now. Get out with your hands in the air."

The man kept driving.

Craig picked up an Uzi and sprayed warning shots on both sides of the truck, making sure not to hit it. The driver kept going.

"We have rockets," Craig called out. "We'll use them."

That got the driver's attention. He slammed on the brakes, then jumped out and ran onto a narrow path between grapevines. Craig told Julio to land the chopper on a grassy area.

Once they were down, Craig leapt out and raced toward the vineyard path in hot pursuit. The man had a fifty yard lead, but Craig was faster. He was gaining ground. Suddenly, the man stopped, raised a gun and aimed. Craig leapt into the vineyard, scratching his face and arms as he hit the ground. His cheek was flush against the dark brown soil. Bullets flew over his head.

Craig clutched his own gun and fired back taking care not to hit the bomber who began running again.

They were approaching a small wooden shed. The man ran inside, leaving the door open. He looked out through a window and opened fire. Craig kept low and ran in an "S" route until he reached a drainage ditch. He jumped into it. The bomber wouldn't be able to hit him now.

Craig removed a smoke grenade from his jacket pocket, pulled the pin and jumped up for an instant to toss it through the door.

Craig saw the smoke. Then he heard a single blast of a gun, but he didn't see the shooter. The shot wasn't aimed at Craig.

"No," he cried out. "No."

Wildly, he tore across the ground toward the shed. Inside the smoke was heavy. Craig was choking and gagging. Even through the haze he knew he was too late. The dark, olive-skinned bomber had shot himself in the head.

His eyes watering, Craig dragged the man outside, then checked for a pulse. He was dead.

Craig searched his pockets. No ID. Not even a single piece of paper. No cell phone. All he found was the remote control device, about half the size of a television remote. Craig immediately recognized the technology. State of the art Chinese.

Who the hell are you? Who sent you?

Craig returned to the pick up truck and searched it carefully. Again, no identifying papers. No cell phone that would give Craig info on the bomber's contacts. He made a mental note of the license plate, convinced it would be a dead end. Undoubtedly a stolen pickup. Musa was smart and organized. And he had persuaded the bomber that he couldn't be taken alive.

Still, Craig had one other possibility of using the dead bomber for information. He checked the man's hands. Fingers looked normal, which meant he'd have prints. Craig called for a forensic police investigating team from Seville.

"We already have teams en route to the train bombing site," the Director said. "We'll divert one to your location."

"Once they arrive," Craig said, "have them immediately take prints from the bomber. Circulate them throughout the EU. Then take the body away. Wherever you stash it, I want armed security around the clock. And let me know by e-mail if you get a match on the prints."

Despondent and angry at himself for not capturing the bomber, Craig climbed back into the Apache and asked Julio to return to the site of the train bombing. There, medivac choppers were on the ground next to the train. A score of ambulances were roaring toward the site. Craig directed Julio to land ten yards from the twisted mangled cars that had taken a direct hit.

The carnage was the worst Craig had ever seen. Bodies and limbs had been thrown through the ragged glass of shattered windows. The dead or dying were scattered near the tracks. Cries of pain and muffled groans cut through Craig like knives.

He joined workers struggling to bring out the wounded and dead from the three most heavily damaged cars. It was tough work in tight quarters, trying to extract the maimed and screaming from the twisted metal.

He carried out an elderly man, the front of his shirt covered with blood. His whole face was bloody.

Craig returned for a small girl, maybe eight, in shock, her right arm severed at the elbow, bleeding from the chest, her glasses smashed against her face. "What kind of people do something like this?" he asked himself.

Surveying the site, his guess was there were at least thirty to forty dead or seriously wounded. Perhaps many more in the cars. He had never had a personal failure like this.

Craig's cell phone rang. Elizabeth. "I heard about the train bombing," she said, sounding grim.

"I screwed up. I got there too late."

"I'm sorry. You did what you could."

"Has Musa contacted you?"

"Nobody."

"That's too bad. I'm at a dead end here. The bomber killed himself before I could capture him."

He had another incoming call. Alvarez. "Gotto go, hon. Time to face the music."

He hooked into the Alvarez call. "You created a fucking mess," the Defense Minister said.

Craig shook his head. Alvarez was a piece of work.

"The Prime Minister wants to meet with the two of us in his office. How soon can you get there?"

"I'm at the bombing site helping with the rescue."

"Others will do it. Have a chopper bring you back to Madrid."

This time Craig didn't argue with Alvarez.

ATLAS MOUNTAINS, MOROCCO

Musa had two large screen televisions on tables in his office, one tuned to CNN, the other to a Madrid station. Everything was unfolding exactly as he had hoped. The attack was a stunning success.

The CNN screen showed Craig, looking weary, trudging from the train debris to a military helicopter. The reporter said, "There's Craig Page, the Director of the EU Counterterrorism office." He raced up to Craig blocking his way to the Apache and shoved a microphone in front of him. "Mr. Page, what can you tell us about how the bomb was set off? Was there a bomber in the area?"

Musa leaned forward, straining to hear the answer, studying Craig's face and trying to pick up the inflection. Ibrahami's orders were to try and escape, then return to the base in Morocco. If not, to kill himself, but in no event to try and communicate with Musa. He wanted to learn something from Craig about Ibrahami's fate. Craig replied, "It's an ongoing law enforcement investigation. I'm not at liberty to divulge that information."

"But can you tell us …"

Craig pushed past the reporter nearly knocking him over and climbed into the chopper.

Musa breathed a sigh of relief. If Craig had captured Ibrahami, he would have said he had someone in custody and he wouldn't be flying off himself.

Omar came into his office and pointed to the television. "What are they saying?"

"Forty four dead so far. Another fifty seriously wounded."

"Any information about Ibrahami?"

"From what Craig Page said, I think he either escaped or killed himself rather than be captured."

Musa refused to use the term martyred. He wasn't an Islamic fundamentalist. Not a religious man. He was secular. He didn't view himself as an agent of Allah. Rather, his course was worldly. Justice for Muslims in Europe.

"Who are the media attributing the attack to?"

"As we expected, speculation has focused on Al Qaeda and Basque separatists." Musa checked his watch. Yasir should be standing in the center of the pont de l'Alma in Paris. "I'm about to end that."

Musa picked up his cell phone and dialed Yasir's cell. "Now," he said. No need to say anything more. Yasir knew what to do. He would go to a public phone booth in the heart of fashionable Paris, another world from Clichy. There he would call CNN and play for them Musa's prerecorded message hoping it would be taped. Musa's voice was garbled to prevent him from being identified. But the words would be understood: "This is Musa Ben Abdil. Our Group, the Spanish Revenge, is responsible for the Spanish train bombing. Our objective is to resume the war between Muslims and Christians in Europe."

Five minutes later, Yasir called back. "Done."

Musa turned up the volume on the CNN screen. He didn't want to miss the broadcast of his recorded message.

He heard, "The death toll from the Spanish train bombing has risen to fifty six, with many more in critical condition." And nothing else. Must be too soon to get it on the air. He was confident CNN would never pass up a chance to broadcast something like that.

"Fifty six," Omar said, pumping his fist into the air. "Time to crack open the champagne."

"Absolutely. Get a bottle of Dom Perignon."

While Musa popped the cork, he smiled. He was struck by the irony of celebrating with a wine supposedly created by a monk, which it wasn't, of course.

As he and Omar raised their glasses and drank, Musa said, "To more successes."

The cold liquid tasted wonderful.

"Did you ever have any doubt we'd succeed?" Omar asked.

"Not for an instant."

"What's next?"

"I've been thinking about that. Has to be something even bigger."

"Blowing up an airplane?"

"Not creative enough."

"The Eiffel tower or the Louvre?"

"No real significance for the Christian world. We have to hit them at their heart. A target that has enormous symbolic and emotional value."

"But what?"

"Don't worry. I'll think of something. We can't be in a hurry. Deliberate and meticulous planning was the secret to our success today."

They finished the bottle of Dom Perignon and opened a second. Midway through that, Omar said to Musa, "Lila, Kemal's sister."

"What about her?"

"If Kemal gave her information about our location here in

Morocco, she could be a real threat. Perhaps ..." Omar was selecting his words carefully. "Perhaps we should eliminate Lila."

"I don't think Kemal told her anything."

"But we can't be sure."

Musa laughed. "You never did like her, because she wouldn't sleep with you. Now you want to get even with her."

Omar looked embarrassed, "How do you know that?"

"She told me. Once when we were in bed together."

Omar looked confused. "You had sex with her?"

"Several times, but in all honesty, you didn't miss much. She wasn't very good."

"That's not what this is about. I do think she could pose a threat and should be eliminated."

Musa had always liked Lila from the time they were young children. He hoped that wasn't clouding his judgment. "Perhaps you're right. Let me think about it. If I decide to act, I know someone in Marseilles who could take care of her."

MADRID

Craig, with Giuseppe at his side, walked in to the Spanish Prime Minister's cavernous office. Photos of Zahara with other world leaders lined one wall. On another, hung a portrait of the Prime Minister. Alvarez and Carlos were already there.

Looking pale, the Prime Minister remained seated behind his red leather-topped desk. "The death toll has risen to seventy fatalities," he said grimly.

"I'm very sorry," Craig said. "I don't have words to express how sorry I am."

"You should be," Alvarez retorted. "I wanted to cancel all the trains this morning, but you insisted they were safe."

Flabbergasted, Craig was framing his response to that blatant lie when the Prime Minister said to Alvarez, "Shut up. I don't want to hear anymore from you."

"Humph," Alvarez snarled, his face beet red.

At that moment, Craig's respect for the Prime Minister increased. He obviously knew his Defense Minister. Zahara turned to Craig. "I don't blame you. I blame myself. I could have cancelled all the trains this morning. You told me everything. I knew the risks. It was my decision."

"Thank you sir, but still ..."

"Tell me what happened."

Craig described in detail the bombing and the death of the bomber. He explained that the bomb was sophisticated, state of the art, produced in China, and activated by remote control.

"Judging from the bomber's appearance, what do you think? Basque or Arab?"

"Ethnically, from North Africa. Arab or Berber. Perhaps Somali. Possibly Iranian."

"But he could be a Spanish citizen?"

"For sure."

"I assume he didn't have any ID?"

"Correct. But I've had your forensic people from Seville lift fingerprints and circulate them throughout the EU. They're supposed to notify me if they get any hits."

Craig pulled the Blackberry from his pocket and looked at it. Nothing. He laid it down on the table. The Prime Minister asked, "Has any group claimed responsibility?"

"Not to my knowledge."

"It's probably the Basques."

"Al Qaeda would be my guess."

Zahara ignored Craig's words. "I've done everything to mollify the Basques, but I won't dismember this country ... even through there are many in Catalonia who would like that."

"Perhaps someone will step forward and take credit," Craig said.

The Prime Minister was walking around the office, deep in thought. "I guess we have to assume there will be other attacks."

"Unfortunately, that's correct."

"We owe the people some explanation. I'll have my press secretary prepare a statement which I can give on Spanish television. I'd like you to review it."

"Be happy to."

"Meantime, I want you to arrange a CNN interview for yourself. I want people around the world to know how aggressively we moved to try and stop this attack. And how vigilant we will be in the future. You're better able to deal with an international audience."

Giuseppe said, "Perhaps Craig should do the CNN interview back in Paris. Let people know that Spain is not alone in this. That the European Counterterrorism Agency is involved as well. And that the next attack could come anywhere in the EU."

"Excellent points." The Prime Minister said. "I'll have my plane fly Craig back."

As Craig stood to leave, he picked up his Blackberry. It began vibrating. A message from the Seville forensic people. "French police matched the bomber's prints with those of Ibrahami Shabelle, arrested in Paris on October 30, 2005. This is a precise match."

Craig read the message aloud. Carlos immediately grasped its significance. "If we could find out whom Ibrahami was involved with, we could get a lead on Musa."

"Precisely.

Zahara pounded his fist into the palm of his hand. "So we might be able to find and capture these bastards!"

Though Alvarez was sulking while twirling his mustache, the others now seemed hopeful. Craig tried to temper his own enthusiasm. He had seen enough leads like this dry up over the years. He turned to Carlos, "Check with all Spanish agencies. See if they have Ibrahami in any of their databases."

Then Craig called Jacques in Paris. After explaining what he just learned, Craig said, "I need your help."

"You don't have to ask. I'll get right on it. I'll let you know as soon as I have a bio on Ibrahami."

As he flew north, Craig closed his weary eyes and held his head. His was a cruel job, with no margin for error. Failure was measured in numbers of lives lost. That made today a disaster.

Musa was dreadful, contemptible. A monster. What kind of person kills innocent children ... women ... men ... so cruelly? Craig vowed to hunt and to kill the man calling himself Musa Ben Abdil, if it was the last thing he ever did.

10

PARIS

Craig was dismayed. As soon as he entered the CNN studio on the elegant Avenue Montaigne in Paris in the early evening, the petite news director, Marie Laval, clipboard in hand, met him and said, "Jean Claude Moreau will be interviewing you."

Craig didn't like doing television interviews. He realized they went with the job, but they were among his least favorable activities. And he detested Jean Claude. The man was abrasive and self aggrandizing. His primary motivation was making a splash and maximizing his ratings. He wasn't interested in obtaining facts. In his desire to make himself look good, the often bombastic Jean Claude was hypercritical of his interviewees, constantly denigrating them. Craig's previous two interviews with Jean Claude had ended in shouting matches.

"Why Jean Claude?" Craig asked. "His program finishes at 8:00 p.m. It's already 8:10."

"He decided to stay late. Just to do your interview."

"I guess it's my lucky day."

Marie wasn't amused. "You asked for this interview. We're accommodating you. We'll start at 8:30."

Jean Claude was tall, six-two, and handsome. At forty-nine, he had incredibly thick, wavy, brown hair, which Craig suspected was a toupee. He dressed in expensive suits and ties along with bright-colored, striped shirts. He had a wide smile, and Craig guessed he spent a lot time bleaching his teeth. Craig had never seen teeth so sparkling white.

"It's an honor to have back the world's greatest terrorist hunter," Jean Claude said, while a technician hooked a microphone to Craig's lapel.

"Very amusing."

"Sounds like you're having a bad day."

Craig realized he had sounded irritable. And no wonder. He hadn't slept last night. Then so much had happened today. Still, he had to pull together. He'd be talking to millions of people.

Craig and John Claude sat next to each other at a long wooden desk, permitting the cameras to capture both at the same time or to zoom in on either one. Behind the cameras were scores of wires and cables. Marie, with her ubiquitous clipboard, raised her hand. At exactly 8:30 she lowered it.

Jean Claude began his segment on the Spanish train bombing with a grisly film of the wreckage—inside the train and on the ground. "This is not for the squeamish," he said, as the film depicted the maimed and the dead. Bleeding bodies. Severed limbs accompanied by screams of the victims.

When it was over, Jean Claude said, "We are fortunate to have with us this evening Craig Page, the EU Director of Counterterrorism who is responsible for thwarting attacks like this."

Thanks, Jean Claude.

"Welcome to CNN, Craig. Would you like to make an opening statement?"

"I want to say that the Spanish government and all of the EU nations will be doing everything they can to find the perpetrators of this horrific attack and to bring them to justice. At the same time, we will be moving aggressively to prevent future attacks."

"Do you know which group is responsible?"

Craig was ready for this question.

"I can't share our confidential information with you. However, we are pursuing some very active leads."

"Have you ever heard of an organization called The Spanish Revenge?"

Craig wondered what the hell Jean Claude was talking about. Better tread carefully, he thought.

"Again, I can't share information with you."

"Then let me share something with you and our viewers."

Jean Claude raised his hand, signaling Marie, who was standing near a technician. They focused the camera on Craig while an audio tape began playing. "This is Musa Ben Abdil ..." The voice was garbled, but understandable.

Craig looked calm, but inside he was seething.

"Our group, The Spanish Revenge, is responsible for the Spanish train bombing. Our objective is to resume the war between Muslims and Christians in Europe."

Craig was furious at Marie and Jean Claude. How could they have blindsided him? They should have given him the opportunity to hear the tape before the interview. And they had withheld critical information from law enforcement officials.

Jean Claude was smirking. Craig wanted to strangle him.

Jean Claude asked, "What can you tell us about the group called The Spanish Revenge?"

"As I said, I'm not at liberty to discuss our ongoing investigation."

"Do you believe that this Spanish train bombing is a prelude to a larger war between Muslims and Christians in Europe as the tape says?"

"I do not think so. The vast majority of Muslims living in Europe are peaceful law-abiding citizens."

"But unlike other immigrant groups, they haven't integrated into the mainstream society. Have they?"

"Your question is outside my area of expertise in combating terrorism."

"That's an easy answer, but isn't there a blurred line between riots in an Islamic area of a European city and an act of terror?"

Of course, Jean Claude was right, but Craig didn't want to admit it.

"Can we return to the train bombing?"

"Sure." Jean Claude was smirking again. Craig was ready for another blast. "What can you tell us about Chinese involvement in the Spanish train bombing?"

Again Craig had to be careful. "I have no information to suggest Chinese government involvement."

"Will you confirm that the bomb wasn't an IED, an improvised explosive device, but instead a sophisticated state-of-the-art Chinese bomb activated by remote control?"

How the hell does he know that? Alvarez? Had to be. What's Alvarez's game? To make me look bad.

"It is true," Craig said, "that the bomb was manufactured in China. That doesn't establish Chinese government involvement. The bomb could have been obtained from a country with which China has a military supply agreement."

"Was the individual who activated the bomb Chinese? Or an Arab?"

"We're still trying to establish his identity."

"But you have someone in custody."

"He killed himself before he could be captured."

Jean Claude didn't seem surprised. Had Alvarez told him that as well?

"How did that happen?"

"He shot himself."

"Well what did he look like?"

"As I said, we're still trying to establish his identity."

Craig had enough of this interview. He decided to end strong. "I wish to emphasize that my agency, in coordination with the Spanish and other EU governments, is making every conceivable effort to find and punish the perpetrators of this heinous crime. At the same time, we have stepped up our vigilance to prevent another attack. Now I must go back to work."

Craig unhooked his microphone clarifying that he wouldn't take any more questions.

As soon as the cameras cut away, he made a beeline for Marie and led her into a vacant office. He was glaring at her. "You should have let me hear the tape before the interview. That was outrageous. All you care about is your story. Whatever gets your ratings up. You have no moral compass."

She was glaring right back. "Don't tell me how to do my job."

"And you withheld critical evidence from law enforcement officials. I can have you prosecuted under French law." He was raising his voice.

"We're not withholding anything. We only received the tape a little while ago. I wanted to confirm with you that it was genuine."

"Bullshit. You wanted to sandbag me." He held out his hand. "I want the tape now or I'll get a court order."

"Give me a minute."

She left him standing there and returned a few minutes later holding a CD which she handed to him. "This is the original we made. I prepared a copy which we're keeping. This one has the best sound quality."

Craig's anger was tempered by one cold, clear fact. In his effort to use the media to boast about his success, the man calling himself Musa Ben Abdil had given Craig his first clue at finding his identity and locating him. Sure the voice was garbled. But maybe it was his. If not, one of his confidantes. And if they could identify the voice, they had a real lead.

11

CAP D' ANTIBES, FRANCE

General Zhou stood on the balcony of his luxurious estate, blowing smoke into the air from a Cuban cigar and looking at the sparkling lights of the Mediterranean a mile below. He had a clear view between the tall pines that lined the two sides of his property and the red clay tennis court between them. Yachts were gently bobbing in the water. In October the movie stars and other celebrities were gone. The crowds, too.

This place is a bit of heaven, he thought. We have nothing like it in China. He should be grateful for being able to split his time between this house and the comfortable apartment in Paris. Not to mention having unlimited money forwarded by his brother, Zhou Yun, one of the most successful industrialists in China. And gorgeous, sensuous Androshka. Not much competition in tennis, but far more important, after a year and a half, she still drove him wild in bed. Men would give anything for a life like this.

But he was still miserable. He wanted to be back in China. More than that, he wanted to replace President Li as the head of the Chinese government. One day, before long, he would do that. His brother would tell him when to make his move and return with the support of military leaders with whom he regularly communicated. Meantime, he was painfully aware every day of his gilded life that he was in exile.

Ah, the bitterness of exile.

He never forgot who was responsible for his banishment: That bastard, Craig Page.

If it weren't for Page, General Zhou's ingenious plan for Operation Dragon Oil would have succeeded. He would now be in Beijing. Praised and revered by the entire Chinese nation. A hero without equal. A military genius embarking on conquests to exceed Caesar or Napoleon.

But Page had foiled Operation Dragon Oil. Exile was General Zhou's punishment.

The passage of a year and a half had only intensified his hatred for Craig. Not a day went by without General Zhou dreaming about revenge. Getting even with Page—and then some. Sure, he could arrange Craig's murder. But there would be no satisfaction in that. Rather, he imagined scenarios in which he succeeded in an operation and Craig suffered the humiliation of defeat. None of them seemed plausible, until this evening.

As he watched Craig squirming in front of the CNN camera, he realized how painful the Spanish train bombing was for Craig. General Zhou had no idea who Musa Ben Abdil was. Or the Spanish Revenge. But he knew what he had to do: Find Musa and join forces with him to wreak such devastating blows on Page with future attacks that his career would be ended. Page would be regarded as a pariah among governments. Never to be appointed to a position anywhere. That would be revenge. Sweet revenge.

The first step was getting to Musa. General Zhou was pleased he had recorded Craig's interview. He wanted to hear it again.

He returned to the living room, hit the play button, and listened intently.

As he did, he was struck with another idea. This Musa Ben Abdil could have value to General Zhou, apart from being an instrument for his revenge with Page. In his future plans, General Zhou not only wanted to be President of China, but he was determined to make China the preeminent power in the world. That meant surpassing both the United States and Western Europe. Musa had planned and executed the Spanish train bombing so brilliantly that General Zhou recognized in him the potential, if properly supported, to destabilize and weaken Europe, helping China to overtake it. His fertile imagination charged ahead. Europe and the United States, though rivals in some sense, were joined at the hip as the Western Christian forces in the world. While reluctant to admit it, both were at war with Islam. If he helped Musa build an army strong enough to weaken Europe, General Zhou could unleash him on the United States. Musa could be valuable to General Zhou in achieving Chinese world dominance.

All of that was good, but he still had to locate and to make contact with Musa. As Craig's interview played on, General Zhou, puffing on a cigar, heard Jean Claude say, "Will you confirm that the bomb wasn't an IED, an improvised explosive device, but instead a sophisticated state-of-the-art Chinese bomb activated by remote control?"

Excited by what he just heard, General Zhou hit the stop button, rewound, and played it again to make sure he had it right. Yes, he did. And then Craig conceded, "The bomb was manufactured in China."

General Zhou now had the wedge he needed to get into the door with Musa.

Once he turned the power off, Androshka walked into his study wearing a pink lace bra, which covered about half of her gorgeous round breasts, a matching thong with lots of brown bush showing on the sides, and five inch stiletto heels that raised her height to his at six two. He had once read that beautiful women were more erotic in lingerie than nude, and this evening Androshka was proving that. Just the sight of her aroused him.

He stood up, making no effort to tie his blue silk robe, letting his erection jut out.

"You have a problem," she said.

"And I have a solution."

She kissed him on the lips, then pulled away, "Not when we're having dinner at the Eden Roc. It'll keep. Besides, you made me wait for dinner until you watched the Craig Page interview. I'm starving. You should get dressed."

"Five minutes. I have to make one call."

Using his cell phone directory, he looked through the list of top officials in the Chinese military, most of whom were still loyal to him, until he found what he was looking for: Freddy Wu.

When he was still Chief of the Chinese Armed Forces, General Zhou had appointed Freddy the head of China's Office of Military Supply-Western Europe and North Africa. Chang Wu, the Shanghai-born son of one of China's rising wealthy industrialists, had been educated at Oxford, where he renamed himself Freddy. Flamboyant, described derogatorily as a dissolute playboy by hard-line old-timers, high-living Freddy had been spending his time mingling with the rich and famous in Western Europe as "a representative," which meant glorified salesman, for his father's industrial conglomerate. General Zhou concluded that, with training on Chinese military hardware, Freddy would be perfect for the job of cracking the American stranglehold on arms imported by Western European and North African countries.

General Zhou knew he made the right choice when Freddy said, "If you give me a large expense budget, I'll succeed. The Americans are afraid to make payoffs to the key officials because of some stupid foreign corrupt practices law of theirs. They're competing with one hand tied behind their back."

So General Zhou gave Freddy an unlimited budget. As he told people, "Freddy exceeded it, but the arms are flowing." Freddy, based in Paris, kept his job after General Zhou's forced retirement. "I'll never forget what you did for me," Freddy said when General Zhou moved to Paris. "You can always depend on me." General Zhou had seen Freddy from time to time in the last year and a half.

He dialed Freddy on his cell.

"Oh, General Zhou, it's good to hear from you."

He loved it when people still called him General.

"I need some help."

"It would be an honor. Please tell me what I can do."

"There was a train bombing in Southern Spain today."

"I heard about it. A terrorist act."

"Correct. Please keep everything I'm about to tell you confidential."

"Of course."

"I've learned that a sophisticated Chinese bomb was used."

"I had no idea."

"I'm trying to find out who directed this terrorist attack. It would be helpful if I had a list of all customers and delivery points in the last six months for sophisticated bomb devices activated by remote control."

"Just in Spain?"

General Zhou thought about the question. It might have been brought into the country. "No. Your entire sales territory. Western Europe or North Africa."

General Zhou recalled Elizabeth Crowder's article in this morning's *International Herald.* She had written that the warning note was signed by "Musa Ben Abdil." The reporter was Craig Page's whore. General Zhou bitterly recalled how she helped Craig block

Operation Dragon Oil. So she must have gotten her information about the Spanish train bombing from Craig.

General Zhou told Freddy, "The customer's name may be Musa Ben Abdil, but don't limit the search to him."

"I understand. How soon do you need the information?"

Before General Zhou had a chance to respond, Freddy answered his own question. "I'm sure as soon as possible."

"Correct."

"You'll have it within twenty four hours."

The next morning was a gorgeous, sunny day, perfect, blue sky, and unseasonably warm. Androshka was sunbathing nude next to the pool in back of the villa. Meantime, General Zhou sat at a table on the patio, poring through the pile of newspapers his aide, Captain Cheng, had brought from Nice early this morning. He was looking for any other tidbits about the Spanish bombing, while he sipped another double espresso, which he now enjoyed. He doubted if he'd ever drink tea again, even when he returned to China.

His cell phone rang. Freddy Wu.

"Yes," General Zhou said anxiously.

"I have the information you wanted."

"Tell me."

"A month ago, four very powerful, sophisticated bombs, which we call the Rock Blasters, with remote control activators, were delivered to Musa Ben Abdil. Payment was in cash. Four hundred thousand euros."

"Excellent. Where was delivery made?"

"In Morocco. On a road twenty kilometers east of Marrakech."

"Do you have any contact information for the purchaser?"

"He refused to divulge it. I'm sorry."

"No need to be. You've given me plenty."

General Zhou hung up the phone. He climbed down the stone

stairs to the pool. Androshka was on her back reclining on a chaise, eyes covered with damp tissues to minimize the sun.

"Androshka," he said, "I have to go to Morocco with Captain Cheng for a couple of days for business."

She uncovered her eyes and sat up. "Can I come … Please. I've always wanted to go to Morocco. Mikhail would never take me. But you're not like he is," she said it in a sugary-sweet voice that made him smile.

He didn't care what her former boyfriend, that Russian thug, once a barbarous general in the Soviet army, now a murderous oligarch, did or didn't do. But as he thought about it, taking Androshka could be an advantage. Though he and Captain Cheng hadn't worn military uniforms in the year and a half since they left China, even posing as Chinese businessmen might attract Moroccan government surveillance. But tourists. That was the best cover.

"OK, Androshka. Start packing." She jumped up, threw her arms around him, and kissed him. "I'll be good for you there," she said.

He laughed. "You're always good for me."

He was waiting for Captain Cheng to bring the car around for the ride to Nice airport when he heard the distinctive "ping … ping … ping" of the encrypted cell phone he used only for calls with Zhou Yun, his brother in China.

"I heard the most incredible good news," Zhou Yun said. "You won't believe this."

"Tell me."

"President Li has been diagnosed with colon cancer. It's being concealed from everyone in the country."

"How did you find out?"

"I made his personal physician a very wealthy man by letting him invest in one of my real estate deals. In return, he keeps me informed of President's Li's health."

His brother's thoroughness always amazed General Zhou.

"What's the prognosis?"

"The fool rejects surgery which his doctors are recommending. If he doesn't have surgery, they're giving him a year to live."

General Zhou wanted to celebrate President Li's impending death, but he was thinking more about the presidential succession.

As if reading his mind, his brother said, "Once the news gets out, the struggle will begin for the next President. Fortunately, we don't have a democracy. The Central Committee will decide. I will immediately begin talking to each of the members of the Committee. Lining up their support for you ahead of time. I can persuade some by calling in personal obligations that must be repaid. Gifts will buy the support of others. I'll do my best to secure your selection as the next President of China."

"I have maintained good relationships with the military leaders."

"That'll help."

"Will my exile be a factor?"

"Absolutely not. Enough people now dislike Li that being his enemy is an advantage. I'm feeling confident."

"Keep me informed."

"Of course. Meantime, do you have enough money? Or should I increase the deposit in your account each month?"

"I have plenty."

General Zhou turned off the phone and thought about his close relationship with his brother. Their unbreakable bond had been forged in 1967, at ten and twelve, when Mao unleashed his Cultural Revolution. Their father, the National Economic Director, had been a rival of Mao for power. Mao, that monster and villain, responsible for the deaths of more Chinese than the total number killed by Hitler and Stalin, didn't tolerate rivals. He sent the boys' parents to the countryside in the north, near the Siberian border, for reeducation and indoctrination. General Zhou and his brother were forced to remain in Beijing.

"We can only trust each other," Zhou Yun, the older had told General Zhou. And they supported themselves in the struggle to survive. Six years later, their father returned, a broken shell of the man who had gone. No longer a rival to Mao. He explained to the brothers that their mother had died of malnutrition.

The irony was that, when Mao had seized power, their father had relinquished a comfortable life in San Francisco to return home for the rebuilding of China ,with a dream of it one day becoming the dominant power in the world.

Together, General Zhou and his brother dedicated their lives to realizing their father's dream, General Zhou as the Commander of the Chinese Armed Forces, his brother as one of the wealthiest and most powerful industrialists in China, with tentacles reaching into construction, real estate, energy, and military supply.

Riding in the car to Nice Airport, General Zhou thought about how the stakes had grown with his brother's call. His chance to become Chinese President was no longer a vague dream, off in the indefinite future. It was real, and it was immediate.

Last night after dinner and sex with Androshka, General Zhou had uncoupled his naked body from the gently snoring Androshka. He had woken and summoned Captain Cheng from his bed in the visitor's house on the estate grounds. With Captain Cheng at the computer, General Zhou learned from the internet about the great Islamic General Musa Ben Abdil in the fifteenth century and the battle for the Alhambra in Granada in 1491. What was clear to General Zhou was that Musa Ben Abdil wasn't the real name of the perpetrator of the Spanish train bombing. He was Islamic and determined to restart the battle with Christians in Europe, and perhaps even in the United States.

All of this underscored General Zhou's conclusion of last evening. When he became the Chinese President, he would be locked in a struggle for world supremacy with the two other great powers: the

US and the EU. Both were struggling to control militant Islam. With proper help and guidance, this Musa Ben Abdil could strike a dagger at the heart of Europe. And that would have a spill over effect to the US. Despite President Dalton's protestations, the two were blood twins united in their birth. The origin of Western civilization. Now his trip to Morocco was even more important.

12

PARIS

Waiting for Jacques to arrive, Craig sat at his desk, thinking about the call made to CNN after the Spanish train bombing. The receptionist had passed the call to Marie Laval, who immediately recorded the caller's number from caller ID.

Craig had that number checked last evening. It was a payphone near the pont de l'Alma, in a fashionable area of Paris across the river from the Eiffel Tower. He asked Jacques to have police canvass the area to see if anyone remembered anything unusual. So far, he hadn't heard from Jacques.

Then there was the report of the audio expert on Craig's staff, which Craig stared at, resting in the middle of his desk.

Marie immediately began recording the call. The man said, "Marie Laval?" Once she replied, "Yes," he turned on some type of machine and played a prerecorded garbled-voice message from a second man, claiming to be Musa Ben Abdil and taking responsibility for the bombing.

The audio expert concluded that both men were from North African backgrounds. Moroccan, Algerian, or Berber. But their French also contained Parisian inflections. The expert believed both lived or had lived in the Paris area for a significant period of time. He was clear they were not Spaniards.

None of this made sense. Why were Frenchmen of North African descent bombing a train in Spain? It would be as easy … no, easier, for them to bomb a French train.

He was shaking his head in bewilderment when Jacques walked into the office dripping in his raincoat.

"Sorry it took so long," Jacques said, "But the Dutch were a pain about Ibrahami. Took their good time getting back to me."

"The Dutch? What do they have to do with him?"

"Get me some coffee. I'm soaked, and I'm chilled to the bone. All that from walking from my car to your building."

"You ever heard of an umbrella?"

"For wimps."

Craig buzzed his secretary and asked for two cups of American coffee, which Jacques preferred, although he hated to admit it.

Once Jacques had coffee and gulped some down, Craig said, "OK now tell me about Ibrahami."

"He was born in Somalia. In 2001, at the age of twenty, he managed to get to Holland by himself, where he was given asylum as a refugee of a war zone. Became a Dutch citizen two years later. Moved to Paris in 2004 to work in construction. He was living alone in a one-room apartment in Clichy-sous-Bois, a Paris suburb inhabited mostly by Muslims. He was arrested in the riots of October 2005 for fire-bombing a police car."

"Obviously showing gratitude to Europe for its hospitality."

"You said it. Not me. The French police drove him back to

Amsterdam and turned him over to the Dutch, who promptly released him."

"Makes sense. Wasn't one of their police cars."

"Then he seems to have fallen through the cracks in the system. The Dutch police have no record that he stayed in Holland. And the French have no record of him returning to Paris."

"How about showing his picture in the neighborhood in Clichy?"

"While you were sleeping this morning, to rest up after your dazzling interview last evening on CNN …"

"Ouch. That hurt."

"You did as well as you could. Jean Claude's an asshole."

"I couldn't agree more."

"Anyhow, we showed the picture around and got the usual reaction. Lots of blank stares and slammed doors. Even if people in places like that know anything, they won't talk to the police."

Craig sighed. His hope that Ibrahami might lead him back to the man who called himself Musa was proving futile.

He called Carlos in Madrid. "Does Ibrahami show up in any Spanish database?"

"I was getting ready to call you. Unfortunately not. What about in France?"

"A dead end."

"Sorry to hear that. Two more on the critical list died."

Craig shook his head in sadness.

"For what it's worth, I thought you did a good job on CNN."

Craig decided not to share with Carlos his suspicion that Alvarez had passed info to the network. No sense putting Carlos in even more of an awkward position with his boss.

Craig turned back to Jacques. "What about the police investigation of the area around the pont de l'Alma where the call was made to CNN?"

"Nothing."

As a heavy mood of gloom settled over the office, Elizabeth burst in. "I think we may have gotten a break," she said, sounding excited.

"We need something."

"I received a call from a woman in Marseilles. She told me that she had gotten my telephone number from the article in the *International Herald* in which I published Musa's note. She said she's worried her brother may be involved with the group responsible for the Spanish train bombing."

"Involved how?" Craig asked.

"She wouldn't say. She refused to talk to me on the phone. She wouldn't even give me her name. She sounded terrified."

"Will she come to Paris to meet with us?"

"I suggested that. She'll only talk in Marseilles. She'll meet with you and me at ten this evening at a brasserie along the port. Brasserie Duquesne. She said she'll be carrying a bag from Galleries Lafayette."

Jacques said, "You think she's on the up and up?"

"You worried about a waste of time?" Craig replied.

"No. A trap. We can't underestimate Musa Ben Abdil. The port in Marseilles is the perfect place to kill or abduct someone."

Elizabeth wrinkled up her nose thinking about it. "I don't know. That's your business. I'm just a reporter."

"If you decide to do this," Jacques said. "I'd advise strong police backup in Marseilles. I can arrange it."

Elizabeth shook her head, "The woman said no police. If she sees any, she'll run and won't talk to us."

"I don't like it," Jacques said. "Smells bad."

"Suppose Elizabeth and I are both armed?"

"I still don't like it."

"Come on. You told me a little while ago these people don't like to talk to the police. She's our only chance."

"I can see I won't be able to talk you out of it."

"Don't try and play big brother by sending some cops who just happen to be in the neighborhood."

"I'd never do that."

"Look Jacques, I've put my life on the line lots of time over the years in worse situations."

Jacques pointed to Elizabeth. "What about her?"

"You won't believe what she did in Iraq and Afghanistan. And I'll bet she's a better shot than you."

Jacques sighed in resignation. "I'll keep my cell on all night. Don't be a stubborn lone cowboy. If you need help, ask for it."

13

MARRAKECH, MOROCCO

Exotic Marrakech is Morocco's main port of entry for tourists. A fantasy city, known as the Red City, because of its natural red stone walls. A city of immense beauty, with its huge medina of low, flat-roofed buildings, a mere six kilometers from the airport.

General Zhou asked Captain Cheng to arrange a car and driver to take them to the La Mamounla hotel. Riding in the back with Androshka while Captain Cheng rode up front, with a pistol concealed under his jacket, General Zhou kept thinking about the problem that had plagued him since he decided to make this trip: How to locate the man calling himself Musa Ben Abdil. He couldn't go to the spot on the road east of Marrakech where the bombs had been delivered. He had to find another way to meet the perpetrator of the Spanish bombing, who would no doubt be hiding and wary of strangers, even Chinese ones.

General Zhou had a solution. Risky. It meant putting their lives on the line. Still, he had plenty to bargain with.

They checked into the hotel, an eighteenth-century palace, luxuriously redone in the classic Moroccan style. General Zhou and Androshka had a suite. Captain Cheng the room next door.

Zhou then arranged a guide to take them on a tour of the city. On foot, he led them through the open air Jemaa el Fna, the first sight for any tourist, an area full of vendors hawking a myriad of goods and street entertainers, including acrobats, musicians, and snake charmers. As they walked along a path passing between narrow stalls filled with fruits, vegetables, herbs, and spices, Androshka pulled in close to General Zhou and gripped his arm tightly. The area was mobbed. "Crowds make me nervous," she whispered. He shared her anxiety. Perhaps it was the time of year, but there were very few tourists. And almost no Asians.

Strong foreign odors invaded his senses. He didn't understand the lure of this place, which the guide extolled.

"How about if we stop for a coffee?" General Zhou asked the guide.

He led them to the terrace of the Café de France, with a view of the plaza below. After they were seated and ordered Turkish coffee, Androshka had to go to the ladies room. General Zhou motioned for Captain Chang to follow. Alone with the guide, who was puffing away on a cigarette, General Zhou said, "I want your help with something."

"What's that?"

"An introduction to Musa Ben Abdil."

General Zhou watched the guide's face tense up. But he didn't say a word.

"I would make a considerable payment to you."

Still no response.

General Zhou reached into his pocket and took out a roll of bills. "A thousand euro."

"Sorry. I never heard of that man."

General Zhou was convinced he was lying. "Five thousand."

The money was tempting, General Zhou could tell. The guide was weighing the risks. Finally, he shook his head. "You're a nice man. Stick to touring. Then go home. You understand?" The fear was evident in his voice.

General Zhou nodded.

They finished the coffee and toured for another two hours, looking at the Koutoubia Mosque, with its sixty-five-meter-high minaret and an eleventh century Almoravid building. Then the guide took them back to the hotel.

Paying him, General Zhou asked, "Have you changed your mind about that introduction?"

The guide shook his head vigorously.

General Zhou told Androshka to go to the room and rest. Meantime, he went to the hotel bar with Captain Cheng. The hour was still early, the bar nearly deserted. While sipping a scotch with ice at the bar, General Zhou took aside the bartender. Then placed his room key and a pile of Euros on the polished wood.

"You want a woman?" winking, the bartender asked. "Maybe two with that much."

"No woman. I want to meet Musa Ben Abdil."

The bartender eyed the money. "Are you certain?"

"Yes."

"He's not an easy man."

"I want to help him. Give him that message."

The bartender glanced at the key, then pocketed the money. "I can't promise. I'll make inquiries."

General Zhou wasn't sure whether the bartender would do anything. Or whether he was happy to play along for the money.

Perhaps he'd receive a call from Musa this evening. If not, he'd try another approach tomorrow.

For today, he'd done all he could. He dismissed Captain Cheng for the evening. He and Androshka would have dinner in the hotel. That was safe.

General Zhou liked walking into a dining room with Androshka. She was so strikingly beautiful that men's heads turned and they gaped, while their wives looked irritated. This evening was no exception, as the maître d' led the two of them to a corner table on the patio of La Francois, the hotel's posh restaurant.

While they sipped drinks, hers a vodka and his a scotch, she told him, "When you were out this afternoon, I read a guidebook. I have a great program of touring tomorrow."

She sounded so excited that he didn't want to rain on her parade by telling her he hoped she'd be touring alone while he went off to a meeting with Musa. That depended on the bartender setting up the introduction.

The chef came from Paris and the menu looked like lots of others General Zhou had seen in France. They both ordered duck confit followed by rack of lamb and a 2000 Cheval Blanc. General Zhou had come to appreciate French food and wine. He didn't know what he'd do when he went back to China. Maybe bring along his own French chef.

Midway through the rack of lamb, between bites, she was giving him a lesson in Moroccan history—what she'd learned from her guide book—but he wasn't paying attention. All he could think about was Musa Ben Abdil. He'd waited eighteen long months to gain revenge with Craig Page. Musa was the vehicle for doing that. But he had to get to the man.

Suddenly, without any warning, she laid down her fork. Her face was white as a sheet. She slipped down in her chair while holding the napkin in front of her face.

"What's wrong?" he said.

"I don't feel well."

Abruptly, she stood and made a beeline for the patio stairs, leading to the pool area, rather than going back to the dining room entrance where the bathrooms were located.

After she was out of sight, he turned and surveyed the room to see what frightened her. Entering the dining room and heading in their direction was a powerful looking man, walking arm in arm with a gorgeous blonde woman, a carbon copy of Androshka. They were followed by three beefy men talking Russian very loudly, who had to be bodyguards. The couple sat down at a table not far from General Zhou. The bodyguards at a nearby table.

These had to be Russians Androshka knew from her former life.

General Zhou got up and walked to the entrance to the restaurant. "My friend's not feeling well," he said softly to the maître d'. "Add a twenty five percent tip and charge the bill to my room."

"I'll do that. I hope she feels better."

When he reached the suite, he found Androshka packing, her suitcase on the bed. "I have to get out of here."

"Who is he?"

She didn't answer.

"Mikail Ivanoff?"

"Yes."

"Don't worry. Captain Cheng's in the next room. We can handle him."

"Not with his three bodyguards. And you don't understand. Nobody's as cruel as Mikail. He used to beat me with his belt."

General Zhou didn't want to tell her how he treated his enemies.

"And I was one of the lucky ones. Before he became a businessman, he was a general in the Russian army. In the war in Chechnya, he was called the Butcher of Grozny. Known for his vicious attacks on Muslims in mosques during prayers on Friday. 'You can kill more of them that way,' I once heard him say."

General Zhou had used a similar strategy against Muslims in Western China.

"And this is the worst," she continued, a horrified look on her face, "If he wanted to find out where resistance fighters were hiding, he'd go into a house, line up the children, and shoot them one by one until the parents told them the hiding place."

"How do you know all this?"

"When he got drunk, evenings with his old army buddies, he'd brag about it. He didn't care that I was there."

"Why'd he quit the army?"

"To get rich in the new Russia. And he was right. He has billions."

"What's his business?"

"Minerals, iron, zinc, phosphate. Stuff like that. He stole a lot of it from the Russian people in so-called privatization. Then sold it."

"That could by why he's in Morocco."

"What do you mean?"

"To make a deal for their minerals."

"Figures. He never had enough money. That's why I know he'll kill me. When I ran away from him, I took money from his desk. As much as I could pack. I felt I was entitled to it. If he saw me tonight or he does while we're here, he'll kill me. We have to leave Marrakech immediately."

General Zhou closed up the suitcase and put it on the floor. "Get hold of yourself. It's almost midnight. We can't leave now."

Besides, he had no intention of going. Meeting Musa was critical. He couldn't pass up his chance to do that.

"Tomorrow at six a.m. we'll get up. Captain Cheng and I will take you to the airport. We'll put you on the first plane to Paris. I'll return as soon as my business is finished. How's that?"

"But he might come for me tonight."

"He couldn't possibly have seen you. Think about it. You left through the patio before he was in the room."

"If I saw him, he could have seen me."

"If he had, he'd already be here."

"You don't know him. He's a patient man."

"I'll have Captain Cheng sleep in the living room of our suite."

That seemed to satisfy her. He just hoped he wasn't underestimating Mikhail's hatred for her.

14

MARSEILLES

During his CIA days, Craig had developed the three turn rule. When he was concerned about being followed, he'd begin walking and make three turns. If the same man—although occasionally a woman—was still behind him, he acted accordingly. This evening he was worried that Musa had somehow learned that Craig and Elizabeth were meeting with Lila. Musa might send someone to follow them to the meeting. Then kill Lila before she could talk.

To avoid this, Craig parked half a mile from the Brasserie Duquesne, south and west of the huge stone Fort St. Nicolas, built by Louis XIV to keep the residents under control. Craig and Elizabeth, both with their hands in their raincoat pockets clutching pistols, set off along the narrow roads, from the car park to the brasserie through an industrial area.

Glancing over his shoulder, Craig saw a gray Citreon park along the side of the road. The driver wearing a black leather jacket, got out and was walking in their direction.

A strong breeze was blowing off the sea. Craig expected it to rain before long.

For now, heavy cloud cover kept the sky dark. Craig couldn't see the man in the black leather jacket clearly enough to get a look at his face.

"We might have company," he whispered to Elizabeth.

"You always draw a crowd."

Craig and Elizabeth turned left at the corner. Black leather jacket followed, hanging back, keeping twenty yards between them and trying to conceal himself behind parked cars. Craig and Elizabeth made another left then a right. Black leather jacket was still there.

"Definitely being followed," he told her.

"What do you want to do?"

"I'm thinking."

He was looking around. Up ahead on the right, at the next corner, was a dilapidated warehouse that looked deserted. As they walked by, Craig studied the lock on the door. It would be easy to disable with a strong shoulder. Craig motioned Elizabeth to duck down next to him behind the front of a parked pick up truck.

Peeking out, Craig saw black leather jacket stop dead alongside the pick up. He was looking around, trying to find them. Swiftly, Craig made his move. He jumped up and smashed his fist hard into back leather jacket's kidneys. Then his foot into the man's groin, dropping him to his knees. He was screaming in agony. Craig moved behind him and looped his arm around the man's neck to keep him quiet. He was olive-skinned. An Arab, Craig guessed.

While Craig dragged him toward the entrance to the warehouse, Elizabeth was slamming her shoulder against the warehouse door, which easily gave way. By the time Craig entered the dark room with his captive, Elizabeth had removed the flashlight from her pocket and was shining it around. She found a wooden chair and some old rope on the floor. She dragged them to the center of the room and waited for Craig to bring over black leather jacket. Craig forced him down in the chair and held him tight. Elizabeth tied him to the back

He was screaming. Craig slapped him hard with the back of his hand.

"Shut up or I'll break your jaw."

The man was silent.

"What's your name?"

"Mohammed."

"Where's Musa?" Craig said.

"I have no idea."

"You're lying."

"I swear I'm not."

Craig removed the gun from his coat and held it up. "First I'll shoot your right knee. Then your left. I'll keep going with other body parts until you tell me. Now where's Musa?"

The man was terrified. Tears were running down his cheeks.

"No. No."

"Where's Musa?"

"Jacques sent me," he stammered. "I'm with French intelligence."

What the hell?

"Prove it."

"I have ID in my pants pocket. If you untie me, I'll get it."

Craig nodded to Elizabeth to untie him while he kept the gun on the man.

"Stand up," Craig said. "And don't put your hands in your pocket."

When he was on his feet, Craig told Elizabeth to fish around in the man's jeans pants pocket for the ID. "Ah … Ah… You hurt me."

Finally, Elizabeth fished out a black leather wallet from the side pocket. She looked at it and said, "His name is Mohammed, and he does work for French intelligence."

Craig called Jacques. Furious, he said, "I told you not to send anyone to protect us."

The Frenchman laughed. "I guess you met Mohammad."

"He was so afraid of blowing his assignment that I damn near killed him."

"I'm not surprised. He's a good man, though inexperienced. I hope you didn't hurt him."

"He'll survive. Now will you tell him to go home?"

"Let me talk to him."

Craig handed Mohammad the phone. Sheepishly, the man said, "Sorry, he found out about me."

"Yes … Yes … Yes …"

He handed the phone back to Craig, who asked Jacques, "Do you have any others in place?"

"Two near the brasserie. A man and a woman."

"Dammit, Jacques. I told you …"

"It's a rough part of town. I've gotten to like Elizabeth. Not you."

"Call them off."

"You sure you want to take a chance?"

"Damn sure. If Lila gets wind of them, she'll cut and run."

"OK, It's your call, but if anything happens, I don't want a lawsuit from your next of kin. You Americans always sue for everything."

"You're safe. I don't have a next of kin. I'm all alone in the world."

Since Francesca's death, that was true.

"OK, I'll call them off," Jacques said reluctantly.

Mohammad was happy to limp away from Craig. He and Elizabeth resumed walking toward the port and the Brasserie Duquesne. When they were on the Quai du Port, the heavens opened with a powerful rain storm, drenching them. "Where is this damn place?" Craig asked.

Elizabeth pulled out a map, which immediately was soaked. She looked up and pointed to the red awning in the next block. Despite water running down his head and into his eyes, Craig saw the sign.

When they were both under the awning, Craig peered inside. The place looked like a thousand other brasseries in France, with a cluster of men around the zinc bar and cigarette smoke heavy in the air. To hell with the smoking ban.

Off to one side, he spotted a beautiful olive-skinned woman around thirty, sitting alone at a table, her head covered with a black scarf. A bottle of water on the table. Beside her on the banquette, a Galleries Lafayette shopping bag. He surveyed the rest of the brasserie. Nothing suspicious.

"She's here," he said to Elizabeth, "but we can't talk inside this joint." He glanced around. Across the street was the Hotel Tonic, which looked decent. He pointed to it. "I'll get a suite there under the name of Charles Winters. Bring her up with you."

"What if she won't come?"

"You're persuasive. Tell her it'll be safer for all of us."

"And if that doesn't work?"

"I'll throw a smoke bomb into the brasserie."

"You're kidding? Right?"

"I don't know what I'll do."

"That's what I like. A good plan B."

Elizabeth headed into the brasserie while Craig walked across the street to the hotel. He rented a seedy suite with frayed carpet and dirt stained beige walls on the second floor facing the brasserie.

A few minutes later, he saw Elizabeth leave with the woman, who pulled an umbrella from her bag and opened it over Elizabeth's head as well as her own.

Inside the living room, Elizabeth said, "Craig, this is Lila Dahab. Lila meet my friend, Craig Page."

"I recognize you from the CNN interview, Mr. Page."

He flinched. "Not my best moment."

Lila took off her coat but not her headscarf.

"Elizabeth said you can help us. Before we talk, can I offer you something to drink?"

Craig opened the mini bar.

"I don't drink alcohol."

"Soda then?"

She shook her head. "I just want to talk." Her voice was cracking. "Then leave quickly."

Her hands shaking, she sat down on a straight-backed chair. Craig glanced out of the window, saw nothing suspicious, and sat down next to Elizabeth across from Lila on an old battered sofa.

"I was born in Clichy-sous-Bois, a banlieue, a suburb of Paris," she said speaking softly.

Craig leaned forward, straining to hear.

"There were two of us. Me and my brother Kamel, two years younger. Our parents are Berbers from Morocco who moved to Paris when they were first married. My father was a carpenter. He and my mother both died when we were teenagers. So I always felt an obligation toward my brother … He's a good boy, but a follower. Not a leader. You know what I mean."

She paused, looking at Craig. Once he nodded, she continued. "From the time he was five, he was good friends with another boy his age from the street. Ahmed Sadi. And there was a third boy, Omar Ramdane. They were inseparable." She held up three fingers pressed close together. "But they weren't equals. Ahmed was the leader. He told them what to do. The others always complied.

"Even when Ahmed went to a private school in the city for high school, they remained close friends. After high school, Ahmed went to Columbia University in the United States. My brother tried to find a job, but he couldn't. For our people it's difficult. He tried to be a carpenter like our father, but he wasn't good at that, and he had no one to teach him. So he hung out. I had a job cleaning in a dress shop in Paris. My brother and I lived together, but I worried about him.

"When Ahmed came back from the United States after Columbia University, he started an organization to help people in banlieues like Clichy. He gave my brother and Omar jobs helping him. He raised money, and they were paid.

"Then the riots came to the banlieue." She took a deep breath and sighed. "When the two boys died in October 2005 … Are you familiar with what I'm talking about?"

Craig had been in the Middle East at the time with the CIA. He never received detailed reports. "Tell us," he said.

"One night in our town, in Clichy-sous-Bois, two teenage boys, Zyed and Bouna, were riding their bikes. They believed the police were chasing them. So to escape, they broke into a fenced-off area that held a power transformer. They were electrocuted. That was what led to rioting in Muslim communities throughout France and elsewhere in Europe. In the next two weeks, hundreds of buildings were smashed. Eight thousand cars were burned. Three thousand rioters were arrested. The police behaved brutally, beating people to break up protests. They would never say how many died or how. I saw them with my own eyes. The boys and girls being buried. The broken and bloody bodies."

She shook her head sadly. "It was terrible. Violence every night. The rioters were young Muslims. They had no jobs. They don't feel a part of society. They have drugs. So they made trouble. But the police reacted too forcefully. It all got out of control."

Elizabeth asked, "Was your brother rioting?"

"Not at first." She was sounding more confident and at ease. "Ahmed used my brother and Omar to try and keep our neighborhood quiet. Then the police shot and killed an eight-year-old boy and arrested many innocent people in a roundup. So the three of them joined the rioters, despite my pleas to my brother. He came home bloody and charred from fire, but he kept going. I was relieved when it ended. I thought he would go back to work with Ahmed. But the riots changed Ahmed.

"Before that, he had a lover. A blonde Catholic girl, Nicole. She worked with him and marched with him. The police beat her into a coma. She died.

"Afterwards, he lost interest in his organization to help our people. He began filling my brother's head with nonsense about how the Christians had taken over land in Europe from Muslims and we're now suffering because of that. Then one day my brother said he was going away with Ahmed and Omar. He refused to tell me where they were going or what they planned to do. I knew it would all lead to no good and I tried to persuade my brother not to go." She sighed again. "It was hopeless."

Craig was hanging on each word. He guessed where this was heading. That Ahmed was Musa Ben Abdil. "When did they go away?"

"About a year ago. My brother and I stayed in touch. Our last call was two days ago."

"Did he ever tell you where he was?"

She shook her head.

"When did you move to Marseilles?"

"About six months ago." She looked away and continued speaking. "Monsieur Rene, the man who owned the shop where I worked in Paris began touching me and saying what he wanted to do to me. I don't want to repeat it. He was a Christian man. Old, fat, and bald. With a bad smell. I told my brother. He said I'll talk to Ahmed. He'll know what to do.

"The next day, Monsieur Rene was found dead, shot in his apartment. The police called it a burglary, but I was convinced Ahmed arranged it. So I ran away to Marseilles. Here I have a job cleaning rooms at a hotel."

"What happened in your phone call with Kamel two days ago?"

"He called me early in the morning. My brother asked if I had heard anything about a threatened Spanish train bombing. He sounded scared. I told him it was on the news. I asked him if this was some of Ahmed's doing. He wouldn't answer. I told him to run away from Ahmed and come to me in Marseilles. He said he would think about it."

"Did he call you back?"

She shook her head. "After I heard about the train bombing, I tried calling him several times on his cell phone. I got a recording. 'This number has been disconnected.' Finally, I called Elizabeth."

She reached into her purse, removed a picture, and handed it to Craig. "This is my brother, Kamel. Please keep the picture to help you find him."

Craig showed her a photograph of the man who shot himself in the shed after the train bombing.

"Do you recognize him?"

"No."

"Do you have pictures of the other two, Ahmed and Omar?"

"I'm sorry. I don't."

Elizabeth interjected, "Did you ever have a relationship with Ahmed?"

Lila turned away and looked at the ground. "You mean like … that way?"

"Yes, sexual."

Lila looked back up and squarely at Elizabeth. "I have nothing to be ashamed of. After the death of Nicole, Ahmed wanted to and tried to persuade me several times. Not with force. With his fancy words and vague promises. I turned him down."

She smiled. "Omar tried as well. I rejected him, too. I'm waiting for marriage, which hasn't happened." She shrugged. "But who knows."

Craig asked, "Was Ahmed involved with religious fundamentalists?"

"Not at all. I doubt if he ever set foot in a mosque. He was constantly ranting on about 'those people.'"

Craig removed from his jacket pocket the CD of the call to CNN and a small battery powered CD player. He played the recording, stopping after the first voice, the man who called CNN and said, "Is this Marie Laval?"

"Do you recognize that voice?"

She shook her head.

He replayed it. Same response.

He played the rest of the tape. She was listening intently to the slightly garbled words of the second man. "This is Musa Ben Abdil. Our group, The Spanish Revenge, is responsible for the Spanish train bombing. Our objective is to resume the war between the Muslims and Christians in Europe."

At the end, she said, "It's Ahmed Sadi. The man calling himself Musa Ben Abdil."

"Are you sure?"

"Positive."

Craig was pleased. He now knew the identity of Musa Ben Abdil. The perpetrator of the Spanish train bombing. Finding him was another matter.

He had exhausted his questions. He looked at Elizabeth. She had nothing else.

They thanked Lila for her help. Craig added, "Please call Elizabeth if you hear from your brother again."

Elizabeth offered to arrange a cab to get home.

Lila said, "No thanks. Where I live, in the Eastern part of town, the North African area, a cab would create trouble for me. Don't worry, I'll be okay. Just find my brother."

When she was gone, Craig called Philippe, one of the researchers in his office. He asked her to obtain pictures of Ahmed and Omar from their schools, the Passport Office, or Motor Vehicle Administration and post them with Interpol. "Distribute them widely among Spanish and French law enforcement agencies. 'Wanted for questioning. Armed and dangerous.' Also put together a dossier on Ahmed." He gave Philippe what she'd need, including Columbia University.

"I'll get on it right away."

He hung up the phone and looked at Elizabeth, who was running her hand through her hair. "Musa Ben Abdil," she said somberly, "wouldn't quit fighting as long as life pulsed through his veins. He would keep going. On and on, inflicting death and destruction on Christians until his last breath. Ahmed will be the same. It's only a question of time until he does something even more horrible."

"I'll talk to Jacques in Paris tomorrow. Also to Carlos. We'll start a huge manhunt for the two of them in France and Spain. Particularly in Paris. I agree we're racing against the clock."

15

ATLAS MOUNTAINS, MOROCCO

General Zhou was awakened by Androshka screaming in Russian on the other side of the bed. Loud, blood curdling screams.

He bolted to an upright position. As he did, he felt a cold wet cloth against his face. And the sickening smell of Chloroform. He reached up and tried to yank it away but a powerful hand was holding it. Another was forcing his head forward.

He thrashed his arms wildly to strike whoever was doing this. In response, he felt a hard chop on his wrist. Androshka's screams stopped.

He was losing consciousness. All he could think was: Mikail has come for us. "Androshka," he cried out. She didn't answer. Then everything went black.

Groggily, General Zhou regained consciousness and tried to get his bearings. In his navy silk pajamas, he was sitting on the floor of the back of a fast-moving van. One wrist was handcuffed to the side of the van. The metal was cutting into his wrist.

With his other hand, he rubbed his eyes and looked around. Androshka was in a nightgown handcuffed to the van. And Captain Cheng as well. No one else was in the back of the van.

"I told you that you were underestimating Mikail," she said. "He's going to kill all of us."

General Zhou didn't argue with her.

After they had driven for what seemed like another hour, General Zhou felt the air changing. They were rising into the mountains. Now, he became convinced Mikail hadn't abducted them. The Russians would have killed them closer to town and dumped the bodies by the side of the road.

He was sure they were Musa's prisoners, but he didn't share that with the others.

Without a watch, General Zhou couldn't keep track of time. They kept driving up and up.

Finally, the van stopped. Two Middle Eastern-looking men opened the back door. They put blindfolds on the three of them, cuffed their wrists together, and yanked them out of the van.

Captain Zhou's senses confirmed they were high in a mountain area. Breathing was difficult. The air cool.

They were led inside a building. Rough hands forced General Zhou into a chair, then wrapped a rope around his chest, tying him to its back. The blindfold was removed.

He looked around and saw Androshka and Captain Cheng tied to chairs as well. Staring at him was a man in scruffy civilian clothes, dark shirt and jeans, neat beard and mustache, holding a Beretta. In the corner were two other men, similarly dressed, holding AK-47s.

General Zhou decided to seize the initiative. "Musa Ben Abdil."

"Craig Page sent you to locate me. Didn't he?"

The idea was so preposterous that General Zhou laughed, which infuriated Musa.

"You think it's funny. When I kill your assistant first, then the girl, you won't think it's funny any longer."

Musa raised his pistol and pointed it at Captain Cheng. General Zhou was convinced he would pull the trigger unless Zhou dissuaded him from his ridiculous surmise.

"I was laughing because what you said is absurd. I hate Craig Page. He destroyed my whole life. You defeated him with the train bombing. With my assistance, you'll score many more victories over Craig Page. That'll give me a measure of revenge."

"You're lying."

Again Musa leveled the gun at Captain Cheng.

General Zhou continued, now speaking rapidly, "A month ago you bought four very powerful Chinese bombs, called Rock Blasters, for 400,000 euros. They were delivered to you on a road twenty kilometers east of Marrakech."

"So what?"

"I can supply you with as much as you want of the most sophisticated weapons. And for no fee."

Now Musa lowered his gun. "Who are you?"

"General Zhou, formerly head of the Chinese Armed Forces."

"And now?"

"An exile living in France. Stripped of my military position, because of Craig Page."

"But you still call yourself General Zhou."

"Always. One day I will return to China and be President of that great country. Even now, key members of the Armed Forces are loyal to me. My brother, Zhou Yun, the CEO of Zhou Enterprises, is one of the leading industrialists, the most powerful and wealthy man in all of China. Between my brother and my military friends, we can give you everything you need."

"What did Craig Page do to you?"

"As Commander of the Chinese Armed Forces, I negotiated a

secret agreement with Iran. As you no doubt are aware, imported oil is the lifeblood of the United States economy."

Musa nodded.

General Zhou continued, "Working together, China and Iran intended to cut off the supply of imported oil to the United States. I conceived this plan and named it Operation Dragon Oil. We would block shipping routes. Sabotage oil pipelines. Most important, we planned to attack the oil fields of Sunni suppliers in the Gulf, like Saudi Arabia. Also to corner the market from other, smaller oil-supplying nations."

"Why were you doing this?"

"To leapfrog China over the United States economically. To make China the dominant military and economic power in the world. I had everything in place. I even paid off the CIA Director, Kirby, to help me. He concealed any intelligence the United States received about our agreement. So Washington would be caught totally off guard. They wouldn't have a clue about what we were doing until it was too late. Their oil spigot would have been turned off. We were set to go. Then Craig Page got into the act."

"When was this?"

"A year and a half ago."

"Why didn't I hear about it in the media?"

"Both Brewster and President Li put a tight lid on any publication."

"But Craig was no longer with the CIA at the time."

"Correct. He had been fired by Kirby and was operating a consulting business in Milan."

"I don't understand how he could have thwarted you."

General Zhou scowled. "Bad karma. Craig's daughter, Francesca, a newspaper reporter working for Elizabeth Crowder at the *New York Tribune,* had gotten wind of our plot. She was snooping around trying to uncover the story. She happened to die. Bad karma.

"After her death, Craig got hold of her notes. He investigated and uncovered my agreement with Iran. Craig then went to US President Brewster. Once Brewster threatened Chinese President Li, that gutless scum refused to support me. He canceled my agreement with Iran. If it weren't for Craig Page, the agreement would have been implemented. Without imported oil, the US economy would be in shambles. China would be dominant. And I would be a hero for all of China and the rest of the world that hates the United States. "

"Then why were you exiled?"

"Because Brewster demanded that President Li punish me. And Li was terrified of the United States."

General Zhou took a deep breath and continued. "Now you know why I hate Craig Page more than I've ever hated anyone, including Mao, who destroyed my parents. Your success will be his defeat and disgrace. I want to help you achieve that. You have an Arabic expression, 'the enemy of my enemy is my friend.'"

Musa looked dubious. "I don't believe you came all this way at such great risk merely because I could help you settle your score with Craig Page. You have something else in mind. Don't you?"

General Zhou was impressed with Musa's acumen. He resolved never to underestimate the man.

"The answer is yes. But with what I have to offer you, I should not be subjected to this humiliating treatment. We must sit together and talk as equals."

Finally, after what seemed like an eternity, Musa was nodding. "I'm persuaded."

General Zhou exhaled with relief, overjoyed when Musa said to his colleagues with the AK-47s, "Untie them. Treat them as honored guests."

He turned back to General Zhou. "I am sorry. Please forgive me."

"I understand. You have to be careful."

"In the custom of my people, we will eat. All of us together. Then you and I will go off and talk."

Musa led them across a dusty field toward a one-story, stone building that served as a mess hall. Looking around, General Zhou concluded this was a community Musa had created for his group, The Spanish Revenge. He saw about twenty young men and women. No children. All dressed in civilian clothes. All olive-skinned. Arabs and Berbers. Women's heads weren't covered. A secular Islamic terrorist group.

Musa was regarded with great deference, General Zhou observed. They ate simple, but good, food. Fruits, vegetables, rice, and lamb.

Afterwards, Androshka and Captain Cheng remained behind in the community dining room while Musa led Captain Zhou to a gazebo on the crest of the mountain. An incredible view stretched out on all sides. It wouldn't last. Fog was descending from the snow-covered mountain peaks. They sat on wooden chairs with thick cushions.

"Now tell me your other motive for wanting to help me," Musa said.

General Zhou hesitated for a second choosing his words carefully. He couldn't give Musa the impression that he wanted to use Musa to help achieve Chinese dominance, though that in fact was what he intended. Musa was a proud man. He'd balk at that. Instead, General Zhou had to approach the matter as if they would be partners.

"As this century unfolds," General Zhou said, "it is clear there are three great power blocs in the world: China, Islam, and the West, which includes the United States and Europe. If China and Islam cooperate, they will destroy the West. That is my dream."

"What about Russia?"

"They are nothing. Too corrupt. Crime ridden. Ineffectual army. Unable to control the Muslim nations of the former USSR. The world's greatest underachiever. But let's come back to the point. Based upon the Spanish train bombing, I see you having the potential with my assistance of coalescing the forces of Islam in Europe."

"Specifically, what kind of help can you provide?"

"First, I must understand your objective."

"Justice and equality for the Muslims in Europe. Part of Western Europe was under the control of Islam for hundreds of years. Southern France and Spain. And we treated Christians fairly. Then the Spanish Catholics, led by Queen Isabella and King Ferdinand, defeated and humiliated us in the fifteenth century. Since then, Christians have ridiculed Islam and treated our people harshly. Like second class citizens. The Spanish train bombing was the prelude to an attack at the heart of the Christian world so daring and devastating that they will have to change how they regard us."

General Zhou was disappointed in what Musa had said. Terrorist attacks had only limited ability to destabilize Europe. Something more was required. An invasion to capture a portion of the continent. Now that would be something. He became excited thinking about it.

"How much manpower do you have?" General Zhou asked.

"I brought my core of supporters from Clichy, outside of Paris. But here I can recruit from Morocco and Algeria plenty of young Arabs and Berbers who hate Europe. As many as I want. You don't understand how much they despise the West."

"Could you create an army, not merely a terrorist cell?"

Musa looked wary. "Why do you ask?"

"I think you should expand your objective beyond terrorist attacks. Do something much larger."

"Like what?"

"Retake a part of Southern Spain. A moment ago, you said that Islam once controlled it."

Musa shook his head. "Trying would be suicidal. My men and weapons are no match for the Spanish army."

"But if you had Chinese military experts to train your men. If I were to supply you with the most sophisticated weapons. And money to pay soldiers."

Musa shot to his feet. "You could do that?"

"Of course. The Chinese government already trains and supplies rebel groups in many places. In Africa—Nigeria, Darfur, Somalia, the Congo—and elsewhere in the world."

"But you're not with the Chinese government any longer."

"My friends in the Chinese military could conceal our activities from the civilian leadership."

General Zhou was confident that Freddy Wu would supply whatever Musa needed.

"You're a military man, General Zhou. How long do you think it would take until we were ready to attack Southern Spain?"

"Six months."

"But I've been planning a dramatic terrorist operation in Europe on Christmas Day. Two months from now."

"What's the target?"

Musa pressed his lips together and shook his head.

"Either we're partners or we're not."

After a full minute, he opened his mouth. "The Vatican and the Pope," he said hesitantly. Then added, boldly, "The spiritual heart of the Christian world. If I succeed with a daring operation there, the whole world will take notice of the Spanish Revenge. Islam will be on the rise."

"What kind of operation are you planning?"

"I'm still developing that."

"Do it in the Spring. Easter Sunday. At precisely the same time you launch the attack to retake a portion of Southern Spain."

Musa's face lit up. "Perfect. Once we establish a beachhead in Andalusia, I can encourage Muslim communities in major cities throughout Europe to rise up and join us."

"And when you have control of Southern Spain, you can use your position and prestige to support Islamic terrorists in the United States. You'll be more of a hero to your people than Osama Bin Laden."

General Zhou's mind was racing ahead to operational logistics. "I see only one problem."

"What's that?"

"Will the government of Morocco block you from bringing in military equipment?"

"King Hassan is ill and ineffectual. I have been paying off Prime Minister Farez. We have reached an understanding. As long as I don't launch any attacks here, he won't bother me or my supporters. With the expanded activities you're discussing, he'll want more money. I don't have it."

"I can supply that to you. But I want something in return."

"What's that?"

"Also staying at our hotel in Marrakech is a Russian businessman, Mikail Ivanoff, three body guards and a young woman. My blonde friend Androshka is afraid Mikail will try to kill her. He is …"

Musa's eyes were blazing. "General Ivanoff, formerly in the Russian army."

General Zhou was alarmed. "You know him?"

"Only by his reputation. The butcher of Grozny. He ordered his men to attack mosques during prayers. He killed children in front of their parents to make them talk. Of all the despicable Russian pigs, he was the cruelest towards the Muslims in Chechnya. I would gladly give him the justice he deserves. Not as a favor to you, but on behalf all those he killed."

Musa paused for a moment, then continued, "You'll stay here tonight. Tomorrow you will see how I deal with Mikail Ivanoff. I promise you he will not be a threat to Androshka or anyone else."

16

ATLAS MOUNTAINS

At sunrise, one of Musa's men woke General Zhou, Androshka, and Captain Cheng. A woman handed each of them a cup of scalding, strong coffee, then led them to a flat, rocky field on which General Zhou had seen men playing soccer yesterday. The goals were gone. In the center of the field stood four wooden stakes, each about six feet high.

The morning air was chilly. General Zhou was shivering.

Standing next to a magnificent gray horse, Musa, robed in a multicolored vest, was waiting for General Zhou.

"My Berber ancestors knew how to deal with their enemies," Musa said. He pointed to the three chairs along the side of the field. General Zhou sat in the center with Captain Cheng on one side and Androshka on the other.

Musa climbed onto his horse and raised his hand. That was the signal for Berber guards to bring Mikail and his three Russian bodyguards onto the field from an adjacent building. The four were bound at the ankles with rope. Their wrists were tied behind their backs. The guards dragged the Russians by heavy ropes wrapped around their chests, stopping in front of Androshka.

Mikail was glaring at her. He fired off a string of curses in Russian. She glared back and returned his diatribe. Then she got up and boldly moved forward. She spit in his face. "For all the beatings you gave me."

Before he could spit back, she retreated.

"I'll kill you, bitch," Mikail cried out.

"You're done killing people," Musa shouted. "Now you're getting justice for what you did in Chechnya."

He signaled the guards, who pulled the four Russians to the stakes. The men were forced to their feet. Each was tied tightly with his back to a stake.

From across the field, three other Berbers were approaching Musa on roan horses, carrying spears. One of them had two spears. He handed one to Musa.

General Zhou had heard that a sport like this was practiced in Muslim mountain areas of China, but he had never seen it.

He watched in awe as the four horsemen rode to the far end of the field. Then, with Musa in front, each spurring his horse, one arm outstretched, a spear in his hand, the four galloped toward the Russians, their horses kicking dust in the air. At a distance of fifty yards, they split, with each of them heading toward a separate captive. Musa was on a beeline for Mikail, the terror on the Russian's face visible to General Zhou.

In a swift motion, Musa plunged the spear into Mikail's chest. He left it stuck there. The others did likewise with their prey. The four Russians were screaming in agony, blood pouring down their bodies.

Ignoring the screams, the horsemen turned and rode back to the far end of the field where they picked up new spears. Two more times they repeated the exercise. By then all the Russians were silent.

One of the Berbers walked from one to the other checking pulses. "All dead," he announced.

Watching Musa dismount, it occurred to General Zhou that Musa was truly amazing. He was a man trying to span six centuries. One leg was in the twenty first—thoroughly modern using high tech resources—the other back in the fifteenth.

Musa walked over to General Zhou. "Your friend Androshka never has to worry about these Russian pigs."

"I thank you for that."

"I know how to treat my friends ... and my enemies."

The words hung in the air. General Zhou now understood that Musa had an additional objective with this morning's show.

17

PARIS

Craig sipped espresso from a china cup and glanced at Elizabeth and Giuseppe across the conference room table. Both were completely absorbed, reading the report Philippe had compiled on Ahmed Sadi, now calling himself Musa Ben Abdil.

When they were finished, he asked, "Well, what do you think?"

Giuseppe responded, "She did a thorough job. We now know everything about Musa ... let's call him that ... from the time he was born in 1978. From his Arab mother and Berber father, who moved to Paris from Morocco in 1970."

"Until a year ago," Craig replied. "When he disappeared."

"Went underground," Elizabeth corrected. Then thoughtfully she added, "But what do we really know? He was like millions of other poor Muslim kids growing up in the slums outside of Paris, London, Amsterdam, Rome, whatever. All of Western Europe has this incredible problem of Muslims, children of immigrants who can't or won't assimilate into mainstream society."

She paused to take a breath. "You have to understand these people. How hopeless their plight is. They realize they've been marginalized by mainstream European society. The Paris riots in '05 were kid stuff. The next one will be far more bloody. They're now controlling expanding crime-ridden, poverty-infested areas within large cities, where the police are afraid to go."

"I've seen it in Italy," Giuseppe said. "But what's the solution?"

"There isn't one," Elizabeth said. "It's too late. We're sowing the seeds of well meaning, but failed, policies. When the immigrants began arriving *en masse,* the Western European governments were unwilling to require assimilation as the price of entry, or even citizenship. That wouldn't have been PC. Let them follow their customs, even if it meant circumcision of girls on the kitchen table and wife beating." She was raising her voice.

"This is obviously a hot-button issue for you," Giuseppe said.

"Damn right. How these supposedly enlightened governments let them treat their women is outrageous. Nor did the Christian leaders think about demographics. You don't need a Ph.D. in math to realize that, over time, the Muslim immigrants who have many children, some with more than one wife, will multiply exponentially, while the children of the current majority, hell-bent on careers, upward mobility, and leisure, often decide to have no children, or one at most. We're typical. Craig had one child. I never had any. Giuseppe, what about you?"

"One. Paolo is twelve."

"My point exactly. In mostly Catholic France, Muslims are already more than ten percent of the population. Most of them are descendants of immigrants from Algeria, Morocco, or elsewhere in Africa. In the Paris suburbs and Marseilles they're a much greater percentage. In Brussels, where a fourth of the residents are foreigners, sixty percent of the children born last year were born to Muslims. In Amsterdam and Rotterdam, Muslims will be a majority by 2020. In Berlin and Manchester, England, the governments have virtually ceded areas to Muslims."

"But haven't the European governments shut off the flow of new Muslim immigrants?" Giuseppe asked.

"They want to, but they can't anymore than a seawall can stop the waters from a tsunami. Look at the facts. Millions of impoverished Muslims live, not only in North Africa, but in strife-torn Iraq, Afghanistan, Pakistan, and Iran. For them, Western Europe, with its generous welfare states and the promise of jobs, is paradise. Those most determined will get there. Some by boat, risking their lives on the Mediterranean or Atlantic. Others over land, crossing the border between Turkey and Greece, some of which is being fortified with barbed wire and armed EU troops. It won't succeed in blocking the flow. The Muslim Turks, furious at the EU for denying them membership, are facilitating the movement of these illegal immigrants across their border into EU Greece. From there, they can easily travel to Germany, France, or England."

Craig turned to Giuseppe. "Elizabeth's doing a book on the subject. *Heads in the Sand—Europe Ignores Its Islamic Threat.* Everything she told you is right."

"But how's it help us locate Musa?" Giuseppe asked.

"We know he's a lot smarter than most," Elizabeth said. "Thanks to benevolent teachers and scholarships, he has an educational background that very few in the *banieues*—the poor suburbs of Paris—ever obtain."

"That may explain why he's never taken up with the religious nuts," Craig said. "According to the report Philippe prepared, and Lila confirmed this, Musa has no interest in going to a mosque or observing religious practices."

"Clearly a belief in Allah isn't motivating him," Elizabeth said, "If indeed he believes at all."

Craig said, "I think the riots of 2005 and police brutality turned him into a terrorist. A French psychiatrist, who read Philippe's report, reached that conclusion."

Elizabeth shook her head. "That's only part of it. The key to understanding Musa is back at Columbia University, where he switched from engineering to history. He sees himself as a fifteenth-century warrior, confronting Isabella and Ferdinand."

"You think he's delusional?" Craig asked.

"I'm not a shrink. I imagine he views himself as a visionary."

"All of this philosophical crap is interesting," Giuseppe said, "but we still have to find Musa."

Elizabeth looked at Craig and smiled. "Your friend keeps his eye on the ball."

"Somebody has to," Giuseppe replied.

"Alright," Craig said. "I want to take stock of our dismal situation. Jacques's people are pressing every source they have in the Paris *banieues.* So far, they haven't gotten squat. No one has any idea where Ahmed and Omar are. It's as if they vanished into thin air. I hate to admit it, but we're stymied."

Elizabeth said, "I'll bet they're holed up somewhere in the Spanish countryside. And Musa's planning his next attack."

Craig thought she was right, and he hated hearing it. Alvarez would never cooperate with Craig. Somehow he had to work around the mustache-twirling Spanish Defense Minister and get to Musa before he launched that attack.

18

SOUTHERN SPAIN AND PARIS

Musa flew to Seville, rented a car, and drove to Granada. He had been there twice before. Now, under the ambitious plan proposed by General Zhou, the Alhambra was key. He had to see it again. To Musa, seizing a portion of Southern Spain meant retaking the Alhambra.

As he approached the exquisite red palace, which had been the home of Moorish kings for centuries, he felt pride and bitterness. Pride that such an awe-inspiring structure was built by his Islamic ancestors. Bitterness as he thought about January 2, 1492, when Queen Isabella and King Ferdinand planted a cross on Alhambra Hill and occupied the building. The final conquest of the Catholic sovereigns. The final defeat of the Muslims in Europe.

It gnawed at him that *they* took over *our* palace and converted it to *their* own.

Musa parked in a public lot, purchased a ticket, and followed the crowd of tourists moving slowly inside.

He walked through the corridors, astounded by the beauty and opulence of the magnificent palace constructed by the Nasrid kings, the last Muslim dynasty in Southern Spain. They drew upon the finest architects and artisans of their beloved Al Andalus.

Musa walked from room to room, amazed by the incredible craftsmanship. Walls were adorned with carved plaster, lacy and delicate abstract patterns, and Arabic inscriptions. Floors covered with intricate mosaic tiles. Ceilings of carved wood and ornate plaster.

As he moved from chamber to chamber, he saw numerous ponds and fountains. Light from outside, filtering through the arches, danced on the shimmering water.

He thought about his medieval hero, Musa Ben Abdil. Tried to imagine what he felt like in the final days and hours before his death. How he must have beseeched his dispirited colleagues to keep fighting. To no avail. A man of courage, death became his only option.

This time it would end differently, Musa swore. With General Zhou's support and his own genius for leadership and ability to mobilize an army of discontented Muslims, he would be victorious. The Alhambra his prize.

At one in the afternoon, he left the building and walked back toward his car. As he entered the parking lot, he noticed a policeman across the road looking at him. The policeman removed a piece of paper from his pocket, studied it, then stared at Musa. At that moment, a group of children around ten or twelve years old, passed between Musa and the policeman heading toward their yellow bus parked close to Musa's car. Musa moved with them, trying to use them as a shield to block the policeman's view.

As Musa reached the back of his car, the policeman, still holding the paper, sprinted across the road and approached Musa. "Show me your ID."

Musa replied calmly, "Sure. It's in the glove compartment. I'll get it."

The policeman was standing so close Musa could feel his breath. Musa unlocked the car on the passenger side and reached into the glove compartment. Without hesitation, Musa grabbed the Beretta and fired a shot into the policeman's chest. As he fell to the ground, Musa yanked the paper from his hand. The children had not yet boarded their bus. Some of them screamed. Musa raised the gun and fired three shots into the windows of the empty school bus. Children shrieked in terror and raced away. Other drivers saw what was happening, cried out, and scattered in all directions, running into each other in the pandemonium.

Musa got into his car and drove away, heading down toward Granada. Minutes later, he heard the sirens of police cars coming up the hill passing him, the red lights flashing on their roofs as they raced toward the Alhambra.

To avoid arousing suspicion, Musa was careful to drive at the speed limit. Without stopping, he picked up the policeman's crumpled paper from the car seat and glanced at it. What he saw stunned him: An Interpol alert with his name, Ahmed Sadi, and his picture. Underneath were the words: "Wanted for questioning. Armed and dangerous."

Musa was perplexed. Someone, probably Craig Page, had figured out he was responsible for the train bombing. But how? Though that question bothered him, Musa was able to get it out of his mind. It didn't matter what Craig knew. With General Zhou's help, the Spanish Revenge was an unstoppable force.

He would be returning to the Alhambra. The next time would be to retake what rightfully belongs to Islam.

It was ten in the evening, and Craig was on his way to the *Herald* office to meet Elizabeth. She was working on her outline for the book, and they planned to have a late dinner.

As Craig approached the *Herald* building, his cell phone rang. It was Carlos in Madrid.

"A policeman was shot outside the Alhambra at one this afternoon," Carlos said speaking rapidly in an agitated voice. "We believe the shooter was Ahmed Sadi. It appears as if the policeman identified him from the photograph you distributed to Spanish law-enforcement agencies."

"What happened to Ahmed?"

"He got away."

Craig groaned. "Now you tell me. Nine hours later."

"Sorry. Our only witnesses were hysterical ten year olds. It took time to piece together a description and have a police artist produce a picture. We have road blocks up everywhere. We're checking trains and planes."

"You're wasting your time. He's long gone from the area. Probably from Spain."

Craig thought about this development. "This could be useful. He might be planning something that involves the Alhambra. With this shooting, he may have tipped his hand."

"Good point. What do you want me to do?"

"Move an army unit into the area to enhance security. Increase checks on all visitors. If the Alhambra is his next target, we'll be waiting for him."

PART TWO

MARCH, SIX MONTHS LATER

ROME

Omar awoke at four a.m., half an hour before the alarm was set to ring, in the dingy Hotel Manzoni in Rome. He could barely suppress his excitement. Musa had given him an order: "Find out how I can poison the Vatican's water supply." But Musa didn't provide any guidance.

Since his arrival in Rome a week ago, Omar had read a dozen books about the Vatican, taken public tours and made observations from hills outside of the Vatican.

From all this, Omar had learned a great deal. He now knew that Vatican City, or "the Vatican," as it was popularly known, covering only 108.7 acres, was an independent state—the smallest in the world—fully enclosed within the state of Italy. High stone walls surrounded most of the irregularly shaped Vatican. It had its own armed forces, the most famous of which are the Swiss Guards, their yellow, orange, and blue uniforms said to have been designed by Michelangelo.

But most important for Omar, the Vatican had its own water supply. Somehow he had to locate a point of access to that system—a reservoir, a pump, a flange—any place at which a fast-acting poison could be injected.

After six days, Omar was becoming worried. Stating the problem was easy. But he didn't have the faintest idea of the solution. And Musa didn't tolerate failure. He couldn't stay in Rome forever.

Yesterday morning, he decided to hang out in a caffe on Via Aurelia, close to the point where railroad tracks carrying freight in and out of the Vatican pass through the walls. There he had seen lots of laborers who worked inside the Vatican. He hoped to overhear some hint about how he might sneak into the Vatican. To his happy surprise, he heard one of them say that Rossi and Rossi, a Roman contractor, would be starting a project tomorrow to upgrade a portion of the underground piping for the Vatican's water system. The foreman would be hiring about twenty day laborers at six tomorrow morning at the southwestern gate of the Vatican.

Omar figured the six o'clock hiring would be a madhouse. So yesterday afternoon he drove his Vespa to Rossi and Rossi's office and found Ernesto, the foreman. "I have a sick baby and need the work," Omar pleaded. That elicited the response, "Lots of people have sick babies."

Omar took a different tack. He offered to pay up front to Ernesto twenty-five percent of each day's wages. Then he reached into his pocket and pulled out the cash for tomorrow, which Ernesto was quick to pocket.

Omar still wanted to be early this morning. He didn't trust Ernesto. After downing a double espresso in an open all-night caffe, he bought bread and cheese for lunch and jumped on his Vespa. Omar tore across the still, deserted streets of Rome.

He parked the Vespa in a corner of the courtyard outside the entrance. Six men were already in line in front of the metal gate. Before jumping off the bike, he made a quick call on his cell phone. "Rashid, have the boat in place from noon on. I'll call you if I'm coming."

Then he pulled up the collar on his jacket to brace against the biting cold wind and got into line.

By five-thirty, the line broke down. Day labor was tough to find in this economy. About a hundred men, a diverse polyglot of Arabs, Africans, and Asians, mixed in with Sicilians and Calabrianas, were pushing and shoving. At six, Ernesto, holding a police truncheon, accompanied by two armed guards, opened the metal gate. The sea of humanity surged forward. Ernesto began pointing with his baton, selecting men to come inside. Omar yelled, "Hey Ernesto." The foreman spotted him and waved him in. He followed the others into the Vatican, along a narrow road, then down a steep flight of stone steps, badly in need of repair, to a grotto with rough stone walls.

The work was menial and brutal: blasting through stone and concrete with jackhammers. Then shoveling dirt to reach the buried water pipe, much of which was heavily corroded. Omar worked hard for two hours, all the while looking, listening, and committing to memory details about the water supply. Somebody blew a whistle. Time for a break.

As he trotted off to the toilet, Omar passed a small, windowless office that served as Ernesto's command center. Peering inside, Omar could hardly believe what he saw. In the center of an old, battered wooden table, a roll of architect's drawings was spread open with wrenches on each side keeping it flat. Ernesto was hunched over studying the dusty sheets. Omar knew exactly what he had to do.

He labored for two more hours while hearing increased grumbling from other workers who were tired and slowing down. Not Omar. Musa had put all his warriors, as he called them, including Musa and Omar, through rigorous physical conditioning. He could easily handle this work.

Another whistle blew.

"An hour for lunch," Ernesto called.

The workers dropped their tools and moved into corners of the grotto to eat. Omar, munching on his bread and cheese, remained close to Ernesto's office, where the foreman was examining the plans. Five minutes later, Ernesto walked out, heading for the toilet. Omar watched him disappear around a corner.

Now go for it.

Omar stood up. Casually, he strode into Ernesto's deserted office. He moved the wrenches, rolled up the drawings, tucked them under his arm, and bolted toward the stairs. None of the workers made a move to stop him.

Halfway up, he heard Ernesto shout, "Hey you, stop right there."

Ignoring the command, Omar kept climbing. He had to be careful. Chunks of stone were falling off the stairs.

"I'm coming after you," Ernesto called.

Omar peeked over his shoulder. He saw Ernesto stumble as a step gave way. The foreman lost his balance, fell, and tumbled down the stairs. Omar saw him whip out his cell phone.

Oh, oh. This won't be easy.

At the top of the stairs Omar raced through an open doorway. He was on the road leading to the gate he had entered this morning.

Twenty yards from the gate, he heard a shout, "Stop now, or I'll shoot." Omar wheeled around to face one of the Swiss guards. From his reading, he knew these guards might once have been an effective fighting force, but not for decades. And the World War II vintage pistol the guard was holding confirmed that.

"Give me the drawings," the guard called.

Looking intimidated, Omar walked toward the guard. "There must be a mistake. Ernesto, the foreman, asked me to take these to the Rossi and Rossi office. Call the company. They'll confirm that."

While the confused guard reached for his cell phone, Omar raised the paper roll and swung it, whacking the guard on the side of the head and knocking him to the ground. The pistol fell out of his hand. Omar grabbed it and resumed running. He paused for an instant at the gate leading out of the Vatican, saw that the path was clear to the Vespa, and took out his cell phone. He punched in one number. As soon as he heard Rashid's voice, he said, "I'll be there in twenty minutes. Rev the engines. They'll be chasing me."

He strapped the drawings to the back of the Vespa. Police sirens were approaching. As he started the engine, a municipal police car turned into the road and stopped, blocking Omar's path. He saw only one policeman in the car, who was climbing out, gun in hand. "Stop, now," he shouted.

Omar raised the Swiss guard's revolver.

I hope this thing works.

Holding his breath, he fired, striking the policeman in the chest. The man collapsed to the ground.

Omar sped past the police car. He was now on a main street. He heard sirens converging on him from several different directions. Through the mirror, he saw a *carabinieri* car approaching fast from the rear.

Omar turned right onto a narrow road, jammed with heavy midday traffic. The *carabinieri* followed. In the auto gridlock, the police car, even with its wailing siren was no match for the Vespa. Omar sped between lanes of vehicles stopped for red lights. Now there were two *carabinieri* cruisers, both blasting their sirens, but they couldn't get through the traffic.

Omar had spent long hours during the last week memorizing the map of that portion of Rome, leading to the sea and the dock near Fiumicino. He kept zigzagging from street to street, making it impossible for the police to fix a position on his Vespa. His fear was that they'd send up a helicopter armed with rockets, but that didn't happen.

When he was a mile from the dock, he had exhausted the twists and turns. He had a stretch of straight road ahead. No other way to the boat. And behind, he heard a siren and saw two *carabinieri* cars in the mirror. The lead was twenty five yards and the gap was closing fast.

Omar watched the cop on the passenger side reach out his hand with a gun and fire. To avoid a hail of bullets, Omar drove in an "S" pattern. Ahead, he heard the boat's engine idling. Head down, he kept going.

Rashid had lowered the back of the boat. Omar sped up the ramp and braked the Vespa. Rashid immediately gunned the engine and pulled away from the dock.

The lead car kept going, hoping to make it on board. It flew off the dock, its front tires landing on the boat, but it couldn't gain traction. It fell into the sea with the driver cursing and his partner firing wildly into the air.

Meantime, the *carabinieri* from the second car were shooting at the boat. Omar, concealed behind a bulky chair, returned their fire.

When they were out of range, Omar raced over to Rashid at the wheel. "Good work," Omar said.

"It's not over yet."

Rashid pointed to a screen that showed two fast moving objects approaching from the northeast. Rashid was heading in a west-south westerly direction.

"Italian Navy," Rashid said grimly.

"Musa said this Chinese boat is faster than anything they have."

"We're about to find out."

The Navy ships were closing in. They heard shouts on an amplifier. "Stop now."

"Hold tight," Rashid said.

He opened the boat up to full throttle.

Musa was right. The Italian Navy couldn't keep pace.

PARIS

Craig looked into the mirror in the men's room outside of his office. He didn't like what he saw. A very old forty-eight. He had aged five years in the last six months. Deep lines were etched in his face and forehead. Spots of gray appearing in his formerly dark brown hair. He had heavy sacks under his gray eyes. He wasn't eating well. He'd lost ten pounds, and his clothes hung loosely on his five ten frame. Sometimes he couldn't perform at sex with Elizabeth.

He knew why. He was continually haunted by those bloody, maimed bodies in the Spanish train bound for Seville and on the ground alongside the tracks. A total of eighty-four dead. Scores more permanently injured. Despite Elizabeth repeatedly telling him, "You did everything humanly possible to prevent it. Don't give yourself a beating," he couldn't stop himself.

Throughout his career, he'd always been able to compartmentalize, to bury deep in his mind the things that hadn't gone well. To move on. Not this time.

Images of victims, like the eight-year-old girl, in shock, her right arm severed at the elbow, bleeding from the chest, her glasses smashed against her face, kept popping into his mind. He had visited her in the hospital and learned she'd lost her sight. There were others, too. He still saw their faces and broken bodies.

If only he had gotten to the bomber more quickly. If only …

In addition to the past, the future was haunting him. After six months, he was no closer to apprehending the man who called himself Musa Ben Abdil, the leader of the Spanish Revenge. Craig had French and Spanish police combing all parts of their countries. They'd come up empty. This must be how the CIA Director had felt in the hunt for Osama Bin Laden after 9/11. What agonized Craig was his conviction that Musa would strike again. It was only a question of time. Craig was also convinced that Musa's next attack would be far more daring and potentially devastating than the Spanish train bombing.

After the murder of the Spanish policeman next to the school bus in the parking lot in October, Craig had expected that attack to occur at the Alhambra. The enhanced security Craig had arranged with Carlos had been all for naught. A month ago, Alvarez had cancelled it.

While Craig was washing his hands, the cell phone in his pocket rang. Craig checked caller ID: Giuseppe.

"We have to talk. I'm on my way to the airport in Rome. Be at your office ASAP."

"What happened?"

"Let's do it in person. Have Elizabeth there, if you can."

"The Spanish Revenge?"

"You tell me."

Craig hung up the phone and felt a surge of hope.

"I know this will be difficult for the two of you," Giuseppe said to Craig and Elizabeth sitting across the table in Craig's office, "but will you let me tell the whole story without interrupting?"

"Only this one time," Craig said, smiling. "Now talk, for God's sake!"

For the next twenty minutes, Craig and Elizabeth didn't say a word while Giuseppe told the story of the theft of the plans from the Vatican and the chase of the Arab-looking man on the Vespa. At the end, Giuseppe said, "So we have one dead Roman policeman, the guy who tried to stop the Vespa outside the Vatican. Fortunately, we rescued the two *carabinieri* from their cruiser in the sea. Wet and humiliated."

When he was finished, Craig pounced. "I don't understand why the police in Rome or the Italian Navy didn't call for helicopters. We'd now have these people in custody."

"Agreed. I asked the same question."

"And?"

"Machismo. 'I can do it myself.' Italian men get that attitude from their mother's milk. It's in the air we breathe."

Craig sighed. "Which way was the boat heading?"

"On a line toward the border between Morocco and Algeria. Our people didn't get an ID number. But they know it was of Chinese manufacture. Very fast."

"Son of a bitch," Craig said excitedly. "This has to be the Spanish Revenge. We've been looking for them in France and Spain while their base is in North Africa."

"How can you be sure it's the Spanish Revenge?" Giuseppe asked.

"The explosive device used on the Spanish train was state-of-the-art Chinese. Ditto for the boat. Also the guy who stole the plans is an Arab. Only one reason he would want them."

Elizabeth completed Craig's thought. "To launch a terrorist

attack on the Vatican. That's exactly what Musa Ben Abdil would do."

"Precisely," Craig said. "Hitting Christianity at its heart."

"More than that," she added. "Pope Innocent the VIII lent his support and prestige to Isabella and Ferdinand's battle to drive Islam from Spain and Europe. When they succeeded with the fall of Granada, ending eight hundred years rule of Islam in Spain, the Pope celebrated their victory with a solemn procession from the Vatican to the Piazza Navona and the Church of Spain. There he hailed Isabella and Ferdinand as the Catholic Monarchs and declared them to be 'the Athletes of Christ.' So for the man calling himself Musa Ben Abdil, an attack on the Vatican is logical."

"It's a tough place to defend," Giuseppe said. "They refuse to let Italian police or military inside the Vatican. Their Swiss guards have exclusive jurisdiction."

"Can't you get them to waive it under the circumstances?"

"Never. Not this Pope."

"What do you know about the stolen drawings?" Elizabeth asked.

"They're for the Vatican's water supply."

"Which means Musa wants to poison it."

"Or introduce bombs into the pipes," Craig said. "Tell us about the Arab-looking man who stole the plans."

"We don't have a name."

Craig was flabbergasted. "Wait a minute. A contractor like Rossi and Rossi can hire guys without looking at papers or listing them?"

"It's day labor. Under the table. They're mostly illegals. If the contractor demands papers, the market will dry up."

"And they'll have to pay full wages and benefits to Italian citizens, which will drive up the cost of construction projects. I love Italy dearly, but the corruption is mind boggling."

Giuseppe shrugged. "Don't get sanctimonious. I've heard the US has a few illegals doing work from time to time. But this Arab killed a cop, so our prosecutors are going all out. They sent an artist to talk to Ernesto, the foreman. Once he makes a sketch of the Arab, the police will take it to every hotel in the city. To see if someone recognizes him. That way we may get an ID. Also, a copy of a passport. Under Italian law, all hotels have to copy passports and register guests with the police. Even the fleabags do it, or the police will shut them down. Very few places violate this law. I'll work closely on this with the police and let the two of you know."

"If we locate him," Elizabeth said, "he could lead us back to Musa."

Craig was on his feet, pacing, hands behind his back, not saying a word.

"What's he doing?" Giuseppe asked Elizabeth.

"He has a great thought running around in his mind."

"Will he share it with us?"

"Eventually."

Craig stopped pacing and wheeled around. "Listen, you two. Satellite photos of North Africa. That's what we need. The base of Musa's Spanish Revenge must be in the Atlas Mountains in the border region between Morocco and Algeria. Just as Osama Bin Ladin's base for Al Qaeda was in the mountains between Pakistan and Afghanistan."

He turned to Giuseppe, "Do you know whether any of the European governments have good recent satellite photos of that area?"

Giuseppe shook his head. "Negative. Only the Americans. And since Dalton became President, they won't share anything with us. At least not with the Italian government."

"What about with the French? Do you think they would share with Paris?"

"I don't know."

Craig called Jacques. "I'm working on a hypothesis that Musa's Spanish Revenge base may be in North Africa. I need satellite photos of the Atlas Mountains."

"Only Washington has them."

"Can you get them from Norris at the CIA?"

"You've got to be kidding. Dalton won't let the CIA give me a bottle of water. Even after we saved his life."

Craig looked at Elizabeth. "Want to fly to Washington with me?"

"No, but I'll fly to New York. I'd like to meet with Ned, my editor, about the book tomorrow morning. I gave him part one, the first two hundred pages last week. I'd like to get his reaction in person. I'll come down to Washington in the afternoon."

"Perfect."

Her nose wrinkled, Elizabeth was looking at Craig. "Do you really think you can get cooperation in Washington? I mean the way President Dalton hates Europe."

"I'll give it a shot. I have some old friends in the CIA. And I can be persuasive."

Craig called the travel agent.

"I'm on a four thirty Air France to Dulles. You're on their five to JFK," he told Elizabeth. "Time for lunch. Then we go to the airport."

"You and Giuseppe do lunch. I have to finish up something at the *Herald*."

Craig took Giuseppe to a small bistro a block away. When they had ordered, Giuseppe said, "Back in the office you told me you have Italian roots."

"Yeah. I do."

"Page doesn't sound like an Italian name to me."

"It's a long story."

"I'm interested. Tell me. If you don't finish your steak and frites, it won't kill you. The airline will feed you."

Craig groaned.

"Air France isn't bad. C'mon, stop stalling. I want to hear this."

"My dad's parents had a farm between Milan and Verona. They grew grapes and some other fruit. He was the youngest of five children. Four years old at the time the American troops were fighting their way north in Italy and the Germans were retreating.

"The Jews had been able to survive in Italy as long as it was just Mussolini, but once the Germans moved into the country, they rounded up and deported the Jews. Although nobody in my family was Jewish, my grandfather hid in his barn and fed for months a Jewish family he had been friendly with. Two adults and two children. Then one day, the retreating Germans were so close my grandfather could hear them. He hid everybody, his wife and all five of his children. My grandfather put my father at the bottom of a pile of hay in the field. He faced the German soldiers himself, telling them he lived alone.

"The Germans found everyone except my father. The rest of his family. The four Jews. They killed them all with machine gun fire. My father waited hours before coming out. When he did, the Germans were gone. The dead were left behind. Can you imagine what it would be like to deal with that as a four year old?"

Giuseppe was too stunned to respond. Craig answered his own question.

"I can't. I heard the story from my father. He told me that he laid down in his bed and cried. All alone. Not knowing where to go or what to do. Four years old.

"The next day the American troops arrived. When a captain by the name of Page was searching the farmhouse, he found my father, who could barely speak. Captain Page pieced the story together from what he saw. He couldn't leave my father on the farm. So he took him with his unit. A couple of weeks later, Captain Page was hit with a bullet in the shoulder. When they shipped him back to the United States, he took my father home with him to Monessen, Pennsylvania."

Giuseppe asked, "What was your mother like?"

"Blonde-haired and blue-eyed. Her family had been from Sweden. My dad met her when he was in college at Carnegie Tech, where he got an engineering degree. Then they went back to Monessen to live. He began as an engineer and eventually became part of the management team at the local steel mill. My Dad died about two years ago. When I was still with the CIA. My mother a year before that. I never had any siblings."

Craig paused for a minute and swallowed hard. "Behaving honorably meant a great deal to my dad. And he loved the United States. He never stopped being grateful to Captain Page and the American Army. All the freedoms my friends assumed, he wouldn't let me take for granted."

"He must have been proud of what you were doing. I mean a top agent with the CIA."

"He was. I wanted him to come to the White House when I received the Medal of Freedom. He was sick so I lined up a car and driver. But he lapsed into a coma two days before. He died a week later."

Craig paused. Remembering was difficult. He still felt a strong bond with his dad.

"When I graduated from college, he gave me a plane ticket and told me to visit the old family farm, so I would never forget where I came from and if it weren't for the US Army, I would never be alive."

"What'd you see?"

"Not much. Developers had built housing on the spot, but that didn't matter. I closed my eyes and imagined my dad lying in bed when Captain Page found him. That story's been pivotal to my whole life. I had to do something to serve the United States. That's why I joined the CIA. I'd still be there, if it weren't for Director Kirby and his jealousy."

"Kirby always was a miserable son of a bitch. We despised him here in Europe, if that's any consolation."

"Now I'm heading back to Washington. Kirby's gone. Norris has the Director's job. And I'll still be walking into a hornet's nest."

MOROCCO

General Zhou was puzzled when he received the early morning call in Paris from Musa on the encrypted Chinese cell phone. "Can you come to the base to meet with me?" Musa said. He sounded so anxious and eager that General Zhou was on a plane to Marrakech later in the morning.

Now he closed his eyes as Musa's car and driver climbed into the Atlas Mountains. It was dusk, and a blanket of fog was descending over the area. He didn't want to look down, as the driver took one hairpin turn after another at breakneck speed. He was glad Androshka wasn't with him. She'd be in a panic and screaming at the driver to slow down.

General Zhou had a fatalistic view of life's risks. His mission in life was to extend Chinese hegemony against all odds. When forces beyond his control decided to end his life on earth, it would end.

General Zhou's last visit to the base was a month ago, and he was pleased at how the size of Musa's army had swelled with Berber recruits from North Africa. Musa then had an army of five thousand, which was still growing. Chinese officers had been conducting rigorous training exercises. Musa's men had been unloading crates of sophisticated new Chinese equipment.

It was dark when they reached the base. Musa was waiting for General Zhou in his refurbished headquarters outfitted with lots of high-tech Chinese equipment. Computers and monitoring screens filled half the office.

"I have to show you something," Musa said. He sounded exhilarated.

He led the way to a table in the corner where a dusty roll of architect's drawings were stretched out.

Before General Zhou had a chance to inspect them, Musa said, "Schematics for the Vatican's water supply. Omar stole them. My plan is to inject poison chemicals at several points. I need you to supply the chemicals."

As General Zhou studied the plans, Musa continued, "Can you get me something odorless and colorless? It has to kill from dermal contact. The Pope and his Cardinals may drink bottled water, but they surely use the Vatican's water to bathe."

General Zhou was focused on a spot in the center of the drawing. "This is the central reservoir," he said pointing. "Poison injected here will permeate the entire water supply in a matter of hours."

"Then I should inject it at the end of the day to increase the likelihood the Pope will have contact with the water before the poison's detected."

Listening to Musa, General Zhou was getting an idea. "Is this your primary objective. To assassinate the Pope?"

"Absolutely. He more than any other individual is the symbol of the Christian religion. But I'm not wedded to the idea of poisoning the water. If you have another way of achieving this objective, I'm willing to consider it."

"OK. Let me suggest this. On Easter morning, Sunday, March 28, the Pope will go out onto the balcony overlooking St. Peter's Square, as he does every Easter Sunday. There he talks to the huge assembled crowd. Thousands of people. Suppose at the time he was speaking, your men launched four missiles through open windows from different Rome apartments outside of the Vatican facing St. Peter's Square. One aimed at the Pope and his entourage. Another at the Basilica of St. Peter's. Two others at the crowds in the square. The damage would be tremendous. Death for the Pope and his advisors. Destruction to the Vatican. Death for thousands in the crowds from a direct hit and also from pieces of the structure falling on the square. Death will rain down. It will be far more devastating than 9/11. What do you think?"

"I like it," Musa said, his voice pulsing with excitement, while pumping his fist into the air for emphasis. "It will cause much more damage and many more casualties, achieving greater publicity. And most important, it will increase the chances of assassinating the Pope. But how do we manage the logistics?"

General Zhou's mind was racing ahead. "We'll deliver the missile parts to a warehouse in Torino on Friday, March 26. Good Friday. There we'll make the handoff to your people and provide them with instructions to assemble and operate the missiles. Your men can transport them in four separate vans to apartments in Rome. Omar stole the plans for the Vatican water system. He must know his way around the city. He can find the apartments."

Musa was nodding. "With two weeks until Easter Sunday, we have plenty of time to do that."

"Now let's talk about the invasion of Southern Spain. Are you on schedule to launch this attack on March 28, Easter Sunday as well?"

"Absolutely," Musa said. "Fortunately King Hassan has not recovered sufficiently from his stroke to know what's happening. In return for the money I deposited in Prime Minister Farez's Swiss bank account, he's agreed to look the other way and let arms come into the country."

"Is that relationship secure?"

"Definitely. Farez wants to move the country away from a secular state toward Islam and he hates the Christians in Europe. He'll be cheering us on. I've had to agree not to launch any attacks on Moroccan soil and not to do anything impinging on Moroccan sovereignty. But that's no problem."

"Has the Chinese equipment been arriving?"

"Everything except the pontoon boats."

"They're in route."

General Zhou hoped that was true. He had no idea.

"They should have been here by now," Musa said, his voice showing concern. "They're critical for the attack."

General Zhou made a mental note to talk to Freddy Wu as soon as he returned to Paris. For now he wanted to change the subject. "Where will you store the boats when they arrive?"

"I've taken control of a warehouse and pier at the point of embarkation on this side of Mediterranean. We won't have a problem. But …" Musa paused and looked troubled. "I'm worried what we'll encounter in Spain."

"What do you mean?"

"I sent Omar into Southern Spain on a fact-finding mission. He learned that Spain has large land and naval contingents on their southern coast supported with heavy artillery. I'm certain my troops are better trained and tougher than the Spanish army, which idles around growing fat. If my troops make it onto Spanish soil, they'll outfight the Spanish troops. But if they can hold us off even for a short while, they'll be able to call in air support and wipe us out. If I had an air force …"

General Zhou shook his head. Musa had raised this before, and General Zhou had turned him down. Chinese planes meant Chinese pilots. In exile, there were limits to what he could do. "Not possible."

"Then what? I can't expose my men to certain death. You're the military man. You have to give me a solution."

General Zhou was thinking. "Suppose the Spanish Defense Minister were to move his troops out of the area before Easter?"

"The problem goes away."

LANGLEY

Craig realized he had an uphill battle as he glanced at the morning *Washington Post* while waiting in the reception area outside the office of CIA Director John Norris.

Twenty minutes ago, Dale, the gray-haired receptionist who had been on the desk inside the entrance to the building forever, remembered Craig and gave him a friendly greeting. "Good to see you, Mr. Page. I heard we lost you to Paris because the women and wine are better," he said with a broad smile while they were waiting for Craig's escort.

"Who said that?" Craig fired back.

"You know. People talk. That's the word around the agency."

Craig wasn't sure whether Dale was putting him on or whether that was the gossip.

"The wine for sure," Craig responded. "The women are about even."

Dale answered the phone on his desk, put it down, and told Craig, "Your escort will be with you shortly."

After working with the agency for twenty years and roaming freely through this building, it felt strange for Craig to need an escort. He'd had a meteoric rise followed by a sudden plunge.

Waiting for his escort, Craig walked over to the window and looked at the rolling Virginia countryside with spring bursting out. He remembered the first time he'd set foot in the headquarters building, twenty-three years ago. After graduating from Carnegie Mellon in chemical engineering, he was working in Houston for Spartan Oil. He and Caroline were happy, and Francesca was the smartest, cutest, and most athletic five-year-old he had ever seen. Then the agency recruited him for his oil expertise. "Energy is the Achilles heel of this country," the recruiter had said. "You have the knowledge we need. With your background you'll have the perfect cover for a Middle East assignment." He knew Craig's bio. How the US Army had saved his father's life. He appealed to Craig's patriotism. Ultimately, that carried the day. Craig was thrilled to have a chance to serve his country.

When Craig said he was interested, the agency flew him, Caroline, and Francesca to Washington. The final decision on his hire was made by the Director of Personnel, on the fourth floor.

After two years analyzing oil data in Langley, he was sent to Dubai to open an oil development firm, CCF Industries, his cover for an assignment that meant trolling for information that could affect the flow of oil to the United States. With the increased terrorist threat, Craig's job morphed into counterterrorism work. He wasn't surprised. The terrorists happened to be where the oil was. And Craig had distinguished himself in training at the Farm. His natural athleticism coupled with strength and hand-eye coordination made him an effective killer. Equally adroit at self defense.

He loved his work. Everything was wonderful, until Caroline died. He came back to Langley so Francesca could finish high school. Once she started college, Craig went back to Dubai as Director of Middle East Operations. The perfect job, wrecked once that asshole Kirby became Director, or DCI as it is known. A former congressman with no intelligence background, that arrogant prick insisted on controlling everything. When Craig learned that Al Qaeda planned a huge suicide bombing in Madison Square Garden, Kirby wanted Craig to stay in Dubai. He had no intention of doing that. He was the only one who knew the MO of Achmed, the ringleader. So instead, he followed Achmed to New York, killed Achmed, and foiled the attack. That earned him the Medal of Freedom from President Brewster.

Easily the best day of my life, Craig recalled. That morning at the White House, accompanied by Francesca, when President Brewster presented him with the Medal of Freedom in the Oval Office.

"On behalf of a grateful nation," Brewster said, as he held out the medal and shook Craig's hand. Craig could still hear Brewster's words as if it were yesterday.

Unfortunately, Craig's disregard of Kirby's orders and the Presidential award led to Kirby's hatred. Six months later it was payback time. The DCI announced a reorganization that eliminated Craig's job. "A bureaucratic way of Kirby firing me," Craig explained to Francesca.

When Craig had received the Medal of Freedom, Brewster had said, "My door will always be open to you." Craig considered calling Brewster to complain and seek reinstatement. But that seemed inappropriate. Kirby was the DCI. He could run the Agency however he wanted.

In addition, Craig was dismayed that no one in the CIA, none of his so-called friends, except for Betty Richards, were willing to support him. They were all too afraid of losing their jobs. He didn't want to work in the kind of place the Agency had become in the last few years. So he picked up and moved to Milan, where he opened a private consulting firm. How bizarre, he thought, that a year and a half later he ended up back in the Oval Office with Brewster, because of General Zhou and Operation Dragon Oil. That now seemed very long ago.

His reminiscence was interrupted by a sharp voice from behind. "Mr. Page."

He pivoted and saw a thin woman, with a narrow face and a pointed nose, and dyed black hair, stiff from this morning's coiffing, wearing a prissy-looking, mud-brown suit and walking from the elevator toward Craig as if she had a stick up her rear. He immediately recognized Adrian, Norris's secretary. "I'll take you to his office," she said in a frigid voice.

"Happy to see you again, too."

She said not a word in the elevator, then pointed to a chair in the reception area. "He'll be with you shortly," she said tersely.

When the door finally opened, Norris walked out. No smile. No handshake. Simply, "Come on in, Craig."

He led Craig to a small round table in the corner. "Something to drink?"

"How about a cup of hot, black coffee. There's a chill in the air."

Norris ignored Craig's words, hit the intercom and placed the order.

Craig didn't expect to be welcomed with a brass band, but he hadn't anticipated downright hostility. As he thought about it, he understood what was driving Norris. John had always been insecure and a good company man. Dalton was committed to an isolationist foreign policy, and the President had made a point of showing his disdain for Europe. That meant any European representative was the enemy in Dalton's, and hence Norris's, view. Then there was the personal factor. Norris no doubt knew that Brewster had offered Craig the CIA Director's job before Norris. It was only because Craig turned it down in favor of the EU position that Norris was DCI. They'd never gotten along when Craig was with the Agency. This had to exacerbate their relationship.

Sizing up the situation, Craig decided his only chance of obtaining Norris's cooperation was by presenting Musa as a common threat.

"Things have changed a lot since Dalton replaced your friend Brewster," Norris said.

"I gather that."

"The country was ready for a change. We'd been hemorrhaging money. Having our best young men and women killed off in foreign wars we couldn't win. As President Dalton said in his Philadelphia speech, 'Let the rest of the world worry about their own problems. It's time we rebuilt America.'"

Craig saw his opening. "That assumes what happens abroad won't pose a threat to people in the US."

"True. But in the past, those fears have been exaggerated. What brings you to Washington?"

"I want to sound the alarm about a new foreign threat that could reach these shores and seek your help in heading it off."

Adrian returned with coffee. Craig took a sip and waited until she left to summarize for Norris the Spanish train bombing and the theft of Vatican water plans. "At this point, all I'm asking is access to your routine satellite photos of Northern Africa, particularly Algeria and Morocco."

Norris frowned and tapped his fingers on the table. "What's any of this have to do with us?"

"You have a considerable Catholic population. They care about the Vatican."

"You ever heard of the separation between church and state in the American Constitution? Besides, you don't have hard evidence of an imminent attack on the Vatican or anywhere else."

Craig couldn't disagree with that. "I want the photos to shut down the Spanish Revenge before their next attack."

"Sounds to me as if this character Musa is focused on Europe. He's not our problem."

"Do you honestly believe that a powerful Islamic terrorist

organization won't eventually attack the United States? ... The dominant power of the Christian western world."

"We have a long time to worry about that threat."

Craig was feeling frustrated. "C'mon, John. Think about Al Qaeda. These organizations are like cancer. You have to eradicate them when they're still small. If you wait, it's too late. That's precisely what happened with Al Qaeda. We had chances to destroy their organization before 9/11 and didn't do it."

"Good debater's point, but the answer is still no."

Craig decided to take another tack. "All I'm asking is to examine a couple of satellite photos. How big a deal is that?"

"It's the principle."

"Afraid Dalton will find out and sack you?"

Norris reddened. "That was out of line."

Craig kept going. "Dalton won't know about it. I promise you. There won't be any fallout."

"Did it ever occur to you that I agree with the President?"

"Bullshit." Craig was raising his voice. "You've become a damn chameleon. What happened to the John Norris I knew ,who told Kirby he was wrong for disciplining me for disobeying his orders and stopping the Madison Square Garden bombing? You had balls then, John. Dalton's not Putin for God's sake. You know it's right to give me photos. So do it."

"I won't. That's final."

Craig realized it was hopeless with Norris. And going over the CIA Director's head to the President wasn't an option. Brewster was gone. Dalton was in the Oval Office. Craig thought of the biblical line, there came a new pharaoh who knew not Joseph. Even if he could get in to see Dalton, he realized the answer would be no.

"Thanks for the coffee," Craig said bitterly. He stood up.

"Sorry you made a long trip for nothing."

"Looks that way."

Norris stood too. He locked eyes with Craig. "You have lots of friends in this building. I know that. So I'm warning you: Don't try to make an end run around my decision."

"I wouldn't dream of it."

Norris narrowed his eyes. "I'm damn serious. We've gotten tough about enforcing our laws dealing with leaks of classified information. You might not be prosecuted, but you'll be wrecking the career and life of whoever helps you."

"Thanks for the advice."

"I don't trust you. I'll have people watching you twenty-four-seven until you get on a plane back to Paris."

"I'm flattered with the attention."

Norris hit the intercom. "Mr. Page is leaving. Are the guards out there?"

"Yes, sir."

As Craig left the Director's suite and walked down the hall toward the elevator, he had one armed guard on each side. Craig realized Norris had been afraid to have Adrian escort him out, no doubt fearing Craig would break away from her, locate and steal the satellite photos. Craig recognized one of the guards, George Polk, a burly black man from his CIA days.

Waiting for the elevator, George said, "Hey Craig, how are you? Haven't seen you in a couple of years."

"I relocated to Europe. Your son still playing basketball?"

"He's at Duke on scholarship," George said.

"A good choice."

The elevator arrived. Craig got in with the two guards. Satellite recon was on the fourth floor. Craig thought about persuading George to let him stop there. Ostensibly to say hello to another friend. It was tempting—but no. He didn't want to cost George his job.

Craig drove through the main gate of CIA headquarters in his rental car. An unmarked, dark blue Ford fell in behind. He made two quick turns. The Ford was still there, close behind. They weren't making any effort to conceal their mission. Norris wanted Craig to know he was being followed.

As Craig drove, he realized he had only one way of getting those satellite photos: Betty. Thinking of the woman he had called "my company mother," made Craig smile. When he had joined the Agency, she was already a senior analyst. After his training at the Farm, he was stationed at Langley headquarters analyzing Middle East oil data. Craig was in the crowded Agency auditorium when the Deputy Director, in a briefing about Middle East developments, said that the cornerstone of US Middle Eastern policy had to be placating Saudi Arabia, because the Saudis had a virtually unlimited oil supply. "As long as we remain close with them, we won't have an energy problem."

In the Q and A, Craig castigated the Deputy Director for "either ignoring or not being aware of Hubbert's Peak," the bell shaped curve that predicted a decline in Saudi oil production around the turn of the century.

People in the audience gasped. A rookie was criticizing the Deputy Director. Red-faced, the speaker tried to make light of Craig's comment. Afterwards, Betty came into his office, introduced herself, and closed the door. "We need smart people like you," she said. "And I want to make sure you stick around, so I'll mentor you on survival in this minefield we call the CIA. Rule number one is never criticize a superior when anyone else is in the room. Certainly not a hundred people."

"But what he said was so stupid. And his error is basic to our whole Middle Eastern policy."

"I agree. But you won't change it by what you did. I'll teach you how to get around the bureaucracy."

That day they formed a bond that transcended the office. He and Caroline often invited Betty to their house for dinner. For Betty, who had never married, they became like family. She developed a close relationship with Francesca, who called her "Aunt Betty."

Many Saturdays, Betty took Francesca to the movies, sneaking the seven-year-old into what Francesca referred to as "action flicks. Not that G-rated stuff. Aunt Betty told me the 'G' stands for garbage."

Craig pulled into the parking lot for a strip mall on Route 123, parked, and took out his cell phone.

As he punched in the familiar numbers from memory, he visualized Betty at her desk on the sixth floor of CIA headquarters, curtains closed to keep out the sunlight, her eyes peering through Coca Cola bottle-like lenses close to the computer screen, a cigarette in her hand, which Betty couldn't light because she was inside, but would as soon as she stepped out. Her stringy, brown hair scattered on her head. In the years since Craig had known her, she had grown chunky, adding twenty pounds to her five four frame, because she hated to exercise, telling Craig, "It's for jocks like you."

"Yes," she answered in a curt voice.

"Betty. It's Craig."

"What a pleasant surprise. Where are you?"

"In Washington for a short visit. Living in Paris is great, but I haven't found a place that has a good cheeseburger."

She laughed. "We have to do something about that. How about the diner in half a hour?"

"I'll be there. Lunch is on me."

"Damn right. With the way the dollar has been tanking."

Craig settled into a corner booth in the back of the diner sufficiently isolated that nobody could overhear their conversation. A few minutes later, he spotted Betty walking through the door. She waved, then made a beeline for the table. He stood up. "Good to see you."

"Aren't you supposed to kiss me on each cheek?"

"Sorry. I forgot."

He did and they both laughed. "I guess I haven't adapted well enough to the continental ways."

When they sat down she said, "I almost didn't come. I've been so pissed at you for not taking the Director's job. Leaving me to slave for that idiot, Norris. And now I think I'm about to be fired. I can see the handwriting on the wall."

"You're kidding. You're the best analyst they have."

She shrugged. "Part of the pull back to the American shores. If we don't care about the rest of the world, why waste so much money spying on them?"

Hearing the resignation in her voice, he felt sorry for Betty. She had made the CIA her life.

The waitress came over. They ordered cheeseburgers with fries and ice tea.

"And ketchup," he called to the departing waitress.

"How's Elizabeth?"

"We're still living together in Paris."

"The woman's a glutton for punishment."

"She came to the US with me. She's up in New York this morning. She has a contract with Wellington to do a book about Muslims in Europe."

"Good. I like her. What brings you to Washington?"

Keeping his voice down, he summarized what he knew about Musa and the Spanish Revenge. Also his discussion with Norris. When he was finished, she replied with a single word, "Asshole."

"I guess he thinks he's serving Dalton."

"Yeah, well, he's also jealous of you. While you were out in the field thwarting terrorist attacks, he was pushing papers at headquarters. He's also resentful that you were Brewster's first choice for the Director's job."

"I figured as much."

The cheeseburgers arrived. Craig took a bite and savored it. "I miss these."

"I assumed that you'd become a food snob. Fois gras or nothing."

He was ready to ask for Betty's help, but before he had a chance to open his mouth, she said softly, "I can get copies of the satellite photos for you."

"I don't want to get you into trouble. I know Norris is clamping down on leaks. And I was followed here."

"I saw them outside. Two clowns from internal security in a dark blue Ford. They're both wearing Nats baseball caps. I've seen them around the agency, but I'm not worried. If I have to flee the country, I assume you have a couch in your apartment in Paris."

"We'll give you the guest room. But let's be serious. Norris made it clear he'll have people following me around the clock. He'll take action against anyone who helps me."

She didn't flinch. "I'm prepared to take the risk."

"You really are a good friend."

"Friendship is only part of it. I love this country. My father died on Okinawa. My brother in Viet Nam. If Musa and this Spanish Revenge gain traction in Europe, they'll be even a larger threat to the United Sates than Al Qaeda, because they're not trying to mobilize religious nuts. Rather, secular Muslims. Whether we like it or not, we'll be drawn into the nascent struggle in Europe between Christians and Muslims. We tried to close our eyes to Hitler when he was a small thug, pretending he was only a European threat. Lot of good that did us. We were spawned in Europe. The umbilical cord was never cut. Any group that bombs Spanish trains today will hit Amtrak tomorrow. You can count on me for help. I'll get you copies of the satellite photos."

"You want to send them to me electronically? I have my laptop with me."

"Too dangerous. Funny little men spend all night in the CIA computer center reading incoming and outgoing emails. It would be better if I printed hard copies at the office and slip them out in my briefcase when I go home tonight."

He shook his head. "That won't work. They know we had lunch. For sure, they'll search your bag."

"Yeah. Shame I don't have bigger tits. With a 36 bra, I could stuff the photos inside."

He smiled. "You can be funny."

"Gallows humor. OK, let's try this. I'm authorized to look at the photos. Even from a remote location. So I'll access them from my computer at home tonight. Then print them. Where do you want me to meet you tonight for the drop?"

He closed his eyes and rubbed his forehead. He had to come up with something good.

"Well?" she said.

"Don't be so impatient. I'm thinking."

"The mills of the Gods grind exceedingly slowly."

Finally, he had it. "Here's what I want you to do."

23

WASHINGTON

After watching Betty leave the diner, ready to light the cigarette in her hand as soon as she hit the parking lot, Craig called Elizabeth on her cell. "Where are you?"

"Just got off the shuttle at Reagan. I was about to call you."

"How'd it go in New York?"

"Couldn't have been better. Ned loved part one. He'll have detailed notes in about a week. 'Small stuff,' he said. I'm mighty happy and relieved. What about you?"

He had to talk to her, but not in the hotel suite he'd taken in the Four Seasons. By now Norris would have had his men find out where Craig was staying and plant bugs. He also had to be careful what he said on the cell phone. The CIA would no doubt be listening.

"Hey listen. It's warm outside. Perfect for a walk on the mall. Drop your bag at the Four Seasons then meet me at the Reflecting Pool at the base of the Lincoln Memorial."

"How'd it go with Norris?"

"I totally struck out, so we might as well do the tourist thing the rest of the day."

"Sorry to hear that. See you soon."

Traffic was brutal. When Craig arrived, Elizabeth was already sitting on a park bench alongside the Reflecting Pool. "Let's walk," he said.

She fell in next to him.

"Sorry I dragged you down here. We have to talk, and I figure Norris has our suite bugged."

"Are you serious? You're a representative of the United States' best allies."

"Trust me. I know Norris. He'd love nothing better than to nail me for improperly obtaining classified information."

"Then he's crazy."

"The CIA does lots of crazy things. If you look over your left shoulder, you'll see a heavyset guy in a Nats baseball cap. He's been following me since I left CIA headquarters."

She glanced back. "You want to tell me what you did to gain this much attention?"

He summarized his meetings with Norris and Betty. Then told her what he wanted her to do. "But only if you're willing."

"Count me in," she said without hesitation.

"You might end up spending a night in a DC jail."

"It can't be as bad as being a prisoner of the Taliban."

He admired gutsy Elizabeth. Up to any challenge.

When they returned to the suite, Craig raised a finger to his lips, then searched for bugs. He found two of them. A tiny transmitter hooked to the bottom of a painting in the living room. And attached to the bedroom ceiling, a video and audio recorder transmitting to a remote location.

He left them both in place. He could use them to get around the CIA surveillance while obtaining the satellite photos. Elizabeth, who had been watching him, was shaking her head in disbelief.

At seven, they left the hotel and walked three blocks west on M Street to Citronelle for dinner. Even after living in Paris, Craig was convinced Michel Richard's food was as good as any in the world. This evening's meal confirmed it. As the dessert arrived, an assorted chocolate selection for Craig, and a meringue snow man for Elizabeth, he savored the last drops of the splendid Rion Vosne Romanee and felt sated from the great meal they'd had.

Only one thing marred the evening. From their table, close to the glass wall separating the kitchen from the dining room, Craig had a view of the upstairs bar. The heavyset CIA security agent in his Nats baseball cap was seated at the bar turned sideways watching Craig and Elizabeth.

"Maybe we should send him a glass of wine," Elizabeth said. "Clarify that we know he's here."

"Only if you have poison in your bag that I can add."

"I'm glad you're on my side."

They both ordered double espressos. They had to be alert for the long night ahead.

When they finished the coffee, Craig paid the bill and whispered to her, "Show time."

They walked back to the Four Seasons. As soon as they were in the suite, he told her loudly, "I'm going out for that meeting I told you about. Don't wait up."

"Are you kidding? After all that wine, I'll be asleep before you're in the elevator."

Once Craig exited the hotel on M Street, he turned right, walking east, crossing the bridge marking the Georgetown border. As he expected, the blue Ford moved out from the curb, hanging back, but following. Craig wasn't surprised the security agents in the Nats baseball caps weren't making any effort to conceal themselves. Norris would be content with intimidating Craig to block his effort to obtain the satellite photos. But if Craig boldly decided to arrange a transfer, they'd swoop in and break it up, arresting the others involved.

After crossing the bridge, he raised his hand and hailed a cab. "14th and U," he told the driver.

"Looking for a little night life," the driver said.

"Yeah. Something like that."

It amazed Craig that only a few years ago 14th and U was the center of urban decay in Washington. Now the U Street corridor was a racially mixed, hot area, jammed with bars and discos frequented by young people, that stayed open until three or four in the morning. Craig saw a bar that looked busy … The Down Home … With a sign in front that said "OPEN UNTIL 4 A.M." He walked in, adjusted his eyes to the dim light and his ears to the blasting music from a live band, and found an empty table in the back. He ordered a Jack Daniels on the rocks and settled in.

Minutes later, through the corner of his eye, Craig watched one of the Nats caps enter through the front door, spot Craig and take a seat at the bar. Pretending not to see him, Craig checked his watch and looked around anxiously.

After a while, he checked his watch again, while glancing at the front door. He removed the Blackberry from his pocket, looked at it in dismay and returned it. Anyone watching would conclude he was waiting for someone overdue.

Fifteen minutes after Craig left the suite in the Four Seasons, Elizabeth called parking and asked the valets to bring up the car Craig had rented.

She exited the hotel driveway and turned left, driving west, then right up into the streets of Georgetown. Glancing in the rear-view mirror, she made three quick turns.

Confident she wasn't being followed, she drove north and east. Once she reached Connecticut Avenue, she descended a winding road into Rock Creek Park. She didn't see another car. The sliver of moon was covered by clouds. The park seemed eerie.

Craig had told her where the old Adams Mill was. Just north of the stone building she saw a picnic grove. The parking lot was deserted except for a red pickup truck. Elizabeth pulled in and flashed her lights twice. She parked close to the truck and rolled her window down, precisely as Craig had told her.

Behind the wheel, Elizabeth saw Betty puffing away on a cigarette. She snuffed it out and left the pickup holding a thin envelope. She handed it to Elizabeth. "Tell Craig: No problem at my end."

Before Elizabeth had a chance to respond, Betty was back in the pickup, turning on the engine.

Elizabeth held her breath waiting for FBI agents to flood the area with light, then rush in and arrest both of them. The night air was in the thirties. She was trembling from the cold and fear.

Nothing happened. No FBI agents.

She watched Betty pull away.

Elizabeth knew what to do next. From the concierge, she learned of an open all night Kinko's near DuPont Circle—ten minutes away.

With the classified material in her possession, she was feeling nervous. Her left leg was shaking. She knew she wasn't being followed, but she was carefully watching her speed and red lights. The last thing she wanted was DC cops to stop her for a traffic violation and to search the car.

At Kinko's, the clerk on duty behind the counter, a thin black man, was alone in the shop. As Elizabeth approached, he put down a civil-engineering textbook. "How can I help you?" he asked in a Nigerian accent.

She needed access to a computer. As long as she paid up front, he was willing to let her do the work herself, while he eagerly returned to *Principles of Civil Engineering.*

With her hands shaking, Elizabeth scanned the satellite photos and forwarded them to her computer in Paris.

Once the electronic transmission went though, she put the photos back into the envelope. Looking around, she spotted the restrooms in a the back. Calmly, she walked to the ladies room and locked the door. Half expecting the FBI to burst in, she tore the photos and Betty's envelope into tiny pieces. It took three flushes before all the bits were gone.

Elizabeth breathed a sigh of relief, took a long pee and exited the restroom.

Fifteen minutes later, she was back in the hotel suite.

She poured two small bottles of cognac from the mini bar into a glass and took it into the bathroom. As she soaked in the hot tub to unwind, she sipped the amber liquid, then closed her eyes and thought about the strangeness of her life.

Growing up in a tough area of Brooklyn, she dreamed of pitching in the major leagues. The first girl player. For the New York Yankees. She got as far as the boys' high-school team, where she won all four games they let her pitch.

Next stop for Elizabeth was Harvard on scholarship—the first in her family to go to college. Right after graduation, she married a classmate, but that only lasted a year. As soon as they got away from the idyllic campus life, she realized she hardly knew him. He wanted to pursue his own activities and didn't care about her. He was going off to Africa to work for an NGO, and she was trying to establish a career as a journalist. They called it a starter marriage and ended it with an amicable divorce.

She thought about the relationships she had since then and before Craig. A couple of fellow journalists. Too dull. A tight end with the New York Jets. Not smart enough. A surgeon. In bed he treated her like a piece of meat on the operating table. None she wanted to commit to. And the truth was, she loved her work. She was determined never to get serious about a man again. Certainly not to get married.

Then Craig came along.

Ah, Craig. They were so good together. And not just for sex. But of course that for sure.

He shared her daring spirit. He appreciated her and respected her work. Let her thrive in journalism. He was exciting and fun to be with. He was bold and decisive. He had accomplished so much with the CIA and now with the EU. Truly, he had made a difference. She wanted a man she could regard with pride and admiration. That was Craig.

Marriage? To someone who might be killed any day? She didn't know. Don't even think about it, she told herself. Right now you have to concentrate on stopping Musa.

"Hey mister, we're cleaning now," the twenty-something, black-clad, blonde waitress in a mini skirt, said to Craig. "Your girl's not coming. You want to take me home?"

He and the Nats baseball cap were among the six patrons still in the Down Home. Craig smiled. "I don't think so."

"I could give you a good time." In case he had any doubt about what she had in mind, she touched herself in the crotch.

Craig reached into his pocket, took out two twenties and handed them to her. "Maybe another time."

Satisfied, she left him alone. He checked his watch and Blackberry one more time. Then with a sigh of resignation, Craig got up and walked toward the bar. "I could use a ride back to the Four Seasons," he said to the security agent in the Nats cap.

"You've got to be kidding," the surprised man said.

"No harm in trying. We're both going there."

"Fuck off."

"Give my regards to Norris."

Outside, Craig waved down a passing cab.

When he walked into their suite, he saw Elizabeth in a robe, looking anxious, pacing in the bedroom.

"What happened?" she asked while she gave him a thumbs up.

"He never showed. This whole trip was a waste of time." Craig sounded dejected.

"I'm sorry."

"I'll book us on the early Air France flight tomorrow."

"Don't worry. I'll make you forget about your troubles."

"How are you going to do that?"

"Well, first I intend to suck your cock." She was pointing to the recording device attached to the bedroom ceiling.

He smiled. "You're the best."

PARIS

As soon as General Zhou returned to Paris, he called Freddy Wu.

Freddy answered his cell phone. General Zhou heard voices in the background. "Can you talk?" he asked.

"To you, of course. I'm in a meeting. I'll move out in the corridor."

A moment later, Freddy said, "What's up?"

He sounds so western, General Zhou thought. "We have to talk. When can you meet me?"

"I was planning to have dinner this evening at Apicius with a French movie star, but I'll reschedule her. Tell her a business emergency popped up. Can you meet me at the restaurant at nine?"

"I'll be there."

On the way to dinner in the back of his car, with Captain Cheng driving, General Zhou heard the "ping ... ping ... ping" signaling a call from his brother.

"I have good news," his brother said. "President Li's colon cancer has become more aggressive. The doctors are giving him six months at most, unless he undergoes surgery, which could save his life. So far, he refuses."

"That is good. What about your efforts to have me become the next President?"

"I'm developing support. We're gaining momentum. People realize what you tried to do with Operation Dragon Oil. I'm feeling confident."

General Zhou arrived at Apicius promptly at nine and walked up the three steps into the glamorous temple of haute cuisine that resembled an ornate country home. The maître d' led him to a corner table in the prime first dining room, where Freddy was sipping a drink. General Zhou ordered a Macallan. For several minutes, he let Freddy gloat about his sexual exploits with French movie stars. Once they made their dinner choices, General Zhou said softly, "I just returned from Morocco."

Freddy looked concerned. "Have all the goods been arriving?"

"Except for the pontoon boats. Our partner says they're late. He's upset."

Freddy was squirming. "We had shipment delays, but they're over now. He'll have them in two, three days. A week at most."

"Is that real time or salesman's talk?"

Freddy's eye was blinking. "Real time. I promise you."

"Well keep on it. Without them, this is all for naught."

"I understand."

"Have you gotten any questions from Beijing about the arms shipments to Morocco?"

Freddy shook his head. "None at all. The customer designation is 'AR' which is our code for African rebel movements. We're supporting several movements on the dark continent. The leadership in Beijing doesn't want to know the details. That way they can feign outrage when the Americans accuse them of meddling at international meetings. Some of those rebels have stolen so much that they're even paying a good price. The arms business has never been better."

A waiter came over with their crab appetizers. At the same time, the sommelier poured the 1986 Chateau Margaux, Freddy ordered. Freddy put some in his mouth, closed his eyes and rolled it around. Finally he said, "Divine … ethereal."

He's been totally corrupted, General Zhou thought.

When the waiter left, General Zhou said, "I need something else."

"What's that?" Freddy sounded wary.

"I want you to deliver into Italy four missiles. The objective will be to install them in four different locations and simultaneously fire them at a single target."

Freddy straightened up and pulled his head back. "Is the target in Italy?"

"You don't have to know that."

Dots of perspiration appeared on Freddy's forehead. He wiped them with his napkin. General Zhou was staring at him.

"This will be one helluva an attack. If it's going to happen in Europe, perhaps I should get approval in Beijing."

That would ruin everything, General Zhou thought. The issue would go to President Li. Once he found out General Zhou was involved, he'd turn it down. That would end General Zhou's relationship with Musa. Time to get tough with Freddy.

"Now listen up," General Zhou said sharply. "President Li has colon cancer. He only has weeks to live."

"How do you know this?"

"My brother told me. You remember him. He was at your father's New Year's party a year ago."

"Yeah, but …"

"I'm going to be the next President of China … and this is important to me."

General Zhou paused to wave his hand at the dining room. "You like all this European high living. Don't you?"

Freddy nodded.

"Answer me. Dammit."

"Yes, sir. I do."

"Well if you want to keep living this way once I take over, you better come through for me with these missiles. Am I making myself clear, Mister?"

"Yes, sir, you are. Of course I'll do what you want." Freddy now sounded very deferential.

"Good. Then let's talk about the details of delivery."

"What's the range?" Freddy asked.

"Twenty kilometers."

"I can do that."

"Are they difficult to assemble or operate?"

Freddy shook his head. "My ten year old son could do it."

General Zhou was relieved.

"I'll make sure directions are enclosed in Italian."

"No. French."

"Alright. All they will have to do is aim and push a button. When do you want them in Italy and what's the delivery point?"

"I promised we'd deliver on Friday, March 26, to a warehouse in Torino. I assume that is doable."

"Absolutely."

"How will you get them there?"

Freddy rubbed a hand over his chin, thinking. "By air to Istanbul. From there, I'll slip them into Greece. Over land after that. The EU is porous."

"Turkey's not a problem?"

"Ever since the EU spurned them, the Turks have become a center for black-market arms. The Iranians. The Syrians. Everybody's using them in their desire to resurrect the Ottoman empire. They'll look the other way, provided a little cash greases the skids."

"The delivery can't be late. Not even one day. Timing is critical."

"I understand."

"I'll be unhappy if there is a problem."

General Zhou locked eyes with Freddy, who met his gaze.

"Don't worry. There won't be."

Freddy paused to eat. "The best crab dish in the world."

General Zhou wasn't interested in the food. He had something else to discuss with Freddy. "How well do you know the Spanish Defense Minister?"

"General Jose Alvarez. A military man before he became Defense Minister. He's pompous, arrogant, and only has his job because wealthy friends wrote big checks to his party in the last election."

"Is he a rich man himself?"

"No. All he has is his military pension and Defense Minister's salary. But he tries to use his position to lure women into bed. Preferably tall and busty. Blonde is even better."

"Have you sold much to Spain?"

Freddy shook his head. "The Americans have had a lock. I've heard that the Spanish are preparing to place a huge order for military aircraft. To upgrade their aging fleet. Forty planes. Everybody figures Boeing will get it with their F-15s, but I've been trying to compete. The deal is worth $30 billion."

"Will Alvarez be involved in the decision?"

"He'll have the ultimate say."

General Zhou felt a surge of excitement. Everybody could be a winner here. "You've done lots for me, Freddy. Now I want to do something for you."

"What's that?"

"I'll talk to Alvarez and persuade him to give you the order rather than Boeing."

Freddy's face lit up, and indeed it should. His personal commission on that transaction would be a hundred million euros. Enough to satisfy his lifestyle for many years.

"I would like that. I've never been able to develop a relationship with Alvarez. You can talk to him as one military man to another. That might work. By noon tomorrow, I'll get you all the background."

General Zhou required something else for his meeting with Alvarez. A small highly sensitive battery-powered tape recorder. He could easily obtain one in a Paris high-tech shop. He didn't need Freddy for it. And he didn't want Freddy to know.

25

PARIS

Craig found Giuseppe waiting at his office in Paris when he arrived from the airport. He had dropped Elizabeth at the newspaper.

"Did you get the satellite photos?" Giuseppe asked.

"Hopefully. Elizabeth sent them to her computer. We'll know for sure when she gets here."

"Was Norris helpful?"

"I had to find a way around that prick. I felt like Alice in Wonderland. We almost landed in a federal prison."

"Has the CIA Director gone off the deep end?"

"He's trying to mindlessly implement Dalton's policy. An underling trying to get a gold star from the boss. I'm sure you've seen that."

"All the time. I hate it. But while you were dealing with Mad Hatters, we had some success here."

Craig perked up. "What happened?"

Before Giuseppe could respond, Elizabeth burst in the door, waving papers in her hand. "Yes," she cried out. "Yes. The photos arrived and are perfectly clear."

Craig was thrilled. "Hold them for a minute, Elizabeth. Giuseppe was just telling me what he learned while we were gone."

"Sure. Go ahead," she said.

"The clerk at a small hotel called the Manzoni, not far from the Vatican, ID'd the guy who stole the Vatican plans. He was registered under the name Jean Louis Renoir. We checked copies of his passport and hotel registration on file at the local police station."

"And?" Craig asked impatiently.

"He gave a Paris address, which was a phony. Also his French passport was a forgery. Very well done. I hauled in and interrogated the best people in Rome who do passports. I'm convinced it wasn't done there."

"Probably in Paris. That ties in with the story the woman in Marseilles gave us. Ahmed's core group is from Clichy-sous-Bois, a suburb."

Giuseppe reached into his briefcase and pulled out a copy of the passport and other documents. He put them on the table. Studying the picture, Craig thought it looked familiar. Before he could place it, Elizabeth spoke up.

"He's Omar. Musa's friend. One of the three, whom Lila told us about in Marseilles."

"You sure?"

"Absolutely. Pull up his photo."

Craig displayed it on his computer screen. She was right. "So now we have positive confirmation that Musa's planning to attack the Vatican."

"Exactly," Giuseppe said.

"I'll give Jacques these materials. See if he can find out who did the passport. So far, he hasn't been able to locate anyone who knows where Omar is. This may give us a lead. Now, let's look at the satellite photos."

There were three of them. She spread them out on the table.

"This could be Musa's base," she said, running her finger around a built-up area deep in the mountains.

The resolution was incredible. American technology at its best.

Craig saw more than thirty buildings surrounding a short landing strip. Also, three buildings resembling aircraft hangars. There were people on the ground. And vehicles. Lots of them, including tanks and jeeps. The Spanish Revenge was well equipped.

"Where's the border?" Giuseppe asked.

Elizabeth drew a line with her finger. "The entire camp is on the Moroccan side."

"I thought King Hassan was a friend of the West," Giuseppe said.

"He is," Craig replied. "But he suffered a stroke about a year ago. It's unclear what shape he's in now."

Giuseppe was becoming animated, waving his hands. "We have to persuade the Moroccans to roll up the Spanish Revenge and turn Musa over to us for the Spanish train bombing."

"That'll be a tall order," Elizabeth said, "Given King Hassan's condition and that his Prime Minister Farez has moved aggressively to take de facto control of the government. If he has his way, he'll turn secular Morocco into another Islamic republic. My bet is that Farez knows what's going on in the mountains. He's either sympathetic to Musa or Musa's paying him off ... Or both."

"You may be right," Giuseppe said. "But I'm not convinced the Moroccan government wants to do battle with the EU for Musa's sake. We have to find a way to get their help."

Craig was studying the photographs. "We're getting ahead of ourselves. All these prove is there is some kind of military base in the mountains. We have nothing to link it to Musa. For all we know, it could be a Moroccan government installation."

Elizabeth was smiling. "I know what's coming next. Fortunately, I haven't unpacked my suitcase from the Washington trip."

"Ever been to Morocco?" Craig asked her.

"Half a dozen times, when I worked for the New York paper."

"Great. I need a guide. How about going with me?"

"Why not? I'm just sorry now I didn't end up in a Washington jail. I think that would have been far preferable to one in Morocco."

26

RABAT, MOROCCO

Craig had always heard that Rabat, the capital of Morocco, despite its history and shifting rulers, was a boring city in comparison to Marrakech or Fez. The ride from the airport confirmed that. The French designed and constructed the new city in order to have an administrative center for their protectorate as well as a place for foreigners and civil servants to live.

Without calling first, he went with Elizabeth directly to the King's palace. He hoped that would give him a better chance of seeing King Hassan.

They made it past two sets of guards and reached an ornate reception area, which held a score of high-backed, gold-embossed chairs. Paintings of Moorish buildings in Morocco lined one wall.

Sitting behind a gold desk, the King's aide, a thin gaunt man, with sad-looking, sunken gray eyes guarded access to the inner sanctum. He told Craig, "I'll have to see if King Hassan can meet with you."

"I appreciate that. Please tell him I'm here as an official representative of the EU. On a matter of grave importance for Morocco and its relationship with the EU."

The aide nodded, signaling he understood, his face giving away nothing. He stood up, turned, and headed through a heavy wooden door with gold decorations, which closed behind him, leaving Craig and Elizabeth alone with two armed guards in corners of the room.

Fearful the room was bugged, he and Elizabeth kept silent.

The wait seemed interminable.

Craig checked his watch. Only twenty minutes had passed. It felt like an hour.

Finally, the aide returned. Craig held his breath. "I'm sorry, but the King is not available. He suggested you meet with Prime Minister Farez. I'll call to arrange it."

As the aide reached for the phone, Craig said, "I would prefer to meet with King Hassan. If this is a bad time, we could return later or tomorrow."

Still no visible reaction from the aide. Was King Hassan too ill to see them? Or was the aide working with Farez? The Prime Minister had probably been tipped off by immigration that an EU official traveling on a diplomatic passport had arrived. Farez could have vetoed Craig's meeting with the King without Hassan even knowing he was here. Short of barging through the wooden door, which wasn't an option with armed guards in the room, there was not a damn thing Craig could do about it.

Elizabeth bowed out of the meeting with Farez. "You'll have a tough enough time without having a journalist along."

He didn't argue.

The Prime Minister, a former university president, was a handsome man, with a big smile and a neatly trimmed salt-and-pepper beard. He was dressed in a stylish dark western suit, no tie. White shirt open at the neck. Craig had never met Farez before.

From his reading, he concluded Farez fancied himself like Erdogan, the Turkish Prime Minister. He, too, was determined to move his pro-Western nation toward the East. Increased democracy was the Trojan horse leading toward an Islamic theocracy.

"We're honored to have such a distinguished visitor from the EU," Farez said, pointing to two chairs separated by a table. A secretary, her head covered, brought in cups of Turkish coffee.

"What brings you to our kingdom?"

"Do you recall the Spanish train bombing six months ago?"

Farez stiffened. "Of course. A real tragedy. I gather the perpetrators were never captured."

"Correct. But we've now traced them to Morocco."

Farez shook his head. "That's impossible. Our government has strict control over what's happening in the country."

Craig decided to go on the offensive. Assert that the base in the mountains was Musa's and see how Farez responded.

"Let me show you something."

Craig took the satellite photographs out of his briefcase and placed them on the table.

While Farez studied them, Craig sipped coffee. At the end, it was both bitter and sweet.

Farez was frowning, but not saying a word. Craig decided to take control.

"The photos depict a military base in the Atlas Mountains on the Moroccan side of the border. The leader of the group operating the base is Ahmed Sadi, who was born and grew up in a suburb of Paris. He now calls himself Musa Ben Abdil. He was responsible for the Spanish train bombing. We believe he is planning other terrorist attacks in Europe. I came here to ask the Moroccan government to shut down Musa's base and turn him over to the Spanish government for prosecution."

Farez picked up one of the photos and held it close to his eyes.

"Who invaded our air space to take these?" He sounded hostile.

Craig paused for a minute. Norris would be upset if he found out Craig had gotten the photos, but to hell with him. Craig had more to worry about than Norris. “They are from routine United States satellite surveillance.”

Farez tossed the photo onto the table. “They’re a fabrication. You manipulated American photos to show a renegade base on our territory. That’s not difficult, technically. Photos are doctored all the time. One of the great benefits of the digital age. I’m confident of my conclusion. Would you like to know why?”

Craig realized he was about to find out.

“Because I was up there last week. I saw the area with my own eyes. It’s desolate. Berbers graze their goats.”

Farez sounded indignant. His response surprised Craig, who hadn’t expected such a bold-faced lie. However, his words confirmed for Craig this was Musa’s base.

“Let’s travel up to the area,” Craig said. “You and I. Today. We’ll see whether the photos are accurate.”

The Prime Minister shook his head. “I told you I was there last week. You’re calling me a liar.”

“I want to clarify an error. Perhaps you’re confusing the location.”

“There is no error. What happens on Moroccan territory is none of your business. It’s a matter of Moroccan sovereignty.”

“When I report back to the EU leadership, they’ll be unhappy. Some may want to take unilateral action against Musa and his base.”

Farez turned beet red. “Don’t try and intimidate me because I’m the head of a small country. You’re bluffing. You don’t have any evidence to back up your charges. These photos don’t prove a thing. The EU leaders will never attack Morocco based on this … stuff.”

Craig decided Farez had a point. He didn’t have enough evidence to justify an EU attack. He changed his approach. “Perhaps there is a misunderstanding.” He tried to sound conciliatory. “I apologize for that.”

Farez was on guard. “If you really mean that, then it’s accepted.

Now if we're finished, I'll arrange transportation for you and your journalist friend to the airport. We'll get you on the first plane back to Paris."

"I'd like to do something first."

"What's that?"

"I've never been in your country before. I've always heard Marrakech is spectacular. I'd like to take a couple days of vacation there. Tour the area with Elizabeth."

"It is an amazing place. Let me know what I can do to enhance your visit. You should have VIP treatment. I'll put a car and driver at your disposal. A guide, too."

I'll bet you would. Make it easier to keep track of us.

"Thanks, but we'll play the regular tourists. I always get a much better feel for a place that way."

"As you wish."

At the airport in Rabat, Craig led Elizabeth to an outside fountain. Pretending to admire Moorish stonework with a background of cascading water, he told her what he wanted to do. "Stop in Marrakech, then secretly go to Musa's camp. I have to get evidence that this is his base."

She whistled. "Wow. That's a tall order. Going up there without a military escort will be dicey. If either Farez or Musa finds out …"

He clutched her arm. "Listen, Elizabeth, if you don't want to go with me, I'll …"

She pulled away. "You gave me the same crap back in Washington. You don't have to worry. I'm plenty tough. I not only grew up in a rough neighborhood of Brooklyn, but I had four older brothers. As an investigative reporter, I faced plenty of danger. I was one of the embedded reporters to go with our troops into Iraq. And also into Afghanistan."

"OK. OK."

Her face was flushed. "I'm not finished. I know how to fire a gun.

Growing up, I was one of the boys. Went huntin' and fishin' with my dad and brothers. Bagged my first deer when I was twelve. I even killed a Taliban thug in Afghanistan who attacked me. So don't give me any more of that male chauvinism. I find it annoying."

"I care for you. I only meant …"

"Do it again, and I'll whack you with a baseball bat."

That was the Elizabeth he loved.

27

MARRAKECH

At Marrakech airport, Craig rented a black BMW with a good GPS. Elizabeth had told him where they should stay: Ksar Char-Bagh, a small luxury inn, formerly a Moorish palace, ten kilometers from the city. Before going to the inn, Craig drove to the old city. From the moment they left the airport, they were followed by a gray SUV. Craig made no effort to lose the tail.

It was late afternoon when they reached the market area. Merchants had reopened their shops. Under a blazing sun, they milled around the narrow streets crowded with shoppers and tourists.

As Craig expected, the two security men from the SUV, both very dark-skinned, one tall, the other short, were following, hanging back, but in dogged pursuit.

While Craig waited in front, Elizabeth went into a shop. The security men took positions ten yards away. Neither going inside.

Not too swift, Craig thought. They should've split. These guys were not experienced and hadn't been well trained.

Ten minutes later, Elizabeth returned carrying a shopping bag. "Got it all," she whispered to him.

They returned to the car and drove to the inn with the gray SUV following. The sun was setting over the desert in a gorgeous red sky.

As a bellman rushed to take their bags, Craig watched the cars. A valet told Craig, "Your keys will be in the box." He took their BMW to a parking lot in the back. Meantime, the gray SUV parked in the front driveway next to a row of date palms, the only exit from the property.

Craig now understood the setup. One of the two would keep an eye on him and Elizabeth in the inn. The other would remain in the car parked in front. He'd be able to follow quickly if Craig tried to drive away. Not a bad plan, in theory.

Craig immediately searched the room. No bugs.

Before they went to dinner, Elizabeth stuffed the items she'd bought in Marrakech—the video camera, binoculars, maps, two flashlights, duct tape, and rope—into her bag. In case the room was searched, Elizabeth was taking her bag to dinner. Craig slipped his Swiss army knife into his pocket.

When they exited the room, Craig saw the tall security man sitting on a chair at one end of the corridor. The dining room was the other way. He immediately followed them. So far, he had nothing to report, Craig decided. They'd done what any tourist would do. First visit the old city. As they passed the reception desk, Craig picked up his car keys.

Craig and Elizabeth followed the maître d' to a table in the back. The security man sat inside the half-empty dining room. He ate while they ate. Then left the dining room immediately after they did.

"Let's get a little air," Craig said to Elizabeth, loudly enough for the security man to hear. He wanted to confirm the layout.

With his arm around Elizabeth's waist, they stepped into the cool evening air. The gray SUV was still in front. They walked around to the back. Craig looked at the swimming pool with a grove of date palms on one side. The tall man was still following. Craig had seen enough. Back in the room, Craig checked again for bugs. Nothing. It was eleven-thirty. With their clothes on, they slept until three a.m.

Craig stuffed the tape and rope into his jacket pocket, along with one of the flashlights. He gave Elizabeth the knife and watched her load into a duffel six bottles of water and all the nuts, dates, figs, and candy from the mini bar.

"Meet you in front of the inn in fifteen minutes," Craig said.

Craig ignored the tall security man at the end of the corridor and ran out of the back door toward the swimming pool. As he expected, the man was right behind. Craig passed the pool and headed into the thick trees. Anyone would think he was going to meet someone.

The ground was soft and covered with leaves. Craig made no effort to keep still as he trampled deeper into the trees. A branch scratched his arm. He snapped it off.

Craig had the advantage of a flashlight. He used it effectively to draw the man deep into the grove, then circle behind him. Swiftly Craig turned around and smacked the flashlight against the man's head, knocking him out. Craig searched the man and found a pistol, which he took. Then he taped his mouth and tied his arms and legs.

One down and one to go.

Keys in hand, Craig ran toward his BMW.

Clutching her duffel and handbag, Elizabeth quickly walked out of the front of the inn and looked around. The sky was full of clouds, providing the cover of darkness.

Nobody in sight. Perfect.

She raced into the line of date palms alongside the security men's SUV. Then she crouched low, moving close to the ground, until she was next to the SUV, with the trees providing cover. Now for the hard part. Knocking the driver out quietly, before he had a chance to call for help.

Elizabeth sprang to her feet and looked into the front side window of the SUV. Son of a bitch. The guy was asleep behind the wheel. Every once in a while you catch a break.

With the open knife in one hand and the flashlight in the other, Elizabeth flattened on the ground and crawled under the gray SUV. She turned on the flashlight and looked around until she spotted the fuel line. She reached up with the knife and cut through the rubber hose. Then ducked to get away from dripping fuel.

She scrambled out from under the vehicle, brushed off the dirt, and calmly walked toward the front of the inn, duffel and bag in hand. Seconds after she reached it, Craig was roaring around the corner. He stopped and she jumped into the car. As they passed the gray SUV, the engine started. Craig was looking through the rearview mirror. "He's coming after us," Craig said, sounding alarmed. "Didn't you take care of him?"

Elizabeth wasn't concerned. "With a severed fuel line, he'll make it a mile at most."

"Way to go. You're great."

"But I just thought of a weakness in your plan."

"What's that?"

"Won't he call for help?"

"At this hour, it'll be a while. By then we'll ditch this car."

"You're planning to walk to Musa's camp?"

"Actually, I prefer a police or military car."

An hour later, they passed a small Army outpost that was dark, with half a dozen jeeps parked in front. Craig hotwired one with a hard top and told Elizabeth to follow him in the BMW. The road was deserted. Half a mile later, he directed her to drive the BMW into a grove of fig trees. She scrambled out with the GPS in hand and joined him in the jeep.

They were now rising in the mountains. Directly ahead, Craig saw the first rays of sunrise. She was studying maps with a flashlight and fiddling with the GPS.

"What do you figure for our ETA at Musa's base?" he said.

"Hard to tell how good these roads are. Let's say noon. More or less."

ATLAS MOUNTAINS

Musa was in the middle of his usual five-mile morning run on mountain trails when the cell phone hooked to his belt rang. It was Prime Minister Farez.

Musa continued running with the phone up to his ear.

"You may have a couple of uninvited visitors this afternoon," Farez said.

"Who?"

"Craig Page and Elizabeth Crowder. He's the Director of the EU's ..."

"I know who they are."

"He met with me yesterday in Rabat."

Musa stopped running and sat on a rock. "What did he tell you?"

"He knows you're responsible for the Spanish train bombing. He also has satellite photos showing your base. He wanted me to shut it down and turn you over to him for prosecution in Spain."

Musa tapped his foot on the ground nervously. He couldn't believe Craig had found him. He'd underestimated the man. "What did you tell him?"

"That the photos were a fabrication. That I know there is no base in the area. But he didn't believe me. Gave me some phony story about going to Marrakech for a couple of days vacation. I knew he was planning to come up to your base. I had people follow him from the moment he left my office."

Musa was confused. "Then why are they coming here? Can't you hold them in Marrakech?"

"That was the plan, but we had a mechanical problem with our following car."

Musa bristled. Farez was such a fool. Musa had done plenty of research on Craig Page and Elizabeth Crowder. He knew these people never quit.

He had to conceal his anger. After all, his operation depended upon Farez's acquiescence. His payments to Farez had been substantial, but very secret, having been deposited into the Prime Minister's Swiss bank account. And while Musa's forces had grown strong, they were still no match for the Moroccan military, which had an air force. Unlike Musa.

"Page and Crowder are in a black BMW," Farez continued. "We're trying to locate them with helicopters as well as military vehicles. If we find them, we'll detain them. I'll personally put them on a plane to Paris. However, it's conceivable they may elude us. So I wanted you to know."

"I appreciate that. As you well know, the roads are dangerous. The ride difficult, even for someone who knows the area. There are plenty of cliffs and gorges. Wild animals. Fierce mountain natives. Many people have disappeared driving in these mountains."

There was a long pause. Finally, Farez said, "We Moroccans treat our guests with hospitality. Besides, Page is a high-ranking official of the EU. If anything happens to him, the EU could unleash severe repercussions. The King would not appreciate that. Nor would I. That means it would not be good for you. Am I making myself clear?"

Well, Farez is a fool, Musa thought, but not a complete fool.

"You don't have to worry," Musa said. "My ancestors are Berbers. We, too, know how to treat our guests."

And I know what I will do to Craig Page and Elizabeth Crowder, if I get my hands on them.

"I'm quite serious," Farez said. "You better not harm them. You must return them to Marrakech. I will make sure they are sent back to Paris."

ATLAS MOUNTAINS

Craig was gripping the steering wheel hard. The mountain air was cold, but his palms moist. He couldn't ever remember driving narrow roads so treacherous, with hairpin turns and steep cliffs above mountain gorges. Snow-capped peaks towered above. He had to be careful to avoid patches of ice.

Twice they nearly crashed down the mountain as the road gave way because of rock slides or falling snow and ice. Once a mountain goat stood in the center of the road, refusing to budge, even with Craig blasting the horn. Elizabeth got out the car and chased it down the mountain. Craig sensed the brakes were damn near shot. And he never knew what was ahead of the next bend. At least there were very few other vehicles on the road.

Next to him, Elizabeth continually moved her eyes from the map to the GPS and back to the map again. She was an incredible navigator, constantly finding back roads.

"Great scenery," he said.

"Keep your eyes on the road."

Suddenly, he heard a helicopter overhead. Oh oh.

"Don't lean out and look up," he told her. "Must be the Moroccan Air Force. I don't want them to see you."

"You think they'll fire rockets at us?"

"Possibly, if they found the BMW and believe we took the jeep. But that's a risky call. They can't see in the jeep. They must have lots of other Army vehicles on the road. They don't want to hit one of their own."

"There's a rock formation ahead. You want to stop and take cover?"

He shook his head. "That'll give us away. Then we'll have the whole Moroccan military after us. We have to keep going. You OK with that?"

"Your call. You've done a lot more of this stuff."

The chopper was circling overhead. Craig reached into his jacket pocket and pulled out the gun he took from the agent he tied up at the inn. He was straining his ears to hear through the open window. If they came close or he heard anything that made him think they would be firing, he was ready to fire back.

He held his breath.

Elizabeth grabbed his thigh and dug her fingers into his flesh through the cloth.

The helicopter pulled up. Moved away.

"Well done," she said. "I figured the odds were long of our escaping the chopper. Maybe I'll take you to a casino."

"It's not over yet. They may not have wanted to risk killing us with rockets. Now that they know our location, they may cut us off on a road ahead."

She groaned. "Thanks a lot. Just when I was feeling better."

"How long to Musa's base?"

"I figure another hour."

"Tighten your seatbelt. I intend to pick up the pace."

"On these roads?" she asked with alarm.

And he did. After forty-five minutes of white-knuckle riding, Elizabeth guided Craig up a steep, dirt, mountain road. "This should give us a vantage point high above Musa's base."

"Perfect. Exactly what we need."

He pulled over to the side of the road and parked. They took large gulps of water before getting out of the jeep. Craig had the binoculars in his hand, Elizabeth the video camera.

They moved up to the edge of a precipice, then stretched out on the rocky earth. Elbows on the ground. Craig raised the binoculars to his eyes.

"Holy shit." Satellite photos were one thing. Being this close was far more dramatic. They were looking down at a full-scale military base. Stone barracks to house several thousand. Armored cars, tanks, mobile grenade launchers. A landing strip with relatively fresh concrete and piles of snow along the sides. Next to the strip, he saw wooden crates being unloaded.

He increased the magnification on the binoculars to the max and focused on the men's faces. One of them looked familiar. Omar!

He recognized the man's face from his picture. Here was absolute proof that this was Musa's base for the Spanish Revenge. He told Elizabeth to capture Omar on her video.

He kept looking around. Many were Arabs or Berbers, but others were Chinese!

He turned his head to the left, to a firing range. Berbers were practicing with automatic weapons.

Behind each shooter was a Chinese instructor.

He knew the Chinese government had supported rebel groups in a number of African countries, but never Morocco. What the hell was going on? Were the Chinese supporting Musa to take over the Moroccan government? Or perhaps Algeria on the other side of the mountains? Either way, Beijing would gain a foothold in Northwest

Africa, a dagger close to the heart of Western Europe.

He glanced at Elizabeth who was filming. "You getting all this?" he asked.

"Unbelievable. I assume you saw the Chinese. I'm filming a group working with Berbers to unload rocket launchers. That'll make good viewing."

"I'd sure like to know how Musa hooked up with the Chinese."

Craig focused on a large stone building, which he guessed was Musa's house and headquarters. He zeroed in on the front landing. Two men were standing and talking. He immediately recognized one of them as Musa from his picture.

"Quick." He said to Elizabeth pointing. "I see Musa. Get him on film."

She aimed the camera. "Got him. Just before he walked into the building. Now let's get the hell out of here."

Craig wasn't ready to leave. "I want to capture Musa. Drive into Algeria and find a way to take him back to Spain so he can stand trial."

"That's the craziest idea I've ever heard. And since I've known you, I've heard lots of wild ideas."

"Most of which succeeded."

"No, really, Craig. This one is absurd."

"I appreciate your candid assessment. But I had a similar situation in Yemen, and I was able to abduct an Al Qaeda leader from his compound. Let me tell you how it'll work."

"I'm a captive audience."

"OK, smart ass. We now know where Musa hangs out." He pointed to the large stone building. "We wait until evening, which is what I did in Yemen. Then, under the cover of darkness, I sneak down the hill and into the base while you remain up here."

"What about sentries?"

"I doubt if Musa will have much in the way of guards. He probably doesn't think he needs them. Being so remote. If they do,

I'll kill one or two quietly, slip into the compound, and into Musa's house. With the element of surprise, I'll knock him out and bring him up here. We'll drive over the mountains into Algeria."

Her nose was wrinkling. "You really think you can do that?"

"It worked in Yemen. Musa's men put in a tough day. They'll be tired in the evening."

"And what do we do until then?"

"We stay in the car to keep warm. We eat the food you took from the mini bar."

"I don't know, Craig."

From her voice, he thought she was coming around.

"I have to try, Elizabeth. If I don't return in an hour, I think you should drive to Marrakech. Call Giuseppe and tell him what happened."

Craig heard a crunching noise on the rocks behind them. He sprang to his feet and reached for the gun in his jacket pocket.

In the flash of a second, he saw two bearded men in military uniforms, each carrying an AK-47. Before he had a chance to react, one of them turned the gun around in his hand, clutched the barrel and swung it against the side of Craig's head. His whole world went black.

30

ATLAS MOUNTAINS

Craig was regaining consciousness. His mind, still a blur, was clearing. His head hurt like hell. He was lying on a dirt floor. His legs bound together at the ankles. He raised his right hand to the side of his head. Felt the dried blood.

"Craig … Craig," he heard Elizabeth calling. "Are you okay?" He rubbed his eyes, sat up, and looked around. She was in a chair, a rope around her chest holding her in place, her wrist and ankles bound with rope.

They were in a prison cell. About twelve feet by twelve. Two windows had bars. They were at ground level. Outside it was dusk.

He was furious at himself. "Sorry, Elizabeth. I was stupid. Should have been watching our six o'clock."

"It wouldn't have mattered. There were eight of them altogether. We didn't stand a chance. Anyhow, it's my fault. I kept us there too long filming stuff we didn't need. We already had enough good footage."

"Did they hurt you?"

"Just a little rough dragging me into the back of their pickup, but I brought that on by kicking and scratching. No big deal. How's your head?"

"Starting to feel better."

"Why do you suppose Musa didn't have us killed up on the mountain?"

"My guess is he wants to find out whether we have information about his future terrorist attacks."

He raised a finger to his lips, signaling there was probably a hidden recorder. They couldn't disclose that they knew the Vatican was a target. If they didn't make it out of here alive, at least Giuseppe could try to thwart that attack and capture Musa.

"But we don't have a clue about his next attack." Elizabeth said. "That's why we're here."

She understood. He smiled. What continued to grate on Craig was the enigma of Musa's Chinese support.

Without warning, the wooden door opened. Four burly, unshaven, armed men in military uniforms barged into the cell. Perfect timing. Minutes after he regained consciousness. Confirmation that Musa had been listening. So Musa heard Elizabeth say they didn't know anything about the next attack.

They untied Elizabeth. Then cut the rope around his ankles and roughly pulled him to his feet. Led the two of them out of the prison courtyard and across a dusty road to the building Craig had decided was Musa's headquarters.

Musa was waiting in his office in a corner of the building. Looking around, Craig was impressed by the high-tech communications and video equipment. All state of the art. All Chinese manufactured.

"Well, well," Musa said. "The great Craig Page. It's an honor to finally meet the world's greatest counterterrorism expert. And Elizabeth Crowder. Journalist par excellence."

Craig wanted to say, "Cut the crap," but he wasn't in a position to anger Musa, who pointed to two chairs in front of his desk.

They defiantly sat down while the four soldiers took positions along the walls.

"What brings you to my retreat?" Musa asked.

Craig decided Farez must have tipped off Musa. Better play it straight. Sort of. Apart from leaving Morocco alive, Craig wanted to avoid having Elizabeth tortured to get him to talk. The only chance of doing that was to persuade Musa that Craig wasn't holding anything back.

"Since the Spanish train bombing six months ago, I've been searching for you. I figure you're planning something else. I have no idea what it is. I wanted to capture you before you had a chance. Initially, I figured your base was in Spain or France. When that didn't pan out, I got American satellite photos. This camp stood out. I didn't think it was a nudist colony."

Musa wasn't smiling.

"Farez told me I was crazy. So Elizabeth and I decided to see for ourselves."

"Who told you I was responsible for the Spanish train bombing?"

Craig closed his eyes. Lila Dihab's face appeared in his mind. As she was in the hotel in Marseilles.

I won't betray her. Musa will kill her.

He had to create an alternative story. "I captured the train bomber in a farmer's field outside of Seville. Before he killed himself, he gave you up. He told me your real name is Ahmed Sadi and you are from Clichy-sous-Bois."

Musa's head snapped back. "You're lying."

"Why would I? He also told me his name was Ibrahami Shabelle. Formerly a Somali refugee to Holland who moved to Clichy."

Musa seemed stunned. On a roll, Craig kept going, spinning out the story, "I had French intelligence run your bio. When I learned about Columbia University, I turned the recording you gave to CNN over to one of my old CIA buddies. They played it for people at Columbia who confirmed the voice was yours. I decided to come up here and see for myself. To make sure this was really your base. Not another terrorist group."

Musa screwed his face up in anger. "Ibrahami didn't kill himself. You tortured him to death."

Craig thought Musa had accepted everything he said. "That's not true. He had a cyanide pill in his pocket. When I called the Spanish Defense Ministry to relay the information, he pulled it out and put it in his mouth."

"I don't believe it. You tortured him to death. You'll pay for it with your own life. Elizabeth, too."

Musa turned to her. "You made a great video. Too bad I had to destroy the camera."

She shrugged. "I prefer print journalism."

"Then it's a shame you won't have a chance to write your story."

Craig said, "If we don't make it back safely, you'll have the combined forces of the EU flying down here."

Musa shook his head. "Those people couldn't agree on anything, certainly not military action to save two Americans." He laughed. "I'll take my chances."

"I know all about you, Ahmed." Craig recited the story of Ahmed's life.

Musa's eyes were blazing. "So what? You did some research. Well, I did as well. Craig Page, the great American patriot. Sacked from the CIA for insubordination when he was trying to apprehend members of Al Qaeda on a suicide mission to blow up Madison Square Garden. Summoned back to service by President Brewster. Foiled a Chinese plot hatched by General Zhou to cut off the supply of foreign oil to the US. Not content with being the top super spy in the US, in a great demonstration of hubris and arrogance, decided to take his great terrorism-busting talents to Europe where he botched the Spanish train bombing."

Inside Craig was seething. Outwardly, he kept his cool. Musa was taunting him.

Musa continued. "Elizabeth Crowder, daughter of a New York City cop with four brothers who are cops. Once a budding journalist and foreign editor of the *New York Tribune*. Decided to stop her career trajectory and go back to being a reporter, based in Paris. And all for the man she loves. A touching story."

Musa paused to take a deep breath. "So now the three of us understand each other."

"Not so," Craig said. "I don't understand how someone as intelligent as you, Ahmed, with so much to offer his people and the world could become just another Islamic terrorist."

Musa reached for the pistol on his desk. "How dare you." He aimed the gun at Craig. The guards were tightening the grip on their automatic weapons.

Craig didn't flinch. "I'm asking it as a serious question. I want to know."

Musa put the pistol down.

"I'm not a terrorist. I'm hastening the flow of inexorable events. History is change. Remember what happened to Rome it the fifth century. Sophisticated Rome. The apex of civilization. Their economy fell apart under debt. Then the unwashed masses swooped down and made them slaves in their own land."

"What's your point?"

"In this century, the ascension of Islam over Christianity in Western Europe is inevitable. You took us in with your hospitality. With our higher birth rates, the demographics coupled with democracy, permitting the majority to rule, dictate the foregone conclusion. For example, by 2020 Muslims will be a majority in the largest Dutch cities. By the middle of the century, we'll dominate Paris, Berlin, and Copenhagen. Birmingham, England will follow. I'm merely expediting the process. Making certain that mosques take over empty churches in Western Europe in my lifetime."

"You're a hypocrite. You've never been in a mosque in your life. You have nothing in common with the fundamentalists who recruit their young warriors for suicide bombers."

"True, but when they hear about my success, those warriors will flock to my banner the way they did to Saladin."

"You accuse me of hubris. At the same time, you compare yourself with Saladin, the bravest Arab warrior in the Crusades. Maybe of all time."

"But there are differences between me and Saladin."

"How modest of you to concede that."

"When Richard the Lion Heart lost his horse in battle, in the Third Crusade, Saladin gave him another."

He looked at Elizabeth. "You're the student of medieval history. I'm right. Aren't I?"

"Yes," she said softly.

"I would not be so generous to my enemies."

A chill went up and down Craig's spine. He understood the not too subtle message.

"Also Saladin fought his own battles. He didn't rely on the Chinese," Craig said determined to find out how Musa had formed his unholy alliance.

"The enemy of my enemy is my friend."

"And how did you make this friend in Beijing? Have you been there?"

"Sometimes the things closest are the things we don't see."

"What the hell does that mean?"

"We've spoken enough. I want you both to rest this evening. Tomorrow, at the crack of dawn we'll have a medieval sport."

"What kind of sport?" Craig asked.

"Not your American baseball or football. Something more exciting."

31

ATLAS MOUNTAINS

Craig and Elizabeth were placed in separate jail cells for the night. Craig tried to unfasten the bars from the window. Without tools, it was hopeless. The door was locked tight and didn't budge.

He had no choice but to lay on the dusty mattress on the floor and to stare at the ceiling. The only light came from the moon outside.

He recalled other difficult situations he'd endured in his career. In Beirut. In Dubai. In Tehran. In Beijing. None as hopeless as this.

Musa had spoken about "medieval sport." Craig understood. He and Elizabeth would be the sport.

He wasn't terrified of death. He expected it to come at a relatively young age in the work he selected. No one had compelled him to spend his life thwarting terrorists.

What did cause him anguish, however, was Elizabeth. Not merely that he loved her, but he had brought her into all of this. If it weren't for him, she would be in New York as the foreign editor of the *New York Tribune*.

He knew he should sleep. In the morning, he would try to find a way for them to escape. For that, he would need all his wits and strength.

Easier said done. He tossed and turned on the mattress. Sleep didn't come.

Minutes after he saw the first rays of sunlight on the horizon, the door opened. Two burly men grabbed Craig, each by one arm. Two others had automatic weapons aimed at him.

They led him across a dusty road full of rocks. He didn't see Elizabeth. Perhaps, he hoped, Musa had decided to spare her. The sun was rising fast, blinding him as he walked.

They arrived at the edge of an open field, moist in the early morning air. Then he saw Elizabeth sitting on a wooden bench. She stood as soon as she saw him, looking weary from lack of sleep. They locked eyes. Both knew what was coming.

From the side, Musa appeared on a magnificent gray horse, a spear in one hand. "Any final words?" he asked.

They both remained silent. Stoic.

"This is for Ibrahami," Musa said as if he were pronouncing a death sentence.

Craig thought of an expression he had once heard. "There can be dignity in death."

Craig looked out at the field. Two wooden posts stood in the center. By now he understood how the sport would be played. He thought of grabbing Elizabeth and making a run for it, but six armed guards had AK-47s pointed at them.

Musa signaled to two of his men. They led Craig and Elizabeth toward the posts. Both marched with their heads held high, grim expressions on their faces.

The six armed guards followed closely behind. Craig saw their fingers on the triggers, itching to fire if Craig made a wrong move.

In the searing sun, Craig watched Musa ride to the far end of the field where another horseman, also holding a spear, awaited him.

A guard wrapped a rope around Craig's torso fastening his back tight against the post, facing him in the direction from which Musa would ride. Another guard fastened Elizabeth. Omar walked over and checked that the ropes were tight.

After Omar walked away, Craig reached behind, his hands grasping for the knot in the rope while trying not to seem obvious. Straining, he had hold of it. He recognized the knot. Damn near impossible to break.

Craig and Elizabeth locked eyes again. Then she closed hers. Not Craig. His were wide open, hoping, though he realized futilely, that he could stare down his executioner. Meantime, he kept trying to undo the knot.

32

ATLAS MOUNTAINS

Musa tightened his grip on the spear. He glanced over at Ali on his chestnut horse, ready to ride.

"I'll lead and take the man," Musa said.

"Yes, sir," Ali replied.

"Let's go."

Musa was preparing to charge when the cell phone fastened to his belt rang. He glanced quickly at caller ID. Farez. He had to find out what the fool wanted.

He raised his hand, signaling Ali to hold his position.

"Yes," Musa said curtly.

"You're disobeying my orders. I told you not to harm Craig and Elizabeth. To return them to Marrakech, and I would send them home."

"They never arrived. They must have had an accident in the mountains. Perhaps their car fell off the road. What a shame."

"Don't you lie to me." Farez was shouting angrily. "I know you're planning to kill them in a few minutes. The same way you killed that Russian oligarch and his bodyguards."

Musa couldn't believe it. Farez had a spy in Musa's camp. He vowed to find the man and rip him apart limb by limb. Further lying was pointless.

"I won't risk an EU attack on Morocco," Farez said. "You have a choice. Either you release Craig and Elizabeth, or I'll bomb your base. Destroy everything you've worked so hard to build. And don't think I won't. Our planes are loaded with bombs and sitting on the runway. It's your decision. You have five seconds to make it. Or I release the bombers."

Musa had no choice. The latest Chinese surface to air missiles and anti aircraft batteries had recently arrived. But Musa hadn't had a chance to make them operational. And he was convinced Farez wasn't bluffing.

"You win," he said reluctantly. "They will be released."

"Good. I'm sending a plane to pick them up. We'll land on your airfield. I want them placed on board. Only the two of them. The plane will fly them to Marrakech. There I will make certain they're on the first commercial flight to Paris. Is that understood?"

"Yes," Musa replied with bile in his mouth.

Twenty minutes later, grim faced, he watched Craig and Elizabeth climb the stairs to a Moroccan Air Force plane. He would dearly love to hit it with a rocket, but that, unfortunately, wasn't an option.

Once the plane took off, he went to his office and summoned Omar.

"We've suffered a terrible setback," Musa said. "Craig and Elizabeth will now be a constant threat to our success. Even to our survival."

"You did what you had to do," Omar said softly. "We will succeed despite them."

"But we have another problem. Farez managed to plant a spy

in our organization. We have to find out who. Order polygraph machines from Paris. I want immediate shipment. Then we'll interrogate each man."

Omar sighed and took a deep breath. Musa knew he wanted to say something, but was holding back. "What is it? We're close like brothers. You never have to be afraid to speak your mind with me."

Omar remained silent.

"If you don't tell me, I will be angry."

"I think a witch hunt for the spy is a bad idea," Omar's voice was trembling. "It will destroy the morale of our organizations. People will leave us. We can't risk that."

"But how can we continue knowing that Farez has a spy?"

"Limit operational information, plans and strategy to the two of us. Give orders to the others on a need to know basis. At the last possible moment. What they don't know they can't tell Farez."

Musa pondered Omar's words for a full minute. "You're right, Omar. We'll do it that way."

Once Omar left, Musa continued brooding. Yesterday Craig had called him "Just another Islamic terrorist." Those words had deeply upset Musa. He saw himself as far more than that. As a modern day Saladin. An emerging leader of the Islamic world. A military genius who would annihilate Christian armies. But what if others shared Craig's perception, that he was simply another terrorist?

Chafing at those words, Musa put on his shorts and went for a run on mountain trails. While he ran, his mind kicked into high gear. He was able to solve problems. Thirty minutes into the run, perspiring heavily, he had the answer: "Legitimacy."

His movement needed legitimacy.

Terrorists attacked what wasn't theirs. People with a legitimate claim retook what rightfully belonged to them.

Somehow he had to find that legitimacy. He knew where to start. A few months ago he had attended a conference in Tangiers on the changing nature of Islam in the modern world. There he had met Abdil Khalid, a professor of medieval history at the University in Casablanca. Khalid had made a presentation on the incredible accomplishments of the Arabs in the period from the tenth through the fifteenth centuries in Spain. Then he talked about the clash of civilizations now occurring in Western Europe. Khalid will be sympathetic. He hoped Khalid would be sympathetic and would be able to help.

When he returned to his office, he summoned Omar. "I have to go away for a couple of days. I want you to ascertain the status of the four missiles being shipped into Italy for the attack on the Vatican. Also, I want you to make sure our antiaircraft batteries are operational here as well as the ground to air missiles the Chinese sent."

"Are you expecting the EU to attack?" Omar asked anxiously.

"It's a possibility. And I can't rule out an attack by Farez. We have to be prepared for everything."

33

PARIS

Craig and Elizabeth exited the jetway at Charles DeGaulle at five in the afternoon. As soon as they were in the terminal, he stopped and took deep gulps of air. The air of freedom. They were still alive. He'd had a number of brushes with the Grim Reaper over the years, but this morning's was the closest.

He threw his arms around Elizabeth and hugged her tightly. Weak in the knees, she collapsed with him onto a blue upholstered bench in the gate waiting area. Passengers lined up to board were staring at them, but he didn't care.

His heart was pounding with joy. His breath coming in short spurts. In the surge of emotion, he stammered out the words, "We made it."

Tears had filled her eyes and were rolling down her cheeks. "We couldn't come any closer than that. Never. Oh my God!"

He squeezed her hand so tightly that she pulled it away. He

caressed the back of her neck.

"Watching you try to undo that knot," she said, "gave me a reason to hope."

He took a deep breath and blew it out with a whoosh. "Let's get out of here."

They stood up, and he looped an arm around her waist.

Outside, moving toward the cab line, he said to her, "Apartment?"

She replied, "Oh, yes."

Once they were in the door, he kicked it shut, took her in his arms, and kissed her deeply. Then he pulled away. "We're safe," he said. "Safe at last."

"I still can't believe it."

In his mind, he saw Musa on that horse. Musa charging at him. Musa aiming his spear. No, he told himself. It's over. We're both alive. I won't think about it anymore.

He kissed her again. As he did, he was unbuttoning her blouse. Unsnapping her bra and caressing her breasts—while she unzipped his pants. They were on fire. With each other. With life.

He unhooked her skirt, let it fall to the floor, and slipped down her pants. She was soaked and she was grabbing his erect cock, pulling him toward the bedroom.

By the time he pulled the spread off, she was on her back, her arms outstretched. They couldn't wait. He entered her immediately. Their fused bodies moved together in perfect rhythm. Both breathing hard. Perspiration dotting her forehead. He kept moving back and forth, driving her wild, until she cried out, "Now. Yes. Now." And he exploded in her.

Their bodies entwined, sated from lovemaking, they fell asleep. When he woke up, it was eight thirty in the evening. She was still sleeping soundly. He called the Bristol for a table when early diners departed. Then he retuned to bed and kissed her on the lips. "Hey," he said. "Time to wake up."

"What's wrong?"

"Everything's great. We have to finish our celebratory dinner at the Bristol. We were interrupted six months ago."

"I'm on my way to the shower. I don't want to miss that."

They started the same way. Champagne. Then fois gras, followed by the rack of lamb and Grand Marnier soufflé they had to miss. All accompanied by '05 Chambolle Musigny from Dujac. This time something was different: He turned the power off on his cell phone.

Craig sipped the spectacular burgundy and looked across the table at Elizabeth. She was glowing. Positively radiant. If I had any sense, I'd resign my job, stop exposing myself to danger, buy a place in the French countryside, and spend my life living with and loving her. It seemed so tempting. But no. He couldn't. Not yet, at least. He had to capture Musa and put the Spanish Revenge out of business.

He felt a tapping on his arm. Elizabeth said, "I've lost you. You must be thinking about Musa. Not me."

"Actually, I was thinking about both of you. After I finish him off, I want to quit this terrorism business. I'd like us to decide what we want to do with the rest of our lives. How's that?"

"I'd love that, but …" She hesitated.

"Go ahead."

"You won't like what I'm going to say."

"This evening I can handle anything."

"OK, you asked for it. When I was a young girl, my father took me out in a boat. He pointed to the line where the sky meets the water, out in a distance, and he told me 'that's the horizon.' I said, 'can we go there?' He laughed and told me, 'The horizon is always ahead of you. But you can never reach it.'" She said it with a twinge of sadness.

"I understand what you're telling me. But maybe …"

She put her hand on his. "We'll have plenty of time to talk about that after you capture or kill Musa. Now tell me: What's your next move?"

A waiter removed their dessert plates. Another brought espresso.

When they were gone, he answered her. "I want to arrange an emergency meeting in Paris on Sunday of the Defense Ministers of France, Spain, Germany, England, and Italy. I'd like you to be there. Also Giuseppe, and Jacques. I want to present everything we know about Musa. Then get them to take action."

"To do what?"

"Issue an ultimatum to the Moroccan government: Turn over Musa and roll up his base or …"

She was looking at him wide-eyed.

"Or these five countries will send in a commando team to abduct Musa and Omar. Followed by bombers to decimate the base."

She gave a long low whistle. "You'll be asking quite a bit. You really think you have a chance?"

"I have to convince them to do it. You saw how powerful Musa's become with Chinese support. If we don't stop him now, he'll wreak incredible destruction."

For a moment, she didn't respond. Then she said, "You're right to try. God knows you played plenty of long shots when you went up against General Zhou and stopped his Operation Dragon Oil."

She excused herself to go to the bathroom.

As he sat alone, her words, "You went up against General Zhou," reverberated in his brain … General Zhou … General Zhou … General Zhou.

Musa's alliance with the Chinese had all the earmarks of General Zhou's involvement with the Iranians in Operation Dragon Oil. Collusion with an enemy of the West. Secret supply of sophisticated arms. An unlikely, but brilliantly conceived, conspiracy.

The longer he thought about it, the more convinced he became.

As soon as she returned, he told her in an impassioned voice, "I think General Zhou is Musa's connection."

She gave a start. "Based on what?"

"The MO is similar to Operation Dragon Oil. Particularly that Muslims are involved, as they were in Operation Dragon

Oil. General Zhou must see value in Chinese Islamic joint action against the Christian West. I figure it has to be another of his rogue operations, because President Li's Chinese government has tried to placate the United States since the blow-up of Operation Dragon Oil. President Li would never approve another confrontation."

"But at the end of Operation Dragon Oil, Li told Brewster that General Zhou was being relieved of his position. That he resigned from the Chinese military. You were there with me. You heard the phone conversation on speaker in the Oval Office."

Craig raised his hand. "I know all that, but General Zhou is a resourceful SOB. He could have gotten the decree lifted. We have to find out whether he did. What about that reporter friend of yours, Carl Zerner, from the *New York Tribune,* who helped us in Beijing? Is he still there? He might know."

"Carl and I talked last Christmas. No politics, just social chit-chat. How are you, and that sort of thing. He told me he would be in Beijing for another year."

"Why don't you call him?"

"You're barking up the wrong tree. Do you really think …"

"What do you lose? It's just a call."

"I'll have to be careful. Carl's convinced they listen in on his calls."

"You can do it without raising suspicions."

"OK," she said reluctantly. "When we get home."

Once they were in the apartment, he didn't wait for her to take off her coat. "Call Carl."

"God, you're persistent."

She checked her watch. "It's eight in the morning in Beijing. Carl will probably be running in the park."

"Perfect."

She called on her cell and put the call on speaker. "Hey, Liz …"

She cringed. No matter how many times she told him, he insisted on calling her Liz.

"Good to hear from you. How's life in Paris?"

"I just finished one of those dinners you couldn't get anywhere else."

"I'm jealous. Maybe one day I'll come to visit you."

"I'd like that. Listen, Carl. I'm doing an article for the *Herald* on the continued expansion of the Chinese military. I've been able to assemble a lot of facts from various sources, but one thing I need help on is who the decision makers are in the military after General Zhou's resignation."

Carl reeled off the names of three generals.

"Does that mean General Zhou hasn't come back to power?"

"Correct. President Li forced him to leave the country. Exiled for life. He's not allowed to return under the expulsion order. It was all very secretive. General Zhou went somewhere in France to live. The public story here is that he's in the north on the Siberian border under house arrest. But the answer to your question is that he doesn't figure in the current military leadership. You don't have to include him in your article. Maybe you'll run into him one day on the Champs Elysees."

"That's very helpful. Thanks."

She hung up phone. Stunned, she said, "France."

Craig repeated Carl's words, "General Zhou's somewhere in France."

"That is what Carl said."

Craig felt an adrenalin rush. He rolled his hand into a fist. "So I'm right. He's engineering Chinese involvement from France. And Musa even confirmed it."

"How?"

"When he said that the things closest are the ones we don't see."

He could tell she wasn't persuaded.

"That's a large leap. Anyway, how could General Zhou arrange to ship arms and supply Chinese instructors from France?"

"Not a problem. With General Zhou's friends in the Chinese military and his brother's commercial network, he could easily have set that up from here."

"But what's his motive?"

"Maybe he wants to inflict damage on the West. He may hope to return to power in Beijing one day. An alliance with Musa would help him weaken Europe and enhance Chinese world dominance. Dreams like that don't die."

"And perhaps he sees Musa's success as a way of evening the score with you. But, I'm sure you never considered the personal revenge issue. The idea of vengeance and a more complete victory for Francesca's murder never entered into your mind."

She had just said exactly what he was thinking. She knew him so well it was frightening. "Of course not," he said.

"Boys will be boys. The macho fur is about to fly. I better climb into a fox hole."

"You can't. You're on the front line with me."

"Do you intend to include this great revelation about General Zhou in your presentation to the meeting of Defense Ministers?"

He shook his head. "It's too speculative. I don't have a shred of evidence to back it up. Besides, my case is already thin enough."

"Then what'll you do about General Zhou?"

"At this point, I don't know. Let it run around in my mind for a little bit. Sometimes in bed, after sex, I become creative."

She yawned. "If that's a sneaky way of getting into my pants, forget it. We've already had sex once this evening. I'm going to sleep."

She headed toward the bedroom, leaving Craig to think about General Zhou. He was pleased with this development. The end to Operation Dragon Oil had been unsatisfying.

General Zhou, you'll pay for Francesca's death.

34

CASABLANCA

On Casablanca's Boulevard Yacoub El-Mansur, the traffic was fierce. Befitting Morocco's largest metropolis, of more than three million. French cars predominated, but Japanese, American, and others were in abundance, belching exhaust fumes, with drivers honking furiously in a city seemingly without traffic laws. Casablanca, a place of intrigue with networks of spies, was also the commercial center of the country.

To Musa, Casa, as it was known, appeared to be a larger version of Marseilles, which wasn't surprising, because that was the objective of the French architect, Henri Proust, when he planned the city.

Musa was alone in his Citroën, having driven to Casablanca himself. He no longer trusted Farez. The Prime Minister was capable of arresting Musa, if he heard he was in Casa. Or even having Musa assassinated to avoid Musa turning on him over the payments made to the Swiss bank account. So before leaving the base, Musa shaved his beard and mustache. In Marrakech, he bought a gray wig and a pair of eyeglasses with black frames and plain glass lenses. He tucked a pistol into his briefcase.

When he had called Professor Khalid to arrange the meeting, he said his name was Mohammad. He was a graduate student at Harvard, in Morocco for research for his dissertation. Khalid was willing to meet with him in the Professor's office.

Once he parked the car and entered the grassy university grounds, he walked swiftly and purposefully, his head down.

Professor Khalid, in his sixties, was short and rotund, resembling a pear, Musa thought, with thinning black hair and heavy sacks under his eyes. He was dressed in a suit and tie.

The office was a cluttered mess. The shelves overflowing with books, the wooden desk so covered with papers that Musa couldn't see the wooden surface.

While the Professor's secretary brought coffee, Khalid was staring hard at Musa, making him feel uncomfortable. He positioned his briefcase at his feet, ready to go for the gun if he had to.

As soon as she departed and closed the door, the Professor said, "I have a unique ability to recognize faces. Even when they're disguised. You and I met at a conference in Tangiers a few months ago. You're not Mohammad. You introduced yourself as Ahmed Sadi. We spoke. Afterwards, I did some research. This is a small country. People talk. I know exactly who you are. The man who would dare to call himself Musa Ben Abdil."

Musa pulled the gun from his briefcase and aimed it at the Professor, who responded with a smile. "You can put that thing away. I sympathize with your objective, to the extent I understand it. I imagine you've come to me for help. I'll do what I can."

Musa breathed a sigh of relief and put the gun away. He paused to sip some coffee.

"Now tell me what you want," the Professor said.

"I attended Columbia University …"

"I know that."

"There I took courses in world history, but I never studied in detail the history of Islam in Spain. I read a book about the expulsion of Muslims in the fifteenth century from which I learned about Musa Ben Abdil."

"What are you looking for?"

"I don't know. I've read that, for centuries, the Arab Islamic civilization in Spain was glorious."

"It was indeed. Our history began in the Eighth Century, when Abd Al-Rahman had a falling out with the ruling family in Baghdad, then the center of the Muslim world. He moved with an entourage of his followers to Cordoba, with the objective of creating an Arab Islam empire that wouldn't merely rival that of Iraq and the Middle East. It would eclipse them. The man was a dreamer."

"And a bold man. A visionary."

"For sure. Though he never lived to see it, he succeeded beyond his wildest expectations. Students of Western European history describe the period from the Fifth Century to Tenth as the Dark Ages. But for the Arabs and Islam in Spain, even up into Southern France, it was the Golden Age. Not merely of economic prosperity, but of learning and enlightenment. Writers, poets, mathematicians, scientists all prospered. The literary output was phenomenal. Greek works were translated into Arabic. And for the most part there was religious tolerance. Jews, though a minority, thrived as well. For their scholarship and theology it was also a golden age.

"But history is change. Eventually it all came crumbling down." The Professor stood up and opened the window. "It's stuffy in here. Where was I?"

"You said history is change."

"Ah yes, gradually the uneducated Christians from the north swept into Spain, burnt the books, and destroyed our civilization. But we helped our own demise with internal dissention."

Musa knew much of what the Professor was saying, but he hoped by letting Khalid talk, he'd learn something he could use to assert legitimacy.

Khalid continued. "Then the sophisticated Arab leaders in Spain brought in uncivilized Berbers from North Africa to fight the Christians. In a short time, the Berbers were challenging the Arabs for control. The situation reached a decisive point in 1468, when Queen Isabella and King Ferdinand married, uniting the houses of Castile and Aragon and taking control of the Spanish government. They launched a war to conquer all of Spain from the Muslims, working their way from north to south. Driving Islam from its last stronghold in Europe, the Iberian Peninsula, was their determined goal. The battles were increasingly bloody in central Spain, but the Christians kept liberating town after town. Finally, the Muslims controlled only the seemingly impregnable towns in the south like Cordoba, Malaga, and Granada. The site of the Alhambra, our jewel in the crown."

"At that point, did the Muslims become united?"

"Not at all. They were arguing about leadership. Battle tactics. Even to fight or surrender. Meantime, Isabella and Ferdinand effectively led their Christian armies, systematically taking the southern Muslim towns one by one. Granada was last. Our glorious Alhambra."

"I know what happened to Musa Ben Abdil. But, after his courageous death was the battle intense?"

The professor shook his head. "To induce the Muslims to surrender, on January 2, 1492, Isabella promised they'd be able to practice Islam in southern Spain."

Musa was on the edge of his chair. He hadn't heard this before. "Did she keep her promise?"

"It was all a lie and a trick."

The professor sounded emotional, his voice cracking. "Three months later, she issued an edict: Convert to Christianity or die. Many of the Muslims fled to North Africa. Some converted. The others were murdered by the Inquisition under the direction of Tomas de Torquemada, one of the cruelest men ever to justify his crimes by resorting to the name of God."

"So that's the end of the story?"

"I thought so, until I was at a seminar in Paris last year. I was speaking privately with Professor Etienne from the University of Paris. A well respected medieval scholar. He believes that, on her deathbed in 1504, Queen Isabella felt remorse for making this false promise of religious tolerance to the Muslims. Etienne claims that, as her final act, she wrote out on parchment an edict granting to Muslims in perpetuity a swath of land in Southern Spain."

A wave of excitement shot through Musa's body. If he had that parchment, his attack to take Southern Spain would have legitimacy. "Has Etienne published his research about this parchment?"

"Not yet. It's so highly charged that he wants to make certain of his facts. He said he expects to publish next year."

"What happened to the parchment?"

Khalid shrugged. "I asked Etienne."

"And?"

"He said he has an idea, but he wasn't willing to tell me."

I have to find out what happened to that parchment, Musa thought. And I have to get my hands on it.

But if Etienne refused to tell Khalid, he'll never tell me unless ...

Extreme measures are required. I need that parchment.

35

SOUTHERN FRANCE

General Zhou was surprised how easy it was to arrange a meeting with General Jose Alvarez, the Spanish Defense Minister. He called Alvarez and introduced himself as "the former head of the Chinese military who retired then took a position in military procurement."

"I've heard about you, General Zhou," Alvarez said with admiration. "I'm a military man myself. A former General in the Spanish Army. You were responsible for building the Chinese military into the most effective in the world."

"The Americans might dispute that," General Zhou, said trying to sound modest and suppress his surge of pride.

"Time will tell, and time is on the Chinese side. Anyhow, what can I do for you?"

"I want to discuss a matter of mutual benefit. It will be best if we speak in person. Preferably outside of Spain."

He paused. Alvarez didn't respond. That was a good sign.

"I'd like to invite you to my house in the South of France in Cap d'Antibes. When can you come?"

"How about tomorrow? I have to be in Paris on Sunday."

"Perfect," General Zhou said.

That call was yesterday. Friday morning.

Now, Saturday at one in the afternoon on a warm, sunny day, Alvarez walked into the house.

"Glad you could come," General Zhou said. "How about drinks, then lunch on the patio?"

"Sounds good. Scotch for me."

"We are definitely in agreement on that."

"A very nice house," Alvarez said.

"I prefer living this way to a military barracks. At some point those of us who serve our nations have to think about ourselves."

Alvarez raised his glass. "I'll drink to that. Why did you leave the military?"

General Zhou was pleased Alvarez didn't know. That the story of his failure in Operation Dragon Oil had been kept secret. "Political differences with the civilian leadership," he said calmly.

"It happens all the time."

At that point, right on cue, Androshka walked through the front door, accompanied by Masha, one of her expat Russian friends, a strikingly beautiful model—tall, blonde, and busty, precisely what Freddy had said Alvarez liked. They were wearing shorts and tight tank tops. Matching bookends. Carrying shopping bags.

"I see you two had a good time shopping," General Zhou said.

"We spent lots of your money," Androshka said and kissed General Zhou on the cheek.

He introduced the women to Alvarez. "My friend Androshka and her friend Masha."

General Zhou could tell that Alvarez was stunned by the women's beauty.

"We're going down to the pool," Androshka said.

"We'll join you later."

Alvarez was nodding with approval. When the women left, Alvarez said, "I didn't bring a bathing suit."

"We don't wear them here."

General Zhou gave a short laugh. Male bonding laughter, promising Alvarez fun and games with Masha before the day was over. By the time General Zhou and Alvarez moved outside to the patio, where seafood salad was waiting, chilled Mersault in an ice bucket and a bowl of flowers in the center of the table, Androshka and Masha, both nude, were stretched out on their backs on chaise lounges. General Zhou thought Alvarez's eyes would jump out of their sockets, and indeed they should. Though he hated Russia and most Russians, General Zhou was convinced that some Russian women were the most beautiful in the world.

General Zhou nodded to the waiter, who poured wine then quickly went inside.

"Let's eat and talk," General Zhou said. "The women will be there when we're done."

Alvarez turned away from the pool and looked at General Zhou. "I am curious to know what you wanted to talk to me about."

General Zhou took a bite of salad, making Alvarez wait and then put down his fork. "I understand you are planning to modernize Spain's fleet of military aircraft."

"That's correct. We expect to order forty planes. The most sophisticated."

"Has the contract been awarded?"

"Not yet. But I have to tell you that negotiations with Boeing for the F-15s are in the final stages."

General Zhou walked into the house and returned with the packet of materials Freddy had given him. He laid them down on the table and placed a hand on top. "The JF-17 Fighter Jet, which China manufactures with sophisticated avionics, exceeds the F-15 in several critical respects. And I can arrange for you to purchase them for ten percent less than the American planes. Would you be willing to open negotiations with China to explore this alternative source of supply?"

Alvarez's forehead wrinkled. He twirled his mustache, a troubled expression on his face. "I don't know We've always bought American planes."

"You've never had a good alternative."

"Many others in my government are involved."

"But you're the Defense Minister. You'll ultimately make the decision. Wouldn't you like to stick it to the arrogant Americans and their President Dalton who hates Europe?"

Alvarez was nodding. "Of course. Still, you're asking a great deal from me to become involved at this stage."

Alvarez had given General Zhou the perfect opening. "I am asking a great deal from you, but I'm willing to compensate you for your trouble."

Alvarez raised his eyebrows. "Compensate me, how?"

He was definitely interested.

"I'd be willing to deposit ten million euros into a Singapore bank for you."

Alvarez raised his hand to his face and held it over his mouth, weighing the offer.

"Why Singapore?" he finally said.

"Greater assurance of secrecy than a Swiss bank since the United States has been beating up on Swiss banks to disclose their accounts. The Swiss, who are pretty smart at banking have opened up branches in Singapore in the names of subsidiaries. The Americans can't touch them there."

"How will this work? I won't have to go to Singapore. Will I?"

General Zhou could barely control his excitement. Alvarez had taken the bait. General Zhou went into the house again. This time he returned with a cell phone and laptop. He used the cell phone to call Georg Wilhelm, a banker at UBZ, United Bank of Zurich, Singapore Limited.

"A friend would like to open an account," General Zhou said. "He'll give you his information. I trust you will assure him that everything is confidential."

"Absolutely," the banker said. General Zhou handed Alvarez the phone. He listened while Alvarez, in a halting voice, gave his name, address and selected a code … "big fish."

The irony of Alvarez's selection amused General Zhou. That's what he felt he had just landed—a big fish. The banker gave Alvarez a secret numerical code which he wrote down and which General Zhou didn't hear.

Alvarez handed General Zhou the phone. "He said the account is open."

"Good, I'll wire ten million Euros."

General Zhou kept the banker on the line while he used the lap top to transfer the money.

Then he said to the banker, "Please confirm to Mr. Alvarez that his account now has ten million Euros."

Wilhelm confirmed it.

"And explain to him how he can access the account for electronic transfer to his account in a Spanish bank."

Wilhelm did that as well, and General Zhou powered off the phone.

"OK, business is over," General Zhou said. "Time for fun. Why don't you head down to the pool. I'll be there in a few minutes. I'm sure Masha would like to know you."

As soon as Alvarez walked down the stairs to the pool, General Zhou took the centerpiece bowl of flowers into his bedroom where he was alone. Carefully, he extracted the micro recorder from the bowl. He played back their conversation. Perfect. The voice clarity was excellent. He now owned Alvarez. Big fish indeed.

The remainder of the afternoon went exactly as General Zhou

figured. Alvarez and Masha ended up together in one of the bedrooms. By the time the Spaniard emerged an hour later, he was staggering, his clothes disheveled. His eyes had a glazed over look. General Zhou had told Masha, "I want you to fuck his brains out." It looked as if she accomplished her mission.

At six, Alvarez thanked Zhou for a great day. "I'm now prepared to deal with Paris," he said as General Zhou walked him to Captain Cheng's waiting car.

"What's happening in Paris?"

"A waste of time. Do you know Craig Page, the EU Counterterrorism Director?"

General Zhou's face disclosed nothing. "I've read about him in the papers. What are you doing with him?"

"He's convened an emergency meeting of Defense Ministers. He wants us to take action against some Islamist terrorist holed up in Morocco."

"You aren't going to do that. Are you?"

"I sure hope not. But you never know what the French and Germans will decide."

"You'll have to take a hard line. Craig Page is an American cowboy."

Alvarez laughed. "I like that expression. Page already pissed me off when we were discussing the train bombing last October."

I have to know what happens at tomorrow's meeting.

General Zhou said, "I also have an apartment in Paris. We'll be back tomorrow and Masha will be staying overnight. Would you like to meet me there after your meeting? The four of us can have dinner."

"Give me the address."

36

PARIS

Craig and Elizabeth worked late into Saturday night preparing a power point presentation entitled "The Spanish Revenge and its Threat to Western Europe." He had told her to summarize the information they learned from the time Craig received the call in the Bristol dining room. "These people will be skeptical. We have to overwhelm them with facts."

Elizabeth was fabulous. Preparing presentations had always been his weak point. Both organization and writing. It was a task he had loathed from the time he began at the CIA. "I'm not a bureaucrat. I'll do anything in the field. Let others prepare the reports and make the presentation." She also knew precisely how to express each thought. He didn't know what he'd have done without her.

At midnight, they made a dry run. He was talking; she was bringing up slides on the computer.

Halfway through the presentation he stopped. "Something's

bothering me," he told Elizabeth. "I have to discuss Lila. She's the key witness. She recognized Ahmed's Sadi's voice on the tape played for CNN and identified him as Musa Ben Abdil. But I'll be exposing her to risk merely by giving her name to the Defense Ministers."

"Are you worried one of them could be involved with Musa?"

"Not that. But I don't know whom they'll report to about the meeting. I can't control that. They give oral briefings. E-mails start flying. You know how that goes."

"Good point."

"I'll call Jacques first thing in the morning and arrange French police protection for her in Marseilles."

"That's an excellent idea."

"We must have it in place before the meeting."

He returned to the presentation. When he finished, she was smiling. "You are definitely good to go. Break a leg."

"In my business, we don't use expression like that."

Craig waited until eight to call Jacques about security for Lila. The Frenchman was immediately on board. "I'll have it in place before the meeting begins. An armed Interior Security agent in an unmarked car outside of the hotel where she works and her residence around the clock. They'll follow her wherever she goes."

"I better call and tell her."

When Craig explained the situation to Lila, she was alarmed.

"Elizabeth told me I wouldn't be in any danger." Fear was apparent in her voice.

"I have no reason to believe you are. We're doing this as an extra precaution."

"OK," she said weakly.

At noon, Craig watched them filing into the large conference room at the French Ministry of Defense: Pierre Moreau, the French Defense Minister, and his counterparts from Spain, Germany, England, and Italy, Jacques, Giuseppe, and Elizabeth. All men, except for her. Surly, glum faces. Angry about having surrendered a Sunday at home, but unwilling to reject his invitation for fear the next attack might be in their country and their political careers would be wrecked.

He knew he'd have a tough sell. He heard the German Defense Minister, with a beefy red face and an almost entirely bald head, grumbling to his British counterpart, "This had better be important. I had to cancel a day in the country with the family." The Brit replied softly, but just loud enough for Craig to overhear. "Americans always like to yank people around like puppets."

Craig ignored them and looked at Elizabeth booting up the computer.

Two petite young French women in short skirts served drinks. Craig asked one of them to lower the window shades and to dim the lights. Then Moreau pointed to Craig. "It's your meeting, Mr. Terrorism Czar. Proceed."

Craig coughed twice, cleared his throat and began. "Europe is now facing a new and dangerous terrorist threat."

He nodded to Elizabeth who put up the first slide: "Musa and the Spanish Revenge."

Before he could open his mouth, the British Defense Minister interrupted. "I'm not sure I feel comfortable with a journalist in the room. What do the rest of you think?"

Elizabeth stood up. "I'm prepared to leave. Craig can operate the power point himself."

He motioned her to sit down. "Elizabeth Crowder has been with me from the beginning. She has critical information. As you'll hear, she almost gave her life for the EU in this cause. Most important, she sat in on sensitive discussions with the Spanish Prime Minister and Defense Minister at the time of the train bombing and never wrote an unauthorized word." He looked at Alvarez. "Isn't that right?"

"Yes," was the grudging response.

"Will you agree," the British Defense Minister asked, looking at

Elizabeth, "not to publish anything about today's proceedings unless specifically authorized?"

"Absolutely."

"Alright."

No one else said a word.

Moreau told Craig, "Continue."

Thanks to Elizabeth's brilliant work, walking through the first part of the power point, describing what he had learned about Musa and the Spanish Revenge, was a piece of cake. And she always knew when to give him the next slide.

He covered everything. The note before the train bombing. Who the historical Musa Ben Abdil was. Facts about Ibrahami. He played the CNN tape. He described their meeting with Lila in Marseilles. The bios of Ahmed and Omar. The theft of Vatican plans and the Mediterranean chase. His meeting in Rabat. What he and Elizabeth saw in the Atlas mountains. Finally, what happened to them in Musa's camp.

Through his hour long presentation, the Defense Ministers listened closely, taking notes, never interrupting. Looking around, he was certain they grasped what he had said.

Now for the hard part, convincing them to act. Before addressing the words on the next slide, he paused to sip from a bottle of water, then turned to the words on the screen.

"Action steps," he read slowly. "Demand that Morocco extradite Ahmed Sadi, a French citizen, who calls himself Musa Ben Abdil to Spain, to stand trial for last October's Spanish train bombing. If Morocco will not extradite him, then I recommend that the EU send in armed commandos to remove him and fly him to Madrid."

He looked around the room from one skeptical face to the next.

"I am prepared to be part of that commando team," he added.

Alvarez spoke first, "Tell us precisely what evidence you have implicating Ahmed in the Spanish train bombing." The tone was hostile.

Craig had covered that in his presentation. He kept his anger in check and repeated, "Elizabeth and I met in Marseille with Lila, the sister of one of the ringleaders of Ahmed's group. She has known Ahmed since they were children. She recognized Ahmed's voice on the tape played on CNN."

The British Defense Minister said, "I happen to be a lawyer. That's insufficient evidence to obtain an extradition order, certainly not to convict someone of murder."

"Play the tape again," Moreau said.

Elizabeth played it. "That voice is garbled," the British Minister said. "No one could ID someone from that."

Alvarez said, "I completely agree."

"Let's focus on what's coming if you don't act," Craig replied. "We know the water plans were stolen from the Vatican construction project. The only reason for that theft is to plan for a terrorist attack in the Vatican."

The Italian piped in. "We can't let that happen."

"I agree," the German said, "but we have no proof that Ahmed's people carried out that theft. It could be Al Qaeda. It could be Catholics angry about child sexual molestation. It could be anyone."

"The speedboat was heading in the direction of Morocco," Craig insisted.

"Proves nothing," Alvarez retorted. "It's a big sea. They could have turned around and come back to a Southern Italian port, for all we know."

Craig was frustrated. These people just didn't want to deal with the facts in front of them. "But Elizabeth and I saw the armed camp in the Atlas Mountains. We saw Ahmed there. His people are planning to launch a major attack."

Again it was Alvarez. "They might be planning an attack in Morocco or Algeria to take over the government."

Craig was convinced Alvarez was gaining his revenge against Craig for last October's events. He wanted to say, "That's stupid and absurd." But he couldn't. So he replied, "I find that inconceivable under the circumstances."

Moreau spoke up. "The last thing we want is involvement in Northern African politics. Do you know how long and painful it was for us to extricate from Algeria?"

"This is different."

"I suppose you want us to start bombing their base."

"That would be a good idea."

The Frenchman laughed. "I like you, Craig. You were extremely effective in thwarting the assassination attempt on President Dalton last October. Jacques believes you're doing an outstanding job. I agree. But what you're proposing gives away your American background. You Americans always bomb first and think later."

The others laughed.

Craig was thinking: And you Europeans always stand around with your fingers up your ass until your cities are overrun.

"To be serious," Moreau added. "I think your evidence to support this type of a military action is weak." Moreau sounded sincere.

Craig disagreed, but he was convinced Moreau was trying to be objective, unlike that asshole Alvarez. Craig responded earnestly. "I understand your point. Of course I'd like more evidence. More certainty. But in dealing with potential terrorist attacks, unfortunately we rarely have absolute certainty. With thousands of innocent lives at stake, we have to make judgments based upon instinct and experience. For me, both are crying out: Stop Musa now, before it's too late."

For a long moment no one responded. Then, sounding triumphant, Alvarez said, "Come back to us if you get something else."

The meeting broke up without agreement on any action. Craig realized he was on his own with Elizabeth, Giuseppe, and Jacques to stop Musa without official government support.

How in the world will we do that?

<CHAPTER TITLE?>

General Zhou sipped a Macallan neat while he waited impatiently for Alvarez to arrive. His apartment occupied a whole floor of a luxury building off Place de l'Alma in a fashionable part of Paris, with a view of the Eiffel Tower across the river. The television was turned on mute to CNN. He wanted to see whether the Defense Ministers issued a statement following their meeting. So far nothing.

Where is Alvarez? he wondered. The Spaniard should have been here by now. What if he changed his mind? Alvarez didn't know that General Zhou had the incriminating recording, and he had to be thankful for the ten million Euros. No, he'll come. He better come.

I have to know what happened at that meeting.

From one of the bedrooms he heard Androshka and Masha yakking in Russian. Other than being Mikail's moll, he had no idea what her life had been like before she met him. From time to time she'd spin fanciful and wildly inconsistent stories—a child born in poverty; the daughter of a Russian General; a descendant of the Czar; a child of the Gulag. He was convinced she had no idea what was real and what wasn't, nor did he care. She gave him great sex. She never questioned what he told her. And since Mikail's death, her gratitude was limitless.

Half an hour later, General Zhou's cell phone rang. Not the encrypted phone he used only for communicating with Musa, but his ordinary Nokia. General Zhou answered immediately.

"My car just pulled up in front of your building," Alvarez said.

General Zhou exhaled in relief. "Good. I'll tell the doorman to let you come up. Top floor."

Alvarez looked weary, his shirt and tie loosened at the neck. General Zhou thought he'd been run through the mill.

"How about a drink?" General Zhou asked. "I'm having scotch myself."

"Pour me a double over ice."

General Zhou fixed the drink and handed it to Alvarez, who took a long gulp.

"Tough meeting?"

"Craig Page is one of those hard-driving, aggressive Americans who want to run over everybody like a steamroller."

Oh, oh, doesn't sound good. "Did the Defense Ministers stand up to him?"

"We did, but it wasn't easy. He wants us to attack a French Arab, who calls himself Musa, based in North Africa. Also send in commandos to kidnap him. Craig is a wild man. But in the end, he didn't get his way. We're not taking any action."

"What's he think Musa did?"

Alvarez took a drink before responding.

"Craig says he carried out the Spanish train bombing six months ago. According to Page, now he's planning to poison the Vatican's water supply."

"Does Craig have any evidence against this Musa?"

"Not for the Vatican attack. For the Spanish train bombing, Craig claims he spoke to a woman in Marseilles, Lila, the sister of one of Musa's gang, who knew Musa when he lived in a Muslim slum outside of Paris. According to Craig, Lila identified Musa's voice on the recording taking credit for the train bombing."

General Zhou concealed his alarm. "That doesn't sound like much of a case."

"That's what I said."

"Good for you."

"The others agreed ... Still it is troublesome. If Zahara gets wind of it, he might persuade the Prime Ministers to reverse the decision."

"You won't let that happen. Will you?"

"No. Of course not. I tell Zahara as little as possible. You were a military man. I'm sure you operated the same with the Chinese civilian leadership."

"But of course." General Zhou gave a short sly laugh. Two military men tightening their bond.

"What will Craig do now?" Zhou asked.

Alvarez shrugged. "He won't quit. That's for sure. The guy's like a dog with a bone. And he has that woman reporter to do his bidding."

"Elizabeth Crowder?"

"Yeah. Speaking of women, is Masha here?"

General Zhou pointed to one of the bedrooms. "She and Androshka are getting dressed. Meantime, let me put on my jacket and tie, and we'll leave."

"Take your time. I'll enjoy the scotch. I have to unwind."

"I promise you won't think about business any more this evening. Masha won't let you."

General Zhou winked.

In another bedroom, he took the encrypted cell from his pocket and called Musa's matching phone.

"What happened in the meeting?" Musa asked before General Zhou said a word.

"The good news is that the countries aren't taking any action."

"I'm not surprised. They can never agree on anything."

"The bad news is that Craig Page has a witness who implicates you in the Spanish train bombing."

"How can he possibly?"

General Zhou explained about Lila in Marseilles. For thirty seconds, Musa reeled off a string of curses.

"Has Craig taken Lila into protective custody?"

"Alvarez didn't say anything about that. So I presume, no."

"OK, now tell me about the missile deliveries."

"Everything is on schedule. In a few days I'll have precise delivery instructions, which I'll bring to you in person. The pontoon boats will be arriving at the crack of dawn tomorrow. We will be good to go with both operations."

"Unless that cow Lila ruins it. But I won't let her do that."

38

MOROCCO, ATLAS MOUNTAINS

In a white fury, Musa pressed the power-off button on the cell phone. He couldn't believe that Lila was threatening to unravel his entire operation. Craig Page wouldn't quit after his rejection by the Defense Ministers. He'd use Lila to build a case and eventually get some action. Dammit … Dammit.

He picked up a green crockery water pitcher on his desk and flung it hard against the far wall, where it shattered into a myriad of pieces.

Omar came running into the office. "Is everything alright?"

"It's all turning to shit."

Musa explained what General Zhou had said.

"The European Defense Ministers weren't willing to act," Omar said. "Maybe we can tough it out."

Musa snarled. "Craig Page will build on what he learned from Lila. We can't tolerate that. We don't know what else her brother told her."

As he finished speaking, Musa recalled his last conversation with Omar about Lila. Omar had wanted to eliminate her.

"I was a damn fool," Musa said. He pounded his fist on the desk. "I should have listened to you about Lila. Then we wouldn't be in this mess."

"It's not too late. I'm willing to go to Marseilles and kill her."

"Craig's smart. He'll have cops or intelligence agents protecting her."

"I can be resourceful."

"I need you to go to Paris to kidnap Professor Etienne at the University of Paris and take him to my house in Marbella. I was planning to tell you about that when General Zhou called."

"Who's Professor Etienne?"

"I had a meeting with Professor Khalid at the University in Casablanca. He told me that Etienne, a well respected medieval scholar at the University of Paris, has discovered that, on her deathbed in 1504, Queen Isabella wrote out on a parchment an edict granting to Muslims in perpetuity a swath of land in Southern Spain." Excited, Musa was talking rapidly. "That's huge for us. It changes everything."

"I don't understand."

"We're not acting on behalf of any government. Rather, for Muslims throughout the world. This parchment gives us a legal basis for the invasion of Southern Spain."

"But how can we get the parchment?"

"First we have to find out where it is. Khalid didn't know. But he told me Etienne does."

"Now I see why you want me to kidnap Professor Etienne."

"I have to decide which is more important. Having you eliminate Lila or kidnap Etienne."

"I can do both," Omar said with confidence. "Fly to Marseilles, then go to Paris."

If Omar was captured or killed in Marseilles, Musa didn't have anyone else good enough to abduct the Professor. Losing Omar would be like losing his right arm.

"Don't worry. I'll be careful in Marseilles," Omar said as if reading Musa's mind.

"If her protection is too great, I want you to abort and go to Paris."

"I'll do that."

"For the Paris job, get on the internet and learn everything you can about Etienne. As I said, he's a professor of medieval history, at the University of Paris. Also, get help from the boys in Clichy."

Omar turned to leave the office. A powerful idea popped into Musa's head.

"Don't go yet. I want to talk about Lila some more."

"Sure."

Omar sat in front of the desk.

"Sometimes," Musa said thoughtfully, "We can turn what seems like a disastrous development into an advantage. I want to do that with Lila."

Omar looked puzzled. "Sorry. That's a little too mysterious for me."

"Did you ever hear of Florinda, the beautiful young Arab woman in the Eighth Century?"

Omar shook his head. "I didn't go to Columbia University."

"I'll ignore that. Anyhow, she was bathing naked in the Tagus River in Spain. The Visigoth King Rodrigo saw her and raped her. When word spread, enraged Muslim hordes crossed the Strait of Gibraltar and captured the Christians' lands in an act of vengeance."

"Aha. Now I understand."

"Good. Here's what I want you to do."

PARIS

Craig Page rarely dreamt. But tonight his dream was so vivid he might as well have been watching a video. His daughter Francesca, twenty five, his only child, his only family, was driving at night in a blinding snowstorm. Suddenly, a big rig, an eighteen wheeler, came barreling down on her from the front. The truck crashed into her car, folding it up like an accordion.

In a cold sweat, Craig shot to a sitting position, screaming. "No Francesca. No."

That woke Elizabeth beside him in bed. She clutched Craig tightly. "What happened?"

"I had a dream. Francesca's death. In Calgary. Just as it happened. It was so real."

The starkly modern bedroom, all metal and glass, Elizabeth's taste, not his, was warm, because the heat never worked right in the old building, but he was shivering. Elizabeth turned on a light and draped a blanket around him.

"No sense trying to sleep now," she said. "I'll get us some Armagnac. We'll talk."

He followed her to the living room, took the glass she handed him, and sipped the golden liquid.

"I haven't dreamt about her in months."

"You know why now?"

He nodded. "Because I'm convinced General Zhou is supporting Musa. As I've thought about it, I'm even more persuaded."

"I'm still not sure. Musa's arms are Chinese, and the instructors are Chinese, but Beijing could be doing this without General Zhou."

"You think my hatred for him is blinding me?"

"That would be understandable."

"From all my experience, I know he's part of this."

"Face it, Craig. You don't have a shred of evidence."

"Musa's from Paris, and I know General Zhou has been living in France since he was exiled from China. I've had one of my people keep tabs of his location. I have an address for him in Paris and another in the South of France. Also phone numbers."

She looked startled. "You never told me that."

"It's my own little obsession, waiting for him to slip up, so I could lower the boom."

Craig thought about his options. Calling General Zhou in for interrogation was pointless. He'd deny any involvement with Musa, and Elizabeth was right. Craig didn't have evidence to incriminate the man.

Zhou had never become a French citizen or changed his visa to stay this long. Craig was tempted to call Jacques and have him arrange with the Interior Ministry to expel General Zhou. Put him on the first non-stop plane to Beijing. Let him face punishment in China for violating his expulsion order. That would give Craig a measure of personal revenge, but wouldn't advance the ball with Musa.

Besides, there was an advantage to having General Zhou in Paris. It was conceivable that General Zhou could lead Craig to Musa or provide information about what Musa was planning next.

"Where does he live?" Elizabeth asked.

"In Paris, in a chic area off Place de l'Alma. He also has a house in Cap d' Antibes in the South of France."

"The man obviously has lots of money."

"His brother, the wealthy industrialist in Beijing, is probably funneling cash to him."

"Why don't I have a brother like that? Mine are all New York City cops. What are you planning to do?"

"Call Jacques and have him put a tail on General Zhou. Tap his phones. Also plant a bug in his apartment."

"Without proof linking him to Musa, that'll be a tough sell."

"I have to find a way to convince Jacques."

"Good luck."

Craig glanced at the clock on his desk. Only 4:15. Too early to call.

He tried, but couldn't fall back asleep. At six, he called Jacques and woke him.

The Frenchman's initial reaction was "Impossible."

Craig couldn't remember how many times he'd heard that word from French people since he'd been living in Paris. He'd learned to ignore it and push on. "Why not?"

"Because you don't have any evidence that General Zhou is involved with Musa."

"I saw a huge quantity of Chinese arms being unloaded at the base and Chinese instructors." Craig was raising his voice.

"That could have all been orchestrated from Beijing."

Same reaction as Elizabeth.

"In my gut, I know he's involved."

"We have laws in this country. You think anyone in law enforcement who has a feeling a French citizen is guilty can authorize following him around and tapping his phone?"

Craig remembered what Elizabeth had found. "He has no rights in France." Craig had tried to remain calm, but he was raising his voice. "General Zhou's not a French citizen. He's overstayed his tourist visa."

Jacques didn't respond. Craig took that as a good sign.

"You sound emotional," the Frenchman finally said. "I don't want to be drawn into a vendetta from your CIA days."

Craig decided to level with Jacques. "General Zhou and I do have some history, but I firmly believe he's supporting Musa."

"Aha. That's what I figured. I have to know about it before I make a decision."

"Fine. I'll tell you."

"Not over the phone. Since you woke me, you can come here for breakfast. My wife's visiting her mother in Annecy. I think I can make coffee. Pick up some bread at the shop on the first floor of my building."

"You better like espresso," Jacques said. "Because I bought this fancy Italian coffee machine for my wife for Christmas and she hasn't let me near it. Bottom line is, I have no idea how to foam milk for cappuccino."

Craig smiled as he handed Jacques the baguette. "Espresso is what I always drink."

"Good. That's what you're getting."

When they sat down at the kitchen table, Jacques said, "OK. What's the history with you and General Zhou?"

"Do you have any children, Jacques?"

"My fifteen-year-old son, Pierre. He's off in Annecy with his mother."

"I had a daughter, Francesca."

Talking about her was painful. Even a year and a half later.

"I didn't know you were married."

"Once, to a wonderful woman, Caroline."

Craig thought about their storybook romance. Childhood sweethearts in Monessen, Pennsylvania, married a week after they both graduated from Carnegie Mellon. Francesca was born a year later in a difficult birth, leaving Caroline unable to have other children. But that didn't matter to Craig. The three of them were so close, thriving the two years they were in Houston where he worked with the oil company and then in Washington when he started with the CIA.

"What happened to Caroline?" Jacques asked.

"She insisted on moving to Dubai with me when the CIA stationed me there, nineteen years ago. Francesca was eight at the time. I pleaded with Caroline to stay in Washington, but she was too stubborn. So the three of us moved to Dubai.

"Caroline paid for it with her life." He shook his head. "Six years later, she became ill. I couldn't convince her to see a doctor. By the time I got her to a hospital in Dubai, it was too late. Bacterial Meningitis. She died a few days later."

"I'm sorry."

"Thanks. Well, anyhow, from that point on it was just Francesca and me. We became very close, as you might imagine. In our shared grief."

He recalled how he put his career on hold for two years, insisting that the CIA transfer him back to Langley until she finished high school in the United States and began college. Then he returned to the Middle East to become Chief of Operations.

"Francesca was a great kid. Smart. Athletic. Beautiful. I was so proud of her. She wanted to join the CIA, too, but I wouldn't let her. So she went to Northwestern and majored in journalism. She got a job as a foreign reporter with the *New York Tribune*. Elizabeth was her boss.

"When she had been there a couple of years, she was working on a huge story. She had learned that General Zhou, then head of the Chinese armed forces, had entered into an agreement with Iran to cut off the flow of imported oil to the United States. "

"I never knew that."

"After President Brewster convinced Chinese President Li to cancel the agreement, we kept it extremely secret. Francesca had been in Calgary, Canada interviewing General Zhou's brother, an industrialist, who was in it up to his eyeballs. When he told General Zhou that Francesca was close to exposing the agreement, General Zhou planned her murder. Francesca was driving to Calgary airport to fly out with her story in a heavy snowstorm. General Zhou had arranged to have a big rig crash into her car and kill her."

"Any chance it could have been an accident?"

Craig shook his head. "I talked to one of the members of the Chinese delegation who had been in Calgary. He confirmed that General Zhou was responsible. The Canadian police concluded it was a homicide. An intentional hit and run. They never located the driver."

Craig felt tears in he eyes. "General Zhou killed my only child. My Francesca."

Jacques didn't say anything. He sat still and looked down at his hands while nodding his head.

"So you were right," Craig finally said. "General Zhou and I do have some serious history. And I have to repay him for what he did ... though it won't bring Francesca back."

"And that's how you hooked up with Elizabeth. Through the *New York Tribune* connection?"

"Yeah. She was a close friend of Francesca, as well as her editor at the paper. Elizabeth helped me uncover General Zhou's agreement with the Iranians and take it to Brewster."

Jacques tore off a piece of bread and chewed it. "I can't tell you how sorry I am for you. Truly. I had no idea. I'm with you now. I want to nail General Zhou, too. But I'm trying to figure out how to justify the request for surveillance. When I complete the paperwork and it asks me the basis, I can't write: 'A hope and a prayer.'"

"C'mon Jacques. He might lead us to Musa. Or we might be able to obtain information about Musa's next attack, which could be in France."

"'Might' is the operative word."

"It's a chance to hit pay dirt."

"Or come up empty."

"Look at it the other way. What do you lose if we're wrong?"

"You think I enjoy getting hammered by the Minister?"

"You received lots of praise for thwarting the Dalton assassination in October. You owe me for that."

Jacques sighed loudly. Craig figured he was coming around and remained silent.

"OK. I'll do it. Hopefully, I won't get skewered over this."

"You won't. I guarantee it."

"That makes me feel better," Jacques said glumly.

MARSEILLES

Omar knew from her brother that Lila lived on Rue Daughin above the Deluxe Shoe Store, in a dilapidated area of Marseilles east of the port, inhabited mostly by Muslims, who comprised a large part of the population of the city. He also knew that she lived alone.

At six in the afternoon, he parked his car, rented with phony papers Musa had provided, at one end of Rue Daughin. Carrying a black leather bag, he walked along the street.

Three children were kicking a soccer ball. Two dark-skinned mothers were holding babies on their laps on a wooden bench with flaking paint. He looked as if he belonged. No one paid him attention.

The sky had turned gray. Soon it would rain. A typical March evening for Marseilles.

He passed the Deluxe Shoe Store and glanced at the windows above it. No lights. She must not be home from work yet.

He spotted a brasserie across from the shoe store. A spot was free at the end of the bar, closest to the door, providing a perfect vantage point to watch the building with the shoe store. The place was crowded with fishermen drinking hard, filling the air with smoke, and whining loudly about their dismal catch today.

He ordered a beer and picked up a copy of the Marseilles paper on the bar. He knew what places like this were like. He could stand here and nurse his beer for as long as he liked. No one would bother him.

He saw lightning. Heard a blast of thunder. The skies opened with a huge downpour. Good. That would clear the street.

Not wanting to appear obvious, he kept his eyes moving between the newspaper and the building across the street. Dusk fell. Then darkness. No sign of Lila.

He ordered a second beer and thought about what he was doing. From the time Ahmed had killed that bully, Omar had incredible admiration for Ahmed. That his friend had gone to an elite private school in Paris and Columbia University only enhanced his respect. For Omar, Ahmed was mythical. God-like. He could do anything. Omar was thrilled to be close to such a great man. To be thriving in his long shadow.

And thanks to Ahmed's dreams and vision, the Spanish Revenge was on course to change the world. At least to change the face of Europe.

Omar never thought much about the status of Muslims in Europe or addressing the injustice they suffered. Those lofty ideas were spewed by Ahmed. Omar didn't have to believe them. If Ahmed believed, that was enough for Omar.

He felt fortunate Ahmed had made him a confidant. If he wasn't hooked up with Ahmed, what would he have? Nothing. When Ahmed was in the United States at Columbia, Omar had tried to find work in Paris. He was laughed at and ridiculed. Just another poor, uneducated Muslim kid. The only job he found was cleaning the bathrooms at the train station, the Gare du Nord, but he declined that. So he lived with his parents. Hung out with his friends. Smoked pot. Took some drugs. Then Ahmed came back. Omar immediately joined when Ahmed started his community-action organization.

Like Ahmed, he never went to a mosque. That Allah stuff meant nothing to him. If Allah was great, then why were the Muslims the dregs of French life? No one he asked that question had given him a satisfactory answer. His father, a brute of a man who worked as a blacksmith, had slapped Omar hard in the face when he asked it of him.

He looked out at the street. The Deluxe Shoe Store was closing.

It was almost nine o'clock when he saw Lila at a distance of twenty yards, walking quickly in the heavy rain along the deserted street. She didn't have an umbrella, or even a raincoat. Her black hair was soaked and hanging from her head like strings. Her hotel uniform was drenched. Through the clinging black material, he saw her breasts, round and full. The swaying of her hips. He felt himself becoming aroused. He couldn't wait to get his hands on her. On that full ripe body.

Though he'd wanted her for years, he never really liked her. He and Kemal had spent a lot of time together. Often at Kemal's house. He hated the way Lila was always trying to control Kemal. To rein him in. Because their mother had died, she assumed that role. Most of all, he had hated the way she protected what was between her legs like a prize. At least with him. With everybody else as well—he'd thought. Now he learned she was willing to spread her legs for Ahmed. That stoked his anger, working him up to a frenzy. He was on fire, the taste of bile in his mouth. She had humiliated him. Insulted his manhood. She would pay for it now.

Though he was itching to move, he had to be careful. Check for the protection Craig had probably arranged. He saw the car. A dark blue sedan, driving slowly behind Lila, following her.

He had spent enough time dodging Interior Security people to sense immediately that the car was theirs. One look at the license plate confirmed it. Ahmed had taught him that the letters I and S appeared somewhere on their plates. No one else was issued plates containing them.

He watched Lila climb a staircase alongside the building leading to her apartment. The lights went on. He hoped the security car would move on because Lila had arrived home safe. But that didn't happen. The car pulled up and parked in front of the Deluxe Shoe Store.

Omar moved into the brasserie doorway to size up the situation. He didn't see any agents on the roof of her building. Only one man in the blue car. Somehow he had to deal with that man.

Trying to sneak up the stairs without being seen by the agent was too risky. He was willing to attack the agent in his car, but the chances of being spotted by someone in the brasserie or a passerby were too great. Think, he told himself. Then he had it. Sooner or later that agent would have to pee. Where would he go? The brasserie, of course.

Omar had made a quick trip to the toilet in the back of the brasserie an hour ago. He had noticed that the door had a lock on the inside and a window that opened to the alley in back. He had also seen on a shelf above the sink a sign that read. "OUT OF ORDER. USE TOILETTE DOWNSTAIRS." Now he knew exactly what to do.

Fifteen minutes later, the agent, clad in a dark suit and black turtleneck, got out of the car. Quickly, he cut through the brasserie on his way to the toilet. Omar waited until he entered the small room to make his move. Bag in hand, he headed toward the toilet. In the crowded brasserie no one seemed to notice.

He reached for the door knob. If the door was locked, he'd wait until he heard the lock click open. But it wasn't. Omar slipped inside. As he did, he reached into the bag, pulled out a stun gun and kicked the door closed.

The agent was facing the hole in the floor, his back to the door, his cock in his hand, in the middle of relieving himself. He heard the door open and close. "Hey," he said glancing over his shoulder. "Wait your …"

He never finished the sentence. Omar fired once, hitting the agent in the center of his back. He collapsed to the ground. He would be out cold for at least an hour.

Omar quickly put the "OUT OF ORDER" sign on the door.

One hour was all Omar needed. He slid open the window and looked around. The alley was deserted. Happy he was thin and wiry, he tossed his bag onto the ground then pushed himself through the window.

Swiftly, he crossed the deserted street. After climbing the side stairs, he knocked twice on Lila's door.

"Who's there?" she called from inside in a frightened voice.

"Omar, Kemal's friend," he responded through the door.

She opened it a crack. A chain was connecting the door and frame. He could easily break it off by kicking the door, but he didn't want to risk her screaming. "I have news about your brother."

"What news?" she said warily.

"Good news. Please let me in? I'm getting soaked in the rain."

He watched her remove the chain. She was wearing a white hotel terrycloth bathrobe. Cleavage visible. She didn't seem to be wearing anything underneath. She pulled the robe tight.

Water was running in another room.

"Wait here," she said. "I'll turn off the bath water."

Walking softly, he followed her. As she leaned over the tub, he snuck up behind her.

She stood up with a start. "I told you …"

He raised his arm and swung it with all his might smacking her with the back of his hand and a large gold ring, stolen from a hapless pedestrian during the '05 riots, on the side of her face. He felt bones break. Her nose. Maybe her cheek bone. Woozy, she fell backwards onto the toilet seat, blood running down her face. He held her in place and slugged her on the other side of her face. She was barely conscious.

He turned her sideways and grabbed her from behind. Then he dragged her to the bedroom. He yanked off her robe. Then pushed her onto the bed, on her back. Her legs were spread. Her thick brown pubics and slit open and inviting.

"I'm going to finish something I started years ago."

He dropped his pants. Flying to Marseilles, he wondered if he'd have trouble getting hard after he attacked her. But he didn't have any problem. He gave two tugs on his prick and it sprang to life. Ahmed had said, "Use a condom. They have DNA tests." He had no intention of doing that.

She was moaning in pain. He was glad she wasn't knocked out. He wanted her to know what he was doing. He climbed on the bed and entered her. She was motionless, but he didn't care. He moved back and forth feeling the sensation spread from his cock to every part of his body. He came in less than a minute.

He spun off the bed. From his bag, he extracted a pushbutton stiletto. He popped open the blade and stabbed her six times in the chest and stomach, jumping back each time to avoid the spurting blood. He wiped the knife blade on the sheets, reached into his bag again and pulled out a typed note that read, "ALL MUSLIM WOMEN ARE WHORES." It was signed: "Christian Action Group."

Omar removed a rusty nail from his bag and stuck the note to her bloody chest. He took out a throwaway camera, which he had bought in a variety store in Marseilles. He took four pictures of Lila, making sure the note showed clearly.

From the window, he glanced outside. No sign of the agent.

The rain was letting up. In the drizzle, Omar walked casually to his car at the end of Rue Daughin. Behind the wheel, he put on gloves and wiped his prints from the camera, which he placed on the seat.

Still wearing the gloves, he drove half a mile to Marseilles's largest newspaper, housed in an old stone building on the left. As Omar passed by, he slowed the car and tossed the camera at the closed, wooden front door. It hit with a thud and fell to the ground. Omar roared away.

By the time they developed the pictures, he would be well on his way to Paris.

PARIS

Tonight, Craig wasn't dreaming. The cell phone next to his bed woke him out of a sound sleep. He checked the red numerals on the digital clock. 2:05 a.m.

Hoping not to wake Elizabeth, he grabbed the phone quickly and carried it into the study.

Jacques said, "I have awful news."

God, he sounds like hell. "What happened?"

"Lila is dead."

Craig rubbed the sleep from his eyes. "Dead. How?"

Jacques described the condition of her body, the bruises on her face, the strangulation, the knife wounds, male sperm, and the note.

Craig felt himself becoming enraged. "Ga dammit. What happened to the protection?"

"Whoever killed her first disabled the security agent with a very effective stun gun in the toilet of a brasserie across from Lila's apartment."

Craig felt sick to his stomach. A great wave of guilt passed through his body. He was responsible for Lila's death. He felt as if he'd killed her.

He noticed Elizabeth standing in the doorway putting on a robe and listening.

"Tell me again what was on the note."

"'All Muslim women are whores.' It was signed by the Christian Action Group."

Craig was now fully awake, his brain processing what Jacques had told him. "You never heard of this organization. Did you?"

"No. But that doesn't mean anything. These right-wing Christian hate, vigilante groups are springing up all over France."

"I don't believe it."

"You don't believe what?"

"That a Christian group killed Lila. That's too much of a coincidence. They could have picked any Muslim woman in France. Why someone who has Interior protection with the added risk of disabling the Interior agent. It's total bullshit. Musa's responsible."

"I need more to believe it," Jacques said stubbornly.

"You know I'm right. You just don't want accept it. To admit that we fucked up."

Jacques wasn't stupid. He'd come around. And he did. First, a sigh of resignation. Then, "You're right. Musa had someone kill Lila to eliminate her as a witness in the train bombing case."

"When this story and the note come out, all hell will break loose. Expect riots in Muslim communities throughout France and Europe. The spin will be that a beautiful young Muslim woman has been raped and murdered by a Christian group. You realize that. Don't you?"

"All too well. I tried to get the police to conceal the note."

"And?"

"Pointless. The killer took photos with a disposable camera after he killed Lila and planted the note. He dropped off the camera in front of Marseilles largest paper. The police chief tried to persuade the publisher to sit on the photos. He refused. They're running in the morning edition, along with a statement from the police chief that the murderer will be caught and brought to justice."

"That'll help."

"What else could he do?"

"How are they coming on apprehending the killer?"

"So far they don't have a clue. They're going all out. Watching airports and train stations. They have a ring around the city."

"That won't do a thing. He's either long gone or is in hiding in Marseilles."

"They're also searching right-wing Christian areas, which you've convinced me is a waste of time."

"It would make more sense to comb through the Muslim neighborhoods in the eastern part of town where Lila lived."

Jacques coughed and cleared his throat, "They're afraid to do that."

"Great … Keep me posted."

Craig hung up and turned to Elizabeth, sitting in a chair across the room. He told her what Jacques had said.

"Musa is incredibly smart," she responded. "The camera was a great touch. He anticipated the police would try to conceal the note."

Craig was shaking his head. "The whole action was brilliant. He managed to eliminate Lila as a witness. At the same time spark Muslim riots against Christians. That furthers his long-term strategy of a Muslim-Christian war in Europe."

Elizabeth's face lit up. She sprang to her feet. "Florinda."

"What's that?"

"Florinda was a beautiful Muslim woman raped by a Christian king in the Eighth Century. That spark united the Muslim army to defeat the Christians and cost the king his throne."

"Musa must have known that."

"He's always one step ahead of us. We're reacting. We have to go on the offensive."

"Agreed. But how?"

They were both silent for a minute, thinking. Then Craig said, "I've got it. There has to be a leak among the Defense Ministers whom I told about Lila."

"Could be a staff member of one of them, who learned about the meeting."

"Possibly. But, let's assume it's a Minister, because Lila's death followed so closely after the meeting."

"Makes sense. But who?"

"Alvarez. He's had it in for me since we tried to thwart the Spanish train bombing. He was negative at Sunday's meeting."

"Worse than negative. Downright hostile. How do we nail the bastard?"

"Remember his deputy Carlos, who sat in on the first meeting we had in Madrid?"

"Sure. Good-looking young man."

"I got the impression he thinks his boss is an asshole."

"Who wouldn't?"

He laughed. "I'll fly to Madrid and see if Carlos will help us."

"Do what?"

"Spy on his boss."

"Good idea, but you can't do it."

"Why not?"

"You'll draw too much attention. We might as well be posting it on the internet."

"You have a way of killing a good idea."

"Not the idea. Just the implementation. You need someone to go for you. Somebody younger. More like Carlos's age."

"Ouch."

"A writer researching her book."

"How's that coming, by the way?"

"I'm making good progress on part two. Meantime, Ned has been consumed by another project. So he hasn't forwarded his notes on part one yet. Don't worry. I'm ahead of schedule. I can go to Madrid."

"OK. Suppose you meet with Carlos and persuade him to tell us if Alvarez does anything suspicious. If he can't get you on the phone immediately, he should report to me."

"I like that."

"Alvarez may lead us to Musa and what he's planning."

PARIS

At six in the morning, Omar was parked outside of Professor Etienne's apartment on a narrow residential street on the Left Bank, two blocks from Boulevard St. Michel. The gray stone buildings looked as if they'd been built before the revolution. The lights were on in Etienne's apartment, which occupied the entire third floor. In front of the building was a weather-beaten wooden door in need of painting, with a brass handle.

Omar had his eyes riveted on that door. Eventually, the professor would come out. Though he hadn't slept all night, there was not much chance of Omar dozing. He was fully alert, running on the adrenalin charge from what he'd done to Lila, supplemented by caffeine.

Omar saw headlights behind him. It was a cop car with flashing lights on the roof. No way they could have found him. Still he fingered the Glock in his bag and held his breath. The cruiser sped up and passed.

At precisely seven o'clock, the wooden door opened. Though he had never seen Etienne in person, Omar recognized from the pictures on the internet the balding, slight figure, five foot eight, wearing wire-framed glasses and a ridiculous-looking gray, flat cap. He was carrying a heavy briefcase.

No one else was on the sidewalk. Omar watched Etienne turn right and walk in the direction of the history department of the University of Paris. When he turned the corner, Omar started the car. He followed for ten minutes, hanging back, making certain that Etienne was going to his office.

Then he made a U-turn and drove away. Today, he wanted to understand Etienne's routine. Musa had told him professors follow the same schedule most days. Now he'd be able to make plans for Etienne's abduction. I'll be back tomorrow, he thought. Meantime, Omar had something else to do.

He turned north and drove to Clichy. Listening to the news on the car radio, he knew that the police had withheld the name of the victim in the Marseilles murder. That was about to change.

The morning was dark and dreary. At eight o'clock, Omar left his car on the outskirts of the banilieu and walked to a complex of six concrete twelve-story public housing buildings, inhabited primarily by Muslims. Garbage was strewn between buildings. Omar headed for one of them in the center, it's wall covered by graffiti depicting prehistoric birds with long wingspans, done by a talented kid. Maybe he'll break out of here one day, Omar hoped.

The lobby was filthy. The elevator smelled of urine. He rode up to the eighth floor and pounded on the metal door of apartment 802.

A burly man with a bushy, black, unkempt beard, in a white T-shirt and Jeans, opened the door. In the background, Omar heard a child crying and a woman screaming. "Don't you throw your food."

Abdullah, Lila's cousin, hadn't changed in the two years since Omar had last seen him. They were the same age and had been in class together, until both dropped out in the tenth grade.

Abdullah reached out and hugged Omar. "I hear you went off with the great man, Ahmed." His tone was contemptuous. "Are you helping him remake the world?"

"I spend some time with him. I also travel."

"No wife or kids. You can do what you want." Abdullah sounded envious.

"Yesterday I was in Marseilles."

"What's down there?"

"I was visiting a friend, and I heard about the killing of the Muslim girl. You know about that?"

"I heard it on the television. Christian pigs."

"They didn't disclose the girl's name. Did they?"

Abdullah shook his head. "Somebody you know?"

"Lila Dahab."

Abdullah's head snapped back. "No!" He cried out. "No! Are you sure?"

"My friend in Marseilles has buddies in the police. As soon as I found out, I came here to tell you."

Abdullah's face was a mask of anger and grief. "Lila wouldn't hurt anybody. Why didn't they disclose her name?"

"They claim to be waiting until they notify her next of kin."

"That's bullshit. The police always lie. They don't want it to get out. Everybody here likes Lila. They know what will happen. Where's Kemal?"

"I don't know. A while ago, he met some Turkish girl from Germany and took off with her."

"They could have notified me. I'm her kin."

Abdullah grabbed a navy shirt hanging over a chair.

"What are you doing?" Omar asked.

"Making sure everyone knows those Christian pigs killed Lila."

Abdullah was out of the door with Omar right behind.

While Omar stood off to the side of the courtyard in the center of the housing complex, its grass chewed up from kids playing soccer,

Abdullah stopped people to tell them the news. Like a man on fire, he charged into several buildings.

Somebody handed him a bullhorn stolen from the police. Waving it, he climbed on to a wooden platform used by speakers and entertainers. "Listen to me everyone," he called out. "I have important news."

In five minutes a crowd of close to a hundred poured out of the buildings and into the center courtyard.

"The woman brutally raped and murdered in Marseilles," he cried out in an angry surly voice, "was not some nameless Muslim woman. She was our own Lila Dahab, Kemal's sister. And because she's a poor Muslim woman, the police won't do anything to find her killers."

From the crowd someone shouted in Arabic. "You speak the truth."

Someone else, "They won't get away with this. We want justice."

A police car pulled up to the edge of the courtyard. Two white-skinned policemen got out, hands close to the guns holstered at their waists as they walked toward the crowd.

"What's going on here?" one of them called.

Omar watched them anxiously keeping their eyes on the crowd directly ahead. What Omar also saw, but the policemen didn't, was two teenagers, twelve or fourteen, entering the courtyard from behind the policemen, armed with bottles of gasoline. They lit the gasoline and flung them under the police car, which went up in flames, then exploded.

As the policemen turned around to look, other teenagers pelted them with rocks.

The two policemen raced out of the courtyard, barely escaping the surging crowd.

The sparks were now lit for a full scale riot, Omar noted with satisfaction. Even larger than the riots of October 2005.

Omar couldn't wait to tell Musa: "Mission accomplished." He

would be very pleased. Omar had done exactly what he wanted.

But he would have to wait. A cell phone was too risky. Besides, Musa would hear it on the news.

Omar now had to concentrate on something else: Recruiting two men and a van for tomorrow morning's operation. He had money to offer. With so many unemployed in Clichy, finding two men would be easy. They had to be men he could trust. And the van had to be in good shape. Marbella was a long ride.

43

MADRID

Walking through the airplane terminal after her flight from Paris, Elizabeth gazed at the television screen above the bar. Police cars were burning. The CNN reporter, a perky-looking young blonde, hair cut short, was saying "Riots have broken out in Clichy-sous-Bois, a suburb of Paris, formerly the home of Lila Dahab, the innocent young Muslim woman viciously raped and murdered in Marseilles last evening by a right-wing Christian extremist group."

My God, Elizabeth thought. What a choice of words. As usual, the media were fanning the flames of the riot. She wasn't surprised the name of the victim had gotten out. Trying to conceal it in the internet age was a stupid waste of time. Secrets and privacy have ceased to exist.

Elizabeth watched in horror as a picture of Lila's dead body from the waist up with the note attached appeared on the screen. Those television people are shameless.

Elizabeth exited the terminal and got into a cab. She gave the driver an address two blocks from the Ministry of Defense.

At the destination, she spotted a small café, the Toledo, across the street. At eleven in the morning the café was deserted. Too early for lunch.

In the dimly lit Toledo, Elizabeth ordered an espresso at the bar and took it to a corner table. The café walls were lined with Spanish maritime scenes depicting battles with England.

Elizabeth thought she'd have the best chance hitting Carlos cold. Getting through to him was a problem, but with information on the web, she knew the perfect way. Her Spanish was just good enough to pull it off.

A woman answered the phone, "Senior Sanchez's office."

"I would like to speak with Senior Sanchez, please."

"Who is calling?"

"The principal from the school. About his son, Roberto."

"Yes. One minute please."

Seconds later, she heard Carlos's anxious voice. "Carlos Sanchez here. What is the problem?"

"This is Elizabeth Crowder. There's nothing wrong with your son. Forgive me for misleading you, but I had to make sure I spoke with you. Very privately. Craig Page sent me to discuss an extremely sensitive and urgent matter. Please don't mention my name aloud."

She hoped he wasn't furious.

"I see," he said, playing along. "Where are you?"

"A small café, the Toledo. About two blocks from …"

"I know it," he said softly. "Stay there. I'm on my way."

Ten minutes later, she saw him walk through the door, pick up an espresso at the bar, and make a beeline for her table.

"Nobody knows I'm meeting you," he said. "I assume this is about Alvarez."

She liked the question. Carlos was intelligent. She decided to level with him. He was the only option they had.

"Alvarez attended a meeting in Paris last Sunday," she said, keeping her voice down.

"I know. Monday morning, he told me that Craig tried to mobilize the EU countries for an attack on Musa, who carried out the Spanish train bombing and has a base in the mountains of Morocco. You were there as well. Craig's proposal was rejected. The Ministers didn't believe he had sufficient evidence to justify an attack."

"That's a pretty good summary. Did Alvarez tell you that Craig's evidence included a statement by a woman in Marseilles who recognized Musa's voice on the tape he made after the attack?"

"He didn't say anything about a woman in Marseilles." Carlos sat up with a start. "You're planning to tell me that woman was Lila Dahab, the one who …"

"Exactly."

"So she was killed by Musa's people. Not a Christian extremist group."

"That's what we believe."

"Which means someone at the meeting leaked her name to Musa."

She nodded.

"And you think it's Alvarez?"

Rapidly, their conversation had reached the critical point. Elizabeth didn't want to overplay her hand.

"Craig and I believe he's the most likely possibility, based upon his behavior at the Paris meeting and how he acted at the time of the train bombing."

Carlos was frowning. "I was appalled by his behavior in the meetings with Craig at the time of the bombing. I always knew he was arrogant and didn't tolerate anyone playing on his turf. Refused to accept suggestions. Was unqualified for his job and was only in it because of wealthy political supporters. But he outdid himself."

She smiled. "Don't hold back. Tell me what you really think."

"You disagree?"

"I had exactly the same reaction."

"I will admit I'm a little prejudiced because one of my neighbors' children died in that train bombing, but still …"

Carlos paused to sip espresso. "What would Alvarez gain from working with Musa?"

"At this point we don't know. We thought you might help."

"How?"

"Have you noticed anything unusual in his behavior lately?"

Carlos shook his head.

"Any clandestine meetings?"

"I'm not aware."

"Efforts to conceal phone calls?"

Again, Carlos shook his head. "But his office is in a different wing of the Ministry."

She took a deep breath and went for it. "What we'd like you to do is keep track of Alvarez as best you can. If you see anything suspicious, call me. If you can't get me, immediately call Craig. I'll give you all of our contact info."

"You're asking me to spy on him."

That was the same word Craig had used. Of course it was apt. She swallowed hard. "Yes."

He fiddled with his wedding ring. The last time she saw a man do that, he knew he was risking the safety and security of his family. They were in Iraq. She wanted him to take her to one of the Sunni tribal leaders

Carlos no doubt felt the same. Alvarez was a former General with rich friends. If they were powerful enough to make him Defense Minister, they'd be powerful enough to kill his deputy.

"This could get ugly," she said. "If you don't feel comfortable …"

"No. I'll do it."

44

PARIS

At 6:30 in the morning, Omar had everything in place in front of Etienne's apartment building. Based on yesterday, he expected Etienne to come out of the building and turn right. So Omar directed Habib to park the gray van ten yards away to the left of the entrance. That way the van would be behind Etienne when he began walking.

Habib was behind the wheel. Omar in the front passenger seat. And Attia in the back of the van.

Though the morning air was chilly, Omar had his window rolled down. The smell of burning rubber was in the air. All night Muslims had rioted in the poor suburbs of Paris, burning tires and police cars. The radio said it was possible that Charles DeGaulle Airport might be closed because the road leading to it passed near "those areas."

Last evening, Omar had watched television in Habib's apartment. Rioting was occurring in many other Western European cities with large Muslim populations. Amsterdam, Marseilles, Seville, and several cities in Germany and England. The police were powerless to stop the rioting. Their objective was to contain it to Muslim areas.

Omar checked his watch. Two minutes to seven.

Then he saw Etienne. Clutching the same large briefcase as yesterday, the professor walked through the front door and turned right.

Omar sprang from the van. On the toes of his feet to avoid detection, he was following Etienne. When Omar was right behind his prey, he said, "Professor Etienne." Startled, Etienne dropped the briefcase and turned around. Omar pulled the stun gun from his pocket and fired a shot into Etienne's stomach.

He grabbed Etienne's limp body before it hit the ground. The van was moving up quickly. In a flash, Attia was out of the van helping Omar lift Etienne. They flung him into the back like a sack of potatoes. Attia was in with him.

Omar was preparing to climb in the back and slam the door when he noticed Etienne's briefcase in the middle of the sidewalk. Leaving it would be a mistake. He scrambled back out, grabbed it, and threw it inside. As he did, he looked around. Nobody in sight. They might have been seen from an upstairs window. But they'd be long gone before the police could begin a search. The cops had their hands full with the riots. Besides, the van had a license plate Habib had stolen at five this morning.

As Omar was slamming the van door from the inside, he shouted "Go" to Habib. His old friend hit the gas. He was driving fast, but not fast enough to be stopped.

Traffic was light. In minutes, they were on the periphery road that circled Paris. The van had recently been used to haul produce. The back smelled from onion and garlic.

Half way around, they picked up the main road heading south.

Forty five minutes later, they pulled into a Total gas station and parked in a deserted corner of the lot. Omar paid Attia five thousand euros. He jumped out of the van, planning to hitch a ride back to Paris. In about five seconds, Omar changed the license plate. Taking off the stolen one and putting on the original.

Omar remained in the back of the van with Professor Etienne, who was beginning to stir. "Drive," Omar shouted to Habib. They were on the road again, heading south.

Omar reached into the groaning Etienne's pocket and pulled out his cell phone. With rope, he tied Etienne's ankles together. He put on a set of handcuffs stolen from the police. As Habib drove, Omar waited for Etienne to wake up.

When he did, the Professor began screaming. "Help me. Help me."

Omar pointed the stun gun at him. "If you keep hollering, I'll put you out again."

Etienne looked terrified. "What do you want? Money? I'll give you everything I have."

"We need your help."

"With what?"

"I'll tell you when we arrive."

"Where?"

"I can't tell you that, but I want you to do something right now."

"What's that?"

"I'll dial your home on your phone. Tell your wife that you had to make a quick trip to London for your work. You'll be back in a couple of days. I'll hold the phone while you talk."

"No," Etienne said stubbornly.

"No, what."

"I won't do it."

Omar wanted to smack Etienne hard in the face with the handle of the gun, but Musa had said, "Bring him here uninjured." So that wasn't an option. Still, he had to get Etienne to make the call.

"If you don't, I'll have someone kill your wife, Jacqueline, and your twelve year old daughter, Mina. Now make the call."

"Who are you people?"

"In time, you'll find out. Now make the call."

The van came to a sudden stop. Etienne lunged for the door handle. Omar smashed the gun barrel against his wrist.

The professor screamed, "Ah … Ah …"

Omar took out his own phone, "OK you made your decision. I'm calling two of my people to tell them to kill Jacqueline and Mina."

"You won't do that."

"Watch me."

With a determined look on his face, Omar dialed.

"No," Etienne cried. "No … I'll do it."

Using the Professor's phone, Omar dialed Etienne's house and held up the phone to the Professor's ear and mouth. Omar was prepared to yank the phone away if Etienne didn't follow the script. That wasn't necessary. Etienne told his wife he was off for London. She didn't question him.

Omar wasn't worried about crossing the border into Spain in the Pyrenees. All those border-guard stations had been removed as EU integration took hold. They had on open road to Marbella.

Say goodbye to France, Professor Etienne, Omar thought. You'll never see this country again.

45

PARIS

"Dealing with the Vatican is the most frustrating experience," Giuseppe said to Craig and Elizabeth. It was ten in the morning, and the three of them were in Craig's office.

"Cardinal Donatello, their Director of Security, insists on total autonomy in matters affecting the Vatican. He has to take each decision to a Committee of Cardinals. Meantime, he rejects every proposal of mine."

"What do you want to do?" Craig asked.

"I know a top firm of civil engineers in Milan. I want them to take control of the Vatican's water supply and set up a procedure for constant monitoring. If Musa slips any poison into the system, we'll detect it immediately. That way it won't do any damage. We'll establish a hookup for an alternative water supply from Rome and furnish huge quantities of bottled water."

Craig was pacing and thinking.

"What's bothering you?" Giuseppe asked.

"Musa does everything on such a grand scale. He set off riots throughout Europe. I can't believe that, if he wants to attack the Vatican, he'd focus on their water supply."

"Then what would he do?"

Craig stopped pacing and sat back down.

"I don't know. But we have to find out, and I'm sure we don't have much time."

Elizabeth said, "Maybe Alvarez will lead us to what we need."

"Giuseppe doesn't know about Alvarez and Carlos. Will you tell him about your meeting with Carlos in Madrid?"

Once she was finished, Giuseppe's eyes lit up. "That could give us a lead."

Craig glanced at the calendar on the wall. Today was Thursday, March 25. Sunday, the 28th, was shown in bold red letters. Easter Sunday. He focused on it.

"If you were going to attack the Vatican, when would you do it?" he asked. Before the others had a chance to reply, he answered his own question: "Easter Sunday."

"Wonderful," Giuseppe said. "That means we have three days and not a single lead, except for the theft of the water plans, which you tell me is taking us down a rabbit hole. Add to that, Vatican security people are giving me fits."

"Also, remember Musa is planning to use the army he's assembled for an attack somewhere," Craig said.

Elizabeth added, "Meantime, what can we do about the riots?"

"They're not as bad in Italy," Giuseppe said.

"You have a smaller Muslim population," she retorted.

Craig responded, "I can't very well go on television and say a Muslim, one of Musa's people, killed Lila. I don't have any evidence. That would only fuel the flames. We have no choice. We have to let them run their course."

"What we really need is to find Lila's killer," Elizabeth said. "That'll stop the riots."

"So far Jacques and the French police haven't made any progress."

The three of them looked at each other glumly.

Craig's cell phone rang. He checked the caller ID. Jacques. Maybe he had something on Lila's killer. "Yes Jacques."

"Are you in your office?"

"Yeah. With Elizabeth and Giuseppe. I'll put you on speaker."

"Look at your computer. I want to send you something."

Elizabeth and Giuseppe joined Craig behind his desk. In a few seconds, he saw General Zhou walking in a grassy area with another Chinese man.

"What are we looking at?" Craig asked.

"Real time feed from two of my men tracking General Zhou. They're walking in the Tuileries. No doubt talking there because General Zhou knows we've got bugs in his apartment and taps on his phone."

Craig didn't recognize the man with General Zhou. "Who's the other guy?"

"Freddy Wu. The Director of Military Sales for the Chinese government in Western Europe and North Africa. Based in Paris."

"So General Zhou could be placing an order for more weapons for Musa," Craig said, thinking aloud.

Giuseppe picked up. "Maybe arms to use against the Vatican."

"Can you step up Italian border surveillance?" Craig asked Giuseppe.

"We can, but only on non EU entries. Sea ports, airports and the like. If they move the stuff by land, say from France, we no longer have checkpoints. Isn't the EU wonderful?"

Craig returned to Jacques on the phone. "This is very helpful. Have the taps or bugs given us anything?"

"Not yet. Part of the time he uses an encrypted phone."

"Probably for calls with Musa."

"It's Chinese technology. We haven't been able to crack it. We're still working on it."

"Let me know."

"OK. And something else. We checked airplane manifests since October. General Zhou has made six trips to Marrakech. The first a day after the Spanish train bombing with his Russian girlfriend, Androshka. The rest alone."

Craig was weighing Jacques's words. He could try to persuade Jacques to arrest both General Zhou and Freddy Wu, interrogate them separately, hoping to break Freddy. That might work, but Craig doubted Jacques would do it. Freddy was a Chinese government official. The French would never risk an incident with China.

Another choice was for Craig to inform President Li of Freddy's activities with General Zhou. That would get Freddy fired. But what good would that do? Musa already had most of the arms he needed.

The best alternative, Craig decided, is simply maintain surveillance on General Zhou. At some point, Musa will leave his base and move to the place of action. Anyone who took the name of a war hero wouldn't watch from the sidelines. But Musa had no battle experience. He'd need General Zhou, the military man, to advise on strategy. Following that reasoning, General Zhou would link up with Musa very soon. If they follow General Zhou, he would lead them to Musa's headquarters for the operation. Somewhere in Europe. No longer under the protection of the Moroccan Prime Minister.

"Have your men stick close to General Zhou," Craig told Jacques. "Let me know immediately if he leaves Paris, and follow him wherever he goes."

46

PARIS

General Zhou had met Freddy Wu in front of the Hotel Crillon. They walked across the majestic Place de La Concorde with the 107-foot gilded obelisk in the center, a gift from Egypt in 1833. Looking over his shoulder, General Zhou saw the gray Citroën following. Two men in the car with a black-haired guy driving; a blonde brute beside him. There might be others on foot. General Zhou wasn't willing to chance it.

He figured they'd have privacy on the path cutting through the Tuilleries, the garden with grassy areas filled with statues, rows of trees, flowers, and fountains. At ten in the morning, commuters had already crossed on their way work; it was too early for tourists. General Zhou watched the blonde getting out of the Citroën, following on foot, hanging back twenty yards, making no effort to conceal himself. The Citroën, keeping pace, moved slowly along the Rue de Rivoli.

At the midpoint of the path, Freddy stopped to admire the yellow tulips. General Zhou was standing next to him.

"Everything is on schedule," Freddy said. "We'll be bringing the missiles in by truck from France at the Italian Riviera border point near San Remo. All four missiles in one truck, carrying Chinese computers. They will be in four of fifty sealed crates marked on the outside as computers. They can only be discovered if someone opens all fifty. Which will never happen."

"Unless there's a leak among your people."

"We don't have leaks."

"Where do they go from San Remo?"

Freddy looked around to make sure no one was approaching. Then he said softly, "The truck will drive southeast to Torino. It will pull into a warehouse at number 20 Via Sardegna in an industrial part of town at ten in the evening on Friday, March 26. Four vans will be parked in the warehouse. I'll have someone to give instructions on how to assemble and fire. Make sure your people are there for the handoff. An hour later, the computer truck and the instructors are gone. It's all yours from that point."

"I understand," General Zhou said. "Perfect."

They resumed walking. General Zhou realized he had to pass along to Musa the information Freddy had given him. But it was highly sensitive. He was afraid to use the encrypted phone. Only a matter of time until the French cracked it. For all he knew, they'd done so already.

He had to deliver the news in person to Musa in Marbella. That meant shaking his tail. He couldn't risk leading Craig to Musa.

"You notice the guy following us?" he said to Freddy.

"One in a gray Citroën, a beefy blonde guy on foot behind us."

"I have to shake them."

"When?"

"Today?"

Freddy thought for a minute. "When you go to a restaurant with Androshka, do those guys go inside?"

"They always wait outside."

"Here's what I want you to do. Get Androshka and go to lunch at Apicius. The restaurant we ate at a couple of days ago on Rue L'Artois. I'll make your reservation and take care of the rest."

General Zhou always liked to be in control. "You better explain."

"I'll get to the restaurant at one o'clock with Charlie Ming from my office who looks like you. Or at least close enough. Caucasians always have trouble distinguishing Chinese men."

"Why do you call him Charlie? And you're Freddy?"

"Operating in France and Western Europe, I prefer American names. The Europeans have been buying from the United States for years. If they hear Chinese names, they get nervous. Anyhow, when I was in the office this morning, Charlie was wearing a dark blue suit, white shirt and blue tie. Dress like that. I promise you'll lose your tail."

General Zhou now understood. "Also, I'll need a phony passport, credit cards and French driver's license."

"I'll bring them to lunch."

General Zhou and Androshka were finishing dessert, a caramel assortment. Lunch was winding down. Investment bankers, masters of the universe, and others rich and famous, as well as those who prized great food, were drifting out. General Zhou drained his espresso and paid the bill. He looked across the table at Androshka and said, "Remember how you promised to do anything for me?"

"Of course. After you took care of Mikail. And I meant it."

"Good. I'm going to the men's room. I won't come back to the table. Instead, another Chinese man named Charlie will sit down and pretend to be me. A minute later, the two of you will leave the restaurant and quickly get into my car with Captain Cheng driving. You'll tell him to take the two of you to my apartment. Don't talk to Charlie. Watch television. He'll spend the night sleeping in a separate bedroom and leave at eight tomorrow morning. Do you understand?"

"Charlie won't mess with me? Will he?"

"I'll kill him if he does. Nobody but me gets into your honey pot."

She giggled. Then turned serious. "When will I see you again?"

"I have to go away for a couple of days. Don't try to call me unless you are arrested."

"I understand."

General Zhou felt a debt of gratitude to Mikail. He had taught Androshka well. She didn't ask questions.

Freddy and Charlie were seated in the next room of the three in the restaurant. On the way to the men's room, General Zhou signaled Freddy, who directed Charlie to follow him. In the men's room, they changed ties. He does look like me, General Zhou thought.

From the men's room, General Zhou went to Freddy's table. Charlie sat down with Androshka.

General Zhou glanced at his Rolex. After a minute, he called Cheng to pull up the black BMW to the front of the restaurant. Through the opening connecting the two dining rooms, General Zhou watched Androshka and Charlie leave and walk toward the front door and the waiting car.

Meantime, Freddy strolled to the front of the restaurant and peeked out. He came back and reported, "The gray Citroën followed your black BMW. You're free of the tail."

"Excellent."

"I have a car outside. Where do you want me to take you?"

"Charles DeGaulle Airport."

"That's what I figured."

Freddy removed an envelope from his briefcase and handed it

to General Zhou. "False passport, credit cards, and French driver's license."

General Zhou was tempted to fly to Seville. No, that's foolish. The safer course is to fly to Madrid. Then take a train to Seville and rent a car to go to Marbella.

MARBELLA, SPAIN

Waiting for Omar to arrive with Etienne, Musa stood on the deck of the villa in the hills above Marbella and gazed at the beach below. The Mediterranean glistened in the late afternoon sun. Following the Spanish train bombing, a Saudi Prince had given Musa use of the house along with five million Euros to aid The Spanish Revenge.

Surrounded by a ten-foot stone wall, the villa resembled a British country house, which had been the objective when a London hedge-fund manager built it a decade ago, ironically betting the price of oil would continue to soar. When the price spiked downward, the ruined hedge-fund manager put the villa on the market. The Saudi snapped it up.

Musa watched a gray van pull up to the checkpoint at the black wrought-iron gate. He recognized Habib, Omar's pal, behind the wheel. He called the guard to wave them through.

Omar led handcuffed Etienne into the marble foyer. The professor looked exhausted and haggard. "You can remove the cuffs," Musa said. "Let the professor shower upstairs. Clean clothes are on the bed. Then we'll give him something to eat."

"Who are you?" Etienne said. "What do you want with me?"

"Later we'll have time to talk."

"I want to leave now."

"That's not an option."

Etienne pointed to Omar. "He has my cell phone. I want it back. I want to call my wife."

"Not an option either."

"In other words, I'm a prisoner."

"I prefer to think of you as my guest. Now why don't you go upstairs and clean up?"

Resigned, Etienne trudged up the stairs. Though he doubted the professor would try to escape, Musa whispered to Omar, "Keep an eye on him at all times." The professor was a pathetic little man. He'll tell me or I'll break him.

Fifteen minutes later, Musa sat down at a table for dinner with Etienne. The Professor ate, then repeated his questions: "Who are you ... What do you want with me?"

"My name is Musa Ben Abdil."

"The Spanish train bomber? The terrorist?"

Musa felt a surge of anger. "I'm no terrorist. I'm seeking justice for Muslims in Europe."

"Are you responsible for the riots occurring now?"

"An innocent Muslim girl was brutally raped and murdered."

"Who are you really? I'm curious who would be so arrogant to take on the name of a famous medieval warrior."

If he didn't need Etienne, Musa would shoot the Professor right now. Refusing to be baited, he said calmly. "Who I am isn't the issue. You have information I want. That's why you're here."

"What information?"

"Last year at a seminar in Paris you spoke with Professor Khalid from the University in Casablanca."

Etienne stiffened. "I don't recall. I attend many seminars and talk to lots of people."

"You told Khalid you had discovered that, on her deathbed in 1504, Queen Isabella felt guilty for reneging on her promise to grant Muslims freedom of worship as a condition of their surrendering at the Alhambra. So she prepared a parchment containing an edict granting Muslims in perpetuity a swath of land in Southern Spain."

"I'm sorry. I have no recollection. You made a mistake abducting me. Truly you have."

Musa pounded his fist on the table. The dishes jumped. "Don't play games. Tell me what happened to that parchment."

"I don't know what you're talking about."

"You're lying. You told Khalid you expect to publish an article with this discovery sometime soon."

Etienne was shaking his head from side to side.

Musa lowered his eyes and glared at Etienne. "Either you tell me, or I will submit you to tortures crueler than any you read about in the Inquisition, because now we have modern technology. Who says mankind hasn't advanced? You'll wish you were on the rack. If you still don't tell me after you die from the torture, I will rape and kill your wife and daughter. And do it myself."

Etienne looked terrified but didn't move.

Musa thought about that red-faced policeman beating Nicole on the head over and over. He wouldn't show Etienne any mercy.

Musa called to Omar, seated in the corner, "Take Professor Etienne to the torture chamber in the basement. Start with electric shocks to his genitals. I'll be down in a few minutes."

Omar roughly grabbed Etienne by the arm and led him to the stairs. When they had descended to the first landing, the Professor screamed, "No … No … No … I'll tell you."

"Bring him back," Musa called.

With tears in his eyes, Etienne returned to his place at the table across from Musa.

"Well, I'm waiting."

"I swear to God I do not know for sure. But I believe from research that the parchment ..."

He hesitated.

"Well?"

"I've never told this to anyone. I plan to present a paper in October in London at the Society of Medieval Historians."

"I don't care about your stupid paper. Tell me now."

When Etienne didn't respond, Musa said, "You'll be the first scholar who ever underwent electric shock to protect his research." He looked at Omar. "Take the fool downstairs and put his feet in water to increase the pain."

As Omar stepped forward, Etienne said, "I'll tell you."

"Last chance."

"Are you familiar with Tomas de Torquemada?"

"He was Queen Isabella's Grand Inquisitor. The worst. The cruelest in searching out, torturing, and killing Muslims and Jews. He also stole their property. A real villain. And all supposedly in the name of God."

"That accurately describes him. He wasn't present when she wrote out the parchment. Once he heard about it from the priest to whom Isabella handed the parchment, he went into a frenzy. He seized the parchment from the priest. Then he ordered the priest to be killed as well as Isabella's two servants who had been present when she prepared it."

"What did he do with the parchment then?"

"Hid it during his lifetime."

"And when he died?"

"Arranged to have it buried with him. Not in his coffin, but in a metal box alongside. The parchment and some jewels he had seized from prisoners."

"What was the point of the jewels?"

Etienne shrugged. "Who knows? At the end, his sins made him crazy. Maybe be planned to buy God's forgiveness in the hereafter."

Musa was mulling over what Etienne had told him. "I don't understand why Torquemada didn't simply destroy the parchment once Isabella died. Rather than bury it in his grave."

Etienne shifted in his chair and looked down at his hands. "As I said, Torquemada became crazy. I don't think we can judge him at that point by rational behavior. Anyone who buried jewels in his grave was, of course, insane."

"Where was Torquemada buried?"

"In a graveyard outside a Franciscan monastery in Avila, Spain. I've been there several times. Most recently in January."

Musa picked up a pad of paper and a pen. He plunked them down in front of Etienne. "Draw me a map."

With a trembling hand, Etienne drew two maps. One of the monastery's location. The other showing Torquemada's grave in the cemetery behind the monastery. He slid it across the table.

Musa studied the maps carefully. When he looked up, Etienne was staring at him. "Can I go now? I've given you what you want."

"It's the parchment I want. I don't have it yet."

"But you will with the maps."

"And if I don't, may your God help you." Musa's words were delivered in a hard, cruel tone. "Meantime, I intend to lock you up downstairs as a precaution. When I have the parchment, I'll release you."

Musa had heard from an aide to the Saudi Prince that his master ordered guards to pick up prostitutes on the streets of Marbella. They were locked up in those rooms and available for the Prince's sexual perversions whenever he wanted. After he finished with them, he had them killed. Their bodies dumped at sea. That's what he would do with Etienne.

Once Etienne was locked up, Musa handed Omar the maps.

"I want you to go with Habib in his van tonight to Avila, Spain. Take two shovels, a gun, a flashlight, and a knife. Also, anything else you might need. You should arrive there about midnight. Get into the monastery's grounds, dig up Torquemada's grave, and bring back the parchment. If any monks try to stop you, kill them."

"I understand."

"Do whatever it takes. I need that parchment. And I need it tonight."

Musa paused, then continued. "If we have that parchment, for sure we will succeed. Islam's lawful place in Europe will be restored. Europe and the world will never be the same ... Don't fail me, Omar."

48

MARBELLA

At eleven thirty in the evening, General Zhou got off the train in Seville. Though he was accustomed to cars with drivers and rarely drove himself, he had to minimize the risk of being discovered. He used the phony ID Freddy had given to him to rent from Avis a Mercedes sedan with GPS. As he punched in the address of Musa's villa in Marbella, he thought of an Avis ad he'd seen on French television. "Even an idiot can find his way with our GPS." He hoped they were telling the truth. With his failing eyesight, reading maps of Spain at night would be next to impossible.

Before pulling out of the lot, he called Musa on the encrypted phone. "I should be at your place in a couple of hours. Don't say any more."

Three hours later, General Zhou, bone weary from hunching over the wheel trying to follow the road, trudged into Musa's villa. Musa immediately led him into the study and closed the door.

"What happened?" Musa asked. "So urgent you didn't want to tell me on the phone."

General Zhou tossed Musa the keys to the rental car. "Before I do that, have someone hide the car in the garage."

Afterwards, General Zhou told Musa about the missiles and their delivery to Torino.

"Perfect," Musa said. "I'll arrange to have my men meet the truck in the warehouse."

"What about locations in Rome for firing the missiles?"

"We rented apartments in four buildings. All with clear shots of St. Peter's Square. Different neighborhoods. The distances from St. Peter's Square are five, eight, ten, and twelve kilometers. Each on a different radius. Random points for all practical purposes. Discovery of one won't compromise any others."

"Good. What about the attack on Southern Spain?"

"I have ten thousand troops armed and ready to go. The pontoon boats have arrived and are stored in a warehouse. But I'm still concerned we'll face heavy ground fire from the Spanish side. That will give them time to bring in air support. You promised me, but …"

"You don't have to worry. I have a plan to minimize the Spanish opposition. Everything is in place. I want to wait a little longer for implementation."

Musa's brow wrinkled. "But are you sure …"

"Haven't I delivered on everything I've promised?"

"I don't want my men to be slaughtered."

"They won't be."

"Alright. Now let me tell you what I'm doing to give legitimacy to the takeover of Southern Spain."

Musa reported what had happened with Professor Khalid and Etienne. At the end, he said, "I have Etienne locked up downstairs." Musa checked his watch. "I expect Omar and Habib to be back any minute with the parchment from the grave of Tomas de Torquemada."

General Zhou was skeptical that this parchment would be intact and readable after being in the grave of some religious fanatic who was buried five hundred years ago. Then he thought about the Dead Sea Scrolls. A drier climate. But still. Possible? Perhaps.

Before General Zhou could say anything else, Omar, filthy, an anguished look on his face, staggered into the room and collapsed into a chair.

"Do you have the parchment?" Musa demanded.

"It wasn't in the grave," Omar replied in a halting voice. "We dug it up. I'm sorry."

"Perhaps the monks hid it."

"We searched the monastery. I killed them all one by one. I'm convinced it wasn't there."

"Where's Habib?"

"I killed him too. He was trying to steal jewels from Torquemada's grave."

"You picked him. He was your friend."

"Forgive me," Omar sounded terrified.

General Zhou hoped Musa wouldn't kill Omar in an angry rage. The man was valuable to the operation. It sounded as if he'd done all he could to obtain the parchment. Habib's treachery was immaterial.

Musa reached for the gun in his holster and placed it on the table. "What a complete disaster," Musa was raising his voice.

"Professor Etienne deceived us," Omar said. "He sent us on a fool's errand. He's the one who should pay for this."

Musa was red with rage. "I'll make him tell me where the parchment is."

A look of relief appeared on Omar's face.

Musa turned to General Zhou. "Come downstairs with me. I'll get the truth."

General Zhou followed Musa and two of his men to the basement. He watched as they pulled Professor Etienne from the cot and dragged him into a room that Musa called the torture chamber. There Musa ordered his men to strip off Etienne's clothes. The Professor was screaming. "I told you everything I know. I swear it. Please."

Musa ignored his cries. He ordered his men to stand Etienne up against a metal wall. They tied his arms and legs to posts, put his feet into buckets of water, then hooked up electrodes to his genitals.

"Where's the parchment?" Musa demanded.

"I told you everything."

"You're lying."

"I'm not. I swear it."

"We'll start with a small charge. Then get progressively stronger. I assure you that you will tell me."

Musa turned on the electricity. Etienne screamed. "No … No …" Tears were running down Etienne's cheeks.

He turned off the power. "Now tell me."

"There is no parchment."

"What are you saying?"

"I never heard about a parchment with an edict granting Muslims rights in Southern Spain. I never even heard about the edict. It never happened. I made up the whole story I told Khalid about Queen Isabella, the edict and the parchment to advance my career. I planned to prepare a fraudulent research paper and present it at the London conference in October. Everything I told you was false. I have no proof she issued the edict or prepared a parchment. I wanted to be famous."

"You're lying. The next one will be stronger." Musa adjusted the current and hit the red button.

The scream was piercing. "No … Don't know … No."

Musa was unmoved. "You'll either tell me, or I'll keep raising it until you die."

Musa increased the charge.

"No … No …" A blood curdling scream. Etienne's face was flushed. The smell of burning flesh filled the room. Smoke was coming from his groin. Saliva dripping from his mouth. The professor was on the verge of passing out.

General Zhou put a hand on Musa's arm. "Stop for a minute. Let's talk outside."

General Zhou led Musa into an adjoining room and closed the door. Musa looked like a wild man. This won't be easy, General Zhou thought.

"Let me tell you something," General Zhou said softly. "I've observed the torture of lots of men and women in China. Etienne is not a professional intelligence agent, trained to endure torture and not talk. He's an ordinary man. If he knew anymore about the parchment, he would have told you. I'm firmly convinced he made up the story about Queen Isabella's edict and the parchment, just as he said. Professors cheat all the time to achieve fame in their fields. Mostly scientists, but lots of others as well."

"Then I have no legitimacy. For sure, I should kill the bastard. For lying to me."

"You have another choice. You don't need a genuine parchment prepared by Queen Isabella. With a forger and Etienne's help, you can create a phony parchment that says what he attributed to Queen Isabella. He's an expert in the field. He'll know how to word it. What the parchment, letters, and ink should look like to be consistent with the time and other documents Isabella prepared. Then you can roll it around in the dirt. Make it seem old."

Musa looked intrigued. "Then what?"

"Give it to your friend Professor Khalid in Casablanca. Let him release it to the media."

"But once other experts in the field study it, they'll conclude it's not authentic."

"It doesn't matter. Scholars work slowly. By the time they discover the parchment's a fake, Easter will have come and gone. You will have used it to give legitimacy to your takeover of Southern Spain.

You'll be in control of a portion of Andalusia. They'll never be able to dislodge you."

"I like it," Musa said, now smiling. "Omar knows a forger, Hamza, in Marrakech. He prepared the fake passport Omar used to get into Italy when he stole the Vatican water plans. And he said Hamza knows how to keep his mouth shut."

"Good. Do you think Omar can get Hamza up here to do the job?"

"For money, you can get anything."

Though it was four in the morning, Musa had to begin. Time was of the essence. "I'll have Omar call him now. I have a deal with a man in Marrakech who runs a helicopter service. He'll get Hamza up here immediately."

Musa went back into the torture chamber with General Zhou trailing behind. "Listen carefully, Professor Etienne," Musa said. "If you do what I want, the electric shocks will stop and I'll untie you."

"Yes. I'll do it. Anything. Please no more."

Musa explained about the preparation of the phony parchment. Etienne eagerly agreed to work with Hamza. "I'll tell you what materials we'll need. Also a computer to access other documents from the period, particularly ones authored by Queen Isabella. It will be perfect. I promise you."

Musa ordered two of his men to lead Etienne back to his bedroom cell. Then he went upstairs and told Omar to call Hamza.

Once the arrangements were made, Musa said to Omar, "When you grabbed Etienne, did you take his cell phone?"

"Absolutely." He pulled it out of his pocket. "I'm letting his calls go into voice mail, then listening. So far just routine university stuff. If I hear anything important, I'll immediately tell you."

PARIS

Friday morning, Craig was in his office, studying reports of last night's riots. Eighty-eight police cars were set on fire in the Paris suburbs. compared with ninety-two the night before. Looting was still widespread, and arrests numbered in the hundreds. So far, no sign of the riots abating.

His cell phone rang. Elizabeth.

"Listen Craig, I got a call from Carlos in Madrid."

"And?" Craig was holding his breath.

"He said Alvarez is acting like a guy who just won the lottery. Bought a big new red Audi. Expensive suits. He's looking at brochures for property in Mallorca."

Alvarez is on the take from Musa, Craig decided. "Call Carlos back and ask him to find out where Alvarez banks."

"C'mon Craig. Don't underestimate me. I already have it. Bank National in Madrid. Carlos couldn't get an account number."

"I don't need it. I may come back to you. Where are you?"

"My editor at the paper, Rob, has me working on an article about Europe's tenuous relationship with President Dalton. The 'Death of the Atlantic Alliance' is my working title."

"Haven't you done a couple of those already?"

"Yes, but we have blank pages to fill every day. Have you ever noticed how top columnists for the newspapers repackage the same stuff over and over? And I don't want to hear one of your anti media diatribes."

"I wouldn't dream of it. I save those for CNN."

"I'm happy to interrupt if you need me."

Craig walked down the hall to IT. Clarissa was the best computer whiz he ever met. Not exactly the usual-looking geek. She was a tall, statuesque redhead.

"Clarissa," he said, approaching her desk. "Let's break into a bank."

"Sure, Craig. I love doing banks. Whose account?"

"General Jose Alvarez at Bank National in Spain. One of the Madrid branches."

"Piece of cake."

In admiration, he watched her move her long thin well manicured fingers over the keys.

"Look at this," she said pointing to the screen. "Two days ago, five hundred thousand Euros transferred into Alvarez account from a Singapore sub of UBZ."

Confirmation, Craig thought. Alvarez is definitely getting paid off by somebody. He had to prove it was Musa.

He turned to Clarissa. "Can you access the account at UBZ Singapore? Find out who put the money in that Alvarez took out?"

She shook her head. "UBZ has an impenetrable electronic wall around their database. The parent and all the subs. At least, I can't get in."

"If you can't, nobody can."

Craig wrote down the number of the UBZ Singapore account, SX23A0, and went back to his office. He picked up the phone and called Hans Schmidt, the President of UBZ in Zurich.

"Mr. Schmidt, this is Craig Page, the Director of the EU Counterterrorism Agency."

"We haven't met, but I know of you Mr. Page."

Craig explained what he wanted.

Without hesitation, Schmidt responded, "As you Americans say, Mr. Page, your request is a no brainer."

"You mean you'll give it to me."

Schmidt laughed. "You have a sense of humor, Mr. Page. Of course the answer is no."

"I could bring pressure from the President of France."

"We both know that would never happen. Besides our Singapore bank is a separate entity. It has to be under Singapore law. I have no control over it. I couldn't obtain and divulge the information if I wanted to, which I don't."

Schmidt slammed down the phone leaving Craig to contemplate his next move.

His cell phone rang. Jacques.

"Craig, you better be sitting down. You won't like this news."

"One time, Jacques, you're going to call me with something good, and I'll probably pass out with surprise. What now?"

"General Zhou slipped our tail."

"I thought you had your best people on him."

"They were outfoxed."

"I don't believe it. I fucking don't believe it." Craig was shouting. "First Lila in Marseilles. Then this. Can't they do anything right?"

"That wasn't justified. These things happen. You want to call me back when you get control?"

"I'm sorry. Give me the details."

"They thought they were following General Zhou and Androshka home after lunch yesterday at Apicius. The two of them went into his apartment. No one left until this morning when another Chinese man who looks like General Zhou came out of the apartment. Our guys got suspicious. They asked to see his ID. His name is Charlie Ming. Works for Chinese Military Sales. Says he's a friend of Androshka's. He was keeping her company last night because General Zhou is out of town. He has no idea where. They checked the apartment. General Zhou was gone."

"Have you been leaning on Charlie?"

"He's in a police station. We've been pressing him for the last hour. I waited to call you, hoping to have more info, but he won't budge from his story. He's threatening to call the Chinese Ambassador. What do you want me to do?"

"Release him. No point holding him. General Zhou is too smart to have Charlie know where he went. That's all we care about. And we have no chance of getting records from Chinese military sales. They work under the Embassy's umbrella."

"Let me give the order. I'll be right back."

When Jacques returned to the phone, Craig said, "General Zhou probably left Paris. Maybe the country."

"I agree. We have people watching his house in Antibes. No sign of him. We've checked airplane manifests out of Paris. He wasn't on any of them."

"Probably using a phony passport."

"That's where I was an hour ago. I have people examining the feed from security cameras at Charles DeGaulle and Orly."

"That's a helluva job."

"Fortunately, we're working with a narrow time window and not many Chinese men go though our airports."

"Smart move."

"I have to do something to redeem myself. I'll let you know as soon as I get any info."

"OK. Listen, I need help with a Swiss banker."

Craig outlined the problem.

"I have a solution," Jacques said. "I'll talk to a friend in the Mossad here in Paris. They get stuff out of Switzerland nobody else does. I have no idea how."

"I don't want them to know why we're interested in Alvarez."

"Gideon's always discreet. I would trust him with my son's life."

"Do it then."

Half an hour later, Jacques called back. "The UBZ Singapore bank account is in the name of Shanghai Partners, a Singapore entity. The name on the account is Shen Ling, a Chinese national. That's as far as the trail goes. Not much, I'm afraid."

"It's plenty. It means General Zhou is in this even deeper than I figured. It puts a premium on finding him. He has to be with Musa. How's the airport feed coming?"

"I'll put you on hold and call downstairs."

A minute later, Jacques was back on the line. "They located him at Charles DeGaulle. He boarded Air France 629 at 17:00 yesterday to Madrid."

"How sure are they?"

"An exact match with his visa picture."

"Good. I'll call Carlos and ask him to look at their feed from arriving passengers. Meantime, we have another card to play."

Jacques completed Craig's thought. "Androshka."

"Precisely. Keep tabs on her phone and add personal surveillance. Sooner or later he'll contact her. Then we'll grab him."

Carlos was happy to help. Two hours later, he called back. "General Zhou was traveling under the name of Wei Shu. Yesterday at 18:30, he exited the airport terminal and went to a cab stand. We located the driver, who said he dropped him at the train station in Madrid." Craig was leaning forward in his chair, listening anxiously.

"Unfortunately, the security cameras weren't working at the station."

"Oh, shit! Technology is the bane of our existence! We depend on it then it fails us."

"I agree."

"He has to be in the south. That's where Musa must be launching his attack."

"It's a large area. I'll mobilize all of our intelligence resources down there. Check train station surveillance. Hotels. Car rental agencies. Don't worry. We'll find him."

"Move fast. We don't have much time."

50

MARBELLA

Musa stood in the doorway of the upstairs room in the villa and watched Hamza, about thirty, bearded and wearing a New York Giants T-shirt and jeans torn at the knees, sitting at a table with Etienne, leaning over the parchment, with papers spread out and an open bottle of ink in the center. In a corner, one of Musa's men with an AK-47 stood at ease looking bored and tired. Bright morning sunlight was streaming in through the windows.

"How much longer?" Musa asked impatiently.

"A couple more minutes," Hamza replied.

When he was finished, Hamza said to Musa, "OK. Done. Take a look at it."

Musa stepped forward and read, "I, Isabella, Queen of Spain, do hereby grant into perpetuity to the believers of Islam that portion of Southern Spain bordered by Malaga, Cordoba, Ubeda, and Granada, including the Alhambra." At the bottom, the parchment contained Queen Isabella's signature.

To Musa, the document looked authentic, but he realized he had no expertise. He compared it with a copy of one of Isabella's actual documents Etienne had printed on the computer. They looked the same. He spot checked the letters I, S and T. They were identical. Hamza had done a good job.

"Let it dry for half an hour," Hamza said. "Then you can cover it with dirt for a few minutes to make it look old."

"Excellent," Musa said. He handed Hamza a roll of bills. "One of my men will drive you back to Marrakech. I need the helicopter."

Once Hamza was gone, Musa said to Etienne, "The guard will take you downstairs."

Etienne was staring at the document. "An official edict like this should have a border along the side."

"But the other documents don't have it."

"Those weren't official edicts."

"Why didn't you tell that to Hamza?"

"I'm tired and I forgot. But it's no big deal. I can easily add it myself. It will only take a few seconds. For that, we don't need Hamza."

"OK. Do it. I have to go downstairs and call Professor Khalid in Casablanca. As soon as the document's ready, I'll fly there to meet him."

Etienne was reaching for the pen. Musa said to the guard, "If he does anything other than work on the document … If he tries to escape, shoot to kill."

"I'm going to make you rich and famous," Musa said to Professor Khalid as he walked into Khalid's office and shut the door. It was one in the afternoon.

"I would like that," Khalid said. "I'm struggling on a teaching salary. And no one from a university in a Muslim country gets any respect in the academic world."

Musa reached in to his briefcase, pulled out the parchment, and placed it on Khalid's desk. The Professor's face lit up like a bright bulb.

"Incredible ... Fantastic ... This will change the course of history. Did you get it from Professor Etienne?"

Musa was pleased that, in his immediate reaction, Khalid accepted the parchment's authenticity. Having told Musa that Etienne had discovered the existence of the parchment, Khalid just assumed that Musa had gotten it from Etienne.

"Dodging Khalid's question, Musa said, "How soon can you call a press conference and assemble media people in Casablanca?"

"For something this significant, a couple of hours. Certainly by four this afternoon."

Musa reached into his briefcase again. He pulled out his checkbook and wrote a check to Professor Khalid for one million euros.

When he handed it to the Professor, Khalid broke out into a broad smile.

"And what do I have to do in return?"

"Present the parchment to the world at the press conference and use the script I have prepared for you."

51

PARIS

Elizabeth was typing at the computer in her cubby hole of a work station called an office. "The Atlantic Alliance has been at the heart of US foreign policy since 1945. Until Roger Dalton became President. It was inconceivable that this would change. Now …"

Over her shoulder, Elizabeth heard Rob, the foreign news editor, call from the doorway. "Hey, Liz, c'mere. You have to hear this."

Once she joined him, he turned up the volume on the television on his credenza. The CNN announcer said, "We now go live to Casablanca, Morocco, where professor Khalid is about to begin his press conference."

The Professor stood alone behind a lectern with half a dozen microphones. Elizabeth saw television cameras in the background.

Khalid began: "I have in my possession a document of enormous historical significance. For many years, I and other medieval historians have believed that in 1504 on her death bed, Queen

Isabella of Spain wrote on parchment an edict granting to Muslims in perpetuity a portion of what is now Southern Spain, bounded by Malaga, Cordoba, Ubeda, and Granada, including the Alhambra. She did so because she felt guilty for what she did in 1492. She had promised Muslims they could worship freely in Southern Spain if they put down their arms and didn't continue fighting against her Christian army. The Muslims relied on her promise. Six months later, she reneged and ordered Muslims to convert or leave Spain. Otherwise, they would be killed."

Elizabeth was stunned. What the hell's going on? This can't be right. In the myriad of texts and articles she had read on the subject, no one had ever mentioned this so-called promise of Queen Isabella. All the historians through the centuries couldn't have missed something so critical. Moreover, by all accounts, Isabella was unwavering in her hatred of Muslims to her final breath.

On the television screen, Professor Khalid picked up a parchment resting on the lectern and held it up to the cameras. "Here is the parchment Queen Isabella prepared, which has not been seen in more than five hundred years. I will be willing to answer a few questions."

One reporter asked: "Where did you get this parchment?"

"I promised my source confidentiality. I must honor that."

"What do you expect to do with the parchment?"

"Give it to a museum in Morocco."

"Questions will be raised as to its authenticity. Are you willing to submit it to an independent group of scholars?"

"I will of course consider all such proposals. Until I have one that is appropriate, I intend to keep it locked up."

"Will you make copies of the parchment available?"

He held it up again.

"All of the cameras here are filming it. Those photographs will no doubt be digitalized. So everyone in the world with a computer will have a copy. And now I must leave."

Clutching the parchment in his hand and accompanied by two armed Moroccan soldiers, Professor Khalid strode from the room, looking like a cat who had swallowed a canary.

The CNN announcer was back. "We have just heard a Good-Friday bombshell. An announcement of enormous historical significance for Spain, as well as for Christians and Muslims everywhere. Professor Khalid has told us …"

Elizabeth picked up the remote and turned the TV to mute.

Rob said, "You're writing a book on this subject. What do you think?"

Rob had no idea what she was doing with Craig involving Musa or what she knew about his plans. She had no desire to tell him she thought Musa had ginned up this phony parchment. So she said, "I think it's all a crock. Khalid was wrong when he said medieval historians believe Isabella executed a document like this on her death bed in 1504. I've never read or heard anyone even mention it. And Khalid isn't willing to make the document available now for examination."

"But it could be a new discovery. Those happen from time to time. Look at the terracotta warriors in China. Or the Dead Sea Scrolls."

Elizabeth was convinced the document was a fake. Besides everything else, coming now with Musa undoubtedly searching for legitimacy for his attacks on Europe, the coincidence was too great.

"That's precisely the point," she said. "In China, the Xian farmer who made the discovery told the world how he did it. While digging a well. For the Dead Sea Scrolls, the location, who discovered them, and details of discovery were immediately disclosed. Here, the Professor refused to say a word about any of these. Telling the world that he promised his source confidentiality confirms it's all rubbish."

Rob took off his glasses and cleaned them with a handkerchief. His thoughtful expression told her he wasn't convinced by what she'd said.

"It's an explosive story, Liz."

"I agree."

"The most significant in the world. I'd like you to drop the piece you're doing on President Dalton and move up on this story. That OK with you?"

"Sure." She would be thrilled to use the *Herald*'s resources to assist her and Craig. "With the research I've done for the book, I could hit the ground running."

"Good. Do it. But keep me posted. If you need help, don't be afraid to ask. I'll give you whatever you need."

Afraid to talk in the office, Elizabeth left the building. She walked a block, turned a corner, and called Craig. "Have you heard about Professor Khalid's parchment?"

"I heard him live on TV. I still have it on, listening to commentary. I was planning to call you. What do you think?"

"The parchment's a phony. Put together by Musa."

"I totally agree. Particularly because Khalid is in Morocco. Remember, Musa told us that his goal is to advance the Muslim takeover of Europe. This gives him some basis for a foothold."

"I convinced Rob to let me jump on it."

"Perfect. The best thing you can do is prove this parchment is a phony. And have the *Herald* publish your article. If you do it quickly, we deal a blow to Musa."

"I'll get started right now."

52

PARIS

Elizabeth asked the *Herald's* IT Department to obtain a copy of the parchment and forward it to her electronically.

While she waited, she used her computer to check world reaction to Khalid's announcement. As she expected, the story was dominating the news. European leaders were unanimous in calling it a hoax. Spanish Prime Minister Zahara hastily convened a news conference to denounce the parchment as "an outrageous fraud … a pack of lies," and an attack on Spanish sovereignty.

In contrast, Muslim governments, particularly in North Africa, lauded the discovery. The Algerian President called it "an admission of guilt" for the crimes crusaders perpetrated against Muslims.

Elizabeth switched back to e-mail. Now she had the parchment on her system. She downloaded it, then enlarged the document.

She read it several times, studying each letter and word.

She was shaking her head. She had to admit it looked genuine.

What if it is? Musa would gain a tremendous advantage.

She went into the computer file for her book, from which she located and downloaded four other documents from the late fifteenth century, two of which had been authored by Queen Isabella.

Comparing the documents with the naked eye, she concluded that if this parchment was a phony, Professor Khalid or whoever prepared it was knowledgeable. Extremely knowledgeable. The handwriting on the parchment seemed identical to Isabella's other documents.

Is it conceivable that anyone other than Isabella could have prepared it?

She thought about Professor Khalid's statement that Isabella had prepared it on her deathbed. Would anyone have been capable of writing an edict like this with death imminent? Probably not. If she were dying, would her handwriting be identical to her normal handwriting? Never.

Elizabeth picked up a loupe. Slowly and painstakingly, she searched for and compared words and letters appearing in the parchment with the same words and letters in the documents.

Then it struck her. A subtle difference, but under the loupe a difference nonetheless. In Isabella's other documents, the line on top of all the letters "T" was straight. But in the parchment, the line on top of the letters T had a slight upward curl on the right side.

She went to the *Herald*'s IT room and got a microscope with a greater magnification. When she used that to examine the parchment, she not only saw the slight upward curl on the letters "T", but the curl looked as if it had been superimposed on the original letters "T." Added as an afterthought, or at a later time.

She looked at the original documents again. The curl was definitely missing. Now she was absolutely positive the document was a fraud.

She was puzzled. The rest of the work was so good. How could the forger of the parchment have made such a sloppy mistake?

Maybe he hadn't. Maybe he was being forced by Musa to prepare it and wanted to signal experts who examined the parchment that it was a phony.

And the curl was superimposed. She groped for an explanation. One possibility was that someone other than the forger placed it there.

Regardless, with the curl someone was trying to send a powerful message: This parchment is a fraud.

Elizabeth sat down at the computer and began drafting her article. "An Historical Hoax," was her title. Then she stopped. What I need, she decided, is corroboration from a world-renowned expert on medieval history and Queen Isabella. She checked her watch. Almost five in the afternoon. Her deadline wasn't until midnight.

She tried to decide whose opinion would carry the most weight and might be available in the next few hours. One name popped into her mind: Professor Etienne at the University of Paris. He was one of the most respected people in the world. Internationally recognized. She'd met with him a couple of times in connection with her book. He'd been very helpful in directing her to source material.

She called his office and got voice mail. No surprise there. Professors are usually gone by five o'clock. She called his home. A woman answered.

"This is Elizabeth Crowder from the *International Herald*. I'd like to speak with Professor Etienne."

"My husband's in London on business for a couple of days. I don't know when he'll be home."

Elizabeth wasn't deterred. "Could you please give me his cell phone number?"

Hesitation on the other end. "I don't know. My husband doesn't like to give it out."

"Professor Etienne and I have had a couple of meetings about a book I'm doing. This is a matter of great urgency. I'm working under a deadline. I want to quote him in a newspaper article. It will help his career. I think he'd like that."

"I'm sure he would." She gave Elizabeth the number.

"Thank you very much. I'll call him right now."

Elizabeth dialed Etienne's cell immediately. Got the Professor's voice mail. This time, she left a message: "Professor Etienne, this is Elizabeth Crowder from the *International Herald.* I have clear evidence that Professor Khalid's parchment is a phony. I am planning to write an article saying that for tomorrow's paper. I would like to obtain your corroboration. My deadline is midnight tonight. Please call me as soon as possible." She gave him her office and cell numbers.

Then she went outside for a cappuccino and called Craig.

"I have proof the parchment's a phony. I'll explain when I see you."

"That's great. Will you put that in an article in tomorrow's paper?"

"For sure. I'll spend the evening drafting. Rob will review it. I'm also trying to get corroboration from Professor Etienne at the University of Paris. He's one of the top people in the field."

"Anything I can do to help?"

"Afraid not. I'll be home a little after midnight."

"I'll be up. Bring a copy."

Back in her office, Elizabeth resumed drafting. She left the cell phone on the desk next to the computer. She didn't want to miss Professor Etienne's call. When it rang fifteen minutes later, she grabbed it. "Yes, Professor."

"It's Carlos, in Spain."

"I was expecting someone else."

"I gather that. Sorry to disappoint you."

"No, no. I didn't mean that."

Carlos must have something important. "What happened?"

"Very strange. Bizarre situation in Avila, Spain, in the south. I'm not sure it has anything to do with Musa or The Spanish Revenge. But I figured it might. So you should know."

"Sure. Go ahead."

"In an isolated Franciscan monastery, the police found the dead bodies of four monks in the basement. Some had been tortured before being executed. Eyes gouged out."

Elizabeth winced.

"The police aren't releasing the information. I learned about it from a special alert from Interior to our Ministry."

"Where'd you say that was?"

"Avila, in the south."

"That's where Tomas de Torquemada was buried."

"The police observed fresh earth around his grave. So they dug down."

"And?" she said anxiously.

"Somebody had been digging there a day or so ago. They didn't disturb the coffin. Didn't take the incredible cache of jewels in a metal box. But they buried in that grave another monk who had been beaten to death and a young Arab in his thirties who had been shot and didn't have any ID. The police have no idea what occurred. We're all dumbfounded here."

Not Elizabeth. As the phony parchment on her desk caught her eye, she pieced together what must have happened. Before preparing the parchment, Musa tried to get his hands on the real one, believing that it existed and was buried with Tomas de Torquemada, the Grand Inquisitor, who would have hated the promise in the parchment and tried to conceal it for all time.

She postulated that Musa had acted in reliance on this story. When it turned out to be false, he had someone fabricate the parchment. For Elizabeth, the events in Avila were powerful evidence she was right: The parchment released by Khalid was a phony.

When I meet with Professor Etienne, she thought, I'll ask him about this as well. She couldn't wait for him to call.

Meanwhile, what to do about Carlos's information? Her conclusions were too speculative to share with him or anyone else until she spoke to Etienne. She'd even wait to tell Craig until she saw him tonight. Hopefully, after her meeting with Etienne. She thanked Carlos and told him she needed time to think about what he said and its possible connection to Musa.

After she ended the call, a shiver went up and down her spine. Five dead monks. Eyes gouged out. If she was right, and the more she thought about it the more convinced she became, then what happened in Avila demonstrated how important the parchment was to Musa. His obsession had no limits. If she could prove it was a phony and publish that, she'd be cutting out the ground from under him.

With renewed determination, she turned back to her article, stopping periodically to stare at her cell phone, willing it to ring.

Please call me, Professor Etienne.

53

MARBELLA, SPAIN

Musa heard a knock on his office door. "Come in," he bellowed.

Omar entered holding a cell phone away from his body as if it were a poisonous snake ready to strike.

"It's Professor Etienne's phone. He just received a voice mail from Elizabeth Crowder. You have to hear it."

"Well, isn't that nice."

As he listened, Musa felt increasingly worried. If Elizabeth had the evidence she claimed, the parchment would be exposed as a phony before he gained traction with it. His brilliant plan to confer legitimacy on his attack of Southern Spain would be ruined.

Musa summoned General Zhou, who had been upstairs studying maps and reviewing plans for the attack on Southern Spain.

"We have a problem," Musa said. He replayed the voice mail.

"I can't let her publish that article," Musa said emphatically. "I have people in Paris who can abduct her and bring her here. We'll put her in the room downstairs next to Etienne."

General Zhou shook his head. "Let's talk about this for a moment. Before you take action."

"We have to grab hold of the snooping bitch. That article would hurt us immeasurably."

General Zhou fired back. "You'll lose the benefit of the parchment. So what? You'll be right back where you started."

"Wrong," Musa said bluntly. "Incredible pressure would be brought against Professor Khalid. We have to assume he'd break and admit I was responsible."

"He doesn't know where you are."

"True. But his words would wreck my claim to the moral high ground in the fight for Muslim equality. My enemies would claim I'm a fraud and a charlatan. The popular uprising I'm hoping for in Europe would never occur. Who would risk his life for a man like that?" Musa paused and stared at General Zhou, "Why don't you want me to abduct her?"

"It's not wise to raise the stakes with Craig so close to the time of attack."

Musa spit on the ground. "To hell with Craig Page. He'll never be able to stop me."

"Alright," General Zhou said in a tone of resignation. "What are you planning to do? Have your people walk into the newspaper and pull her out?"

"No. Of course not. We'll have Etienne call Elizabeth and tell her he's on his way home. Have him set a meeting with her somewhere easy for my men to snatch her."

Musa looked at Omar who had been listening. "You picked up the Professor. Tell me where we should do this?"

"In front of the Professor's apartment. It's on a quiet residential street on the Left Bank, close to the University. In the late evening, likely to be deserted."

"Good. Go get Etienne and bring him up. Meantime, I'll write out the script for his call with Elizabeth."

A few minutes later, Omar led Etienne, limping into the room. "Can I go now?" the Professor said. "I've done everything you wanted."

"Not yet. One more day. You'll be home for Easter. Do you have plans for your holiday?"

"Just to be with my wife and daughter."

"You'll be able to do that. Meantime, I have one final thing."

"What's that?" Etienne asked apprehensively.

"Elizabeth Crowder, a reporter for the International Herald, she's …"

"I know who she is."

"Have you ever met her?"

"A couple of times. She spoke with me about a book she's writing."

Good, Musa thought. Their prior relationship would make this go down easier.

"She wants to talk to you about the parchment."

"What do you want me to do?"

Musa handed Etienne a piece of paper. "Call her on your cell. If you get her voice mail, read this statement. If she answers, talk to her, but stick with the substance."

While Etienne read the script, Musa picked up his gun. "If you say anything different, I'll immediately blow your brains out. Then kill your wife and daughter. Do you understand?"

Etienne nodded. Musa was confident the Professor wouldn't deviate from the script. He was a broken man. He'd do anything to save his life and those of his daughter and wife. A pity he had to die.

Musa turned up the volume to max and dialed Elizabeth's cell. He heard her answer, "Elizabeth Crowder." Then he handed Etienne the phone, put his face close to Etienne's so he could hear what Elizabeth said, and pointed his gun at the Professor's head.

Sounding natural, Etienne said, "Elizabeth: This is Professor

Etienne. I just listened to your voice mail. I, of course, heard Professor Khalid's press conference. I'd be delighted to talk to you."

"Great. I'm convinced the parchment is a fraud. I'd like confirmation from you on a couple of points."

"What are those?"

"First of all …"

Etienne interrupted her. "Oh dear. I'm at Heathrow. They just called my flight. I'm on my way home. Tell you what. I'll be back in time for your deadline. Here's my address." Etienne recited it slowly so Elizabeth could write it down. "Nobody's home this evening. I'd like you to meet me in front of the building at ten. I'll be arriving in a cab from the airport. We can go up to my apartment and talk. If I get back earlier, I'll come down for you."

"I'll be there," Elizabeth said.

Musa took back the phone and turned the power off. He was confident Etienne avoided raising any suspicion.

54

PARIS

Elizabeth took a cab to Professor Etienne's apartment and arrived fifteen minutes before ten. It was dark. Heavy clouds covering the sliver of a moon. Two street lamps at the corner burnt out.

She sent the cab away, planning to call another when she finished talking to the Professor. She was thinking about the draft she'd written thus far. A damn good article. With a couple of pithy quotes from Professor Etienne, she'd put it to bed.

Her laptop in the briefcase held the draft. She planned to make the revisions with Etienne in his apartment. Then transmit to Rob.

She was particularly proud of the last two paragraphs. "When scholars like Professor Khalid perpetuate a hoax, the public must search for their objective. Is it merely to enhance their standing in the academic world? Or are they serving some master with a political agenda?

"This parchment is so highly charged, cutting at the heart at

European stability, threatening to destroy the existing order, that suspicion of a larger goal is justified. It behooves the governments of Western Europe to force Professor Khalid to disclose all of his partners in this intellectual crime."

Looking around, Elizabeth felt increasingly vulnerable and nervous. She was the only pedestrian on the sidewalk. In the five minutes since the cab pulled away, no cars had passed. Odd, she thought, Professor Etienne wanting to meet her on the street. She tried to rationalize. If no one was home and he was coming from the airport, perhaps it wasn't so unusual.

She should have insisted that he come to her office. But face it, I never had a chance. Our phone conversation was rushed because his plane was boarding.

She walked over to the front door of his building. Above the doorbell were name plates for the occupants. Etienne was on the third floor. The only apartment on that floor.

She backpedaled to the curb and looked up. Lights were on in the third floor apartment. But Etienne had said no one was home. Nobody goes to London and leaves lights on in his apartment.

Her nerves were giving way to fear.

I was stupid to do this.

Craig. I better call Craig. He'll know what I should do.

She pulled out the cell phone from her bag. As she did, she saw a cab rounding the corner. That must be Professor Etienne. Exactly at ten o'clock, as he said. I was being paranoid.

She put back the cell phone and stood at the curb waiting to greet the professor.

The cab was a gray minivan. It stopped right next to her. The back door slid open. Instead of Professor Etienne, a bearded, swarthy man jumped out. He had a white cloth in his hand. The unmistakable order of chloroform was in the air.

She thought about the monk with his eyes gouged out.

I can't let these people take me.

He was a lot bigger, but she had the element of surprise.

As his left hand lashed out for her face with the cloth, she swung her bag with the laptop as hard as she could at the side of his head. It hit him on the cheek and nose, tearing open flesh. He screamed, blood pouring down his face. The bag slipped out of her hand.

A wild man, he lunged for her. Having grown up in Brooklyn with four brothers, she knew how to fight. She ducked away, then raised her foot and smashed the pointed toe of her black leather pump into his balls. While he was doubling over, she rolled her hand into a fist and threw an upper cut at his bloody chin, knocking him to the ground, clutching his face and groaning in pain.

She would dearly love to haul him in for questioning, but that was too risky. At least one other was in the minivan. The driver.

I have to get the hell out of here.

Her heart was hammering. Terrified, she grabbed her bag from the sidewalk, put her head down, and ran. As she passed the back of the van, two men jumped out. One was holding a two by four like a baseball bat. He swung at her from behind, whacking the wood against her ribs.

"Ah," she cried out. "Ah." The pain was excruciating.

Every instinct was screaming at her to keep running.

Run fast.

He swung again, hitting her on the shoulder, knocking her off balance. She stumbled a few more steps, then collapsed to the sidewalk, landing on her chest.

The other man pounced on her back. He looped a powerful arm around her neck. She was thrashing while screaming for help, but he was too strong. He was squeezing her throat. She felt her windpipe closing. She was gasping for air, the life draining from her body.

I was set up. God what fool I was.

PART THREE

EASTER

55

PARIS

Craig left the office at nine in the evening and stopped for dinner—steak and frites—at a neighborhood bistro on the way home. When he reached the apartment there was no sign of Elizabeth, but he wasn't worried. With her midnight deadline, he often didn't see her until one in the morning.

He settled down in his study and read Jacques's report about the riots, which were now dying down. According to Jacques, the riots began at nine, the morning after Lila was killed in Marseilles. The triggering event was a speech my Mohammad, a cousin of Lila, inciting a crowd about her death. But how did Mohammad know Lila was the victim at that time? Craig wondered. The police were still withholding her name. There was only one explanation: Someone else from Clichy, a pal of Musa, had told Mohammad. And he knew it, because one of Musa's men had killed her. Jacques' report confirmed what Craig had suspected.

He was interrupted by the ringing of his cell phone. Carlos in Madrid. "Sorry to call so late, but I have something."

Craig's hopes were soaring. "It's never too late."

"General Zhou must have taken the train to Seville. Using the phony ID, Wei Shu, he rented an Avis car at Seville train station. We have the license number. All of my men are searching for it."

Carlos's last words pricked Craig's balloon. By now he had hidden the car. And as Carlos had previously said: Southern Spain is a large area. General Zhou and Musa could be anywhere. Craig would have to find him some other way.

He thanked Carlos and returned to the report about the riots, reading about damage to property and injuries in France and elsewhere in Europe. The numbers were staggering. Musa had done a helluva job. At midnight he was tired, but he never went to bed until Elizabeth came home.

At one o'clock, she hadn't appeared and he hadn't heard from her. Craig was alarmed. Elizabeth always came home by now or called. He tried her cell phone.

Damn it. Answer.

Voice mail. Something had happened to her. She always answered her cell. He tried her office. More voice mail. God, he hated voice mail.

Maybe she was in the newsroom going over edits. He threw on clothes and sped across the Paris streets to the *Herald.*

Frantic, he charged down the corridor of the foreign news department, bumping into people scrambling, shirts out, trying to make the deadline, to Rob's office. "Where's Elizabeth?" Craig asked her editor.

Rob was shaking his head. "That's what I want to know. The receptionist downstairs checked her out at nine ten this evening. Since then nothing. I've been calling her cell every ten minutes, but no response. I was holding, front page, top right for her article about

Professor Khalid and the parchment. She told me she had proof it was a phony, but that's all I know. There's nothing on her office computer. She must have the draft on her laptop. In ten minutes, I'll have to let the space go." He shook his head again. "This isn't like Elizabeth. I hope she wasn't hit by a car or something like that."

Christ! Thought Craig. Musa. He knew what had happened to her. Musa had abducted Elizabeth to stop her from publishing the article exposing the parchment as a hoax. Craig had to find her. And fast. Before Musa killed her. If he hadn't already.

Goddamn you Musa. Where did you take her?

Panic stricken, Craig tried to recall what she said when they spoke earlier this evening. She wanted to check her article with Professor Etienne at the University of Paris.

His heart racing, Craig dashed out of the newspaper building without sharing his fears with Rob. On the sidewalk, he took out his cell phone. Though it was past two in the morning, he called Professor Etienne's house. He knew immediately that he woke the woman who answered. "Yes," she said sounding groggy.

"This is Craig Page, the Director of EU's Antiterrorism office. I'm very sorry for disturbing you at this hour, but it's an emergency. I would like to speak with Professor Etienne."

"I'm sorry, but he's not here. He's in London on business."

"Are you his wife?"

"Yes. Jacqueline Etienne."

"I think we have to talk Mrs. Etienne."

"Is it about Gerard, my husband?"

"I'm afraid so."

"Oh God. Is he hurt?"

"We should talk in person."

She gave Craig her address.

"I'll be right here."

Craig parked in front of Etienne's building. Walking toward the entrance, he noticed liquid on the sidewalk. It hadn't rained. He reached down and touched it. Blood.

As he headed into the building, his stomach was churning.

Jacqueline Etienne was about fifty, Craig guessed. Attractive woman, five two, prematurely gray. She'd gotten dressed in a navy skirt and white blouse. The living room was overflowing with books. Not merely the shelves, but the tables. Craig even saw a pile on the floor. Jacqueline's face was drawn tight. "Can I offer you something to drink," she said. As if that was required.

"No thanks."

"What's happened to Gerard?"

"I don't know. A reporter from the *International Herald* was trying to get in touch with him."

"Elizabeth Crowder?"

"Yes."

"I gave her his cell phone number and told her he was in London on business."

"Are you sure he's there?"

"Two days ago, he told me that's where he was going. He's never lied, but …" she brushed back a few strands of hair, "usually he's called me from a business trip. This time he didn't. I just thought he was busy. And I have been as well. I'm an architect, involved in a large project. So you don't think he went to London?"

"I don't know. Did he give you a hotel?"

She shook he head.

"What if you called his cell now?"

"He'd answer it. When he's away, he always has it next to him when he sleeps, in case I have a problem. We have medical issues with our daughter."

Craig was thinking. If Etienne had been abducted by Musa, they'd never let him answer his cell phone, and they'd listen to any voice mail messages. If Musa thought Craig knew that Elizabeth and Etienne had been abducted, he'd probably kill both of them immediately. So he told Jacqueline, "If he answers, tell him you couldn't sleep and realized you didn't know where he was staying in London. See what he says. But if you get voice mail, tell him nothing's wrong. You missed him and wanted to talk. Call when you get a chance."

She nodded and picked up the house phone. Sitting next to her, he heard it kick into voice mail. She grimaced. Then she left the message Craig had given her. After she powered off the phone, she said, "I don't understand. My husband has no enemies. He's a professor."

"Unfortunately, I don't have answers for you."

"I'll bet it has to do with this parchment of Professor Khalid. That's Gerard's field."

"I think so."

"What should I do now?" she asked.

"Do nothing. This is extremely important. Believe me, I'll have all the resources of France and the EU trying to locate them. Anything you do could further endanger them. Don't even tell your daughter. I know it's difficult, but …"

"You don't have to convince me. I'm a professional. I hate it when ordinary people think they know more about architecture than I do. Just please keep me informed to the extent you can. Here's my cell-phone number."

She recited it, and he entered it into his system.

He started toward the door. Then thought about the blood on the sidewalk. "Earlier this evening, maybe around ten, did you hear any commotion on the sidewalk out front?"

"Actually, I thought I heard screams. I ran to the front window. By the time I got there, I saw a van driving away. I didn't call the police or anything like that."

"What'd it look like?"

"Gray. I didn't see the license. You think it involved Gerard or Elizabeth?"

"I don't know."

Out on the sidewalk, Craig took out his cell and called Jacques.

"It has to be Craig. Nobody else calls at three in the morning."

"Musa abducted Elizabeth and Gerard Etienne, a professor of medieval history at the University of Paris."

"Because they'll rip apart Khalid's phony parchment."

"Exactly. I don't have any clue as to where he's taken them."

Craig summarized for Jacques everything he knew about their disappearance. Jacques responded immediately, talking fast. "I'll get an investigative unit over to Etienne's apartment to check the sidewalk and talk to neighbors. Also I'll have all police units in and around Clichy begin searching and asking questions. Musa may have taken them there."

"Good idea. I'll call Carlos and have him on the lookout in Southern Spain."

"Meantime, let's pay a visit on Androshka. She might know where General Zhou is. That'll be a start. Besides, I've been hoping to get at her after she helped General Zhou lose my guys."

"I want to be there. Meet you in front of their building in thirty minutes."

The beauty of driving around Paris at three thirty in the morning, Craig thought, is that there is no traffic. Some street cleaners. Not much else. A light mist began falling. A traffic signal changed to red. Not wanting to risk skidding, Craig blew threw it. All he could think of was Elizabeth. And finding her.

Jacques was waiting for Craig in front of General Zhou's building. No umbrella. The collar up on his tan windbreaker.

"How do we do this?" Jacques asked.

"Bad cop. Bad cop."

Jacques repeatedly rang the bell of the building manager's

apartment. From inside a man shouted, "Wait a damn minute." Jacques was holding up his ID. "French Intelligence. Open up."

The man did. Elderly, disheveled, dressed in black striped pajamas that made him look like a zebra.

"We want to go up to General Zhou's apartment," Jacques said.

"Be my guest."

"Let's skip the elevator," Jacques said. "My doctor told me I need more exercise."

Jacques took off up the stairs with Craig right behind. By the time they reached the fourth floor and General Zhou's apartment, Jacques was puffing so much, Craig was worried he'd have a heart attack. This time, Jacques ignored the bell and pounded on the door. For a minute, there was no response.

"Maybe she's gone as well." Jacques sounded dejected.

"I hope not."

They heard a woman call through the closed door. "Who's there?"

"French Intelligence," Jacques shouted, and held up his ID.

When the door opened, Craig, who'd never seen Androshka before, thought she was one good looking woman, even at this hour with her blonde hair falling over her eyes. She was wearing a blue silk robe tied loosely enough to show some of the sheer peach nightgown beneath, and half of her breasts, in case that would solve whatever problem she had.

Once they were inside, Craig looked around. Ming vases were scattered throughout the room. A sword hung above the fireplace. Chinese art lined the walls.

Jacques said, "Androshka Ilyvich?"

"Yes."

"Where's General Zhou?" Craig asked.

"Not here. I have no idea."

Craig left Jacques alone with her and searched the apartment. No one else was there. He returned and repeated. "Where's General Zhou?"

"I don't know."

Jacques went on the attack. "Show me your citizenship papers."

She looked chagrined. "What papers?"

"Exactly. You entered this country two years ago as a tourist and never applied for citizenship or a visa. Go get dressed. We're arresting you for being in the country illegally and as a material witness to a crime."

"What crime?"

"If you watched more French television, you'd know we don't have to specify. Now get dressed."

"Where will you take her?" Craig asked as if he wanted to know.

"To the jail in the First. Let her share a cell with killers, druggies, prostitutes, and perverts we pick up at night. Maybe that'll help her remember where General Zhou is."

She was shaking.

"Where is he?" Craig asked again.

"I don't know. I swear it."

"Get dressed."

She loosened the tie on the robe. She's certainly not a natural blond, Craig thought, from the dark pubics showing through the thin peach silk.

"Can't we solve this another way?" she said.

"You really are something," Craig said.

She gave him the finger, turned around and headed toward the bedroom.

"I'll get dressed."

"Good," Jacques said. "I'll watch you."

At the jail, a female guard supervised Androshka's changing into an orange prison uniform and handed Jacques her cell phone. She was trying to look defiant. Craig thought she was ready to cry.

They led her into an interrogation room, windowless, dirty beige walls, suggesting an aura of despair, with a phone on a table.

Jacques was holding a file. "Turns out you've been in this jail before, Androshka Ilyvich."

"I don't know what you mean."

He was leafing through pages. "A month after you arrived in Paris, you were giving sex for money to a wealthy Dutch businessman. You stole his watch and five thousand Euros. Obviously, you thought what he paid you was insufficient for the outstanding services. They brought you in here and threatened to deport you back to Russia. I'll notify all the Russian police and security agencies. You pleaded that Mikail Ivanov, a Russian Oligarch, would kill you if you came back. I guess you stole money from him too."

"Mikail was an evil man."

"Was?"

"He's dead."

"Did you and General Zhou arrange his death?"

"I'm not saying any more."

You have a choice," Jacques said, "Tell us where General Zhou is, or we'll begin processing papers in the morning to deport you to Russia. Even if Mikail's dead, I imagine his pals would like to get hold of you."

"No," she wailed. "No."

Jacques pulled a page out of the file. "Hey look at this. On your last arrest, a year and a half ago, the detective left you off with a warning. What'd you do, let him fuck you on the table?" He smacked the palm of his hand against the tabletop. "Sorry, we don't do that. This time you're shit out of luck."

"You can avoid deportation," Craig said. "All you have to do is tell us where General Zhou is."

She began crying, looking at them wide eyed. "I don't know. I swear it. He just left after lunch at Apicius. He didn't tell me."

"That's a shame. I hear it's still winter in Moscow. I hope you kept the fur coats Mikail bought you. Or that you bought with the money you stole from him."

More tears. Louder.

Craig now believed she didn't know where General Zhou was, but he wanted to use her to locate him. "Tell you what," he said, "we're about to give you the biggest gift of your life."

"What's that?" she asked with suspicion in her voice.

"Jacques will give you back your cell phone so you can call General Zhou. You can't tell him you've been arrested. You're calling to tell him how lonely you are without him. All light and personal. Small talk. Most important, you have to keep him on the line for one minute. If you do that, we'll release you and won't bother you anymore."

She looked at him wide eyed. "You want to use the call to find out his location."

The woman was no dummy.

"That's right."

"You want me to betray General Zhou?"

The question hung in the air. Craig waited to see if she would do it. She had to know she was between a rock and a hard place. He felt as if wheels were turning in her amoral mind doing a cost-benefit analysis.

"OK. Give me my cell phone," she finally said.

"It'll take us a couple of minutes to get this set up," Jacques said. "I'll go talk to the techies." He sprang out of his chair and headed toward the door.

When they were ready, Jacques handed her the phone. Craig and Jacques were sitting across the table. Craig had a hearing device hooked to his ear which would permit him to listen.

Her fingers were shaking as she dialed.

General Zhou answered on the first ring. "Why are you calling, Androshka?"

"Because I miss you. I want to talk to you," she said in a soft, sexually enticing voice.

"I told you not to call." He hung up the phone.

She was shattered. She never dreamt it would go that way. She put her head into her hands and down onto the table.

"I guess he doesn't love you as much as you thought," Craig said. "The thing about men is that we're led around by our dicks only so far. Sorry. You just lost your get-out-of-jail card."

She picked her head up. "Go fuck yourself."

"OK. Here's your situation," Craig said. "For now, we're not sending you back to Russia. We'll keep you in jail. A guard will hold your cell phone. If General Zhou calls, you can try to keep him on the line for a minute. If not … Well I guess you'll be here for a very long time. Till hell freezes over."

Once the guard took her away, Jacques said to Craig, "General Zhou is obviously worried that someone's monitoring her calls."

"I was concerned about that. But it was worth a shot."

Craig would try anything to locate Elizabeth, regardless of the odds of success. His cell phone rang.

"Yes, Giuseppe."

"We finally got lucky. An unmarked van was involved in a crash with a car on Victor Emmanuelle in Rome. The driver was a Muslim living in Torino. Name is Rachid Nezzar. He was shaken up, but not seriously injured. The police on the scene found a gun in his possession so they got suspicious and opened the back of the van. Found a single box that said Chinese computers on the side. I've got the Rome police on alert so the officer on the scene called me."

"And?" Craig said impatiently.

"I had the bomb squad open the box. No computer. Instead a Chinese surface-to-surface missile."

"Yes," Craig said aloud. "Yes."

"I thought you'd like it."

"Where's the driver of the van?"

"In custody, in the building I share with the *carabinieri*. He's in a locked cell being watched. We took his belt and shoelaces so he can't kill himself."

"Good work."

"Yeah, I remember what happened after the train explosion. You almost had that guy and he blew himself up. You want me to interrogate Rachid, or you want to be here?"

Craig was torn. On the one hand, he didn't want to leave Paris until he located Elizabeth. On the other, the Arab in the Rome prison might lead them to Musa, which would be a way of locating Elizabeth. Also, Jacques was experienced and had all the French police at his disposal. Not much Craig could contribute to their search.

"Hold on a minute," he told Giuseppe and explained the situation to Jacques.

The Frenchman said, "You have to go. With all due respect, you can't help much here. We'll have the blond Russian princess under close surveillance. I have police units scouring Paris for Elizabeth."

Craig returned to his call with Giuseppe. "I have to stop at the office and pick up something we'll need. Then I'll take the first plane to Rome. Together, we'll squeeze this guy."

56

MADRID

At seven in the morning, the Parque de Retiro in Madrid was deserted. General Zhou left his car in a parking lot off Calle Alfonso XII and walked along a path crisscrossing through the lush park grounds which had once been a 350-acre royal playground.

When he called Alvarez last evening to set their meeting next to the lakeside monument to King Alfonso XII, Alvarez had sounded apprehensive, as indeed he should. Negotiations were proceeding for Spain to purchase Chinese aircraft. Alvarez, whom General Zhou learned had already withdrawn funds from the Singapore bank account, no doubt thought he'd seen the last of General Zhou.

Approaching the monument, General Zhou saw Alvarez seated on a park bench reading a newspaper. Cracks of sunlight were appearing in the eastern sky and reflecting from the lake. General Zhou sat down next to him on the bench.

Alvarez kept the newspaper raised. "I was surprised to hear from you."

"I saw the new red Audi parked in the lot with the license plate ALV-1. Are you enjoying the car?"

"It rides smoothly," Alvarez said awkwardly. "And the acceleration is unbelievable."

"Don't drive too fast. I wouldn't want anything to happen to you."

Alvarez put down the paper. "Why'd you call?"

He doesn't want to risk being seen with me. He'd like to leave as quickly as possible. And I don't blame him.

"I need you to do something for me."

"I've already done something for you. My people are negotiating the airplane purchase. Per our arrangement. That's all. We're finished."

General Zhou pretended he didn't hear what Alvarez said. "This morning I want you to issue an order moving all your troops out of Southern Spain. Immediately. Sending them to the Basque country in the north."

Alvarez picked up his paper and fiddled with it, creasing and uncreasing it. "Why would I do that?"

"You've received secret intelligence that the Basques are planning a military attack on Easter Sunday against government facilities."

Alvarez now understood. "You're working with this terrorist Musa. He's planning an attack in the South on Easter."

"That's preposterous. Stick with what you know."

It was cool in the morning air, but Alvarez was perspiring. "I'm no traitor. Negotiating for airplanes is one thing. This is quite another."

"How about taking a bribe of ten million Euros to walk away from a Boeing proposal and begin negotiating with the Chinese? Which side of the line does that fall on?"

"You can't prove that." Alvarez sounded indignant.

General Zhou reached into his pocket and pulled out a micro cassette. "I recorded our conversation at lunch in the South of France."

All of the color drained from Alvarez's face. "You bastard. You're trying to blackmail me," he said weakly.

"I prefer to think of it as friends helping friends."

"What will happen in the South of Spain?"

"You don't have to know. An attack by Basques in the north is perfectly credible."

"I won't do it." Alvarez sounded belligerent.

General Zhou shrugged. "Your choice. I'm prepared to provide copies of the recording to newspapers and television stations in Madrid."

"Why did I ever get mixed up with you? Chinese bastard."

The words stung, but General Zhou kept calm. "You wanted the money. And you wanted to fuck Masha. It's as simple as that."

"I could call your bluff."

"Not a good move against an adversary who's holding all the cards."

"I could tough it out."

"You'll not only lose your position, but go to jail." General Zhou shrugged again. "You decide."

Alvarez ran his hand through his hair. A desperate man searching in vain for a way out.

"If I give the order," Alvarez finally said in a trembling voice, "I'll be questioned by the Prime Minister and others in the government. They'll want to know about my intelligence sources with the Basques. What'll I do then?"

"Once you give the order, board a plane with your family to Buenos Aires. It's a long-planned vacation."

"You think of everything. Don't you?"

"I try."

General Zhou wrapped his fingers around the micro cassette and shook his hand holding it. "Well, what'll it be?"

"What choice do I have?"

"You don't."

"OK," he said with resignation. "I'll do it."

"I'm glad to hear that. I'm sure you'll enjoy Argentina."

Alvarez got up and stormed off. General Zhou remained on the bench, even after he saw the red Audi roar away.

He should be happy. A large part of his plan with Musa had fallen into place. Without Spanish troops in the south, Musa's forces, with their sophisticated Chinese arms, would establish a beachhead. Then roll north.

But General Zhou was miserable. Elizabeth's involvement confirmed for Zhou that Craig Page was leading the charge to defeat him and Musa. That meant Page was responsible for Androshka's arrest. Again Craig Page. Always Craig Page. Blocking him, foiling his plans. He pounded his right fist into the palm of his left hand. That damned Craig Page. This time, he had to kill Page.

And he also had to find a way to free Androshka. She wasn't just another woman. She made him feel things in bed no other woman ever had. Taking her back to Beijing as his mistress was part of his master plan.

He captured my queen, General Zhou thought. But he had Page's queen as well. In a few hours, Musa's men would be bringing Elizabeth Crowder to the villa in Marbella and installing her in the basement cell next to Etienne. She would be helpless. He'd be able to do whatever he wanted with her as a way of getting at Craig Page. But none of that will get Androshka back.

ROME

Giuseppe was waiting for Craig in the interrogation center of the concrete *carabinieri* building that resembled a large block. Against one wall was a hospital bed. Two computers were on a table. Lots of wires and electronic gear hanging from the ceiling. A large wash tub on another wall. A wooden table with four chairs in the center.

"Anything happen with the prisoner since we spoke?" Craig asked.

"He's spent a lot of time on his knees praying to Allah."

"He'll need all the help he can get. One way or another he's going to tell us where he was taking that missile and what he knows about the overall plan."

"We have to assume the threat of a long jail term won't loosen his tongue."

"Agreed."

"You want to go with water boarding?"

"My experience with it hasn't been great. Often I've ended up with unreliable information. Chemicals are much better. On the way to the airport, I stopped at the office and picked up some Sodium Amytal." Craig reached into his bag and took out a bottle that resembled cough syrup. "This has worked consistently for me, particularly with non professionals, like this guy, the poor stupid dopes who get drawn into terrorist attacks by ideologues like Musa."

"How do you inject it?"

"In his arm. Get me a syringe and a couple of strong officers to hold him down."

Ten minutes later, two powerfully built men in khaki uniforms led the prisoner into the interrogation room. He had a scraggly brown beard, bruises around one eye, and freshly dried blood on the side of his face. Must be from the accident, Craig guessed.

Craig had left the syringe on a table in the corner. Let him see it and know what awaits him. The *carabinieri* pushed the prisoner into one of the chairs at the table. Craig was across from him. Giuseppe on Craig's right.

"Please state your name?" Craig said.

"Allah Akbar. God is great," he responded defiantly.

Craig pointed to the chemical and syringe in the corner. Either you talk to us voluntarily or we have other ways of getting into your brain."

He looked wide eyed. "Allah Akbar," he repeated.

Without any warning, he flung himself across the table, his arms outstretched, hands going for Craig's throat. This had happened to Craig on two other occasions, and he was ready. Before the prisoner reached him, Craig rolled his right hand into a fist and smashed it against man's jaw. Craig heard the crunch of bones breaking. Teeth fell from his mouth. Unconscious, he slipped off the chair on to the floor.

"Good reflexes," Giuseppe said.

"Been there. Done that."

"Takes away the need to strap him down while we inject the chemical."

"True. But before we inject him, let's throw ice water on his face. I don't know if it'll work if he's unconscious."

One of the *carabinieri* pulled the prisoner to his feet and held him while the other poured ice water over his head waking him. They tied him down on the bed. Craig injected the chemical. He checked his watch.

"We have to wait thirty minutes for this stuff to take."

Once the time was up, Craig began the questioning. "State your name."

"Rachid Nezzar." The words were mumbled, but clearly understood.

"Address?"

"Number twelve Via Albert. Torino, Italy."

That coincided with his driver's license. Craig was pleased. This will work.

"Why were you driving the van?"

"I was asked to do it by Omar, an old friend from Clichy."

"Did you ever live there?"

"Until a year ago. Then I moved to Torino, because I found work in a Fiat plant."

"Where did you pick up the van?"

"A warehouse in Torino located at number twenty, Via Sardegna."

"What was your destination?"

"An apartment on the third floor of number seven, Via Paglia in Rome."

"What were you carrying in the back of the van?"

"A Chinese made missile. I was shown how to operate it by a Chinese man in the warehouse."

"What's the name of the Chinese man?"

"I don't know."

"What were you planning to do with the missile?"

"Fire it at the Pope at ten in the morning on Easter Sunday, when he speaks to the people assembled in St. Peters Square."

A gasp went up from the officers.

Craig wanted to believe they had now foiled the attack, but he knew better. He tried to think like Musa. In Musa's position, he would have multiple missiles. So he asked, "Are other missiles to be fired at the Vatican?"

"Yes. Three others. Each of us was given one missile to fire."

"What are the locations for firing those other missiles?"

"I don't know. Omar told each of us only our own location."

"Are you certain of that?"

"Absolutely. I asked Omar and was told it was none of my business."

"Who are the other three people with missiles?"

"I don't know. We were all wearing masks."

Giuseppe wrote Craig a note. "Do you believe him, or should we try water boarding or something else to get the other locations?"

Craig wrote back, "I believe him. Under the chemical he couldn't lie about this. Also, Musa's too smart to give them all the addresses. Only he and Omar know."

Giuseppe nodded. "I don't have any questions."

Craig turned to the *carabinieri*. "Take this piece of dog shit back to his cell."

When they were gone, Craig and Giuseppe sat down across the table.

Craig took out his cell phone and stared at it, willing it to ring. He desperately wanted to hear Elizabeth's voice on the other end.

"What's wrong?" Giuseppe asked.

"Elizabeth was abducted in Paris last night by Musa. Also a professor of Medieval history at University of Paris. Elizabeth was planning to expose Professor Khalid's phony story about the parchment, which Musa no doubt engineered. So I'm a little distracted."

"Why don't you go back to Paris?"

"Jacques is doing everything possible to locate Elizabeth. I'm hoping to get to her by following the thread for the Vatican attack back to Musa."

"You got quite a bit from Rachid's interrogation."

"True, but we're missing a lot more. Have your military people examined the missile?"

"I asked them to and email me. Let me check."

He took out his Blackberry. "It's the latest Chinese. Range is twenty kilometers."

Craig gave a long low whistle. General Zhou's buddy, Freddy, must have made the whole Chinese arsenal available. "I can't even imagine how many potential locations there are in a twenty kilometer radius from St. Peter's Square."

"I can't either, but I intend to use all the cops and law enforcement agents I can get my hands on. They won't be able to search every location, but they can ask people if they've seen anything suspicious. Vans pulling up and being unloaded. Stuff like that."

"You're right to do it. But trouble is, judging from Rachid, the missiles were delivered around two or three a.m. Not many people up then."

"More than you think. This is Rome. We'll start immediately. Also, monitor all cell communications moving out of Rome toward Spain or Morocco."

Another fact was depressing Craig. Musa hadn't assembled an army of thousands to launch these four missiles. Another attack was coming as well. But where? When?

Craig's cell phone rang. He pounced and grabbed it, hoping it was Elizabeth. No. Carlos.

"Elizabeth didn't answer her phone. She said to call you if I couldn't reach you."

"What happened?"

"Alvarez gave an order this morning moving all Spanish troops out of Southern Spain immediately and north into the Basque country. He wants the redeployment concluded by Saturday, eleven p.m. When I asked him why he was doing that, he said he had received intelligence pointing to a Basque attack on San Sebastian and Bilbao on Easter Sunday. He wouldn't disclose his sources. I called my own agents in the Basque community, who are well connected. They say it's rubbish." Carlos was excited, talking so fast that he had to pause and take a breath.

Before Craig had a chance to respond, Carlos continued, "Right after Alvarez gave the order, he said he was leaving for a vacation with his family in Argentina. I knew I had to get the information to you and Elizabeth immediately."

"You did the right thing. I can't thank you enough."

When Craig ended the call, Giuseppe said, "I assume that wasn't about Elizabeth."

"Correct."

Craig told Giuseppe what Carlos said. As he spoke, all the pieces came together. On Easter morning, Musa planned two operations. A missile attack on the Vatican, aimed at the Pope as he was talking to the crowd in St. Peter's Square. And an invasion of Southern Spain, supposedly justified by the phony parchment.

He picked up the phone and dialed the office of Zahara, the Spanish Prime Minister. He got as far as Juliana, the Prime Minister's secretary, who remembered Craig from the Spanish train bombing. When she said her boss was in a meeting, Craig asked if the Prime Minister could meet with him this afternoon on a matter of extreme importance to Spain. They settled on three o'clock. Craig told her, "Please keep this meeting extremely confidential. It must be just the two of us. And nobody can know."

58

MARBELLA

Musa glanced up from his desk and the battle plan he had been reviewing in a notebook when Omar led Elizabeth, arms tied behind her back, into his study. They were followed by the three men who had abducted her from the Paris street. She had bruises on her body, but she looked defiant.

Salim, one of the three men, had bloody towels over his face.

"What happened to you?" Musa asked.

One of the others spoke up. "She beat him."

Musa was astounded. "You let a girl do this to you?"

Salim didn't respond.

"What's your excuse?"

When Salim still didn't say anything, Musa picked up his gun and shot the man. "Get him out of my sight," he barked to the two others who had been in the van.

Elizabeth was still standing erect. Not cowering. He admired her courage.

When the others were gone and it was just Musa, Omar, and Elizabeth, he said to her, "I can't let you publish your article about the parchment. You realize that?"

"Yes," she said in a bold voice.

"What makes you think it was a hoax?"

"It's inconsistent with everything I've read about Isabella's life."

"Specifically what?"

"Isabella's hatred for Muslims. She was vicious and unrepentant to her last breath. The parchment is totally out of character."

"You consider yourself such an expert on medieval history with your Harvard degree."

"I've learned a little. Enough to recognize that killing Lila wasn't a very creative act on your part. You knew about Florinda. It may have led to a popular uprising then. It won't now. People saw through it."

He ignored her taunt. He still wanted to determine whether her conclusion about the hoax was based on her knowledge of Isabella or whether she had found a defect planted in the parchment by Etienne. If Musa could see her draft article, he'd know. "Did she have a laptop with her?" he asked Omar.

"It was in her bag. She used it to strike Salim in the face. After they tied her down, he destroyed the computer."

Musa groaned. "Ah ... What an imbecile."

He turned to Omar. "Blindfold her and take her downstairs. Put her in the other cell."

Musa returned to his battle plan, but he couldn't concentrate. He was anxiously awaiting General Zhou. The meeting with Alvarez was critical to their operation.

An hour later, Zhou arrived. As usual, the man's face showed nothing. Musa slammed the door to the study. "How did it go?"

"Alvarez agreed to do what we want. Spanish troops are already being deployed from the south to the north."

"Excellent."

They began reviewing the final plans for tomorrow morning's invasion.

"My goal," Musa said, "is to retake the Alahambra, the majestic palace that signified the rule of Islam in Spain. Once again that will be the ruling center of Muslims in Europe. With the Spanish troops out of the area, thanks to Alvarez, we'll be able to move fast across the countryside, cutting a path from our landing point to the Alhambra in Granada. Meantime, like Saladin during the Third Crusade, I'll be rallying Muslims throughout Europe to join in my struggle. The parchment will be of enormous help in gaining support. A glorious day awaits us," he said with enthusiasm. "A day where …"

Musa was interrupted by Omar entering the office, a horrified expression on his face. "What happened."

"I've heard from three of the four men deployed in Rome. They reached their destinations with rockets intact and ready to fire tomorrow morning."

"And the fourth?"

"Rachid should have phoned in with a coded message. He hasn't. I don't want to call his cell phone for fear the call will be traced."

Musa shot to his feet. "Rachid is an idiot and incompetent. I don't know why you selected him for such an important job."

Omar's eye was twitching. "I thought I could depend on him. It was an error of judgment. I'm sorry."

"'Sorry' doesn't cut it. We have to assume Craig Page and Giuseppe have seized Rachid and he's spilled his guts." Musa was shouting. "This could jeopardize our whole Vatican operation. How could you have been so stupid?"

"They all had guns. They were supposed to kill themselves rather than be taken alive."

"He doesn't have the courage."

"Would you like me to resign as your deputy?:"

Musa grabbed the gun on his desk. "I don't tolerate failure." He aimed at Omar.

Before he could fire, General Zhou said, "Hold on a minute. I think you're overreacting." He turned to Omar. "Did Rachid know the locations of the other three who will be firing missiles in Rome?"

"No. I was careful to give them only their own addresses. When they were together, they were all wearing masks."

"Suppose Page learned one of the locations, would this lead him to the others?"

"Absolutely not. The four are each on a different radial line from the Vatican. And at varying distances. If you look at a map of Rome, the four would seem like random selections. All they have in common is they are within twenty kilometers of the Vatican."

"Along with thousands of other locations."

Omar nodded.

"This means that Page and Giuseppe have twenty four hours to find three needles in a haystack. They can't possibly locate them, particularly because your people are now in place and won't be leaving their locations."

"That's right."

Shifting the gun from hand to hand, Musa was glaring at General Zhou. "Why are you defending Omar?"

"He's valuable to the overall operation. If his mistake won't jeopardize our plans, I don't want to lose him."

"You think I'm becoming too emotional. Too erratic. A commander who's losing control on the eve of battle."

"I didn't say that."

"Humph." Musa gripped the Beretta tightly and glared at Omar.

Suddenly, he put down the gun. "Perhaps I did overreact. Omar, you've worked hard and been loyal. We're so close. I just don't want it to slip away now."

"I understand," Omar said, relief in his voice.

Musa turned back to the open notebook on his desk with the plans for the invasion.

"We'll talk about the landing point," Musa said. "I want our troops to come in just to the east of Gibraltar. That will cut down on the time we'll be on the water."

"I think that's a mistake," General Zhou said. "It will be better to make land further to the east. To the east of Malaga. With the element of surprise and the cover of darkness, being at sea is not risky. The advantage is that it will reduce enormously the distance our troops have to cover on land to get to the Alhambra. Those will be tough kilometers, each one bitterly contested. It has another advantage. They'll be expecting us to come in close to Gibraltar. This will fool them."

Musa thought about what General Zhou said. He was right, of course. "We'll do it that way."

Musa leafed through the rest of the notebook. Then he said, "We're ready. I'm going back to Morocco today. I want to lead my troops in the invasion. At the front of the lead boat. Omar, you'll come with me."

"I'll remain here in Marabella," General Zhou said. "I want to be close by in case I can help with the battle."

"Good. I'll call if I need anything."

Omar asked, "What should we do with two prisoners downstairs?"

Musa was tired. He'd forgotten about Elizabeth and Professor Etienne. Now he focused.

Musa had to decide what to do about the two of them.

"We'll go downstairs and I'll kill the Professor," Musa said, pronouncing an immutable death sentence. He picked up his gun.

"And Elizabeth ?" Omar asked

"We should use that hellcat for sport."

"What do you mean?"

"After I kill the Professor, we'll strip off all her clothes. Yours too.

We'll lock the two of you in her cell for a fight to the death. You'll have fun. Right?"

He knew Omar was afraid to disagree with him.

"Yes. Fun," Omar said glumly.

"You don't sound like you mean it. Afraid she'll get the better of you?"

"That'll never happen."

Musa noticed General Zhou frowning. "What's bothering you? Against fun?"

"It's OK with me."

Musa turned back to Omar. "General Zhou and I will be watching from the outside through the glass in the bars. We'll see whether you're man enough to subdue her, then rape and strangle her as you did with Lila. But if she kills you, then I shoot her. Either way she dies."

Now fully alert, Elizabeth sat on the bed in the cell like room trying to assess her situation. They hadn't killed her in Paris. They hadn't gouged out her eyes. Not yet. At least they'd taken off the ropes from her wrists and ankles. The blindfold was gone.

Her whole body hurt like hell. She was certain she had several broken ribs. She hoped no internal injuries. Her shoulder ached. She didn't have a mirror, but she was sure her neck was severely bruised, because breathing was difficult. She recalled Musa shooting Salim. I'm better off than the guy I hit with my bag, she thought. For now, anyhow. Maybe not for long.

Elizabeth had only a vague recollection of how she had gotten here. She had been bundled into a small plane and put into a large box. After the flight, someone placed a blindfold over her eyes and led her to another car. In the backseat he tied her wrists and ankles. She heard someone say, "It's half an hour drive to Marbella." It was useless knowing where she was. She had no way of reaching Craig or anyone else for help.

She recalled her bizarre encounter with Musa upstairs after

they took off the blindfold. He was a madman, killing her bleeding attacker, capable of anything.

She didn't know whether Professor Etienne was still alive. In the event he was, she was glad she protected him. Not telling Musa how she discovered the hoax.

Thinking about her next encounter with Musa sent shivers up and down her spine. A rat ran across the floor. That terrified her even more. In Brooklyn as teenagers, her brothers used to hunt rats. When they did, she ran and hid.

The room had a bathroom on one side. A while ago, a man had deposited a tray of food inside the door and gone away. He wasn't wearing a facemask. He didn't care that she saw him. That confirmed Musa was planning to kill her. Her death was the only way Musa could ensure that she didn't publish the article.

No one will ever find me, she decided. She blamed herself for being stupid. For being so intent on her story that she'd gone to the Professor's house without anticipating the risk. If only she'd told Craig about the strange meeting that had been arranged. He would have sent bodyguards with her. Well, it was too late for that.

She heard knocking on the wall. She moved closer, making sure she wasn't imagining it. More knocks. She knocked back. Then put her ear against the wall. A muffled voice called out. "I'm Professor Etienne. Who are you?"

He had to be in the cell adjacent to hers.

"Elizabeth Crowder."

"Please forgive me for getting you here. I had no choice."

"I know that."

"Did you notice the curl on the letter "T" in the parchment?"

"Yes. How did it get there?"

"I put it on. I realized Musa would kill me regardless of what happened. I had no chance of saving my life. So I tried to signal that the parchment was a fraud. To get back at him that way. Did you let others know?"

"I didn't have time, but scholars will find out. Just as I did."

"That's good."

"Don't give up hope." She recalled being tied to the stake in Musa's base while he and the other horseman held their spears. "Never lose hope. Salvation is always possible."

She heard loud voices coming down the stairs toward her cell and the Professor's.

The men with the loud voices, Musa and two others, went into Professor Etienne's room.

She heard the professor scream. "No. No. Don't kill me. I did everything you asked ... No ... No ... Please."

"You're no longer of use to me. Only a threat."

"But I won't tell anyone. I swear."

"Get off your knees. Stand up straight. Die like a man."

Then the unmistakable sound of a gun firing. Once. Twice. Three times. Elizabeth was trembling.

She heard Musa say, "He's dead. Now we'll have fun with Elizabeth. Then kill her."

She couldn't summon the hope she had urged Etienne to embrace. She was resigned to her death. Willing to face it with courage.

With alarm, General Zhou watched Omar strip off his clothes. Was Omar planning to enjoy this sadistic game of Musa's or was he too terrified of Musa to object? More bizarre behavior on Musa's part. This could have serious repercussions.

General Zhou had failed to block Elizabeth 's abduction, which led to Page seizing Androshka. For sure, he had to stop this crazy sport. He couldn't let Musa kill Elizabeth. Not while Page had Androshka. Elizabeth was his only bargaining chip to get Androshka back. But he couldn't tell Musa that. Musa would laugh at him and tell him he was a fool. One woman was no different than another.

Besides, Musa was a hothead, as he had shown with the man he killed upstairs and by almost killing Omar. General Zhou had to be careful, or Musa would turn the gun on him. Tell him, "I no longer need you." Unquestionably, Musa was becoming unglued as the attack drew closer.

While they were leaving Professor Etienne's cell, the smell of gunfire in the air, General Zhou clutched Musa's arm. "Let's talk for a minute. Just the two of us."

Musa looked at naked Omar and said, "Wait here. Stroke your prick. Get it ready."

General Zhou led Musa down the corridor to a deserted room. He had to approach this carefully. "I've been involved in a lot of military operations over the years," he said.

"And?" Musa sounded impatient. "Omar's waiting. I want to start the game."

"Everything rarely proceeds exactly as planned."

"I know that. I'm no fool."

"As Sun Tzu declared in *The Art of War*, over two thousand years ago, it pays to keep every option open. Every resource at your disposal."

"What the hell does that mean? Do all you Chinese talk in riddles?"

General Zhou swallowed hard. "Having Elizabeth alive and under our control gives us leverage over Craig Page if we need it at a critical point. We gain nothing by killing her."

"Wrong. I'll get pleasure from watching the bitch die." Musa had wild look in his eyes. "She's arrogant, and she's been a thorn in our side. Almost as much as Craig Page. They've been in this together from day one."

"Precisely my point. The two of them have a tight bond. They're much more than lovers. Page's wife died. His daughter was killed. He has no family. Without her, he might not be able to continue. He'd do anything to save Elizabeth."

"Like what?"

"I'm confident we'll prevail in battle. But there's always

uncertainty. Suppose it all goes to hell. You'll need something to trade with Page for your own life."

"You really think he'd ever make a deal like that?"

"Of course. He'll tell himself that he can come after you in the future. But meantime, he'll be giving you a chance to begin anew. In an Islamic bastion in Europe."

Musa didn't respond. General Zhou pressed ahead. "You have no downside to doing it my way."

"I lose the satisfaction of watching her die. Right now."

"We're talking about a short delay. A matter of days. Once we succeed, we'll kill her immediately."

"You think I should take her with me back to Morocco this afternoon? And in a pontoon boat when we move into Spain in the morning?"

General Zhou shook his head. "She'll be in the way. Better to leave her with me locked in this cell. She won't be able to harm us. I have a gun. When I hear that you've retaken the Alhambra, I'll kill her."

General Zhou could see that Musa still wasn't convinced. "You have to believe me on this, based on my military background. Haven't I successfully guided and supplied you to get to this point?"

"OK," Musa said reluctantly. "I'll follow your advice."

59

MADRID

"I appreciate your seeing me on short notice," Craig said to Prime Minister Zahara, once he entered the huge wood-paneled office and Julianna had departed.

"Today is a bad day for me. As you may have heard, on Thursday our stock market fell like a rock in a pond. I was hoping that, with the Easter weekend, we could pull the financial markets together. Then this morning I learned that one of our largest banks is in trouble. But from the message you conveyed to Julianna, I knew I had to meet with you."

Your day is about to get a lot worse, Craig thought.

"Have you received information about another terrorist attack in Spain? Like last year's train bombing."

"Worse than that. As you know, the man responsible for that bombing calls himself Musa Ben Abdil. He has assembled an army of thousands in the Atlas Mountains of Morocco, equipped with the latest Chinese weapons. I've been watching him for some time. Unsure of his objective. Today I put the pieces together. He's planning to attack Southern Spain tomorrow and seize part of your country."

The Prime Minister was on the edge of his chair, listening carefully, his eyes blazing with intensity. "I assume the business with the parchment is related to this attack."

"Precisely. Musa arranged its fabrication."

The Prime Minister reached for the phone. "I have to get General Alvarez in here. We have to prepare to defend our territory."

"Alvarez is a traitor. He's on the take from Musa."

Craig felt as if he'd tossed a live grenade on the desk.

The Prime Minister's head snapped back. "What are you telling me?"

Craig summarized the phone calls Carlos had made to Craig and Elizabeth, Craig's bank investigation, the troop deployment order, and Alvarez's trip to Argentina. "He's probably on a plane to Buenos Aires right now."

"I'll have him extradited. He'll face a firing squad."

"I agree with that, but right now you have a more immediate problem. Defending your country."

"When do you think Musa will attack?"

"Tomorrow morning. Easter Sunday."

The Prime Minister reached for the phone again. "Then I better get Carlos in here. I'll appoint him Acting Defense Minster. He'll have to reverse the deployment order and mobilize our troops."

Waiting for Carlos to come, the Prime Minster called his wife. "We have a problem. I don't know when I'll be home … Yes, I know about the dinner tonight … Start without me," he said sharply. "I'll be there when I can."

He put down the phone and shook his head. "Even after all these years, she never understands … Are you married, Craig?"

"No, sir."

"Oh that's right. You're in a relationship with that newspaper woman. Sorry. I'm terrible with names."

"Elizabeth Crowder." Even mentioning her name underscored Craig's anxiety bordering on desperation about Elizabeth. Before entering Zahara's office he called Jacques for about the thousandth time. They didn't have a damn thing. The blood on the sidewalk wasn't hers. The police couldn't get any information in Clichy. Camera feed at Charles De Gaulle, Orly, and train stations hadn't turned up a thing.

"Before you marry her," Zahara said, "make sure you have an understanding about your work. Of course, I couldn't do that. I needed Lina's money and family connections. Ah. Well ..."

The door opened. Briefcase in hand, Carlos bounded into the office, looked at Craig and nodded. Craig said, "Mr. Prime Minister, I want to tell you how valuable Carlos has been in uncovering Alvarez's treachery."

The Prime Minister turned to Carlos, "Craig thinks Musa's army will be attacking Southern Spain tomorrow morning. I'm appointing you Acting Defense Minister. I want you to reverse the order deploying troops to the North. Also, convene a meeting of the top Generals of the Army, Navy, and Air Force in my office in one hour. I don't care what they're doing. They must be here or they'll lose their rank. Together, we'll develop a war strategy."

"I've been doing some checking," Carlos said. "It'll take time to get the troops back into the South."

"I understand. Let's get moving."

Craig said, "I don't think you should fight this battle alone. You could get help from other EU countries. France, Germany, and England could send planes and troops. They could be here in a few hours."

"No," the Prime Minister retorted quickly, angrily, and firmly.

"Why not?"

"We are a sovereign nation," Zahara said with lots of pride and arrogance, Craig thought. "We defend our own nation."

Craig glanced at Carlos, hoping for support. The young man met Craig's gaze, then looked way, unwilling to challenge his leader. Machismo and obedience rules again.

Craig realized it was impossible to change the Prime Minister's mind about accepting help. There was nothing else for him to do in Madrid. He just hoped the Spanish military was up to the task.

Meantime, he'd go back to Rome and help Giuseppe thwart the attack on the Vatican. Or, heaven forbid, deal with its consequences and the thousands of casualties.

Craig and Carlos left the Prime Minister's office together. Out in the corridor, Carlos said, "I hope you understand why I couldn't join in your suggestion of calling for foreign troops."

"Of course. No need to apologize."

"I also want you to know I have police, military, and intelligence forces searching for Elizabeth in Southern Spain. We're dealing with a difficult terrain and lots of territory. So far we haven't learned anything. I promise we'll continue at an intensive level. I like that woman. I want to find her."

On the way to the airport he called Jacques again. No news. A heavy, dark cloud enveloped him. He had heard nothing about Elizabeth, and he was no closer to gaining her release. With each passing hour, the chances of her being alive grew dimmer. But he didn't know what else to do.

60

ROME

The sun was setting when Craig climbed the stairs of the *carabinieri* building and rode up to Giuseppe's command center on the third floor.

"Good timing," Giuseppe said. "A few minutes ago, I received a call from a policeman in the area of Piazza Navona. He was walking around questioning people. An elderly man said he's in pain with arthritis; he can't sleep. So he often looks out of the window. Last night, about three in the morning, he saw a van pull up to a building across the street. He said an Arab carried out a cardboard box. Looked like it had a picture of a computer on the side. He carried it into the building across the street, then drove the van away. He returned in a cab an hour later."

"Our second shooter," Craig said.

"It all fits."

"They must be stashing the vans in a garage."

"Probably planning to use them for their getaway."

Giuseppe tossed Craig a Kevlar vest and put one on under his jacket.

"I have police watching the shooter's building. I hope unobtrusively."

"What floor's he on?"

"Don't know. It's an old three-story building. One unit to a floor. We'll start at one and work our way up."

"Agreed. I'll bet he's on three. A better shot at the Vatican."

"I'm figuring that, too."

Giuseppe handed Craig a pistol. "Let's go. I told the cops, 'If this guy runs, grab him. We don't want kill him. We want to talk to him.'"

"Based upon our interrogation of Rachid, chances are this guy won't know the other locations."

"We can always hope. People get sloppy. They talk. Others listen."

Rush-hour traffic was dreadful. "Welcome to Rome." Giuseppe said. "It's like this every evening."

He slapped a flashing light on the roof of his car and activated the siren. It didn't do much. He couldn't get around the cars in gridlock. A fifteen minute ride took thirty, with Giuseppe cursing all the way. Craig learned lots of new Italian words and phrases.

Thirty minutes later, they arrived at the Piazza Navona. Craig didn't see a police car. Good. They were keeping out of sight. Two cops were inside the front door. One in the back. When Giuseppe went into the front with Craig, the cop said, "No movement. We talked to a woman on the first floor who was going out. She said her third floor neighbor moved out a month ago. Somebody rented it. She doesn't know who."

"Did you ask her about the second floor?"

"Elderly couple. Lived here forever."

Giuseppe looked at Craig. "My city. I'm going first."

Giuseppe told the cops to remain at the doors in case something went wrong.

The ancient wooden stairs creaked as they climbed, guns in hand.

Craig wondered whether Giuseppe would give any warning before they went in. He didn't. He took a locksmith's tool from his pocket and used it to quietly unlock the door. He twisted the knob softly, opening the door slowly. Craig, gripping his gun tightly, was standing behind Giuseppe. They didn't hear a sound. Keeping still, they stepped into the apartment.

Guns in hand, Craig and Giuseppe tiptoed into the living room. They couldn't see anyone. A pizza on the table looked as if it had been recently eaten. An empty bottle of water was next to it.

One bedroom was to the right; another to the left. Craig motioned that he'd take the one to the right. Stealthily, he moved down the hall. The bedroom door was ajar.

From the corridor, Craig saw a bearded Arab looking man sitting on a bed playing a portable video game, a gun resting next to him. At the window, a missile launcher was aimed at the Vatican.

Craig was preparing to shout, "Hands up," when the man spotted him. He tossed the video game at Craig. As Craig ducked, the Arab grabbed his gun, jumped up, and held it to his own head.

"Wait," Craig cried out. "You don't have to do that. I can get you immunity. You'll be free."

The man had a crazed look on his face.

Craig thought about aiming for the Arab's gun, but it was flush against the man's temple.

Only one way to stop him.

Recalling his football days, Craig left his feet and hurled his body through the air going for a flying tackle. At the instant he made contact, the Arab pulled the trigger, splitting open his head, splattering brain and tissue against the wall.

For Craig, the noise of the Arab's gun blast was deafening. Dazed, Craig fell to the floor, the Arab's blood on his head and face, holding his ears. The sharp stinging pain in Craig's ears was almost unbearable.

In a blur, he saw Giuseppe rush into the room. Giuseppe's lips were moving. Craig couldn't hear a word.

Giuseppe was using his cell phone. He helped Craig to his feet, placed an arm around his shoulders, and led him out of the building.

On the street, an ambulance was waiting. Medical personnel standing next to it. They put Craig on a stretcher and cleaned off his face. A doctor was taking his blood pressure; another was examining him.

They were talking to him. "Can't hear you," Craig said. "Can't hear you."

They loaded Craig into the back of the ambulance, with Giuseppe next to him. The ambulance roared away. The pain was still intense. Craig wondered if he'd ever hear again.

At the hospital, a doctor checked him and inserted ear drops. He went through an MRI. Then another exam. Three doctors in hospital blues were consulting.

The pain was starting to ease. He heard faint sounds.

Half an hour later, a doctor was talking to Giuseppe. "He'll be OK," the doctor said.

And Craig heard every word. Albeit faintly.

"Yes," Craig shouted. "Yes."

The doctor explained, "It will take a little while, but your hearing should return to normal."

Craig was straining to hear the muted words. The doctor handed Craig a bottle of eardrops and a prescription.

"Let's get out of here," Craig said to Giuseppe.

"Don't you want to rest?"

"No time for that. Tomorrow's Easter."

In the car, Giuseppe said, "Sorry, I couldn't get there in time to help."

Finally, Craig clearly heard every word.

"No way we could have done it better. Besides, chances are this guy wouldn't have known any more than his own location. The good news is that we've taken the second missile out. You saw his missile setup?"

Giuseppe nodded. "The guy had a clear shot at the Pope on his balcony."

"The other two will have equally good shots."

"We have to work all night to find them."

Craig shook his head. "You're always an optimist, Giuseppe. I love you for it, but the odds of finding the other two are between slim and none."

"So what do we do? Give up and let them kill the Pope and lots of innocent people who happen to be in St. Peter's Square tomorrow morning?"

"No. We have to convince the Pope to cancel his appearance and lock the gates to St. Peter's Square."

"I'm all for that. Cardinal Donatello is in charge of security for Vatican City. Let's go talk to him."

They decided Giuseppe should make the pitch to Donatello in the Cardinal's Vatican City office. Better to use the home-town boy.

Donatello was distinguished looking. Tall and thin. In his seventies. He had intense, gray eyes behind wire-framed glasses. The room was small and crowded with bulky, wooden furniture that must have been created in the Renaissance. When he didn't see a computer or any high-tech equipment, Craig wondered how Donatello could possibly manage security. A glass case in the corner held a magnificent gold cross studded with rubies.

As Giuseppe summarized the situation and its urgency, Craig studied Donatello for body language. There wasn't any. Giuseppe was talking to a stone wall.

At the end, the Cardinal said, "Do you realize what you're asking."

"I do, sir," Giuseppe said politely and deferentially.

"Are you a Christian?"

"I am."

"Then you understand the sanctity of the day you're asking me to profane."

"I'm trying to save the life of his Holiness and many other innocents. Also, the Vatican's priceless structure."

"We have never done anything like this."

"I realize that, sir. This is an unusual situation."

"I understand that, but I can't agree to your request."

"Perhaps I didn't make it clear." Giuseppe continued, "The man calling himself Musa Ben Abdil is determined to renew actively the war between Christians and Muslims in Europe. If he succeeds tomorrow in killing the Pope and damaging the Vatican, he will achieve his goal. The Christian response against Muslim communities will be violent and severe. They will then respond in kind. Bloodshed and death among both religions will be horrendous. Surely, you don't want that to occur?"

"Of course not," the Cardinal said. "But canceling the Pope's appearance would mean surrendering to a terrorist. For that's what Ahmed Sadi is. To reward him with victory is unthinkable. The armies of the lord will not prostate themselves before this infidel."

"I'm not asking you to do that. By calling off tomorrow, you will give us time to capture him. Time to avoid further bloodshed."

"Today's discussion," the Cardinal said, "proves the great wisdom of the Vatican's independence. We cannot be buffeted by temporal forces. I'm sorry, but I have made my decision."

Craig admired Giuseppe's polite perseverance. He wouldn't have been as gracious. But Giuseppe wasn't getting anywhere. Craig decided to speak up. "Since the Pope's life is at stake, perhaps we can talk with him."

The Cardinal seemed indignant.

"Security matters are under my control."

"Will you at least consult with him? I doubt if you'll be on that balcony tomorrow. Certainly not after what you just heard."

Shaking his head in anger, Donatello stood up. "I'll speak with his Holiness." Then he stormed out.

Giuseppe turned to Craig. "One thing I've always admired about you Americans is your tact and finesse." Then he smiled.

"I figured at this point it couldn't hurt."

"I agree. We were dead in the water. I like to kid you."

Fifteen minutes later, Donatello returned, a smug look on his face. Craig knew the answer before he opened his mouth.

"I've consulted with his Holiness."

"And?" Giuseppe asked anxiously.

"He refuses to change the plans for tomorrow. He asked me to thank you for your concern and to tell you that he is not worried. The matter is in the hands of God."

61

ROME

Despondent, they returned to Giuseppe's office.

"Ready for Plan B," Giuseppe said.

"Sure."

"Suppose we make an announcement in the media telling people we have information about a possible attack in St. Peter's Square tomorrow morning."

Craig shook his head. "Won't accomplish a thing. After so many vague terror alerts, people ignore them. Some might stay home, but most will be there. Remember, they're coming from around the world to hear the Pope. A once-in-a-lifetime experience. And he'll be there, for sure. The rockets will kill him. Damage the structure. Kill thousands."

Giuseppe sighed. "Yeah. You're right. The crowds will come. Also, I'd be in trouble with my government for not honoring the independence of the Vatican. Definitely a non-starter. I'll call my police contacts and tell them to redouble their efforts to find the other two missiles. Work all night. Even though we think it's futile. What else can we do? We can't build an impenetrable missile shield around St. Peter's Square."

"Wait a minute," Craig said in a burst of enthusiasm. "You just gave me an idea. We do have another alternative."

"OK, I'm listening."

"The high-tech approach. The most advanced planes are equipped with heat-seeking air-to-air missiles. Each of the two launchers we recovered was equipped with only a single missile. Presumably that'll be true for the other two. So we put planes in the air a little before ten with heat-seeking air-to-air missiles. Musa's shooters will fire their missiles, but they'll never reach the target. Our planes will blast their missiles out of the sky."

"The Star Wars approach." Giuseppe's face was flushed with excitement. "I love it. But we have a problem."

"What's that?"

"I am concerned that we couldn't get the Italian Air Force mobilized in time. The US Air Force has planes based at Magdalena off the coast of Sardinia with that capability. They are on alert around the clock. That would be a better alternative."

Giuseppe was right. United States assistance was the only way.

Craig didn't have a relationship with top officials in the Pentagon or in the US Air Force. The lines of communication for his agency with the United States ran to the CIA.

Craig recalled his last encounter with Norris. He hated having to go back to that asshole, but he didn't have a choice.

"Norris?" Giuseppe said, reading Craig's mind.

"Uh huh. Given how he behaved with the satellite photos, it'll be a tough sell."

"There is a difference. Now we have a definite and immediate threat."

"If we were dealing with a rational person, that would carry the day."

"Can you go around him?"

"I know how Washington operates. He has the point. If Brewster were still President, I could go over Norris. I never even met Dalton."

Giuseppe pushed the phone across the desk. "Bite the bullet."

Craig called Langley. Though, it was Saturday afternoon, the Director was in his office.

"We need your help, John," Craig said to Norris in a polite tone. "You're on the speaker with me and my deputy, Giuseppe." Craig explained to Norris the serious immediate threat, confirmed by the capture of two of the four missiles. Also, the necessity for involving US planes. When he was finished, there was a long pause.

"Well," Craig said. "Italy is an ally of the United States. I'm asking your assistance to stop an attack on Italian soil."

"I'd like to help you," Norris said. "I really would. But you're aware of President Dalton's strong views about disengaging from European matters."

"Don't you at least want to talk with the President?"

"I have a clear sense of his priorities."

Craig was flabbergasted that Norris would do this on his own. He was becoming enraged. "You're a fuckin' idiot, John."

Norris slammed down the phone.

"Well, that certainly worked," Giuseppe said.

"I felt better saying it."

"Happy to provide an outlet for your therapy."

"It's inconceivable he wouldn't check with Dalton."

"I guess we're stuck. You said a minute ago that you don't know Dalton."

"Correct. I can't call the President."

Craig was thinking. He'd be damned if he'd let that twit Norris block him. There had to be a way around the CIA director. Then it hit him. Yes! That was the solution.

"But I do know somebody who can call Dalton," Craig said.

"Who?"

"Your Italian President Cerconi."

Giuseppe was looking at Craig wide-eyed. "And how are you planning to do that at eleven o'clock on Saturday evening, the night before Easter?"

"I'm not. You are."

Giuseppe took a deep breath, sounding like a child pushed onto a high diving board, who now had to leap. "OK. Stay here."

Left alone, Craig was thinking about Elizabeth. He had to find her and free her. But right now he didn't have the faintest idea how to do that. My only choice, he concluded, is to stop Musa's attack, then capture him or General Zhou. One of them has to know where she is, and by God, I'll get the information out of him. He didn't even want to contemplate the alternative: that they had killed her.

Giuseppe returned fifteen minutes later. "Cerconi is hosting a dinner at the Quirinale. I spoke to Fabrizio, his top aide, who's there to field calls. I told him how extremely urgent this is. If we come now, he agreed to pull Cerconi out of the dinner. 'Cerconi won't be happy about this,' he told me. 'He doesn't like to be disturbed during dinner.' If Cerconi doesn't think this merits dragging him out of dinner, Fabrizio threatened to cut off my nuts. Because that's what Cerconi will do to him."

"That's a good way to run a government."

"In Italy we play hardball politics. No pun intended. Let's go."

62

ROME

Craig had never before been in the Palazzo del Quirinale, the ornate residence of the Italian President.

Walking from Giuseppe's car toward the pale-yellow-stone sprawling structure, Craig passed the fountain lit with floodlights in the piazza and the ancient Egyptian obelisk moved here from the mausoleum of Augustus. The Quirinale was on top of the highest of the seven hills of Rome. Spread out below in the clear night sky were the sparkling lights of the city, as far as the eye could see. A great metropolis that would be in mourning in less than twelve hours if we don't stop the attack.

As Craig stepped into the richly furnished marble foyer, history smacked him in the face. This palace had once been the residence of the Pope. Ironic, in view of tonight's mission.

Then, until World War II, the Quirinale was the home of the King of Italy. Nearly every famous Italian architect since the renaissance had worked on the structure.

For Craig, with roots in Italy, being in the palazzo had powerful emotional significance. He thought about his grandfather and his father. They would have been proud of him now, standing in the Quirinale.

Fabrizio, a tall, balding, taciturn man in his sixties came down the marble corridor to meet Craig and Giuseppe. He led them up a heavily polished, dark wooden, winding staircase to a second floor study containing a red leather-topped desk with a phone and four bulky, brown leather chairs.

"You two wait here," he said. "They're still at the dinner table. I'll go get him."

"We appreciate your help," Giuseppe said.

A few minutes later, Cerconi entered the room followed by Fabrizio. He was a handsome man, with movie-star looks, who reminded Craig of Cary Grant at fifty. Dressed in a dark gray cashmere suit molded to his body. Swaying as he walked. Craig guessed he'd had a lot of wine. And why not? It was almost midnight on Saturday night.

When he opened his mouth during the introductions, he slurred his words, making Craig nervous. He'll never be able to do this.

But the politician's instincts and graciousness kicked in. "I'm sure the two of you wouldn't be here unless you had information about an imminent terrorist attack. I appreciate your coming. I know it wasn't easy."

Giuseppe pointed to Craig who said, "That's right, Mr. President. Let me quickly review what we know. We don't want to keep you any longer than necessary."

"Don't worry about that. Francesca will entertain our guests without me."

Craig winced at the name. It drove home for him the stakes.

In his summary Craig talked slowly, figuring that Cerconi's mind was dulled with alcohol. He was astounded by the crisp, pointed questions the President asked. He clearly understood the gravity of the situation. He arrived at the action item before Craig. "So you want me to call President Dalton and ask him to put those planes in the air tomorrow morning?"

"Precisely."

"Do I have any leverage?" Cerconi was thinking aloud. The politician's proclivity for the deal. "I could threaten to terminate the base leases on Magdalena—but he might say—'Alright. We're happy to pull out'—Definitely not an option—I'm as well to play it straight. Appeal to his sense of decency. I met him once. He's not an ogre." Cerconi smiled. "Well, maybe not totally."

Craig always formed snap opinions of people. He liked Cerconi.

The President looked at Fabrizio. "Get Dalton on the phone and put him on speaker."

Craig was pleased they'd passed the first hurdle: Cerconi agreed to call.

The next hurdle was getting past Dalton's Chief of Staff. Fabrizio kept pushing until he succeeded.

Once Dalton was on the line, Craig's hope rapidly dissipated. Dalton was cold, if not rude to the Italian President, who talked about their prior meeting when Cerconi visited the United States. Cerconi promptly got to the point and told Dalton, "Craig Page, EU Director of Counterterrorism, has solid evidence that a missile attack is planned for tomorrow morning at ten against the Vatican in an attempt to assassinate the Pope, destroy the Basilica of St. Peter's and kill thousands of people. Craig tells me the only way we can prevent this attack is if the United States puts planes with heat-seeking missiles into the air over Rome. You have those planes based at Magdalena."

Dalton snapped back, "Have you discussed this matter with John Norris?"

"I did, Mr. President," Craig said. "He refused my request or even to take the issue to you."

"So you decided to go over his head."

Craig swallowed hard. "Yes sir. In view of the urgency of the situation and the threatened harm."

"Well, John understands my position about this country not becoming entangled in European matters."

"We're not asking you to become entangled," Cerconi interjected. "It's simply a question of two airplanes for an hour or so."

"These matters always begin small."

"My government has no other way of thwarting this attack."

"Craig, you were born in the United States and lived there much of your life. You know how much of our resources we've squandered in recent years in foreign engagements. We've lost thousands of our best people. Destroyed our financial stability. Vietnam. Iraq. Afghanistan. I don't have to tell you about these. As a matter of principle, I feel strongly that we have to pull back."

Craig felt his blood boiling at the stupidity of what he was hearing. "This issue is totally different. We're not asking for American troops."

"But it's only a first step. Our planes could be shot down. Our pilots killed. Next you'll want us to spearhead an attack against the terrorists."

"I wouldn't do that, Mr. President. I can assure you."

"The American people," Dalton continued while ignoring Craig's words, "agree with me on the need to scale back our foreign involvements."

Time to play the only card I have.

"That may be true," Craig said, "but as you pointed out a minute ago, I was born and lived in the United States for much of my life. I know a great deal about the country. You'll be running for reelection in November. Less than eight months from now. One thing I know is that the United States has millions of Catholic voters. With all due respect, Mr. President, they'll be very unhappy if they learn that you had a chance to stop the Pope from being assassinated, the Vatican blown up, thousands of pilgrims killed while you refused to lift a finger to help."

"Nobody will find out about it," Dalton quickly retorted.

"You're aware that these anonymous leaks happen, Mr. President," Craig said. "Somehow the press gets hold of the information. Nobody knows exactly how."

Cerconi was smiling and nodding with approval.

Craig thought he heard Dalton mutter the word "bastard," in a low growl.

Dalton was silent for thirty seconds. Finally, he said gruffly, "OK, two planes for an hour. Craig, coordinate logistics with Jim Perry, my National Security Adviser. I'll tell him to expect a call from you. Is there anything else President Cerconi?"

"Nothing. I want to thank you for your assistance."

"Alright then."

The line went dead. Cerconi was laughing. Deep belly laughs. He took a cigar from his jacket pocket and lit it. "You really nailed him with that Catholic voter point."

"Thank you, Mr. President."

Cerconi blew smoke into the air. "I owe you two a great debt of gratitude. I can't imagine how awful it would be if those bombs strike. I just hope you can stop them."

"We'll do our best, sir."

Cerconi stood to leave. "Giuseppe," he said. "Keep Fabrizio informed. He'll arrange to have all our hospitals and medical resources on alert without creating a panic. And he'll report to me." He looked at his aide. "Right?"

"Yes, sir."

Craig was glad he'd be working with Perry, rather than Norris. When Craig had been in the CIA, Perry had been an Air Force

General and Craig's point man in calling for strikes against suspected terrorist bases in the Middle East. Perry was professional. He'd get the job done.

"Let's go back to your office," Craig said to Giuseppe. "By then hopefully Dalton will have called Perry. Jim's a good guy. No bullshit. This will work."

When Craig called, Jim Perry was in the loop. For the next hour, Craig and Giuseppe coordinated with Perry and General McCallister, the base commander at Magdalena. By three a.m. Rome time, all the details had been hammered out. Two US planes would be on the runway, fueled and armed, at six in the morning in case they were needed earlier. The Pope's appearance was scheduled for ten. At nine thirty, the planes would take off for Rome. From nine fifty on, the planes would be circling over Rome, ready to take out the missiles as soon as they were launched.

Then Craig called Carlos in Madrid. "How are your preparations to resist Musa's attack?"

"To be honest, confused and disoriented. Alvarez's redeployment order made everything much more difficult." He sounded weary and frustrated. "Army, Navy, and Air Force officers are squabbling. I'm sorry I didn't speak up and urge Zahara to bring in military assistance from France, England, and Germany."

"I doubt it would have made a difference."

"Right now I feel as if I live in a country of lovers, not warriors."

"Anything I can do to help."

"Unfortunately not. I'm flying down to Seville to our command center. I'll call when the attack starts and keep you posted."

Craig and Giuseppe moved cots into Giuseppe's office in the hope of getting a couple hours sleep.

Tomorrow would be a long and brutal day.

Elizabeth tried to sleep in order to maintain her strength, but it was futile. So she got up from the bed and paced back and forth across the windowless cell, totally disoriented, not knowing whether it was day or night.

She had no idea why Musa had shot Etienne, but not her. Food was brought to her periodically and trays taken away by a polite, bearded, young Arab man. Though she had no appetite, she forced herself to eat. At any minute she expected Musa to barge in the door and execute her. But until he did, she refused to lose hope.

She recalled her captivity with the Taliban, when she had been a reporter in Afghanistan. She had kept constantly alert and vigilant. When her guards became careless, arguing about Afghan politics while she was exercising, she ran into the forest. By the time they realized she was gone, she had a good start. She ran fast. Tearing past branches that scraped her while ignoring the shots from behind. Finally, she made it back to NATO-controlled territory. Here, too, she might get an opportunity to escape. Guards became board and sloppy. When that happened, she'd make a break for freedom.

63

ROME

At five thirty, Craig was lying on a cot, dozing when Carlos called. He sounded frantic. "The attack has started. They're making land east of Malaga in fast boats. General Bernardo, our chief of staff, insisted they would come in close to Gibraltar. So our troops are out of position. We're trying to catch up. Rushing more men to the East. The fighting is fierce. They're advancing."

"What about air support? Do they have planes?"

"No. We have complete control of the skies. The only good news. We were hitting them in their boats. But it's dark. Once they're on land, our air force will have a tougher job. Too many civilians in the area. Lots of places to hide. We'll be limited to pinpoint bombing. The main battle has to be fought on the ground."

"Casualties?"

"Many killed on both sides. They've shot down a dozen planes.

We're astounded at how good their army is. And well equipped. We expected a ragtag motley crew."

Craig wasn't surprised. General Zhou was responsible for supplying and training Musa's army. And General Zhou had built the Chinese military into a rival of the United States.

"Which way are their troops moving?"

"In his last report, General Bernardo wasn't sure. Let me check with him."

A few minutes later, Carlos was back on. "They're heading in a Northeasterly direction."

Craig recalled Musa's killing of the Spanish policeman in the parking lot in October. Musa was obsessed with the magnificent Alhambra, the red palace finished in the fourteenth century after a hundred years of construction, with its thirteen towers and fortified walls.

"That's what I figured," Craig told Carlos. "Musa's heading straight to Granada. He wants to retake the Alhambra."

"That means if we shift troops to the Granada road, circle behind the fighting, we can cut them off before they reach the Alhambra and destroy their army."

"Precisely."

Maybe I should fly to Spain, Craig thought. No, not now. I have to remain in Rome until we resolve the attack on the Pope and the Vatican.

After Craig relayed Carlos's depressing report to Giuseppe, his Deputy said, "The Spanish obviously underestimated Musa and General Zhou."

"Yeah. I hope we're not making the same mistake here."

As the sun rose over Rome, Craig and Giuseppe climbed to the top of the six-story *carabinieri* building, each with binoculars in hand.

The sky was robin's egg blue. Not a cloud for miles. Craig lifted the binoculars to his eyes. He had a clear view of the Vatican balcony above St. Peters Square, where the Pope would make his appearance at ten o'clock.

He called General McCallister. "What's the status?"

"Both planes are on the runway. The pilots understand their mission."

After Craig put the phone back in his pocket, Giuseppe said, "Once Musa's two guys with the missiles see the planes overhead, you think they'll figure out what we're planning and abort?"

Craig considered the question. "If Musa or General Zhou were here, I'd say that was a real possibility, but you saw Rachid, whom we interrogated with chemicals. He didn't have military sophistication. And I doubt if they'll be in cell phone contact with Musa. He must have told them no cell phone calls. Besides, he's tied down in his battle in southern Spain."

"Yeah. I guess they're robots. They won't be thinking."

Giuseppe called to check on the search going on in Rome to locate the other two shooters. Craig heard him say, "Nothing ... You don't have a single lead ... Keep going. We still have time."

Craig wasn't surprised. Rome was a large city. They had gotten lucky twice with Rachid and the guy who blew himself up. Four times was too many.

It all comes down to the two United States planes.

At nine o'clock, Craig called Carlos. "What's happening?"

"I'm in Seville with General Bernardo at the command center. Our estimate is that Musa started with ten thousand men. He's down to about five thousand."

"That's good."

"Agreed. Not good is they've broken through our defense line northeast of Malaga. They're headed in the direction of Granada, as you predicted."

"Were you able to fortify the roads outside of Granada to cut them off?"

"We didn't have time. They were moving too fast. We had some troops in the area, but not enough to stop Musa's advance."

Craig asked Carlos to put General Bernardo on a speaker phone. When he had both of them, Craig said, "Listen. I know Musa. I was his prisoner a few weeks ago. I understand his goal. He wants to take the Alhambra. Then use his conquest as a rallying cry to Muslims throughout Spain and all of Europe to begin an insurrection against their Christian rulers. He'll use the media to do that. Do you understand what I'm saying?"

Both men responded, "Yes."

Craig continued. "I intend to alert law enforcement people throughout Europe of the threat. And urge them to keep the peace and avoid bloodshed.

"If the widespread insurrection doesn't occur, we will be able to isolate and surround Musa and his troops in the Alhambra. That means we have to do two things. First, as they march toward the Alhambra, kill off as many of his men as possible with pinpoint bombing and artillery while minimizing your own casualties. Second, clear everybody out of the Alhambra and the immediate area. This is critical. We can let Musa take control of the Alhambra. We can't let him take prisoners."

General Bernardo spoke up, "You're saying we should surrender the Alhambra to him." He sounded incredulous.

"Yes. We can't run the risk of damaging the building. Or permitting him to seize hostages."

"But by surrendering the Alhambra, we'll look weak and inept to the rest of the world," General Bernardo said. "Also to our own people. The Spanish military will become the butt of jokes. Laughed at throughout Europe."

"I'm not talking long-term surrender," Craig said emphatically. "I'm talking short-term tactics. We want Musa to make exactly the same mistake the Muslim General Musa Ben Abdil made in 1492. Trapping himself and his troops in the Alhambra. The Muslims lost then, and Musa will lose now if we play it smart."

"But," Carlos said. "What if Muslims around Europe respond to his call for a uprising?"

"Then heaven help us."

"We'll follow your recommendation," General Bernardo said reluctantly.

Craig next called Jacques in Paris. "Talk to each of your counterparts in the other EU countries," Craig said. "Tell them Musa will be calling for a Muslim insurrection."

"I'll make sure they have troops near the Muslim areas."

"Also, have them work with Muslim community representatives. There are millions of decent law abiding people in those communities. Enlist their help in avoiding bloodshed."

64

ROME

For Craig, the time dragged, each minute seeming like an hour. He thought his plan to stop the missiles was foolproof, but what if Musa had a surprise in store? Also high tech military equipment wasn't perfect. Malfunctions occur. Human error, always a possibility.

"Stop worrying," Craig told himself. "You did everything you could. The US Air Force is damn good."

Finally, nine fifty. Craig looked up. No planes. Where the fuck are they? He grabbed his cell to call General McCallister. Then he saw them. He picked up his binoculars. Two gorgeous F-35's, sparkling in the bright sun. Circling over the city, manna in the sky. Thank you President Dalton.

Captain Goldini, from the *carabinieri*, Giuseppe's liaison, joined them on the roof. Also binoculars in hand. "Everything's set," he said. "I have men scattered around the city. Once I get the location of the missile shooters, we'll arrest them. We'll get firefighters to the scene of falling debris. The President's office has dozens of ambulances with supporting medical personnel close to St. Peter's Square."

"Let's hope we don't need them." Giuseppe said grimly.

Craig recalled a recent dinner at Giuseppe's house. When he arrived, Paolo, twelve, was in front of the television, totally engrossed in a video game trying to blast missiles from the sky with other missiles. And he was good at it. The boy had fabulous hand-eye coordination. He got most, but not all of them. Unlike Paolo, we have zero tolerance for error.

Craig lifted the binoculars and focused on St. Peter's Square. Mobs of people, thousands, from around the world, were milling around, waiting for the Pope, for his words and blessing. They had no idea of the danger threatening them. Craig located the line of ambulances a block away.

He glanced up at the balcony above the square. The door opened. The Pope, looking frail, walked outside accompanied by an entourage. No sign of Cardinal Donatello. The Pope raised his arms and began speaking.

Craig scanned the city. Suddenly he saw it. From Trastevere, southeast of the Vatican, a missile streaking through the air on a trajectory for the balcony above St. Peter's Square.

It was moving fast. "Now. Fire now," Craig cried out.

As if the pilot heard him, one of the F-35s released a heat seeker. It raced toward the missile headed for the Vatican. A bullseye! Blasting it apart. The debris falling onto Janiculum Hill.

At that instant, a second missile was fired from the northeast, about twelve kilometers away. It was tearing through the air heading directly toward the Pope.

The second plane hadn't released its heat seeker. What the hell was happening?

Oh, shit. Maybe the firing mechanism jammed. Technology failing us.

The missile was getting dangerously close.

Craig thought about the Spanish train bombing. He had failed to stop that.

Not again today.

I can't fail today.

Damn it. Fire.

As if Craig had willed it, he saw a flash from the second plane. The heat seeker streaked through the air. Bam! Another direct hit. The debris dropped into the Tiber River, less than a mile from where the Pope was standing.

Craig breathed a sigh of relief.

Captain Goldoni was on his cell phone barking orders. "Move fast," he said.

He put down the phone and turned to Craig and Giuseppe. "I've got a location on both of them. We'll have the shooters in custody in minutes."

One of them might have another missile. The two F-35s remained overhead, circling.

Craig looked at the square. Amazingly, the crowd was orderly. Many remaining in the square. Some left. But there was no panic. The Pope was still talking.

"Fortunately," Goldoni said. "The first one fell into a sparsely populated area. The second into the Tiber."

Moments later, the captain's phone rang. "We found both missile shooters. After firing, they killed themselves. Bullets to the head. We seized their equipment."

Craig called General McCallister. "Your pilots did a great job."

"Thanks. I got their report. I plan to leave them in the air until the ceremony is over."

Craig knew that wasn't necessary, but he didn't argue.

Craig remained in place for another uneventful twenty minutes. Until the Pope was finished speaking and went back inside. Then he told Giuseppe, "I'm flying to Southern Spain."

"I have an Italian Air Force plane waiting for you at Fiumicino."

65

MARBELLA

General Zhou watched CNN on the large screen in Musa's villa with increasing frustration and misery.

In Rome, it must have been Craig Page who foiled the attack on the Pope and the Vatican. General Zhou should have anticipated Craig would use airplanes with heat-seeking missiles and tried to counter them. That part of the attack was an absolute failure.

Damn that Craig Page.

From looking at battle scenes in Southern Spain, General Zhou had a clear picture of the situation: Musa's troops had fought valiantly. The pinpoint bombing had decimated their ranks. They had now seized the deserted Alhambra with a force of about four thousand, CNN estimated. Down from the ten thousand Musa had brought from Morocco. Surprisingly, the Spanish army made no effort to engage in combat with Musa's troops at the entrance to the palace. They backed away, letting Musa have it. Then moved into defensive positions surrounding the Alhambra.

For a moment General Zhou was puzzled. Why didn't the Spaniards fight to the death to keep Musa from taking over the enormously significant Alhambra? Then he realized how brilliant the Spanish strategy was.

Musa's trapped. His only hope is for a general uprising of Muslims in Europe.

General Zhou switched the channel to French television. If the insurrection had any chance, it was in the Paris suburbs like Clichy, where Musa had his strongest supporters.

In Paris, the French reporter announced, "The man calling himself Musa Ben Abdil has adroitly used the media by calling CNN with his message that, just as Muslims flocked to and rallied around Saladin during the Third Crusade, Muslims throughout Europe should now join him in his war against the Christians. To gain their support, Musa has relied upon the parchment allegedly prepared by Queen Isabella, but so far that hasn't led Muslims to flock to his banner.

"CNN broadcast his words, but so far nothing has happened. Muslim areas in large cities are tense. Troops have surrounded them. Some rabble-rousers have issued a call to arms. However, community leaders have asked for calm. Bottom line, no general uprising has occurred."

The television shifted to Clichy, where a reporter was interviewing people who knew Ahmed Sadi, the man calling himself Musa Ben Abdil.

General Zhou listened to them expressing sympathy for Ahmed, but the scene was generally peaceful. Only three police cars had been firebombed. No widespread rioting.

Musa's finished, General Zhou decided.

Craig Page has defeated him.

Time to cut and run.

Fortunately, General Zhou had Elizabeth in a cell downstairs. His insurance policy.

General Zhou called his brother in Beijing on their encrypted phone. "A disaster," he said. "A fucking disaster."

"I know," his brother replied. "I've been following it on television."

"I can't stay in Europe."

"I figured that. You need a place to hide only for a month at most."

"What happens then?"

"President Li has changed his mind and decided on surgery for the colon cancer. He'll have it done sometime in the next month. My intention is to make certain Li does not survive that surgery."

"How will you accomplish that?"

"I don't know yet, but I have some ideas."

General Zhou didn't press his brother, who continued, "Meantime, I'll solidify your support in the Central Committee. My objective is to have you return to China to take over the presidency the day after Li's death."

"Excellent. Where do I hide until then?"

"Bali. I've paid plenty to arrange comfortable living conditions. Most important, no extradition. Their laws don't provide for it. And they've given me an ironclad guarantee."

"I can't thank you enough."

"We've always stuck together and we always will." His brother added, "Our bond is unbreakable. Until one of us dies."

"Correction. We'll go together."

"Let's not think about death. A wonderful opportunity awaits you in Beijing."

"Both of us. We always operate together. I'll make sure your wealth and power double. But now I need something else," General Zhou said.

"What's that?"

"I want to execute a prisoner swap with Craig Page. He arrested Androshka in Paris. I want her back in return for Elizabeth Crowder, who's my prisoner in Southern Spain. How can I do that?"

"Why waste your time with that nonsense. Kill Elizabeth and forget about Androshka. She's easily replaced. With your money, you'll have no trouble finding another beautiful Russian whore. Or Chinese for that matter."

No one else would dare talk to him this way.

"She's become more than that to me. I've gotten used to her."

"Like a pair of old shoes. Don't become a sentimental fool. Kill Elizabeth. Ditch Androshka, and get on with your life."

But he couldn't. He didn't know why. He wanted Androshka.

"Listen, I hear you but …"

"When you get stubborn, I can't reason with you. Alright. I'll help you make the exchange. You'll need an intermediary. Someone Craig will trust."

"But who?"

"Let me think."

There was a pause. Then General Zhou's brother continued, "I'm now involved with a British firm in a huge real-estate deal in London. The developer needs my money badly, and he's well connected with the Prime Minister. Let me talk to him. I think we can work this out."

Musa should have been delirious with joy. After more than five hundred years, the greatest prize in all of Europe, the Alhambra, across the river from the modern city of Granada, was again under the control of Islam.

He walked the corridors, stopping to touch the intricately carved plaster walls. He marveled at what the artisans had created. Feeling light headed, he bowed down on an elaborate mosaic tiled floor in which blues and greens predominated. He lowered his head and kissed the cold stone.

For Musa, illusion mixed with reality. Past and present were indistinguishable.

History reached out and grabbed him. He was catapulted more than five hundred years back in time. He was in the capital of

Islam in Europe. Granada, the last Muslim city to fall in 1492. The Alhambra, the final surrender.

He was a man of destiny, some of whose ancestors built this structure, he imagined. While others died defending it. Now, after more than five hundred years, he had restored what was lost. The desecration and sacrilege ended at last.

With all of that, Musa was still rational and a pragmatist. The reality of his situation was painfully clear. The attack on the Pope and the Vatican had been a complete failure, undoubtedly because of Craig Page. All that brilliant planning for naught. An utter and total waste of time. He was furious at himself for not killing Page in Morocco when Page and that nosey reporter Elizabeth discovered his base. He had the two of them tied to stakes. He should have killed them both and taken the consequences with the Moroccan government.

Even more infuriating was that in Spain and throughout Europe, his call for an insurrection using Queen Isabella's parchment as a linchpin, had so far not produced results. Muslim warriors weren't rushing to him as they had to Saladin. Even in Clichy. He knew because of calls he made, Mohammad, Lila's cousin, and others were calling for riots, but community leaders were angrily opposing them, arguing that the 2005 riots and the ones prompted by Lila's rape and murder accomplished only "destruction in our neighborhood."

Cowards. All of them. Too shortsighted to realize that he was providing them with an alternative to their second class-citizenship.

Musa was still hopeful this would change in the next couple of days, as he continued his pleas for support in the media. That the masses would rise up and disregard their leaders.

But now he had a pressing problem: How to hold on until that occurred. His troops were desperately in need of re-supply. They were low on ammunition. They needed grenade launchers and other sophisticated weapons. So much had been destroyed on the march to Granada. They would also be out of food in a couple of days.

Only General Zhou could arrange this re-supply. He could airlift in what Musa desperately needed. Frantically, he called Zhou on his encrypted phone.

"I was sorry to hear about Rome," General Zhou said.

Musa tried to sound upbeat. "We've achieved a great victory. I've retaken the Alhambra. The capital of my nation of Islam in Europe. I expect the Muslim masses to join my call for an insurrection within the next day. I'm calling because I need re-supply of arms and food. And I need them tonight. Can you arrange to airlift them in?"

Musa expected General Zhou to resist. To his surprise, General Zhou said, "I anticipated that. I spoke to my brother in Beijing a few minutes ago and asked him to begin working on it. I expect him to call back any minute."

"What about the logistical problems?"

"Don't worry. Don't underestimate Chinese ingenuity. We'll take care of those." General Zhou said with confidence.

Musa was very pleased. He still had a chance.

Fifteen minutes after he hung up with Musa, General Zhou sat in the study, smoking a cigar, when his brother called. "It's all set. I personally spoke with James Ferris, the British Governor of Gibraltar. He agreed to be the intermediary. He called Craig Page to arrange the terms of the exchange. You and Page will each deliver your prisoner to Ferris. At his residence. At six this evening. Can you do that?"

"Yes."

"Once he has both under his control, he'll deliver each of them to different locations. Neither side will know where the other is being taken."

"Thank you for arranging this."

"You should know it cost me dearly in terms for the London real estate deal."

General Zhou ignored that. His brother could afford it. "What about my transportation?"

"I've arranged a high speed boat to pick you up off the cost of Gibraltar. Ferris will deliver Androshka to the boat. From there you can begin your trip to Bali."

The encrypted cell phone he used with Musa was ringing. Musa must need something else. General Zhou turned off the phone. He had no intention of talking to Musa again. When he got on the boat, he'd throw it into the sea.

66

SOUTHERN SPAIN

Craig had flown into Malaga a few minutes ago and was in the back of a car, speeding to Granada and the Alhambra, when his cell phone rang. The caller ID was blocked.

"Yes," he said

"This is General Zhou. I have something you want. And you have something of mine."

Craig felt a surge of hope. If General Zhou was telling the truth, Elizabeth was alive. "I assume you're speaking about Elizabeth and Androshka?"

"Correct. I want to arrange a swap, and I have the logistics worked out."

Craig wanted to scream with joy. "Yes. Yes. Let's do it," but his professional training dictated caution. Prisoner exchanges were always risky. The potential for a trick. For a hostage dying. "First I need some assurance Elizabeth is alive and unharmed."

"I appreciate that. Give me a minute to take the phone to her."

Craig glanced at his watch. It took a full minute. Then he heard Elizabeth. "I'm OK, Craig. I haven't been harmed."

Her voice was clear and strong, though she sounded weary. He also knew Elizabeth. No way she would have uttered those words if they weren't true.

"I'm working on your release," Craig said.

"That would be wonderful."

General Zhou got back on. "Satisfied?"

"Yes. How do you want to do this?"

"By six this afternoon, you deliver Androshka to the residence of James Ferris, the British Governor of Gibraltar. I'll hand Elizabeth over to him. He'll then transport Elizabeth to a location of your choice. And Androshka to a location I designate. Neither of us will know the other's location."

Craig played it back in his mind. Everything seemed right. It was better than he had hoped. Still, he couldn't be lulled into dropping his guard.

"Terms are acceptable," Craig said. "What happens to you?"

"I leave Europe for good."

Craig desperately wanted to kill General Zhou or to prosecute him for his involvement with Musa. He realized that wasn't an option. He had to swallow this bitter pill. If he turned down the deal, he was confident General Zhou would kill Elizabeth, leave Androshka to rot in jail, and escape from Europe. This way at least he would be saving Elizabeth. Freeing Androshka was of no consequence.

"Suppose I deliver Androshka to Ferris," Craig said. "And you don't deliver Elizabeth?"

"You haven't lost a thing. Ferris is a British official. He'll return Androshka to you to be sent back to prison. But that won't happen."

Craig couldn't find any flaws in the deal General Zhou had

put together. He just hoped it wasn't a trick. That, as a result of his emotional attachment to Elizabeth, he wasn't missing something.

"OK," Craig said. "I'll deliver Androshka."

Craig and Androshka were in the back of the car from the airport. Craig was behind the driver. Her large, black Valentino bag between them.

"You didn't think he cared about me, did you?" she said.

Craig wasn't interested in talking with her. He was thinking about what would happen next. One possibility was General Zhou would try and seize Androshka before Craig turned her over to Ferris. General Zhou could have his men stop the car, shoot Craig, and pull her out. Craig touched his jacket making certain the gun in the shoulder holster was in place.

"Well you can answer," she said sounding very pleased with herself.

"You're right. I didn't."

"Because you think I'm just another whore."

"I didn't say that."

"You don't have to. I know what you're thinking. But in truth, my family was descended from the Czar."

"Yeah, right."

"Don't underestimate General Zhou. He's a great man. One day he'll take you down."

When Craig didn't respond, she turned to the right, away from him, and stared out of the window. This was the moment Craig had been waiting for. He reached into his pocket and withdrew a tiny round object, the size of a button, resembling a camera battery. Deftly, he slipped it into her bag.

Thank God they arrived. Five minutes more and he would have found it difficult to avoid strangling her. They were pulling up in front of the British Governor's majestic stone house, evidence of the grandeur of the former British empire. Craig checked his watch. Five minutes to six.

Craig told the driver to remain behind the wheel. He got out on one side and walked around the car in the back, his eyes searching the area, looking for anything suspicious. Ready to go for his gun. All seemed normal. Tourists on the street in bright sunlight. Residents walking past the house. Ten yards away, two British soldiers with rifles stood at attention on either side of the black wrought-iron gate.

Craig opened the car door for Androshka. She got out and stood erect in the five inch stiletto heels she had worn when he and Jacques took her to jail.

OK, here we go. The last ten yards.

General Zhou was capable of grabbing her now. Craig reached inside his jacket, hand on the gun, eyes scanning the area like lasers. Nothing happened.

They reached the British soldiers.

Androshka turned to Craig and said, "An American friend once taught me one of your expressions. 'It's been swell.'"

He didn't respond. The gate opened. Two more soldiers came out of the building and accompanied her inside.

Craig looked around. No sign of Elizabeth. He had spoken to Ferris before moving Androshka. Ferris had promised that Androshka would be returned if General Zhou didn't bring Elizabeth. Following the agreed upon procedure, Craig walked four blocks to the Imperial Hotel and stood in the lobby. The point he had designated for Elizabeth's delivery.

Craig paced on the red carpet, worn and in need of replacement, like the rest of the lobby of what had once been a four-star destination during the height of the British empire and had later fallen on hard times. A large picture window provided a breathtaking view of the Rock and the sea below. The lobby was crowded with tourists, mostly elderly Brits on Easter holiday.

Every minute Craig checked his watch.

At six twenty, with no sign of Elizabeth, he became worried.

I'll kill that fucking General Zhou with my bare hands if he doesn't bring her.

He pulled out his cell phone, preparing to call Ferris, when he saw her. Walking wobbly through the front door, her neck black and blue, accompanied by two British solders.

The instant their eyes met they raced toward each other. He hugged and kissed her.

"Oh my God. You're free," he said. "I was worried he'd pull a trick. Up to the end."

"Me, too. And relieved. Like you, I couldn't believe it until it was over. It was awful. Musa killed Professor Etienne."

As he squeezed her tightly, she grimaced.

"What's wrong?"

"Just bruised ribs from when they grabbed me. I tried to escape."

"What else?"

"A sore shoulder and neck. That's all. Now tell me what happened with Musa."

"Not until a doctor examines you.

"Don't be silly."

He called Ferris, thanked him for his help, and asked the governor to find a doctor who could see Elizabeth right now.

Ferris put him on hold. While he was waiting, Craig looked out through the window. He saw a boat racing away from the harbor. Craig grabbed binoculars on a table in front a gray-haired woman in Bermuda shorts having tea. He turned them up to the maximum magnification and pressed them tightly against his eyes. The crew was Chinese. He saw Androshka's blond hair blowing in the wind. Standing next to her and waving, a gloating smile on his face, was General Zhou.

Trying to pursue him was pointless, Craig realized.

He felt a surge of overwhelming anger. The pill was even more bitter than he had anticipated. That bastard General Zhou was not only the mastermind of Musa's vicious operation, which had killed thousands in Southern Spain. He was responsible for Francesca's murder. Brilliant, beautiful Francesca. His only child. His only family. And now General Zhou was escaping.

The revenge which Craig so desperately wanted had eluded him again. Just as it had eluded him at the end of Operation Dragon Oil.

But maybe not for long this time, he hoped. With the tracking device he had placed in Androshka's bag, it might be possible to locate General Zhou and gain that revenge.

Then he heard Ferris's voice on the phone. "I located a doctor two blocks away."

As Craig walked there with Elizabeth, he refused to bend. He wouldn't tell her what had happened with Musa until the doctor examined her.

The verdict was, "Broken ribs but no internal damage. A severely bruised neck and shoulder."

The doctor taped the ribs to help the healing. "Not much else we can do."

He gave her pain pills which she buried deep in her bag.

"OK. Now tell me what's with Musa and General Zhou?"

"We have a long ride to Granada. I'll give you a full report on the way. And I want to know what happened to you."

67

SOUTHERN SPAIN

It was almost eleven o'clock when Craig finished his report, interrupted by questions from her. A few minutes later, they reached the Spanish military command center in the living room of a farm house on a hill with a view of the Alhambra a mile away. General Bernardo and Carlos were poring over maps.

"Thank God, you're safe," Carlos said. He came over and kissed Elizabeth on each cheek. Then he introduced her to the General. "Because of Elizabeth and Craig, we exposed Alvarez as a traitor. The Justice Minister is already seeking his extradition from Argentina."

"Where are you on strategy?" Craig asked.

"We were just discussing that," Carlos said. "Musa and his men have to be short on food. We destroyed their food convey. The soldiers we captured had very little in their backpacks. They were more interested in speed. We have to decide whether to wait for

Musa and his people to surrender rather than starve. Or to go in now with tear gas and kill them all or take prisoners. General Bernardo and I are divided on the issue."

The General spoke up. "It's night. They have to be tired. I say at three a.m. we mount a full attack under the cover of darkness. Lots of troops with tear gas and masks. We'll try not to harm the building, but we'll end this war of theirs."

Carlos shook his head. "I don't like that. It'll result in damage to this priceless structure. Also casualties for our soldiers that are unnecessary. If we wait, all that will be avoided. Sooner or later they'll all come out with their hands in the air."

The General was scowling. "Waiting for days will make us look weak. We have to show strength, particularly since they blasted their way to the Alhambra without our being able to stop them. The world is already laughing at us."

"I don't agree." Carlos replied firmly.

The General's face was turning red.

He's obviously unaccustomed, Craig thought, to opposition from a young civilian on a military matter.

"You don't have to agree. You're not the commanding officer. It's my decision."

"Correction," Carlos fired back, waving his arms for emphasis. "It's Prime Minster Zahara's decision. I'll call him and see what he says."

"You better tell him that, if he sides with you and he's willing to wait for days, then I'm resigning."

To Craig, the argument was familiar. He'd heard numerous renditions between American generals and the civilian Pentagon leadership

Carlos reached for the phone on the table. "I'll put the phone on speaker so you can present your own position."

"Fine, do that." Bernardo said, his voice dripping with venom.

Before Carlos placed the call, Elizabeth said. "Hold up. There's an alternative. A better way."

Carlos looked at her with a puzzled expression. Craig, too. He had no idea what she had in mind. General Bernardo was shaking his head. An expression of contempt on his face. Craig read his mind. Now I have to listen to a woman. This young punk Carlos was bad enough.

Tell us," Carlos said.

"Ahmed, the ringleader of the group in the Alhambra, took on the name Musa Ben Abdil. His medieval hero. When the other Muslims wanted to surrender in 1491, that medieval warrior raced out of the safety of the Alhambra and attacked the Christian enemy surrounding it. He knew he faced a certain death. He preferred to die fighting on the attack. We have to assume this Musa will do the same. That he'll emulate his hero to the end."

She paused to take a deep breath. Craig could tell from her face that talking was painful.

Still she continued, "So, I believe very soon Musa, and perhaps some of his followers, will come racing out of the Alhambra firing in all directions, trying to kill as many Spanish troops as possible."

"I think she's right," Craig said,

Carlos was nodding.

"When will this happen?" General Bernardo asked.

Elizabeth replied, "I believe very soon. I don't know exactly. Musa's intelligent. He has to understand the situation. He has to make his move fast. Every minute he delays, he becomes weaker physically. Also, he risks your troops rushing into the Alhambra and making him die in total defeat and humiliation. By storming out firing, he can persuade himself he is dying a courageous death as well as emulating his hero."

General Bernardo ran his hand through his coarse gray hair. They all looked at him expectantly.

"I'll give this Abdil or Musa or whoever the hell he is twelve hours. If he's not out by noon tomorrow, Carlos, you'll have to make your call to the Prime Minister. Meantime, I'll tell my troops to be vigilant. Nobody sleeps. We have to be prepared for a frontal assault against hopeless odds … in case Elizabeth is right."

"Exactly," Elizabeth responded. "It could come at any time."

GRANADA

From a sitting position on the cold, gray, stone ledge of a watchtower facing east, Musa saw the first rays of light appear in the sky. He hadn't slept all night.

The resupply General Zhou had promised never came. Four times he had tried to call Zhou, but there was no answer on the encrypted phone. At the first sign of trouble, that coward had deserted him.

He had made calls to Muslim friends around Europe. All provided the same report: There would be no widespread insurrection, merely a number of solidarity rallies. Even the parchment didn't help.

Walking around the Alhambra through the night, he heard the grumbling of his troops. They were hungry. Their ammunition was low. "Our situation is hopeless," he overheard one of them say.

Musa was a pragmatist. He knew the man was right. The situation was hopeless. In a matter of hours, his troops would begin to surrender in groups, walking out of the Alhambra, hands raised, holding white cloths. He would be powerless to stop them.

As a student of history, the irony struck Musa. He was in precisely the same situation as Musa Ben Abdil in 1491.

He walked over to an adjoining tower where Omar stood looking out over the rolling countryside. "It's a beautiful land," Omar said. "I wish it could be ours again."

"Unfortunately it cannot," Musa said grimly. "You've been a wonderful friend and supporter. In truth, I've failed you. Under my leadership, we accomplished nothing."

Omar shook his head. "Not so. You called attention to the plight of Islam in Europe. That's significant. A hundred years from now Islam will be predominant in much of Europe. Then you will be viewed as a man of vision who dared to dream and had the courage to try and advance our inevitable victory with the Christian world."

Musa was moved by Omar's words. "Perhaps, but we have to deal with our situation today."

He knew how his medieval hero, Musa Ben Abdil, would have responded to this situation. He was Musa Ben Abdil. There was only one possible action.

He asked Omar to assemble the troops in the Hall of Kings, the site of entertainment for the Sultan and his retinue. There Musa climbed up on a table. I have to be honest with them, he decided.

"You have been brave and loyal warriors," he said, his voice cracking with emotion. "Landing in Spain, fighting our way to Granada, and retaking the Alhambra. All are incredible accomplishments.

"However, without the Muslim uprising I had hoped for, we now have no chance of surviving here. The resupply I was promised is not coming. If we remain inside this palace, we will starve to death or the Spanish Army will come in with tear gas and kill those of us weary, hungry warriors who are still alive."

He paused. The room was deathly still. "Another choice is surrender. For me that is not an alterative, but I will not judge harshly any man who selects it.

"For me, there is only one course of action. To rush out of the Alhambra with guns blazing. To kill as many Christians as I can. I am prepared to face my destiny. Those who wish to join me may do so. The others may surrender after I have died my hero's death. Whoever wishes to fight at my side, please come forward."

Only Omar stepped to the front.

Musa was sorely disappointed, but he didn't show it.

"Come Omar," he said. "We will pray. Then prepare our weapons."

Craig, Elizabeth, Carlos, and General Bernardo stood on the verandah of the farmhouse in the cool morning air. Craig was sipping coffee, looking at the beautiful Alhambra, hoping Elizabeth was right.

It would be tragic if the building were damaged or destroyed. Tragic if more men died in what was now a futile exercise of defending it.

Elizabeth said, "I expect Musa to make his move first thing this morning. That's when the medieval Musa rode out."

"My troops are in place," the General said.

Half an hour later, Craig saw activity near the entrance to the Alhambra. Musa was running out of the building, shrieking in Arabic, an automatic weapon in each hand, firing as he ran. Behind him was Omar, firing as well.

With the element of surprise, they hit eight Spanish troops before the Spaniards unleashed a ferocious barrage, their bullets flying toward Musa and Omar. Craig watched them hit the two men repeatedly. In the head. Face. Body. Head. Face. Body.

Musa's knees buckled. He fell, landing on his back. Omar on his face. Blood flowing on the ground. Neither moving.

General Bernardo called the commander on the scene. "Make sure they're dead."

The return call was, "Both dead."

Once the firing stopped, Musa's warriors straggled out of the Alhambra unarmed. Hands in the air, some with white flags. General Bernardo gave the order, "Hold your fire."

"It's over," Elizabeth said to Craig. "It's finally over."

The two of them walked down the hill. Over to Musa's still body.

PARIS

Two days later, Pierre Moreau led Craig and Elizabeth into the large conference room in the French Defense Ministry—the same one in which Craig had struck out trying to persuade the EU Defense Ministers to attack Musa in Morocco.

The defense ministers of England, Germany, and Italy were at the table, along with Carlos from Spain. Jacques and Giuseppe as well.

As soon as Craig and Elizabeth entered, the others all stood and clapped their hands with enthusiasm.

One by one, the Defense Ministers expressed their gratitude to Craig and Elizabeth for stopping the attack on the Vatican and for arranging the defeat of Musa's Spanish Revenge in Southern Spain.

When they were finished, Moreau turned to Craig. "Would you like to respond?"

Craig stood and looked around. "First, Elizabeth and I are deeply touched and very appreciative of all your thanks.

"Jacques, Giuseppe, and Carlos," he said, stopping to point, "played an enormously important role in this success. Without them, we would never have prevailed. This truly was a pan-European operation and victory. Precisely what the formation of the EU hoped to accomplish.

"Second, while we undoubtedly prevailed and avoided incalculable damage, we must not forget the terrible price that was paid. Eighty four innocent people were killed in the Spanish train bombing. Thousands of soldiers and civilians died in the south of Spain. Also, Professor Etienne. Four Franciscan monks. One Roman policeman. And Lila, a courageous young Muslim woman in Marseilles.

"We cannot ignore the fact that, while the leader of the Spanish Revenge is dead, the issue that inflamed Ahmed Sadi, namely the ongoing battle between Islam and the Christian West, is far from over. I am not a policy wonk and have no magic solutions. Elizabeth's book will be published in a year and will illuminate the topic.

"From my limited perspective as a counterterrorism expert, I know that, as part of this battle, some Muslims will launch terrorist attacks on Europe and the United States. We must be vigilant to stop those.

"What seems clear to me is that the ongoing war between Christians and Muslims throughout the world … not merely in Europe and the United States … but in Egypt, Asia, and Africa, is only in its nascent stage. Like the Crusades, I fear it will continue for decades, if not centuries. One tragic difference is that both sides are now in possession of weapons of mass destruction."

Craig stopped talking and sat down to stunned silence. As the meeting was breaking up, Pierre Moreau said to Craig. "You're analysis was sobering. To say the least."

"I wish I could be more optimistic."

"And I wish I could disagree."

It was a beautiful spring day in Paris. A day for lovers. A day when everything seemed possible. So at odds with Craig's grim and dreary assessment.

He and Elizabeth left the Ministry of Defense and wandered down Boulevard St. Germain to the square next to the church, St. Germain Des Pres.

They sat down at a small outdoor café. Craig looked at the artists in front of the church selling their paintings. At tourists in short sleeves, wandering aimlessly. At elaborately coiffed women entering fashionable boutiques.

Once they each had a cappuccino, Elizabeth said, "I was surprised you didn't talk about the Chinese involvement with Musa."

"I didn't want to get away from the main point. Besides, we have no evidence that General Zhou had help from the Chinese government."

"I agree. It was all the venal General Zhou. I feel badly that, on my account, you had to surrender your chance to kill him and avenge Francesca's death. So stupid to let them capture me."

He placed his hand on hers. "C'mon. Don't give yourself a beating. You were amazing in all of this. We're good together. As for General Zhou, one day he'll pay for all he's done."

"I hope you're right," Elizabeth said thoughtfully. "But if General Zhou gets back into power in China, there will be major problems for Europe and the United States."

ACKNOWLEDGMENTS

Pam Ahearn, my superb agent, helped me shape and write this story with enormous wisdom and insight. My wife, Barbara, supplied ideas for revisions on numerous drafts, while always adding encouragement. Joseph Pittman, my editor, provided valuable notes which improved *The Spanish Revenge*.

Turn the page for a special preview of
Allan Topol's next Craig Page Thriller,

THE RUSSIAN ENDGAME

PROLOGUE

NOVEMBER, SIX MONTHS AGO, MOSCOW

ENRAGED, DIMITRI ORLOV stood in Red Square at noon watching Russian President Fyodor Kuznov's motorcade leave the Kremlin through Savior Gate and race past. Heavy snow was falling. Orlov paid no attention to the flakes caking in his blonde hair, the water running down his face, past the scar on his right cheek, the result of a knife wound in a battle with a Chechnya terrorist. At six two, and powerfully built, standing tall in his military coat, which he had found in the back of his closet, and staring at the Kremlin, Orlov was a forbidding presence. People crossed the street to avoid him. Orlov ignored them.

I won't take "no" for an answer, Orlov vowed. He had always refused to take "no" for an answer. That was part of the reason for his meteoric rise to Major in the Soviet army and then to section head in the KGB in the good old days of the Soviet Union. "Yes I can" was his creed. "Yes I can," was his answer to any question. For example, "Orlov, can you break though the defense lines of the Chechnya rebels?" Or, "Orlov, can you force the American spy to tell us whom he's working with?"

After the breakup of the Soviet Union, which would never have happened but for that self-aggrandizing coward, Gorbachev, and that worthless drunk Yeltsin, Orlov moved on. He took his can do approach to Vasily, "the venal" Sukalov, an oligarch in the new Russia, who became incredibly wealthy, five billion dollars' worth, as a result of stealing the telecom monopoly from the State. After ten years of being Vasily's enforcer, while skimming twenty million euros he socked away in a Swiss bank, Orlov severed his relationship with Vasily. He was now ready to serve Mother Russia. And he knew exactly how.

Orlov had only one problem: He needed a meeting with President Kuznov, and he hadn't been able to get through Kuznov's layers of bureaucrats to schedule it. Orlov even knew Kuznov from his KGB days when Orlov played a minor role in a Kuznov operation to spread disinformation to the Americans in Germany. He was confident Kuznov would remember him.

Though Orlov explained that to the secretary to Kuznov's secretary, he received the stock answer given to any lunatic who tried to approach the President's suite in the Kremlin. "Submit your request in writing. You will receive an answer in six to eight weeks." Unfortunately, using Vasily to gain access to Kuznov wasn't an option. Those two hated each other. Vasily was even worried Kuznov might issue an order for his arrest for theft of State property.

Submitting a request in writing wasn't an option. What Orlov had to say to the Russian President couldn't be put in a letter. Besides, he guessed all those letters were routinely dumped, unread, into a trash can. So he had only one choice: To force his way past

Kuznov's layers of protection. That would be next to impossible to do if Kuznov was in the Kremlin. But today was Friday and two days ago when Orlov sat cooling his heels for the fifth time in the office of the secretary to the secretary, he overheard the fat, redheaded, swine say in a phone conversation, "President Kuznov will be leaving for his country home Friday afternoon."

Orlov decided that must be where the Presidential motorcade was now headed. He zipped up his black leather jacket, climbed on his Harley, and sped off following the motorcade. He was hanging back far enough to avoid attracting suspicion.

As he rode, Orlov thought about Kuznov. The Russian President, like Orlov, had been a distinguished army officer who was recruited by the KGB. But unlike Orlov, who fought against the changes convulsing the Soviet Union with the rise of the so-called democratic movement, Kuznov, with loyalty to no one, manipulated the new system for his own advancement. He became the Director of the FSB, the KGB's domestic successor, then Mayor of Moscow, and finally President of Russia. In his early contact with Kuznov, Orlov found the man impressive. Yes, but President of Russia? Orlov would never have imagined it.

Orlov had to admire Kuznov. Somehow, he was now in a Presidential motorcade while Orlov, binoculars pressed against his eyes, was stretched out on the snowy ground on the crest of a hill, literally freezing his dick, while watching the motorcade pass the guardhouse at a break in the twelve foot high stonewall that surrounded Kuznov's country estate on three sides. On the fourth, it bordered a circular lake roughly two kilometers in diameter.

Orlov focused on the guardhouse. Four men were inside, all armed with machine guns. He considered his options. Forcing his way through the guardhouse would be tough. It meant killing or incapacitating the four guards. They would no doubt sound an alarm and bring every other security man on the property. And no doubt, there were plenty of them. Scaling the wall under the cover of darkness was more likely to succeed, but if he was spotted at or near the top, he'd be a sitting duck.

He didn't like either of those. Then it hit him. He had a third way.

Orlov rode back into the center of Moscow to gather what he needed.

ORLOV HAD ALWAYS been a student of history. It was his favorite subject in school. Even in the KGB, he was a voracious reader of history books about each area in which he operated.

He was convinced that people shaped world events. Not just leaders. But others. Those with courage and daring. The assassin of the Austrian Arch Duke in Sarajevo was responsible for the outbreak of the First World War. Philbrick and his colleagues who spied on England for Russia. The American scientists who beat Germany in the race to develop the atomic bomb.

Orlov had always dreamt that one day he would be someone who influenced world events. In that way, he would achieve immortality. That was why he had joined the KGB.

So far, he hadn't affected the course of the world. He had merely been a low level agent. Now, finally, his time had come. He was determined to take advantage of it. And something else was motivating Orlov as he prepared for this evening's encounter with Kuznov. He had money, but he sought power. He wanted to be the head of a new revitalized and even more dreaded KGB, making him the second most powerful person in Russia. If he accomplished this mission for Kuznov, delivered what he was promising, a grateful Kuznov would readily accede to Orlov's request.

At eleven thirty that evening, with the sliver of a moon concealed by thick clouds, he rode his motorcycle back to a park across the lake from Kuznov's estate. The snow had stopped. Orlov parked the bike in a thick clump of trees and pulled out the materials he'd packed in the side bags. First the black wet suit, mask and flippers. Then the Glock, knife and rope in a water tight container, which he tied around his waist. Orlov donned the wet suit over his slacks and shirt and dove in. He swam on a straight line toward Kuznov's house with smooth strokes. No splashes to alert anyone to his presence in the water.

As he approached the other side, Orlov saw two guards, sitting on lawn chairs facing the house, their backs to him. They were each holding a bottle and talking loudly. They had to be drunk, he decided, from the sounds of their voices.

He pulled the Glock from the pouch at his waist. All I want to do is knock them out, Orlov decided. No need to kill the fools. But I can't give them a chance to call for help.

On the toes of his feet, gripping the gun by the barrel, he advanced stealthily across the wet grass. He was right behind them. Neither man had turned in his direction. The man on the right looked larger and tougher. Orlov decided to attack him first. In a single swift motion, he swung the gun and smashed it against the side of the man's head. Before he passed out, the cry of "Ah...Ah..." came out of his mouth. Enough to alert his colleague who shot to his feet and wheeled around to face Orlov.

"Who the hell..."

Before the startled man could finish the sentence, Orlov slammed a fist into his stomach doubling him up. Orlov followed that with a viscous kick to the balls. The guard dropped to the ground. Orlov fell on top of him, raising his pistol to smash against the man's head and finish the job. Before Orlov had a chance, the man lunged for Orlov's face, scratching and punching, going for Orlov's eyes. The gun fell from Orlov's hand. Momentarily stunned, Orlov recovered quickly and fought back. They rolled on the muddy ground. Orlov ended up on top. The guard was trying to force him off, but Orlov had his hands around the man's thick neck. He was squeezing tightly. Squeezing and squeezing until the man stopped moving. Still squeezing until the man stopped breathing.

Orlov stood up and peeled off his wetsuit. He tossed it on the dead man's body, recovered his gun, rope, and knife, and looked at the house. No one was at any of the rear windows. Chances were no one had seen or heard what happened. Orlov breathed a sigh of relief. He studied the house some more. Undoubtedly, Kuznov's bedroom suite faced the back. That way he'd have a view of the lake. Lights were on in only one room facing that direction. It had to be Kuznov's. The Russian President was well known to be an insomniac.

With the knife in one hand, gun in the other, and rope over his shoulder, Orlov snuck to the back door. He could pick most locks with a knife, but maybe I won't have to do that. Maybe I'll get lucky.

He turned the doorknob slowly and the door opened, without creaking, leading into the kitchen. The house was quiet. He saw a young woman, in her twenties, dressed in a pink flannel robe leaning into the refrigerator, her back to the door. She must have heard him because she suddenly turned around. Orlov saw she was preparing to scream. He lifted his right hand with the gun and pointed it at her. At the same time, he raised the forefinger of his other hand to his lips, signaling her to be quiet. She stood mute, frozen to the spot.

"Who are you?" he asked.

"One of the maids."

"If you tell me what room President Kuznov is in, I won't harm you."

She pointed to the ceiling confirming what he suspected. The room faced the back.

"How do I get there?"

She gestured toward a closed door in a corner of the kitchen, "A staircase behind the door," she stammered in a frightened whisper. "Will you kill him?"

"That's none of your business. I'm going to tie you up."

She nodded. He used the rope to tie her torso to a chair, legs and arms as well. He grabbed a kitchen towel and tied it around her mouth.

Then he opened the door, concealing the wooden staircase. Climbing the stairs, Orlov heard the sound of a television. A movie was playing in English. He had read that Kuznov liked Americana movies.

When Orlov reached the second floor landing, he saw five closed doors in a dimly lit corridor. On the tips of his toes, he walked softly toward the room in which the television was playing.

Gun raised, Orlov twisted the doorknob, kicked open the door and looked inside. He saw Kuznov leaning back on a sofa. With him was a gorgeous, busty, blonde woman half Kuznov's age at best. Definitely not the frumpy Mrs. Kuznov. The Russian President's pants were unzipped and she had his dick in her mouth. The Manchurian Candidate was playing. The Russian President pushed aside the blonde, grabbed a cell phone from the table, and shot to his feet.

Kuznov was not a dominating physical presence, Orlov recalled from their prior meetings. He was thin with a receding hair line. No more than five eight. A contrast to the strapping Orlov. But Kuznov did have those hard, cold, black eyes. And they were boring in on Orlov while the blonde raced behind the sofa to hide.

"All I have to do is press one button on the phone," Kuznov said, in a steely cold voice, devoid of emotion and fear, "and four armed guards will come. You'll be a dead man."

"I'm not here to harm you."

"Who the hell are you? And what do you want?"

Orlov realized Kuznov was staring at him. The President's face showing partial recognition.

"Dimitri Orlov. We were..."

Kuznov completed the sentence. "In the KGB together. You worked for me on a disinformation project in Berlin involving the Americans."

"You have a good memory."

"You did an outstanding job. And now you've become insane, breaking in like this."

"I didn't have a choice. I was desperate to talk to you about something extremely important and confidential. Those morons who guard your access refused to schedule me. I had to take matters into my own hands."

"Why should I believe you?"

Orlov handed the gun to Kuznov. The former KGB operative kept the knife in his hand. If he thought Kuznov intended to shoot him, Orlov planned to open the knife blade and hurl it at the Russian president.

Orlov held his breath for a long minute while Kuznov stared at his surprised visitor and moved the gun around his hand.

Finally, Kuznov looked behind the sofa and called to the blonde, "Wait for me in the bedroom and don't tell anyone about this."

She practically flew out of the room.

Kuznov pointed to a chair. When Orlov sat down, Kuznov settled into the sofa facing him. He rested the gun on the end table where Kuznov could easily reach it. Now confident of the outcome, Orlov put the knife in his pocket.

"Are you still working with Vasily Sukalov?" Kuznov asked.

"I quit two months ago."

"Good for you. Sukalov's a gangster. A criminal. Since then?"

"I'm freelancing."

"Who sent you to talk to me?"

"Nobody. This was my idea."

"It better be good."

"It is."

"Start talking."

Orlov took a deep breath and began. "Most Russians believe that the events of 1991, culminating in the collapse of the Soviet Union were a tragedy. Even that spineless Gorbachev, who is referred to in the media as Jell-O, has conceded that the Soviet Union could have and should have been preserved. Yeltsin, after him, was a disaster for Russia."

"You're here to give me a history lesson."

Orlov ignored the sarcasm and continued. "Under Putin, Medvedev, and now you, our economy has prospered. We are once again an economic force in the world. Thanks in part to our energy resources, but also because of the drive of our top businessmen. The State has created stability in the country, which is key. Every recent survey shows that the Russian people don't want democracy or human rights. They want order and stability. The FSB, while not as effective as the KGB in our day, has solidified domestic control."

"So you're telling me that Putin, Medvedev, and I have been successful. We've given the people the order that they want as well as economic growth."

"That's true, but…"

Orlov paused for a minute and looked at the Russian President. He was confident Kuznov wanted to hear what was coming next.

"But," Orlov continued, now treading carefully because his views could be considered criticism and Kuznov was thin skinned, "We are still viewed as a joke militarily. The sick man of Europe."

"Are you aware that I have been quietly rebuilding our army, navy, and air force?" Kuznov sounded defensive.

"Of course. But no one in Washington regards Russia as a resurging superpower. Prepared to compete with the United States and China."

"The American arrogance is unbelievable. They view themselves as the dominant superpower. The world's judge and police. All this from a country whose own government is dysfunctional."

"I couldn't agree more. That's why I'm here. I have a plan to restore

Russia to its prior greatness before Afghanistan, Gorbachev, and the fall of the Berlin Wall. And at the same time, to inflict a mighty blow on the U.S. The Russian people will revere you for doing this. Most look back longingly and yearn for the good old days when we were a world force."

Kuznov walked over to the credenza, poured two glasses of vodka, and handed one to Orlov. They each took a gulp. Kuznov said, "That's an extremely ambition objective. How do you propose to do this?"

It was a lob up to the net. Orlov was ready with his response. "We form an alliance with China. Then in a joint operation, we strike at the United States and Europe."

Kuznov was shaking his head. "I'll be very frank with you, Dimitri. I've met Chinese President Li twice. I've never been able to develop a relationship with the man. He's gutless and two faced. An alliance with China is out of the question."

"Change is in the wind in Beijing. A beneficial change for us. Li will not be the President of China much longer. He will be succeeded by General Zhou."

"You're wrong. Zhou was exiled."

"Respectfully, I hate to disagree with you. Zhou will be back in Beijing sometime next year. And he will become the next Chinese President."

Kuznov looked skeptical. He finished his vodka. "How do you know all this?"

"My sister Androshka is General Zhou's mistress living with him in Paris. Though I'm ten years older, we always had a close relationship, in part because our father died when Androshka was only a year old."

"I've heard of your father. He was well respected as a high ranking Communist Party official."

"Thank you. Well, anyhow, I had a secret meeting with Androshka last March in the south of France. She told me precisely what I told you about General Zhou's plans to become the next Chinese president. She also told me that General Zhou hates the United States."

While Kuznov paced with one hand in his chin, undoubtedly assessing what he had just heard, Orlov recalled that meeting with Androshka.

He hadn't seen or heard from her in two years and he hadn't been able to locate her. It was as if she had vanished from the face of the earth. The last he heard, she was in a relationship with Mikail Ivanoff, another Russian oligarch. Word had reached Orlov that Androshka had stolen money from Ivanoff and fled the country. And that Ivanoff wanted to find and kill her. None of that made sense to Orlov, who had plenty of money to give to Androshka. All she had to do was ask.

Then out of the blue, she called and asked him to meet her in the south of France. "I'm staying at the house of Chinese General Zhou. He's away for a few days. Come now. Please."

So Orlov took the first plane to Paris where he connected to Nice. In a huge estate, with a swimming pool and a red clay tennis court, in the hills above the town of Cap d' Antibes. Androshka, with tears running down her cheeks, told him how, back in Moscow, Mikail had beaten her when he was drunk. One night it was too much for her. While he slept, she gathered up the money he had in the house and fled to Paris. There she had no choice. She had to earn money the way good-looking women have since the beginning of time.

"You were a prostitute?" Orlov said horrified.

"I had no choice. But I had good luck. I met General Zhou. He's been good to me."

"You should have called me," Orlov said angrily.

"I didn't want to make trouble for you. I know that Vasily and Mikail were friends."

"They were. Now they hate each other. But why did you call me now?"

"Thanks to General Zhou, Mikail is dead."

Orlov stopped thinking about his meeting with Androshka and looked at Kuznov, who was staring at him.

"Alright," the Russian President said. "I'm willing to accept everything you've told me about General Zhou and his hatred for the Americans. If and when he becomes President of China, I would like to meet with him. Here in Moscow. But I can't arrange that meeting myself. And it can't be a public meeting. That would raise suspicions around the world. Feed paranoia. Particularly in Washington. They'll see it as Stalin and Hitler joining forces and take strong action. We have to form our alliance secretly. Do you understand?"

Kuznov's words were music to Orlov's ears. "Absolutely. That's where I can help you." Orlov added.

"How?"

"Androshka promised to get me access to General Zhou...As your representative of course...As soon as he becomes Chinese president, I'll call her and arrange to visit Beijing. To meet with Zhou and invite him to Moscow. If that's what you want."

Orlov was trying to sound deferential.

Now Kuznov was smiling. And he almost never smiles, Orlov thought.

"I like that plan. Good you came to see me. I promise you won't have trouble getting in the next time...By the way, how many of my guards did you kill to get his meeting with me tonight?"

"One dead. One unconscious. Both on the back lawn."

They were just the beginning as far as Orlov was concerned. He was prepared to kill more—as many as necessary to fulfill his mission and make himself the second most powerful man in Russia.